In the Heat of the Moment

A Black Horse Campground Mystery

by

Amy M. Bennett

Aakenbaaken & Kent

In the Heat of the Moment

A Black Horse Campground Mystery

Aakenbaakeneditor@gmail.com

ISBN: 978-1-938436-85-7

Prologue

The Black Horse Campground, Bonney County, New Mexico, early February

He looked through the window of the rental RV as he sipped at the bourbon-laced coffee in his cup and smiled. The view wasn't one that would normally elicit that reaction; dry, dead tree limbs shook in the wind; gray leaves that had fallen weeks earlier skittered across the dusty road; brown tufts of grass, brittle and parched, stirred in the icy breeze. He drew back when Corrie Black, the campground's owner, stepped out onto the porch of the campground store although it was unlikely that she would see him, even if she happened to look in his direction. His smile widened and he couldn't repress a chuckle as she tugged her jacket tighter around herself and looked up into the bleak sky, a worried frown on her face. He knew what she was thinking.

The entire state of New Mexico, principally the south-central region where Bonney County was located, was facing a severe drought. Not only had neither rain nor snow fallen in the area for over a month, there wasn't any moisture in the forecast for at least another three weeks. The ski resort in nearby Ruidoso had managed to keep a few trails open with manufactured snow—at least it was cold enough for that—but the US Forest Service had issued strict fire restrictions for the entire Lincoln National Forest and the surrounding areas. No open flames of any kind, from campfires to propane grills and camp stoves, were allowed due to the dry conditions. Even smokers were restricted from lighting up cigarettes outdoors. Not that there were many guests under these conditions.

He watched Corrie shake her head dejectedly and go back inside. In the five days that he had spent at the Black Horse, under the guise of being a businessman who needed some quiet time away from his big-city office, he'd been able to observe the flow—make that trickle—of business at the Black Horse. No campfires or grills meant many people didn't want to camp, especially with the daily temperatures hovering at the freezing point and dropping into the teens at night. At the present, only he and three other guests, all in RVs, were at the campground and he was the only one who wasn't a year-rounder. The only other accommodation that was occupied was the cabin rented by police detective J.D. Wilder. He'd become acquainted with the law enforcement officer during his daily visit to the campground store for a cup of coffee and a complimentary breakfast snack, but he was careful not to get too chummy. He didn't have to worry; it was obvious from the start that the detective was far more interested in Corrie and her problems. Still, he knew that he was only there to make discreet observations and report them to his partner, not get entangled in the locals' business.

He heard the rumble of Wilder's Harley starting up and he watched as the detective pulled up beside the door of the campground store and went inside. He wished he could be a fly on the wall and hear what was being said, but he expected a call from his partner momentarily. He sensed that his time here at the Black Horse was almost over. That meant the next phase would be kicking in soon.

He turned from the window and sat at the tiny table in the kitchenette. He hadn't made his daily trip to get coffee this morning; it was too cold and there was nothing more he could learn, so he'd brewed his own and had already consumed half the pot, lacing it liberally with liquor. The list he'd been given of things to look for lay next to his cell phone, with all but one item having a red checkmark next to it.

Meghan.

He raised a brow then he raised the cup of bourbon coffee and drained it. Soon. Very soon. Then, as he contemplated refilling it, his cell phone rang.

He smiled.

Chapter 1

"Should I ask how it's going?" J.D. Wilder asked as he picked up Corrie's empty coffee cup from the counter and made his way to the courtesy table.

Corrie gave him a lop-sided smile and he returned a similar one as the smell of piñon coffee rose from the cup he refilled. "Do you really have to ask?"

He shook his head as he filled his thermal cup and brought both back to the counter. The fact that both coffee pots—one with piñon coffee, the other with regular—as well as the platters of banana bread slices and blueberry muffins were still almost full at nearly eight in the morning told the story. He took a sip of his coffee and sighed. "No new reservations?"

"Nope," she said. "Lots of inquiries, but once people hear about the fire restrictions, not to mention that the forest service has shut down hiking trails and prohibited off-road vehicle use, they change their minds. Even the skiers and snowboarders aren't making the trip, since the resort only has a few trails open. They take their business north up to Taos and Red River and Colorado. This has to be the worst drought we've had in years." She grimaced as a stiff gust of wind rattled the windows, prompting her dog, Renfro, to stir from sleep and let out a whimper. Oliver, her black-and-gray tabby, was curled up moodily on the black Lab's back. Their earlier trip outside to take care of "business" had been quicker than usual since neither pet liked the icy wind. "I don't think people understand how dangerous it is when the wind is kicking up like this, even in the winter time. It wouldn't take much for a fire to start and spread."

J.D. nodded. During one of his exploratory rides through the mountains around Bonney and Lincoln counties, he had seen the devastation wrought by the Little Bear Fire that burned for nearly two months in 2012 and destroyed over 44,000 acres. It would be decades before the forest recovered from the damage. He could understand why the Forest Service and the people in Lincoln and Bonney counties were worried about the dry, windy conditions; though no lives were lost in the Little Bear Fire, people lost their homes and entire communities were threatened. However, it was a bitter pill to swallow that the measures implemented to lessen the fire danger also lessened the number of visitors to the area—visitors that provided the income and livelihood of many business owners in Bonney and Ruidoso. "So how many guests do you have right now?" he asked.

"Besides you?" she said dryly. "Only one that's actually staying here. My three year-round guests have all taken off for warmer climates, even the Westlakes. I was fortunate that they opted to leave their RVs here, so I'm still collecting rent from them. Then I've got the guy that's been here a week and I think he's getting ready to take off, too. He didn't even come in for coffee today," she added glumly.

J.D. grimaced. That had to be hurting her bottom line. He'd seen Jerry and Jackie Page, Corrie's long-time friends and employees, come over at seven, the campground's official opening time and then go back to their RV less than fifteen minutes later. Red and Dana Myers, her other friends who were also employees had returned from an extended vacation after the first of the year, but had yet to work more than a couple of days a week. Their restored Airstream usually had a cheery awning with lawn chairs and a couple of other ornaments under it to make it look homey and inviting, but the strong winds had prompted Red to take down the awning and store all their outdoor items to prevent them from blowing away. As retirees, neither the Pages nor the Myers really needed a paycheck, but Corrie hadn't been able to schedule her regular employees full time hours since mid-January. J.D. knew the guilt was eating her up… and her savings, as well.

"Where's RaeLynn?" he asked, noting that it was unusual not to see the young woman bustling around the campground store, dusting and rearranging displays and making sure that everything was spic-and-span. Not that the store ever looked the slightest bit messy at any time, but even more so since Corrie had hired her on full-time. After RaeLynn Shaffer had moved in with Corrie back in December, J.D. knew that she had taken her work ethic to a whole new level in an effort to thank Corrie for her kindness.

"I gave her the day off. She earned it and her therapist had to rearrange her appointment schedule this week," Corrie said. "In a way, I'm glad I'm not that busy because she would have been tempted to cancel if she thought I needed the help, but she's doing so well after all she went through that there was no way I was going to let her miss her appointment." J.D. nodded; he knew all too well that it was nothing short of a miracle that RaeLynn had recovered as well as she had from her harrowing experience of being kidnapped and left for dead on the highway. The subsequent events ended up putting both J.D. and Sheriff Rick Sutton in the hospital. The sheriff was still on desk duty, no doubt impatiently waiting to get a clean bill of health from the doctors who operated on him after he ended up with broken ribs and a punctured lung with massive blood loss.

A condition that put J.D. in the hospital after he donated more than a safe amount of blood to save the sheriff's life.

Corrie smiled. "I told her while she was out, she might want to stop by DeeDee's salon. Her birthday is next week and I told her that her present was a makeover—a haircut and a mani and pedi. She's never had that before and I think it will give her a much-needed lift."

J.D. returned the grin. He knew it was an expense that Corrie could ill afford but was glad to pay—she wanted to make up for a lot that RaeLynn had gone through. He cleared his throat. "You heard from Sutton lately?" he asked tentatively.

A look of pain flashed in Corrie's eyes for a split second and J.D. regretted having asked. "Not since I saw him at church on Sunday," she said, her indifference sounding forced. "Why?"

"No reason, really," J.D. admitted. Ever since they had discovered that the sheriff's marriage had been ruled valid by the Catholic tribunal—for the third time—thus extinguishing any possibility of him being able to rekindle his relationship with Corrie, things had been, to put it mildly, awkward among the three of them and J.D. couldn't really explain why. He straightened up. "So, uh, I guess I'd better be on my way to work. I'll see you tonight. Uh, do you want me to pick up some dinner for us? I mean, I can get enough for the three of us, if RaeLynn wants to join us." He stopped before he ended up inviting the Pages and the Myers to join them as well.

Corrie gave him a strained smile. "You don't have to do that, J.D.," she said. "RaeLynn put a roast in the slow cooker for dinner tonight before she left. She's been insisting on doing all the cooking since she moved in. I'm sure there will be more than enough for you to join us."

"Okay," he said and winced inwardly. Dinner with Corrie had been his plan but he was starting to realize that, short of asking her on an official date, RaeLynn would always be included now that she lived in the same apartment. "Need me to bring anything?"

"Just a big appetite," Corrie said with a laugh. "RaeLynn came home from a used-book sale at the library last week and must have bought every cookbook they had. She always cooks enough for an army."

"All right," he said. He set his cup down and debated on how he should take his leave. Should he try anything other than a simple good-bye? Would she accept a hug? Something more? And would he be able to do anything without making things even more awkward?

She settled the issue for him. "Be safe and have a good day, J.D.," she said as she picked up her coffee cup, sat back on her stool behind the counter, and gave him a gentle smile. "Give me time," she whispered. She blinked and looked away.

"Sure," he said. Time was all he had anyway. He repressed a sigh. "See you tonight."

"Sheriff, do you have a minute?"

Rick Sutton looked up from the reports on his desk. Deputy Dudley Evans stood in the doorway of the sheriff's office, his normally placid face lined with concern. Though he was only a year or two younger than Rick, with five years of service under his belt, he was often mistaken for a young rookie and was usually carded whenever he'd taken his wife, Myra, to dinner anywhere other than in Bonney. Since Evans rarely encountered anything he couldn't handle personally, Rick's pulse quickened. "Something wrong?" He pushed the reports aside and beckoned the deputy to enter.

"Not sure, Sheriff," Dudley admitted, stepping in and closing the door behind him. "There's a gentleman here to see you. It's in regard to, er, Ms. Stratham."

Rick winced and for once it wasn't due to the lingering soreness in his ribs. "Meghan? Who is it, her attorney?" *And what is she doing back in Bonney?* He bit back the last question. Deputy Evans was shaking his head.

"No, sir, it's not. Says his name is Alex Durán."

Rick frowned. The name meant nothing to him. "What does he want?"

"He wouldn't say, sir. Says it's personal."

Rick sighed. The last thing he wanted to do was to talk about his ex-wife with some stranger. He supposed he could have Dudley tell the man that he was too busy to see him and to get in touch with Rick's own attorney, but.... He shook his head; he might as well face it, whatever it was. "All right, send him in."

Dudley nodded and stepped out the door. Rick stood up as a man about his age entered the room. He was classically handsome, with smooth copper-colored skin, jet-black hair, and a trim, well-built physique which was set off by a well-cut designer suit. He didn't smile, but he reached out a hand toward Rick. "Sheriff Sutton? I'm Alex Durán." He had a slight, well-educated Spanish accent. "I hope I'm not intruding on your time."

"How can I help you, Mr. Durán?" He shook the man's hand then indicated the chair in front of his desk. He had to admit that he was intrigued. The man seemed ill at ease, but at the same time, completely business-like. He took a seat and seemed to be sizing Rick up, his piercing hazel eyes taking in the details of the sheriff's office, and in no hurry to start talking. Rick sat down, clamped down on his impatience, and waited.

Finally, Alex Durán spoke. "I'd like to get right to the point, but I'm not sure how to begin, Sheriff. I really don't like making trouble for people and... well, it's a situation that has been pretty much unknown for over ten years." He cleared his throat. "I understand you know Meghan Stratham."

Rick raised a brow and reined in his initial response. "Quite well," he answered dryly. He didn't ask, but the question of how Alex Durán happened to know Meghan was apparent.

Durán allowed a grim smile. "She was in Cabo San Lucas many years ago with several other young women for a," he paused, his eyes locked with Rick's, "bachelorette party."

"Yes," Rick said, his heart crashing hard against his ribs, making it hard to breathe. He remembered Meghan planning her bachelorette party, "one last fling", she'd laughed, before she became a married woman. Rick hadn't been pleased—she had narrowed it down to either Las Vegas or Cabo San Lucas—and he had refused to have a similar event with his groomsmen, whom he barely knew because they were simply the escorts of Meghan's bridesmaids. She had to have a fairytale wedding with eight couples as attendants and Rick just didn't have enough friends to fill the bill. He dragged his attention back to the present and got his emotions under control. "What about it?"

Alex Durán shifted in his seat. He seemed reluctant to fill in the details. Perhaps he hoped that Rick would do the honors, but Rick wasn't about to admit that he knew next to nothing about what went on during Meghan's weekend in Cabo. A weekend that ended up lasting eight days. He should have questioned it at the time, but Meghan had brushed it off as an extended spa day with very little that would interest Rick. He'd wanted her to be happy; at the time, that had mattered to him. Though his patience was waning fast, he forced himself to wait and let Durán take the lead. Durán took a deep breath.

"I worked at the resort where she and her friends were staying. I was a bartender," the man said, looking squarely at Rick. "I met her the first night they arrived. She was a very beautiful woman." Rick didn't react. Durán went on, "She didn't mention that she was getting married. She just said that it was a girls' weekend getaway. She... gave me a lot of attention. I didn't know she was engaged to be married," he repeated.

Rick wondered what she had done with the ten-thousand-dollar emerald-cut diamond engagement ring she'd insisted upon. Surely Alex Durán would have noticed it; she was always flaunting it. With a sick feeling in his stomach, he realized that when she said she was having "one last fling"... he cut off the thought. "So you hooked up with my fiancée during her bachelorette weekend," he said. He felt numb. It didn't matter now, he told himself. That was ten years ago, she had left him five years ago, they were divorced, even if the Church had found their marriage valid. It shouldn't sting the way it did. Even if Rick hated being played for a fool.

Durán jumped to his feet and started to pace. Rick watched him, wondering if the man expected him to react more strongly. Well, he guessed he'd just tell Durán that all was forgiven, it didn't matter anymore, and if he was still interested in Meghan, to get in line behind however many other men she was stringing along. It didn't affect Rick in any way.

Alex Durán stopped pacing and turned to face Rick. "We got married," he blurted.

Rick blinked.

Durán's expression didn't change. Rick wondered if he'd heard the man correctly. Durán drew a deep breath. "Yes. Meghan and I got married."

"What?" The question slipped out before Rick could gather his thoughts. Surely he was imagining things. Or he was misunderstanding what Durán was saying. There was no way....

"Two days after she arrived in Cabo," Durán said.

Rick stood up. "I think you need to leave Mr. Durán." He was surprised that his voice wasn't shaking. Durán frowned.

"You don't believe me."

"I don't know what you think you're doing," Rick said, keeping his emotions under tight control. "I don't know if you're trying to pull some kind of prank, if Meghan put you up to this, if she's trying to play some kind of mind game with me, but you need to leave. Right now."

Durán put his hands up. "Sheriff, I wasn't sure if you knew what happened, but I see now that you didn't. I can explain, if you'll let me."

"I'd love to hear it," Rick said tartly and shook his head. "Meghan and I were married a week after she returned from her trip. There's no way you and she...."

Durán pulled an envelope from his pocket and held it out to Rick. "Here's the proof. A notarized copy of our marriage license." Rick didn't make a move to take it. "It's all legitimate and legal, Sheriff. Meghan and I are married."

Rick's eyes narrowed. "What do you mean, 'are married'?"

Durán sighed and dropped the envelope on Rick's desk. "I mean what I said. 'Are married'. Present tense. We have been since then."

"Wait a minute," Rick said. He put his hands on the desk and leaned toward Alex Durán. He felt as if his head was going to explode. Nothing was making sense. "You're saying that you and Meghan are STILL married? That's not possible. She and I were married ten years ago. She divorced me five years ago and she's been married twice since then. That wouldn't be possible if she were married to you."

Durán looked miserable. "I know this is a shock to you. Let me explain." He cleared his throat. "Like I said, Meghan came on to me when she saw me at the resort. She and her friends, well, they were drinking a lot. I kept serving them because they were tipping extremely well and they were staying on site, so I didn't have to worry about them driving. She asked me what a good-looking guy like me was doing tending bar at a resort. She seemed so... I don't know. Caring. Attentive. Flattering. At some point, she told me she wanted to marry me. I could tell by this time that she had money." Durán's bronzed face turned red. "I guess that was wrong of me, but I was bartending to pay off my college expenses and support my family. I found myself telling her about my financial problems. She was so sympathetic. I saw that she was drunk but I was thinking more about a way out of my financial mess... and the fact that she was beautiful and very interested in me, well, that just made the prospect even more inviting." He cleared his throat. "I thought that surely she was joking, and when she sobered up, she'd be embarrassed about her behavior, but she asked me if I was willing to fly to Vegas to get married. The very next day. I decided to call her bluff and I said, sure, of course. She told me to meet her in the lobby the next day and be ready to leave. So I did." Durán raked his fingers through his hair. "She showed up, we grabbed a cab, we went to the airport and she booked us a flight to Vegas. We flew out that morning, took a cab to a wedding chapel, got married, and literally flew right back to Cabo."

Rick's head was spinning. He held up a hand. "You flew out of Mexico just like that," he snapped his fingers, "with a woman you barely knew and went to Vegas and got married? I'm supposed to believe this is true?"

Alex Durán sighed. "I know it sounds crazy. I'm actually an American citizen, I was born in San Diego but I was living in Mexico because my mother was deported along with my dad who was caught dealing drugs when I was fifteen. Mom needed me to help make ends meet when my dad died and then she got sick. I have a dual citizenship, I could have lived in the U.S. but I couldn't leave my mom. And I had a passport because I had to take my mom to a specialist in the States from time to time." He shook his head. "Meghan said we could fly to Vegas and get married immediately. So we did. I'll be honest... it was crazy, it was impulsive, and at the time, it seemed like an answer to prayer. I needed money, and it literally walked up and threw itself at me. We spent five hours on a plane each way from Cabo to Vegas and she never once mentioned you." He cleared his throat and glanced away. "She bragged about how much money she had and that I wouldn't have to worry about anything. I saw her ring... she claimed she bought it on impulse because she liked it. I told her I didn't have the money to buy her a wedding ring and she laughed and said she didn't need another ring. She made me believe that she was rich... and single. I was young and dumb enough not to question why a rich, beautiful woman would want to marry a poor bartender...."

Young and dumb. Rick could identify, all too well. "So what happened after you got back from Vegas?" Rick asked. "Obviously, she didn't stay with you." Durán flinched.

"No, she didn't," he said, his voice thick with emotion. "We got back to the resort and I was getting ready to go tell my boss what he could do with his job. Her friends were all sitting around the pool when she walked up to them. She turned to me, gave me her key, and told me to go up to her room and wait for her there. I walked away and then I looked back. She pulled out our marriage license and waved it at them. 'See?' she said. 'I did it. Now pay up!' They all stared at her and... I didn't know what to think. I

14

didn't understand what was going on. I went up to her room like she said and I waited." He drew a deep breath. "About an hour later, she came up and she had an envelope in her hands. She handed it to me and said, 'Listen, thanks for everything, your problems are over, but forget we ever met.' She handed me the envelope and then took our marriage license and tore it up. I didn't know what was going on." Alex Durán shook his head, his expression one of hurt bewilderment, as if he were reliving the moment. "I just stared at her and said, 'What?' And she laughed. She told me I helped her win a bet with her friends and that my cut of the winnings was in the envelope. Forty thousand dollars," he said, shaking his head. "She got each of her bridesmaids to put up ten thousand dollars apiece if she found a guy and got married within forty-eight hours. She kept her half and... I don't know, went off with her friends to spend it all, I guess."

Rick stared at him. Durán's face grew redder. Rick drew a deep breath. "I'm not sure why you're telling me all this, Mr. Durán, but...."

"Meghan is my wife, Sheriff Sutton," Durán broke in. "She tore up our license, but she never filed for divorce. She and I are still married. Which means...."

Rick froze.

Which means she and I never were.

15

Chapter 2

RaeLynn Shaffer felt giddy as she pulled into the parking lot of the salon where DeeDee Simpson worked. She had never gotten a professional haircut in her entire life; her mother had always done it, with varying results. And a manicure or pedicure? Not even in her dreams. She stared at her fingertips, curved over the steering wheel of Corrie's old Ford pickup truck, and felt her face burn. The thought of going inside and letting the beautiful DeeDee Simpson see her raggedy hair, her rough hands, and her acne-scarred face made her want to cancel her appointment and just go back to the campground. What difference did it make what she looked like there? Only Corrie and the Pages saw her every day. And the Myers. And Rick. And J.D. And... she felt her cheeks grow redder.

Her therapist had been pleased that she was going for some "self care", as she put it. She had been emphasizing to RaeLynn that her life wasn't ruined by what had happened in the past, that she was capable of a fresh start, that she could have a happy, successful life. What made her feel happy and successful was entirely up to her; only she could make that decision. And she had to start by believing that she was worthy of having a happy and successful life.

And Corrie gave her a gentle nudge with a gift certificate for a lot of "self care" at the Bella Vita Salon, hinting that it was time for a fresh start at a beautiful life. RaeLynn took a deep breath and got out of the truck, pulling the winter coat she had borrowed from Corrie a little tighter around herself.

Once inside the salon, she felt even more insecure. Unlike the rustic simplicity of the campground store, the salon was decorated with opulent gold, crystal, and plush velvet and satin in shades of lavender, purple, and mauve. A few of the local women were at various stations having services done by stunningly beautiful technicians who all called out a friendly greeting to RaeLynn. She managed to stammer out a response but she felt overwhelmed by sights and smells she was unfamiliar with. She stood, feeling lost, until DeeDee approached her, moving incredibly fast on her signature stiletto heels.

"RaeLynn!" DeeDee squealed as if greeting a long-lost friend. As always, DeeDee looked every bit the movie star she aspired to be. Today, she was sporting a deceptively casual looking messy bun, every strand of her dishwater-blonde hair perfectly in place. Despite the almost natural look of her face and nails, RaeLynn could see that DeeDee had used every service the salon offered to attain that appearance. What was it going to take for her to get to that point? Would she even be capable of getting halfway to that point?

And did she want to?

"Hi," she said feebly, praying she wouldn't blush. It always made her acne scars more noticeable. "I'm here."

"And I'm so excited!" DeeDee clapped her hands like a little girl at a party. "Let's get you started! I've got a station all set up for you! Oh, this will be so much fun!" She grabbed RaeLynn's hand and hauled her in the direction of the luxurious multi-service stations.

Within minutes, RaeLynn had her hands and feet soaking in tubs of lusciously scented warm water and bubbles, while DeeDee expertly tipped her chair back and started massaging a delicately floral scented shampoo through RaeLynn's hair, prattling away a mile a minute. RaeLynn barely registered what DeeDee was saying and wasn't sure how to respond, but it was soon obvious that DeeDee didn't expect more than "Oh, really?" or "Wow!" to any of her chatter and RaeLynn allowed herself to relax a little.

She wasn't sure what she would say when DeeDee asked how she wanted her hair cut and styled, but DeeDee was perceptive. She offered a "low maintenance" cut that didn't require a lot of time or styling tools or products to achieve at home. As DeeDee clipped away several inches of hair, RaeLynn felt as if the weight of years of stress and fear dropped from her shoulders. She noticed DeeDee scrutinizing her in the mirror as she expertly wielded the blow dryer and curling iron. "Let's do a little skin care while you're here," DeeDee said casually. "If you keep your skin moisturized, you'll be able to make those scars less noticeable without having to use a lot of concealer."

RaeLynn gave up trying to tell DeeDee that she didn't want a lot of fuss; DeeDee was on a mission. In less than two hours, DeeDee had RaeLynn's blond hair bouncing in waves that framed her face and ended just below her shoulders. She had shown her how to use very light makeup to minimize her scars and bring color to her face, emphasizing her tawny "tiger eyes". And as she worked on RaeLynn's toes, she offered advice on what colors to wear. "RaeLynn, honey," she drawled. "I know you admire Corrie a lot, but you can't copy her color style. She can wear those bold jewel tones," she pointed her scrubbing tool at the red sweater

RaeLynn was wearing, "but those colors wash you out. You need soft pastels and neutral, natural colors. That'll bring out your best looks." RaeLynn felt herself blush; it was true that she tried to mimic Corrie in a lot of ways. She did admire Corrie's confidence and no-fuss good looks. But her therapist had said that she eventually did have to find out who she, RaeLynn, was and be the best at that, not someone else.

It wasn't until DeeDee settled on RaeLynn's hands that her conversation turned more to gossip than instruction. "You really have no idea how much work a lot of people—and not just women—need to look their best," she confided. "And then others, well, it just comes naturally to them. Corrie, for one. She looks good without even trying. It's 'cause she's good people, you know? Being a good person brings out beauty better than makeup." She pointed her nail file at RaeLynn. "You know you got that going for you, right? You have to hold your head up, RaeLynn. You're a strong woman. Nothing I'm doing today is going to make you any prettier than you already are inside. All's I'm doing is giving you the pampering and respect you deserve. So when you walk out that door," she said, nodding in the direction of the salon entrance, "you better make sure you don't make me look bad. I have a reputation to maintain," she teased. "People think I make them beautiful and I don't want to lose my job."

RaeLynn felt a laugh bubble up in her throat when DeeDee winked at her. For once, she felt like a regular person, one who was accepted and could have friends and be like other women who had normal lives. Then she glanced over DeeDee's shoulder and let out a gasp.

Meghan Stratham stood staring down at them, with a bemused smile on her face.

RaeLynn swallowed hard and wished she hadn't reacted so strongly. It seemed like the entire shop had gone silent. DeeDee looked over her shoulder and put on a bland expression. "Hello, can I help you, ma'am?" she asked with a clipped, professional tone.

Meghan stood straighter, running an impeccably manicured hand through her silky blond hair. "I need to have a blowout done as soon as possible," she said. She kept her eyes hard on RaeLynn even though she was addressing DeeDee. RaeLynn fought the urge to squirm and she wasn't sure where to look. It seemed rude to stare right into Meghan's face but she didn't know what else to do.

"We're pretty booked up today, but I'll see if we can work you in," DeeDee drawled as she resumed brushing a base coat onto RaeLynn's nails. "Go ahead and have a seat in the waiting area and one of us will be right with you."

Meghan's beautiful features twisted into a sneer as she looked down her nose at RaeLynn. "You're almost done with this one, aren't you?" she snapped. "I'm in a hurry."

"Sorry, ma'am, but I don't rush my clients," DeeDee said, pausing in her work to give Meghan a cold glare. "And I'm in the middle of a service so you'll have to wait till I'm finished or someone else will help you. Either way, you're going to have to wait a few minutes."

Meghan's mouth dropped open in shock. DeeDee continued to ignore her. Then Meghan let her breath out in an exasperated sigh, spun on her heel, and marched away. RaeLynn heard the bell over the front door ring and then the low murmur of voices and hushed whispers came from the other salon stations. DeeDee shook her head. "You know who that was, don't you?" she whispered. RaeLynn nodded. DeeDee sighed as she bent over RaeLynn's hand. "Every time she comes to Bonney, she comes in here like she owns the place. And for some reason, she always comes to me. She tries to get me to talk about Corrie and Rick... but I don't gossip about my friends," DeeDee said, looking RaeLynn straight in the eye. "When she was married to Rick, I did go out of my way to be nice to her and accommodate her... but that was more for Rick than for her, to be honest. He never asked me to, but I got the impression she'd go give him grief and I didn't want to put him in a spot." She lowered her voice and leaned closer and RaeLynn suspected that she was about to break her own rule about gossip. "I've known Rick and Corrie since we were all kids, you know. And I have to admit I was totally shocked when they broke up. I don't know if anyone ever really warmed up to Meghan, but she didn't make it easy for us, you know, acting the way she does. I don't know what Rick ever saw in her," she said, shrugging her shoulders. "I guess things happen, but...." She paused as she carefully brushed French tips onto RaeLynn's nails. "I think this will be a nice look for you. Not flashy but classy. What do you think?"

"I like it," RaeLynn said. DeeDee nodded happily and began brushing on the top coat. RaeLynn drew a silent breath. "Does she come back often? Meghan, I mean?"

"Oh, yeah. Especially in the last year," DeeDee said. "Every few weeks. I don't know why, she always looks like she comes straight from getting her hair and face done... and at a much higher end place. Always asking about how well the Black Horse is doing. She knows I work there part time. I don't tell her much," DeeDee added as she finished RaeLynn's nails. "Just sit there and let them dry for a while." She began gathering up her instruments and towels and picked up the thread of her previous subject. "Like I said, I don't know why she keeps coming back. I hear from other sources," she tipped her head toward the other clients in the front area of the salon, "that she comes back and stays in town for a few days at a time. I don't know where she stays or why she keeps coming. I told Gabe about it last month and he said Rick's never mentioned it. So I don't guess she's coming to see him, but it's weird, you know? She hated Bonney the whole time she lived here when she was married to Rick, so why keep coming back now? And why does she care much about how the Black Horse is doing?"

"Meghan? She's in Bonney now?" Corrie blinked in confusion. When RaeLynn had burst through the door at the campground store, Corrie hadn't even had time to compliment her on her new haircut before RaeLynn was stammering out what she had seen and heard at the salon. Corrie's initial reaction had been to say she didn't care one bit about the fact that Rick's ex was in town or had been coming to town frequently—or at least, she shouldn't care—but when RaeLynn mentioned that Meghan always asked about the Black Horse at every visit, her suspicions were aroused. "Why is she asking about the Black Horse?"

"I don't know and neither does DeeDee," RaeLynn admitted. She twisted her hands together and a slight blush crept into her cheeks. "I'm sorry, I must sound like a terrible gossip, but it seems weird to me that she's asking about the Black Horse, especially after her boyfriend was offering to buy it a few months ago... I just thought it was something you should know."

Corrie nodded absently. It was true that Conrad Englewood, Meghan's boyfriend/lawyer, had been hanging around Bonney several months earlier and had even been a suspect in three cold case murders that J.D. had been investigating when he first joined the Bonney police department. Englewood had been persistent in asking Corrie if she was interested in selling the campground, despite Corrie's repeated firm refusals to entertain any offers, but he had just as firmly denied that Meghan had any knowledge of his inquiries. So why was she asking about the Black Horse now? Did she think Corrie had taken Conrad Englewood up on his offer? And why should it matter to her?

"I wonder if she's still with that boyfriend," Corrie mused. RaeLynn looked chagrined.

"I didn't think to ask DeeDee that," she said and Corrie shook her head and laughed.

"RaeLynn, don't think for one minute that I'd ask you to go fishing for that kind of information for me! Besides, who cares? Nothing Meghan does matters to me anyway. If she wants to know how the Black Horse is doing, she's more than welcome to walk in the door and ask me directly. I've got nothing to hide."

"But what if she's changed her mind and does want to buy it?" RaeLynn asked worriedly.

"Just because she, or anyone else, wants to buy it doesn't mean I have to sell it," Corrie said. "Not unless I want to." RaeLynn stared at her, her tawny eyes widening.

"You don't mean you'd actually consider selling the Black Horse, do you?"

Corrie blinked. She wouldn't have thought that the idea of the Black Horse being sold would bother RaeLynn so badly. She was wringing her hands so much that Corrie began to fear for her fresh manicure. It was then that she saw what the Black Horse meant to RaeLynn—a safe haven, a place where she had purpose, the place where the happiest memories of her life resided. A home. She smiled at her friend. "RaeLynn, there is no way that I would consider selling the Black Horse," she said firmly. "It's not just a business or just my home; it's my parents' dream, my dad's legacy. He left it to me, it's a part of him and my mother... and me. So you don't have to worry," she said, taking RaeLynn's hands in hers and squeezing them reassuringly. "The Black Horse isn't going anywhere, not as long as I'm around to keep it going."

RaeLynn blinked back tears and looked relieved. "Guess I'd better get to work," she said. "And check on dinner!" She hurried away and Corrie watched her go with a smile.

And a slight nagging feeling of unease.

Chapter 3

Rick paced his office, chewing on his lower lip furiously. As soon as Alex Durán left, Rick had told Dudley Evans he was unavailable for calls or to see anyone. Deputy Evans' dark face registered curiosity and concern that fought with his professional demeanor. Rick knew that his deputy wanted badly to ask what was wrong, but Dudley also knew that Rick wouldn't say anything if he didn't want to talk about it.

He forced himself to stand still for a moment and draw a deep breath. He had to think clearly. Few things had ever rattled Rick Sutton in his entire life. The last time was when he had received the judgment from the marriage tribunal regarding his appeal on his annulment petition. The Church had found, much to his dismay, that he was validly married to Meghan until death they did part. He had no one to blame but himself for that. He'd done everything in his power to make sure that he was really and truly married. At the time, that had mattered to him. The fact that Meghan had left him and divorced him didn't change the fact that they were married. She wasn't Catholic; she didn't understand or care about that. She went on to get married twice more while Rick steadfastly refused to consider that option. He couldn't. Not if he wanted to be true to his conscience. He'd already done enough to compromise it, he though grimly.

He looked down at the copy of the document that Alex Durán had left on his desk. The names stood out in bold relief as if they had been written with a paintbrush: Juan Alejandro Durán and Meghan Leigh Stratham. "Certificate of Marriage" arched across the top in Old English lettering. No, Durán hadn't given him a certified copy; he'd availed himself of the copy machine in Rick's office. He had assured Rick that his copy was one he'd requested from the chapel in Las Vegas after Meghan has unceremoniously torn up the one they had received at the ceremony. He equally assured Rick that there was no record, either in the U.S. or in Mexico, that Meghan had legally dissolved the marriage. As far as he, and the law, was concerned, he and Meghan were still husband and wife.

Rick sank into his office chair. The whole situation had him feeling more than just rattled. He was disoriented, confused, and— most dangerously—hopeful. If Meghan had been legally married to someone else when she and Rick had gotten married, then his marriage to her was not just illegal. It was invalid in the eyes of the Church. Which meant that, now that they were divorced, he was free to get married in the Church. He just had to present the proof to the tribunal, even if it meant another appeal, and then....

He snatched his cell phone out of its holster and paused. As much as he wanted to accept this at face value, he knew that he had to be sure, be positive, that Alex Durán and Meghan had been really, truly, legally married. And that Meghan hadn't obtained a divorce without Durán's knowledge. He almost laughed. What difference did it make? She had obviously lied to him, lied at the altar, to Father Eloy and the entire village of Bonney, pretended that there were no impediments to her marrying Rick. Pretended that marriage meant something serious to her. Just after having had a fling and married a bartender she had known for less than a day during her bachelorette trip to Mexico. Even if it was a Vegas wedding, even if she'd been married by Elvis, it was a legal marriage....

He stopped and took another deep breath. He needed to think rationally. He couldn't make another mistake and jump the gun again. Before he made another attempt to reconcile with Corrie, he had to be absolutely sure. Even before he contacted the tribunal. He needed to talk to someone. Someone with a clear head who could be brutally honest and trustworthy.

He picked up his phone and grimaced. There was only one person....

"You're kidding me, right?"

"No. I'm not."

"Of course you're not." J.D. sighed and leaned heavily against the adobe exterior of the San Ignacio church. Sutton's call had caught him in between a meeting with Chief LaRue about the village police department budget and doing evaluations for the rookie officers. Neither option had held any appeal for him and he jumped on the opportunity to do anything but be stuck at his desk, even if it meant talking to the sheriff about a personal matter in icy cold weather.

He'd been intrigued by Sutton's request to meet at the church. It was mid-week and probably the only time they wouldn't be seen by any of the numerous volunteers that flowed in and out of the church and parish hall at all hours of the day, except on the day that the office was closed. J.D. fought off a shiver that had little to do with the cold wind and pulled his leather jacket tighter around himself. They were standing at the back of the church where their vehicles weren't likely to be seen and where the building afforded some protection from the elements. Sutton wore a heavy jacket and kept his Stetson pulled low on his forehead. J.D. shook his head. "Tell me again. From the top."

The sheriff did, in agonizing detail. "I know this is awkward," Sutton said, as apologetic as he could sound, "and I know it sounds crazy, but I can't think of anyone else who I can trust."

"Thanks," J.D. said dryly. He held out his hand. "Let me see that certificate."

"It's not a certified copy," the sheriff said, placing the paper in J.D.'s hand. "Alex Durán had a notarized one; I checked and it looked legitimate. He just made this copy for me on my office copier."

"For what reason? What did he expect you to do? What is it he expects to gain from all this? Why not contact Meghan herself?"

"All questions I asked him," Sutton said. He also leaned against the church wall and blew out his breath. "He claims she avoids all his calls, and that all her friends and family have been instructed not to speak to him. He reasoned that I was the best option to get him in contact with her, because he figured she wouldn't have told me about all this."

"And what does he want? He wants her back? After ten years?"

"Apparently he wants either a reconciliation and, in his words, 'resuming their marriage roles'. Or he'll settle for a divorce so he can get married again. He was kind of cagey about his reasons for wanting to contact her, but I got the feeling he wasn't exactly entertaining some romantic ideal of reuniting with a long-lost love."

J.D. nodded with a grunt. "So did that forty grand Meghan gave him ten years ago help him at all?"

"He was well-dressed and sounded well-educated. I didn't inquire as to his current profession or financial status. So I don't know if it has anything to do with the money Meghan gave him or not."

"Easy enough to search online and see what comes up," J.D. said, watching Sutton closely. The sheriff looked away.

"I didn't think of that," he admitted. J.D. saw that the sheriff was so agitated that he wasn't his usual analytical self. He supposed he should be flattered that Sutton had thought of him when he needed someone who could think straight in a stressful situation, but he doubted that Sutton had considered how the situation would affect J.D. He cleared his throat.

"So what, exactly, do you want me to do? Aaron Camacho is good at...." He stopped as Sutton shook his head vehemently.

"I want this kept between us. I don't want to take any chances on anyone else hearing about this. Not until we find out what's true and what isn't."

"And if this," J.D. indicated the paper in his hand, "IS true, then what? What are you planning to do about it?" He was positive he knew the answer and he knew Sutton realized that as well. The sheriff looked him in the eye.

"Then the ball is in Corrie's court. Whatever happens next depends on her. But until we know for sure, I don't want her to know what's going on. She's got enough to worry about right now. So I'm asking you not to say a word to her."

"You know I won't. That's why we're having this conversation." J.D. sighed and raked a hand through his hair and tugged at his ponytail. "Has it occurred to you what this all might mean to ME?" he blurted. He almost regretted his outburst when he caught the pained look in Sutton's eyes.

"Believe it or not, yes, it has occurred to me," he said hoarsely. "I know it seems ridiculously cruel for me to ask for your help. If you say 'no', then I understand and we won't talk about this again."

J.D. almost laughed. Whether he helped Sutton or not, they would definitely be talking about it again. "Okay, let's talk about motive before we look for evidence."

"Motive?"

"Yeah," J.D. said, waving the paper in his hands. "Ten years. Legit or not, why would Durán wait ten years to claim what he believes is rightfully his? He claims he's a legal U.S. citizen so he can't say it's because he was stuck in Mexico and couldn't do anything. Apparently he's moved on and done something with his life, or else he's trying to make it look like he has. And how long has he been contacting Meghan? Has it only been recently? She's never said a word to you, has she?"

"She wouldn't," Sutton said. "She knows if I'd learned about it, I would have been able to have our marriage annulled and she'd have ended up with a substantially smaller divorce settlement since our marriage was illegal. She might have ended up with nothing at all."

J.D. let out a low whistle. He was well aware that Sutton's

family was one of the most wealthy and influential in the state, even though he never acted like it. "So why didn't she take Durán's calls? Or file for divorce instead of just walking away?"

"My guess? She knew that being married and divorced meant she couldn't marry me without going through the annulment process, which would probably result in that we couldn't have gotten married at all."

"I thought the Church didn't recognize civil marriages?"

"It doesn't... for Catholics. Meghan wasn't—and isn't—Catholic. Her marriage to Durán would have been recognized as valid and we wouldn't have been allowed to get married in the Church. A deal-breaker for me. And she knew it."

"So, then what? Did she really think tearing up the certificate made the marriage disappear without having to get the courts involved? Did they, uh, consummate the marriage?"

"I didn't ask," Sutton snapped. "I really don't care and it doesn't matter. It still would have been a legal civil marriage unless either she or Durán filed for divorce or an annulment. If neither of them made a move to legally dissolve the marriage, then they're still married."

J.D. was silent for a long moment, digesting all the information. Meghan had received a very comfortable settlement from the sheriff after their divorce although, as Sutton had once told him, it wasn't near as big as it would have been had she stuck it out till the sheriff turned forty years old and received the bulk of the trust his parents had set up for him instead of just the interest. What had possessed her to jeopardize that with a quickie Vegas wedding to a man she hardly knew? Was it just pre-wedding hijinks with her bridesmaids, fueled by copious amounts of alcohol? Some juvenile reenactment of a stupid rom-com movie that she thought she could make disappear with a snap of her fingers or a rip of a paper? He shook his head. He didn't know Sutton's ex that well, certainly not well enough to know if she had once been an extremely immature party girl that would pull off a stunt like a spur-of-the-moment wedding during her bachelorette party. But he felt he knew Sutton well enough to know he wouldn't have married a woman like that. Something wasn't adding up. "Do you believe Meghan would do something like this? Marry this Alex Durán, I mean?"

Sutton stared at him. "She did marry him."

J.D. shook his head. "That's what it looks like. But let's look at this logically. Is this something that you would believe Meghan would do? You know her better than I do. At any time, did you ever believe she would do something so impulsive and crazy?"

Sutton was quiet for a long time, his eyes faraway. He frowned. "No... she always seemed to be so level-headed and... well, calculating. It took her months to plan our wedding, down to the very last detail. She never left anything to chance, never did anything that she didn't consider what the outcome would be and how it would affect her." J.D. said nothing and the sheriff went on, "She never dated anyone who didn't have money or influence, no matter how good-looking or popular. She had a bunch of guys after her but she was careful who she went out with. A poor university student from the sticks with a scholarship living in student housing? Never. The frat guys who drove expensive cars and had their own apartments and money to burn? That was more her type. She didn't care about their potential to make money; she liked the guys who already had money at their disposal. She checked up on her suitors, made sure they were who they said they were. That's how she found out about me and probably was the only reason she gave me a second look," he muttered, his face darkening.

J.D. nodded. "So... not likely to pick up a good-looking but poor bartender who's trying to make ends meet while supporting an invalid mother and paying off his student debt?"

"Durán said she was drinking heavily," Sutton began then stopped.

J.D. shot him a keen look. "Was that out of character for her, too?"

"She hated to not be in control of herself and the situations around her."

J.D. refrained from pointing out that the same could be said for the sheriff but circumstances sometimes made people act wildly out of character. He cleared his throat. "So far, it's looking like Meghan had good reason to keep this all under wraps... if things actually happened the way Durán described."

"You think he's lying? That he's made all this up for some reason?" The sheriff's disbelief and disappointment was almost palpable.

"No," J.D. said. "I think all this actually did happen, whether it's out of character for Meghan or not. Because if it was all an elaborate lie, why would Meghan keep it to herself? Easy enough for her to disprove it. She was a law student, same as you, right? And even if she didn't know the law, she's had an army of lawyers

28

at her disposal for the last ten years, all of them bound by attorney-client privilege. Durán has kept quiet all these years because it suited him, but now there's a reason why he's rocking the boat."

Sutton held up a hand. "Look, Wilder, isn't this beside the point? What matters is whether or not Durán and Meghan really ARE married."

"And in order to make sure you don't end up being disappointed again, we need to make sure why this happened, if it really happened at all." J.D. was amazed that he was able to remain calm and rational, if not downright impartial, about the whole situation. He had a stake in all this as well; Corrie was, for lack of a better description, in mourning. In spite of all he had ever hoped, J.D. had to face the fact that she had still harbored a hope, no matter how small, that there was a possibility that Sutton would be able to resume the relationship that he had abandoned over fifteen years ago. The tribunal's last decision on his multiple appeals had been the final nail in the coffin, so to speak, of her hope. It was as if Sutton had dumped her again, as he had done fifteen years earlier. She needed time to get over losing him again before she would consider having any kind of relationship with anyone. And J.D. refused to be her rebound relationship. He only wanted her if she wholeheartedly wanted him, not just settled for him because the sheriff was completely off limits. He managed to keep his thoughts and feelings to himself while Sutton mulled over all he'd said.

Finally, the sheriff sighed. "Okay, so now what do we do? Contact the county clerk's office in Vegas to see if this certificate is legitimate?"

"No," J.D. said. "It's legit. It has to be. If it weren't, Meghan would have made this Durán guy disappear… in a legal sense. And you're such a Sir Galahad, Sutton, that if she'd come to you and said this guy was harassing her, claiming they were married when they weren't, you would have moved heaven and earth to get him off her back, even if the romance had all but died by that time. You're a man of honor and you wouldn't have let a lie destroy Meghan's reputation, even if she deserved it."

Sutton inclined his head and nodded. "Then what's our next move?"

J.D. pushed off from the church wall and stood in front of Sutton with his arms folded across his chest. He probably shouldn't enjoy this as much as he did, but he couldn't help it. "YOUR next move," he said, with a poor attempt to hide his glee at the sheriff's predicament, "is to contact your ex-wife and see what she has to say about Durán's claims."

Chapter 4

"I hope you enjoyed your stay here at the Black Horse Campground," Corrie said cheerfully, hoping she was hiding her dismay at the man's sudden decision to cut his weeklong stay short. He had paid in full for seven days, which included a discount of a day's stay, but now that he was leaving two days early, she had to refund him a full day's rent. Not that it was going to make or break her at this point, she had to admit to herself. Still, she was worried; no other guests had reservations for the next week or so. "I hope you'll recommend us to any of your friends or business associates who are looking for a peaceful getaway," she added, hoping she wasn't coming on too strong.

"Sure," he said distractedly. Corrie assumed he had to get back to his office and deal with an unexpected crisis. He probably hadn't heard a word she'd said. She printed out a copy of his receipt and pointed out his refund, to make sure there were no problems down the road. He barely looked at her as he snatched it from her hands and made his way out the door, pulling his cell phone out of his jacket pocket as he went. She sighed. "Well, goodbye," she muttered.

"Are you all right?" Jackie asked her, coming up to the counter. She patted Corrie's shoulder, already knowing what the answer was.

"We're in trouble, Jackie," Corrie answered, keeping her voice low so that RaeLynn, who was deep-cleaning the TV room, wouldn't hear. "No snow or any other kind of moisture in the forecast for the next two weeks. Lots of outdoor events have been canceled due to the high fire danger both in Bonney and Lincoln county. The ski resort in Ruidoso is shutting down, three weeks before spring break season. Everyone is taking a hit right now because of the lack of tourist business. I've got my three year-rounders but their rentals aren't going to pay the bills." She went on before Jackie could ask. "And I've already dipped into my emergency fund. I thought it was a good idea to make repairs and updates on the pool area while we were in the off-season, to be ready for the summer season. Now I'm not sure we'll make it to summer," she finished with a hitch in her voice.

Jackie squeezed her arm. "It will be all right, honey. The Black Horse has survived tough times and so have you. Something will work out."

"It better be soon," Corrie said. She thought about the pile of bills, insurance and taxes, and the financial statements on her desk. She knew she could request a loan to get through the slowdown in business, but her father, Billy, would be spinning in his grave if she did. He'd made sure the campground had been paid for, free and clear, before he had passed away two years earlier. "You might struggle, but no one can take the Black Horse away from you," he'd said to her. He had known tough times, too, but he'd kept his concerns to himself, always focusing on the positive and working to find a way. How Corrie wished she had his wise counsel to turn to! She shook her head. "At this point, I'm going to need a miracle to make it through the next couple of months."

The bell over the door rang, eliciting a welcoming "woof" from her black Lab, Renfro, who was sleeping behind the counter, and her heart leaped with hope. She turned toward the door with a smile that didn't have to be forced. "Hello, welcome to the...." Her voice trailed away in disbelief as her jaw dropped.

Conrad Englewood stood in the doorway, a smirk on his handsome face.

"I said 'miracle', not 'curse'," Corrie said under her breath to Jackie. She managed to wipe the shock off her face before she addressed Meghan's boyfriend. "What can I do for you?" she asked shortly. His smirk widened into a smile.

"Well, where should I begin? I'd think you'd be happy to see someone who could solve all your problems walk in your door," he said as he strolled to the counter, looking disarmingly casual. Corrie wasn't fooled.

"I doubt you know half my problems, much less solve any of them," she said tartly. "What is it you want, Mr. Englewood?" RaeLynn had stepped out of the TV room and gasped when she saw who was talking to Corrie. He turned and flashed a smile at the young woman and she shrank back into the doorway. He turned back to Corrie.

"I don't think it's necessary to repeat the offer I made a few months ago," he said. "Or is it? I thought it might be a good time to stop by and remind you that my offer is quite generous and," he paused and looked around the campground store at the lack of customers, "if I may be so bold, it seems to me you could use some generosity."

Heat rushed into Corrie's face. Her hand, resting on the counter, tightened into a fist. "I don't think it's necessary for you to be here at all," she said in a clipped voice, "and I'd like you to leave, Mr. Englewood. You have nothing I need."

He looked at her with a maddening expression of pity. "I'm sure you can find someone locally who can bail you out of your financial straits," he said, and Corrie clenched her jaw. "However, we all know that's not your style. You don't want to be in debt to a friend, no matter how close you are, to save your livelihood. So I'm here to offer you a deal with me, which you will agree, would not be the same as making a deal with a friend."

"I don't want any kind of deal with you and you can go now."

"A loan...."

"No."

"... instead of an outright purchase."

"I said 'no'. Do I need to spell it out for you?" she snapped. She stood up but decided to stay behind the counter so she could control her impulse to physically throw the man out of her store. "I already know how the rest of this conversation will go. You offer me a loan to help me stay open, suggesting that I use the Black Horse as collateral, despite the fact that business is slow and there aren't any signs that it's going to pick up in the near future and you'll be quick to pounce if I default. No, thank you. I won't risk my home or business falling into your hands. I have no idea why you want my campground so badly and I don't believe that Meghan has nothing to do with your offer, though I have no idea why SHE wants it."

"Meghan?" he said, looking confused and then chuckling. "I told you she has nothing to do with my offer. She doesn't even know about it."

"Oh, really? Then why is she showing up in Bonney so frequently the last few months? I didn't think there was anything here she ever cared about!"

"Well, you'll have to ask the sheriff about that," Englewood said dismissively. "Despite our personal relationship, professionally she and I have separate lives. So anytime she comes to Bonney, it's her business, not mine. I certainly have nothing to say to Sheriff Sutton, nor do I have any desire to see him."

"If you don't get off my property, Mr. Englewood, you'll be seeing him whether you want to or not!" She picked the phone up off the counter. "Do I make myself clear?"

"Very," he said with that maddening smirk. "I'll be seeing you again soon, Miss Black. Or call me if you need to talk to me sooner." It infuriated her that he seemed clearly unaffected by anything she said or did. She wished, just once, she could see him lose his composure.

She got her wish a second later. He turned toward the door just as J.D. walked in.

"Well, well, what a surprise, Mr. Englewood," J.D. said, masking his shock at seeing the lawyer in the campground store. He glanced out the window and raised a brow. "Trade in your sportscar for something more practical?" he asked, nodding at the battered four-wheel drive Toyota in the parking area.

Englewood managed to recover his poise before he answered. "Detective Wilder, of course it's no surprise that local law enforcement is always hanging around here," he drawled. "I just stopped in to see Miss Black about a business proposal."

"Again? Didn't the sheriff warn you about bothering her about your 'business proposal'?" J.D. said. He cocked his head to one side as Englewood gave an elaborate shrug.

"New year, new circumstances. I'm on my way out now, as you can see," he said.

J.D. stepped aside wordlessly and Englewood strode out the door without a backward glance. No one said anything as he got into the gray Tacoma and roared out of the parking lot. J.D. shook his head. "What did I miss?" he asked.

"The usual," Corrie groused. "He's still asking if I'm willing to sell the Black Horse."

"Corrie told him she wasn't interested at all. She was very clear about it, but he wouldn't take 'no' for an answer." RaeLynn surprised them all by speaking up. J.D. did a double-take at the sight of her looking more polished than he'd ever seen her. She flushed and her hands flew to cover her mouth. He noted her manicured nails and had to admit to himself that Corrie's gift to RaeLynn had produced great results. Her cheeks bloomed with embarrassment and she locked her gaze with his before looking away sheepishly. "I mean, Corrie handled it really well," she murmured.

"She shouldn't have to handle it at all," Jackie said firmly. She eyed J.D. "Isn't there a restraining order on him or something? Can't Corrie have one put on him?"

J.D. held up his hands. "Yes, but it would take time…."

"And money I don't have," Corrie blurted before she could stop herself. She shook her head. "Never mind, forget about him. I don't care what he claims, I'm almost positive that Meghan sends him in here just to annoy me and I won't give her the satisfaction of taking legal action. He's not around that much." She managed a smile for J.D. "And what brings you here, Detective? I thought you were on duty."

J.D. paused. On the way to the Black Horse from the church, he'd tried to think of a way to inquire about whether or not Meghan Stratham had been around without rousing curiosity, especially Corrie's curiosity. The sheriff had been adamant that he didn't want Corrie to hear about his current situation, not until he knew exactly what all the facts were. But now he wondered if Conrad Englewood's surprise appearance had given him the perfect excuse to probe without arousing suspicion. He cleared his throat. "I left something in my cabin and I noticed you had someone in the shop. I thought it might not be a bad idea to stop in and check on things. And it gave me an excuse to grab a cup of piñon coffee." He gave Corrie a roguish grin as he moved toward the courtesy table and filled a cup. "So, how long is Englewood in town?" he asked, hoping it sounded like a question that he would naturally ask. Corrie's brows rose.

"I have no idea," she said. "I didn't know he was in town, though I guess it shouldn't surprise me, since Meghan is in town, too."

J.D. nearly dropped his cup. He swallowed the searing hot gulp of coffee he'd taken and tried not to choke. "Oh, she is, huh?" he managed to say through the pain in his throat. He coughed and swallowed hard. "You've seen her?"

"Not me," Corrie said, nodding toward RaeLynn. J.D. turned to the young woman and she blushed and looked down.

"How'd you get so lucky?" J.D. said with a bantering tone, hoping his question sounded indifferent and casual. He tried to calm his galloping heart. He was getting more information than he expected.

RaeLynn glanced up at him shyly. "At the salon," she said. She went on to tell him about the encounter and finished with DeeDee's gossipy revelations.

"So she's been coming to town almost every month," J.D. mused. That was interesting, especially since it was apparent that the sheriff was unaware of that fact. J.D. knew that Sutton often let his ex-wife stay in his apartment in the village whenever she happened to be in town, but J.D. was under the impression that such visits were few and far between. She must have found another place to stay. "And DeeDee didn't seem to know why?"

"Probably to sic her minion on me," Corrie said and J.D.

became aware of her penetrating stare. He tried to maintain a neutral expression on his face as he turned and met the suspicion in her coffee-brown eyes. "You seem awfully interested in Meghan's activities," she said.

"Nah," J.D. said, finishing his coffee and tossing the cup away. He felt his casual act was becoming less convincing the longer he stayed around. "It's a slow, boring day in the village. Anything out of the ordinary keeps my brain from freezing up." He made a show of checking his phone for the time. "I'd better get back. Thanks for the coffee, Corrie. Ladies," he said, making a slight bow toward Jackie and RaeLynn. He headed for the door and tried not to hurry as he made his way to his Harley.

"That was odd," Jackie said before Corrie could voice the same opinion.

"I thought so, too," Corrie agreed. J.D. never felt the need to over-explain his reason for stopping by the Black Horse at different hours of the day. She felt he had stopped by for specific information and, strangely enough, seemed to have gotten it. Whatever it was. "Of course, if he needed something from his cabin...."

"But he didn't even go to his cabin," RaeLynn pointed out. Corrie's brow furrowed.

"Now what is he up to?" she murmured. Jackie shook her head, sending her long silver ponytail swinging as she wagged a finger at Corrie.

"Whatever it is, it's not your business," she warned. "Don't go nosing around something that could create problems for J.D."

"Would I do that? Don't answer that," Corrie said, holding up a hand as Jackie gave her a look. RaeLynn giggled and Corrie made a face at her. "However, if it's got anything to do with Conrad Englewood's visit, then it IS my business."

"And you'll be asked to get involved if that's the case," Jackie said firmly. She glanced at her watch. "I need to go get Jerry some lunch. Red and Dana are joining us for a game of canasta afterward, if you don't need any of us this afternoon. Do you want some lunch as well?"

"I think RaeLynn has us covered," Corrie said, flashing a smile at her friend. "I'll holler if I need anything, but consider yourselves off the clock for the rest of the day." Jackie nodded and went to get her coat from the closet under the stairs. Corrie looked at RaeLynn. "That includes you, too, RaeLynn."

"What? You want me to clock out, too?" RaeLynn said, pausing as she wrangled the vacuum cleaner out of the closet. Jackie shot Corrie an understanding look as she took her coat and hurried to the door, calling a hurried "good-bye" as she left. Corrie took a deep breath.

"Look, RaeLynn, I know this isn't the best time to do this, but I'm afraid I'm going to have to start cutting everyone's hours. Business hasn't been so great lately and I'm in a bit of a bind. I can't afford to pay you for a full forty hours; even Buster and Myra are down to only two days a week. I've already told them if they want to look for another job that my feelings won't be hurt. Seriously, there isn't enough work to keep everyone busy."

"You don't have to pay me," RaeLynn protested. "You're already doing more than enough by letting me live with you. And you can't do everything by yourself." Her faced paled. "You're not really thinking of selling the Black Horse, are you?"

"No, I'm not," Corrie said firmly. "Don't let that Conrad Englewood scare you."

"But, Corrie, what if that's what Meghan's been coming to Bonney for? And why she's always asking DeeDee about the Black Horse? Maybe she's been checking to see how business has been and she knows that things have been slow for a few months."

"Everyone knows business slows down a little after the holidays," Corrie said soothingly, but she had to admit to herself that RaeLynn could be on to something. Why else would Meghan be coming around so much?

RaeLynn said nothing, but she looked unconvinced. She mumbled something about going to check on dinner after she vacuumed the TV room. Corrie turned her attention to her reservation book. Blank page after blank page greeted her. She wondered if any other of her friends in the lodging industry was having the same kind of season.

The roar of the vacuum in the other room assured her that RaeLynn wouldn't overhear as she reached for the phone.

Chapter 5

"You know I don't believe in coincidences."

J.D. had sent a text to the sheriff, asking him to meet with him. Sutton had suggested Rozey's Diner for a quick meal break. They were ensconced in their usual corner table, reserved for local law enforcement officers, that was out of earshot of the other patrons... not that there were many. Diane, the long-time waitress who knew that what most of her customers at that particular table wanted was privacy, deposited two cups and a carafe full of coffee as soon as J.D. sat down. "The usual?" she drawled. "One with, one without?"

"Yes, thanks," J.D. said, grateful that it hadn't taken her long to learn that J.D. preferred his food be free of the ubiquitous green chile that seemed to appear on just about everything from eggs to hamburgers to apple pie in New Mexico. Without preamble, he told the sheriff everything he'd learned from Corrie and RaeLynn at the Black Horse. Sutton listened, his face expressionless until J.D. finished, just as Diane appeared with their burgers. He handed her his credit card and a fifty dollar bill.

"The tab goes on the card, the cash in the tip jar," the sheriff said quietly. "And tell Rozey I'm picking up lunch for the whole department. You know what everyone likes." Diane's face registered surprise and then gratitude. She blinked her eyes rapidly, murmuring a heartfelt "thank you" before she hurried away. J.D. raised a brow.

"Rozey is struggling right now," Sutton said, keeping his voice low. "A lot of small business owners are. You know Corrie is. Everyone is having to cut hours on their employees. Times are tough everywhere. It's like this whenever the weather doesn't cooperate. The area relies on a cold, wet winter to keep businesses going. No winter sports, no tourists. No outdoor fires, no campers." He drew a deep breath and shook his head. "And it's just like Meghan to try to capitalize on other people's misfortune."

"So you don't believe that she isn't in cahoots with Conrad Englewood."

"I'm surprised she isn't more discreet," Sutton said. "So she's in town right now. Wonder for how long? And I don't believe for one minute she doesn't know Englewood's in town."

"What about Alex Durán? Think she's likely to run into him?"

"If Durán's story is true, I'd say she doesn't know he's here

39

and, if she did, she would do everything in her power to avoid him."

"So are you going to let Durán know she's here? I assume you have his number."

The sheriff shook his head and shrugged. "I'll be honest, I'm not sure what to do. My first impulse is to look for her myself and ask her a few questions."

J.D. had taken a bite of his burger, watching the sheriff wrestle with his dilemma. He hadn't touched his food yet. He nudged the sheriff's plate closer. "You'd better eat. We've got work to do after lunch."

"We do?" Sutton asked, reaching for his food. J.D. nodded.

"Yeah. I haven't had time to look up Durán yet, but I plan to do that after I get back to the office. Despite what you might prefer, it wouldn't hurt to get your family lawyer up to speed on what's going on. There's a chance Durán is just playing you and you'd better make sure none of you get blindsided."

"I don't see how Durán can expect to get anything out of me."

"Still, it doesn't hurt to be prepared." A soft buzz came from J.D.'s phone. He checked the screen and grimaced. "I forgot, I told LaRue I'd meet with him about promotion evaluations this afternoon. I shouldn't have put him off last week; now he won't stop hounding me about it. I better get it taken care of. I'll get to checking on Durán as soon as I can."

"Never mind, I'll do it," Sutton said. He shook his head. "I don't know why I didn't think to do it from the beginning."

"You were thrown off. Anyone would have been," J.D. pointed out.

"No excuse," the sheriff said. "I've got my head back on straight. I need to stay focused. One step at a time." He gave J.D. an earnest look. "I have to thank you, Wilder. And apologize. I shouldn't have gotten you mixed up in this. This is my problem to take care of, but I appreciate you stepping up. I needed a clear head in this, since mine wasn't doing so well."

"Don't mention it," J.D. said, meaning it wholeheartedly. He tried to treat this situation like another case, not as personal as it truly was. Otherwise, he'd have bailed by now. "You're sure you're okay to do the checking? You might not like what you find," he warned.

Sutton gave a firm nod. "I'm preparing myself for that possibility. In fact, I realize now that I'd rather be the first to find out about anything like that than hear it from anyone, even you," he said. The fact that there wasn't a trace of apology in his tone made J.D. chuckle.

"You've recovered from the shock very well," he said. They finished up their meal and stopped by the cashier counter to pick up the meals for the sheriff's department. J.D. decided to do the same for the village police department the following day, handing Diane his credit card and dropping a generous cash tip in the jar as well. Rozey came out to thank them personally for the business while Diane answered a phone call.

"Can't tell you how much I appreciate it," Rozey said, pushing his grease-stained ball cap back on his balding head. Roosevelt "Rozey" Dennison had owned the diner for years and was as much a fixture in the village as the Black Horse. "I gotta tell you guys, I haven't seen it this bad in years. State cops pulled me over just outside of Ruidoso last week. I had changed a flat and forgot to secure the chain that holds the spare under my truck. He gave me a warning, said that dragging that chain could throw sparks that could start a fire. They're not messing around. Huge fines if they catch you smoking outside of a closed vehicle, never mind tossing a lit cigarette out a window. Bad enough the tourists aren't coming into town, but everyone is tightening their belts. We need snow badly, even rain, but the dry weather doesn't show any signs of letting up. And the wind is predicted to be pretty bad the next week or so. We need some relief," he said, shaking his head.

J.D. marveled at the differences between Bonney and his old hometown of Houston. He didn't recall any true concern about the effect of drought on local businesses. Houston's weather problems tended to run in the other direction, too much rain instead of not enough. Still, he knew that he'd choose Bonney over Houston, for more reasons than he cared to count.

He was helping the sheriff carry the lunch bags out to the Tahoe when Diane hurried out to them. "Hey, Sheriff," she said, keeping her voice low, "I'm not sure if I'm doing the right thing or not, but someone just called, looking for you. Wouldn't say who it was and I honestly couldn't tell if it was a man or woman calling. I didn't tell them you'd been here or that you were just leaving, but I did tell 'em to check at the sheriff's department. I hope I didn't do anything out of line," she said, shaking her head and sending her bright pink dice earrings swinging.

J.D. and Sutton exchanged a glance. "That's fine, Diane, I'm sure Laura will get in touch with me right away if it's urgent," he said. J.D. knew that the sheriff department's dispatcher, Laura Mays, had an uncanny knack for knowing how and when it was necessary to get in touch with the sheriff when he was 10-7b, out of service for personal reasons. Right now, the only unidentifiable person who was likely to know to seek out the sheriff at Rozey's Diner was Meghan; Corrie would have no doubt identified herself. Diane nodded, thanked them again for their generosity, and headed back inside. Sutton sighed. "I guess I'd better get back to the office before Meghan starts making a nuisance of herself."

"Are you planning to bring up Alex Durán?" J.D. said as he mounted his Harley. Sutton was chewing his lower lip.

"I don't want to, but I also don't want to drag this out longer than necessary. I'll try to call my attorney before I talk to her, unless she's waiting outside the department for me."

"Good luck," J.D. said dryly as he started the engine. The sheriff raised a hand in good-bye and got into his vehicle.

Corrie hung up the phone and stared at the list in front of her pensively. The only motel in Bonney and the bed-and-breakfast were run by people who Corrie considered friends. They often referred guests to each other when any of them were booked to capacity. They also had connections in Ruidoso with other places of lodging. She had called a total of six places and got interesting—and depressing—information.

The depressing part was that all were reporting significant drops in business. The B & B owner admitted to planning on closing up completely for the next month once their current guest checked out. That was the interesting part; it was Meghan Stratham.

Corrie dismissed the twinge of conscience she felt at having been, to be completely truthful, nosy. Besides calling and commiserating with her fellow business owners about the lousy weather and even worse tourist traffic, she had probed gently and was rewarded with the information that, at one time or another in the last six months, they had all had Meghan as a guest. It helped that all the lodging owners knew Corrie's and Rick's history and they expressed outrage over Rick's ex showing up in town after disparaging Bonney so much when she had still lived there. Corrie did her best to pretend to take the high road and insist on not hearing any details but, human nature being stronger than her acting skills, her friends still imparted more information than they probably should have. No, no one was with Meghan; yes, she asked about how business was and if they knew how the Black Horse was doing; no, she didn't mention Rick very much; yes, she seemed particularly interested in Corrie's financial status.

"And let me tell you," Ida Lopez, the manager at the motel, said, her voice shaking with indignation, "I told her a thing or two about nosing into people's business that was none of her concern! Told her it didn't matter one bit how bad things were, it was none of her business how financially strapped we are, especially you, Corrie! I know you wouldn't have cut Myra's hours unless you really couldn't afford to pay her, especially knowing she's got a baby on the way and she and Dudley really could use the money what with having to take care of her grandma and all...." Corrie winced, glad that Ida couldn't see her over the phone. It was easy to forget how everyone in Bonney County was connected to one another and she should have known that Ida, being Myra's cousin by marriage, would have heard about how Corrie had to pare down her work crew due to lack of business. She wondered if she should ask Ida if she had told Meghan that information, but decided that it was a safe bet that she probably had.

After she got off the phone, she stared dejectedly out the window. Buster, she knew, had already applied for a job with the village; Myra had picked up part-time hours at Noisy Water Winery in Ruidoso, although she could only work a few months until the baby was born; Dee Dee had the salon and her part-time dispatcher job at the sheriff's department. She knew her employees would be all right, but could the Black Horse survive this downturn in the economy? What else could she do?

She could ask Rick for a loan, for any amount, and he'd give it to her without hesitation, without interest, and without a due date. He wouldn't even ask her why she needed it. But she couldn't—wouldn't—do that. Not after finding out that he had been hoping that they still had a chance, a chance that they both thought had been gone forever. Maybe it was foolish or hurt pride, but she wouldn't take advantage of him that way. Not now. Maybe not ever. And by then it would be too late to save the Black Horse.

She heard the vacuum shut off in the TV room, but she didn't hear RaeLynn singing or humming like she often did while working. She'd been so happy that she would at least be able to offer RaeLynn a job and a home while she recovered from her ordeal, a refuge after a life filled with insecurity. Now she wasn't sure if she, herself, would have a home and business if things didn't improve. She had been truthful to RaeLynn about having no intention of selling the campground.

What she hadn't been able to be honest about is that she might end up with no choice in the matter, regardless of her intentions.

Chapter 6

Rick hadn't bothered to return to his office after delivering the lunch he'd bought his staff at Rozey's Diner. After verifying with Dudley that no one was there waiting for him, he decided it was time to take the bull by the horns and stop waiting for something to happen. After he made a few phone calls, he found himself pulling into the parking lot of the River's Edge Bed and Breakfast as Meghan was getting into her silver BMW sedan.

"Well, look who finally decided to stop avoiding me," she snapped straightening up from stashing her Givenchy bag in the passenger seat. She tugged her cashmere Burberry trench coat closely around herself and adjusted the Hermès scarf that shielded her face and hair from the wind. She'd never been one to be faithful to just one designer.

She'd never been one to be faithful, full-stop, Rick thought fleetingly as he stepped out of his department Tahoe. He wished he'd found that out ten years earlier. He didn't say a word until he was standing face to face with her. For a moment, he was struck by the fact that her beauty didn't affect him at all anymore. The first time he'd seen her, sitting in a lecture hall at the University of New Mexico surrounded by young men who were vying for her attention, she became the first woman who had turned his head since he had broken up with Corrie. And now he didn't even know why. Maybe it was because, all those years ago, she hadn't worn the veneer that came with money. She had been attractive in a more natural setting, in a less pretentious manner. She'd been a well-bred, well-off young woman who had kept her status under wraps until she had found a young man who met her standards of class and financial standing. She hadn't given Rick a second look until one of her friends, who happened to be the daughter of one of his mother's social acquaintances, clued her in to what was hiding underneath the boots, faded Wranglers, and button-down Western shirts. And then he became her mission.

And that's all I was—a means to an end, he thought, and the realization didn't hurt as much as it once had. He stopped an arm's length from her and tugged on the brim of his Stetson in greeting. "What do you want, Meghan?" he asked quietly, determined to stay in control.

She glared at him. He had no idea why she seemed to be angry with him, but that had been something he had become accustomed to in the last year of their marriage. Now he didn't really care, but he was curious.

"You've been stonewalling me for months!" she snapped. "I don't know why you're making such a big deal of this."

"Let me think," he said, resting his hip against the front of the Tahoe. "Oh, yeah. The fact that you're making such a big deal about wanting to move our daughter, who you never wanted and couldn't even wait until she was buried to file for divorce from me, six hundred miles away so she could be closer to you when you don't even visit her grave when you're here. I can't believe you have the nerve to ask why it's a big deal to me."

She drew back, her ice-blue eyes widening, as if Rick had been shouting at her. He hadn't raised his voice much more than a whisper. He didn't care to have the entire village privy to his personal conversations. He figured she was just surprised that he'd dropped all pretense of politeness and was meeting her head-on about the issue instead of avoiding her. She glanced back at the building as if concerned that the B&B's owners might be listening in on their private conversation. "What's gotten into you, Rick?" she hissed.

"Maybe I'm tired of pretending I care," he said bluntly. Meghan blinked. He pushed off from the Tahoe, ignoring the twinge of pain in his side. "Maybe I'm tired of believing that I owe you some respect just because at one time I cared enough to ask you to marry me. Maybe I'd like, just once, to know that I'm being told the truth, that I don't have to question every single thing you tell me."

"I don't know what you mean."

"The name Alex Durán mean anything to you?"

For a split second, panic flashed in her eyes. When she answered, it came after a fraction of a second too long to sound natural. "Who?"

"You know," he said stonily. "Alex Durán. Your husband."

She forced a careless laugh. "I'm not married. Not right now, anyway."

"That's what you think."

"I don't know what you're talking about."

"Really? Maybe you should call the wedding chapel you went to in Las Vegas. They might be able to jog your memory. Or maybe this will," he said pulling out the envelope in which he'd put the copy of the certificate Alex Durán had given him. To her credit, she didn't reach for the envelope, though he could tell it was taking every ounce of will power she possessed not to. Her eyes narrowed.

"What's that supposed to be?"

"A copy of your marriage certificate," he said. She still didn't reach for it, but her face grew whiter.

"And where did you get that?" she said, her attempt to sound anything but panicked failing miserably. She managed to keep her eyes fixed on Rick's although her answer came through gritted teeth. He fought the urge to smile at her anxiety.

"Mr. Durán was kind enough to drop it by my office this morning."

"He what? Alex is here?" Meghan's façade shattered completely. She snatched the envelope from Rick's hands and tore it open.

"It's not a certified copy," he said as she scanned the paper in disbelief. "But I can request one from the county clerk's office… now that I know the document exists."

"This is a joke," Meghan said, tossing her head and shaking the paper at Rick. "That's all this is. It means nothing, it's just a big joke."

"Oh, I know marriage means nothing to you," he said, his voice hardening. "And the joke is on you, Meghan. You were married to another man while you went through with our wedding. Our marriage is not only invalid, it's also illegal. You and I were never married."

"That's ridiculous!" she snapped. She seemed to have pulled herself together although there was a tremor in her voice. "Of course you and I were married! This," she indicated the paper in her hand, "never happened!"

"Tearing up the original certificate and paying off your husband's debts to keep him quiet doesn't make your marriage disappear," he said dryly. "As much as you'd like to pretend that if you believe that it never happened, it will all go away. You never filed for divorce, Meghan."

"I didn't have to!" she stormed. She pointed at him with the envelope. "The whole thing was a joke, just to win a bet! Nothing about it was legal!"

"The state of Nevada would disagree with you about that."

She started to speak, then stopped, trembling with rage. Rick told himself to be patient. He was surprised at how calm he was… and it wasn't an act.

"This doesn't mean a thing," she repeated, her voice low and controlled. She jammed the envelope into the pocket of her coat.

"I don't care what Alex told you, he is NOT my husband! He never was! He's twisting the whole thing around for some reason."

"What's 'the whole thing' he's twisting, Meghan?" Rick said. "Your trip to Vegas? The visit to the wedding chapel? The bet with your bridesmaids? The fact that not twenty-four hours after you left me to go on your bachelorette trip you were hitting on a bartender you'd never seen before and telling him to marry you, two weeks before our wedding?"

"We're done speaking," she said coldly, turning to get into her Beemer. Rick caught the car door before she could slam it shut.

"Alex Durán is looking for you. He says he's been trying to contact you but you don't answer and you tell your friends and family not to speak to him. Why are you avoiding him?"

"I have nothing to say to him or to you," Meghan said tartly. "Now take your hands off my car or I will call the police."

Rick reined in the impulse to scoff. He raised his hand off the car door and took a step back. "Why now, Meghan? Why, after ten years, is he now approaching me? He must have known about us... why did he wait so long?"

Her response was to slam the door and start the car. He stood watching as she backed out of the parking area and drove away. He shook his head and got back into the Tahoe.

"Interesting," J.D. said. He pushed away from his desk and the performance evaluations he was supposed to be reviewing and gave the sheriff his full attention. "She didn't deny it?"

"First she pretended she didn't know what I was talking about, then she seemed to believe that it didn't matter. 'It means nothing', she said, over and over." J.D. could hear the wind, occasionally drowning out Sutton's words and he wondered where he had gone so as not to be overheard. "I made some calls, first to my attorney, who said he'd do his own checking, then I called the county clerk's office in Vegas. They were swamped but they said they'd look up the paperwork and send me certified copies as soon as they could, which might be a couple of weeks from now, even after I paid the fee. I tried to call the wedding chapel but they went out of business years ago...."

"A wedding chapel in Las Vegas went out of business? You're kidding."

"Nope. I found a newspaper article that said that a fire started in the chapel and all the records from five years ago and farther back were ruined by the sprinkler system. So I'll have to wait for the clerk's office to send me the copies."

"So Durán must have secured his copy before the fire... before you and your ex split up." J.D. tapped his pen on his desk, frowning. "Wonder why he didn't get it from the clerk's office?"

"What makes you think he didn't?"

"I could be wrong but I don't think certified copies of marriage certificates are as ornate as the one Durán had. That looks like one that a chapel would issue, you know, for the couple to put in a frame with their wedding photo. Did they take a wedding photo?" J.D. asked suddenly.

"If they did, I doubt Meghan has it lurking in a scrapbook somewhere," Sutton said dryly. "And Durán didn't show me one."

"And if the chapel took one, it was probably destroyed along with the records."

"You think the certificate Durán showed me was fake?" Sutton sounded both incredulous and defeated. J.D. shrugged, even though the sheriff couldn't see him.

"I'd think that if it weren't for the fact that Meghan kept saying that it meant nothing. I suppose it would be possible that she arranged a mock wedding, for the express purpose of winning her bet with her friends...."

"I was stupid enough to let Meghan keep the copy Durán gave me," Sutton muttered. "But it said it was issued by the wedding chapel and that they had ten days to file it with the recorder at the clerk's office." His voice shook slightly and J.D. felt a hitch in his gut.

"There should have been a stamp or something to show that it was received and recorded by the clerk's office," he said. He heard the sheriff blow out his breath.

"No," he said, a note of resignation in his voice. "The copy Durán had was notarized, but it wasn't certified. Which means...."

"Which means we don't know that it wasn't filed," J.D. said firmly. He had no idea why he was encouraging Sutton to think that Meghan was legally married to someone else. Why wasn't he telling him to forget the whole thing, that it was obviously a hoax, that Sutton was still married to Meghan and Corrie was beyond his reach? He knew the answer before he even finished his questions: because they both wanted the truth. And that Corrie would expect nothing less from either of them.

It always came back to Corrie.

J.D. went on, "It's up to the wedding chapel or the officiant to file the license. Unless Meghan arranged for them not to do so…."

"Which she might have," Sutton muttered. J.D. ignored him.

"…but they would have had to have Durán's agreement."

"Meghan has money," Sutton said. "She had enough back then to have paid someone off to ignore protocol, lose the license, anything to not get it filed."

"So how did Durán get his copy?" J.D. asked. Silence greeted him for a long moment and he went on, "Look, Sutton, Durán said Meghan tore up the license once they were back in Cabo, right? That had to be the commemorative one that the chapel gave them, so of course, the actual license hadn't been filed yet, since they left Vegas immediately after the wedding. By law, they had ten days to file it. If Meghan didn't deny the wedding, if her only response was that, 'it meant nothing', then there probably is still a legit marriage certificate floating around in the county clerk's office in Vegas."

"So why doesn't Durán have it?"

"Beats me. I'm willing to bet that after Meghan dumped him in Cabo and tore up their license, he called the chapel to have them send him a notarized copy of the certificate."

"And held onto it for ten years without acting on it?"

"Hey, I'm not a mind-reader. I'm just spitballing here, trying to figure out how this happened. If you want to know WHY it happened, you'll have to talk to Durán again. Meghan won't talk to you and my guess is she's hightailing it out of town as we speak, especially now that she knows Durán has talked to you."

The sheriff's sigh sounded as loud as the wind howling into the phone. "Let me see what I can come up with. I'll be in touch." And he hung up before J.D. could argue.

Chapter 7

"There has to be a mistake," Corrie stammered. "There's no way I can possibly owe that much in late fees! I've always paid my insurance on time and I have the canceled checks to prove it! And when did my policy premiums increase anyway?"

To give credit where it was due, the young woman on the other end of the line was sympathetic. "Ma'am, I'm sorry, but we did send a notice several times last summer and fall and I have a note here saying that one of our agents spoke to you directly and advised you of the increase in policy premiums on your fire and flood insurance." She rattled off the dates that the conversations took place and Corrie's heart sank. She knew exactly when those events happened... when she was recovering from amnesia after being attacked by Troy Thompson's girlfriend, Elsa Sandoval, and almost ended up being Troy's fourth victim. She hadn't even remembered meeting J.D. earlier that year and her memory was full of blank spots. She should have known that it would have been best to allow Jerry or Jackie to take over the financial operations of the Black Horse while she was recovering—the doctors had told her that it would be a while, possibly months, before she could reasonably expect her memory to recover completely from the trauma. However, she had stubbornly refused to be treated like an invalid.

Now she wondered what else she had forgotten in the last several months.

She thanked the young woman and hung up. She stared at the sum she'd jotted down on the notepad in front of her. She'd circled it in red and underlined it several times, as if that would make it go away or magically be paid off. The wind, rattling the windows, sent a shiver down her spine and drove home the seriousness of her blunder. In all the years that the Black Horse Campground had been in existence, it had always been fully insured against any and all potential disasters. Her father, Billy, had always emphasized the importance of keeping the insurance paid up to date, especially during times of extreme weather, when a fire or flood could easily destroy everything they had spent their lives building. And while they had never, thank God, had to use their insurance, Corrie felt as if she'd let Billy down by not staying on top of things the way he had always taught her.

And now, she was in deep trouble.

The numbers on her notepad seemed to grow darker and more

accusing. She just didn't have the money to get everything up to date and she only had three days before they canceled her policies and then it would cost a fortune to get everything insured again. More money she didn't have, on top of salaries and taxes due. She was thankful she had put off ordering merchandise for the stores for spring break, but the amount she had saved wasn't going to be enough to cover this expense. What could she do?

I could ask Rick for a loan, she thought and immediately shook her head. No, she would not take advantage of their friendship… or whatever their relationship was now. Things were already awkward enough between them; having a debt would only make things unbearable. The bank was out of the question. While she was sure they would give her the loan, the slowdown in business made it difficult to determine if she'd be able to pay it off on time. And defaulting on a loan would make Billy spin in his grave, not to mention possibly mean losing the Black Horse.

She wouldn't take that chance.

Jerry and Jackie had a nest egg set aside. They were both in their late sixties and should have been enjoying life instead of helping her run the Black Horse. To them, it was just as much their home and business as it was to Corrie and had been to Billy, having stepped in to help him raise Corrie when her mother had died. But it wasn't their responsibility and she knew they were waiting for the day when they didn't have to set an alarm clock and their days weren't scheduled around the campground. She wouldn't jeopardize their future by asking them to do more than they'd already done for her.

She pushed the notepad aside and a business card fell to the floor. She picked it up and felt a sharp stab in her gut. *Conrad Englewood, Attorney at Law.* She almost dropped the card as if it had burned her fingers and the polished script seemed to taunt her. His offer would most certainly cover the expenses she had, possibly save the Black Horse, but would it still be hers? Or would it belong to the person to whom she owed money? Well, there was no question that if she was going be in debt to someone, it wouldn't be Conrad Englewood or, more likely, Meghan Stratham. Having to ask Rick for a loan would be hard enough; the thought of his ex-wife holding the future of the Black Horse in her hands would be too bitter a pill to swallow.

"Corrie, what's wrong?"

Corrie gasped and jumped, RaeLynn mirroring her actions on the other side of the counter. She hadn't heard her friend come down the stairs and walk up to the counter. "Oh, RaeLynn, you startled me!"

"I'm sorry," RaeLynn said, her face turning red. "I didn't mean to. But you already looked like you'd seen a ghost and I was worried about you. Did something happen?"

Corrie cursed her transparent face and emotions. But the truth was she couldn't keep RaeLynn in the dark about the situation. She took a deep breath. "Yeah, kind of," she said, trying to force a smile. "I guess I really messed up when I didn't let someone take over my office work when I was recovering from amnesia." She found herself telling RaeLynn about her conversation with the insurance company and how she had found herself in even more dire financial straits than she had been before. RaeLynn's face paled and she shook her head.

"Oh, Corrie, that's awful! What are you planning to do? You're not planning on closing down the campground, are you?"

"I might not have a choice, RaeLynn, but even then...."

"You can't sell it!" RaeLynn cried, tears streaming down her cheeks. "You just can't! Oh, Corrie, you can't give up your home and business!"

"I don't want to," Corrie said, dangerously close to tears herself. "But if I can't get the money in three days, it might be the only thing I can do."

"No!" RaeLynn actually stamped her foot. "You are NOT going to call that Conrad Englewood and ask him for help! I'll help you! I have money set aside and I won't take no for an answer! Just tell me what you need!"

"Wait, what are you talking about?" Corrie stammered, stunned by her friend's passionate reaction and offer. "What do you mean you have money set aside?"

"Oh, Corrie, what do you think I've been doing with my paychecks since I've moved in?" she said. "You won't charge me rent and you hardly let me pay for anything! I have money put away and you can have every last penny, if that's what it takes to keep the campground open!" She grabbed Corrie's hands and squeezed them hard. "I know you don't want my help, or anyone's help, for that matter," she said. "But I *want* to help and you've done so much for me that I'll never be able to repay. Please, Corrie, please let me help," she implored.

"I don't know what to say," Corrie breathed. She was humbled and blown away by RaeLynn's offer. But did she have enough to help? Was she only getting her hopes up to be disappointed?

"Well, start by telling me how much you need!" RaeLynn said, bouncing impatiently. "I can't help you if you don't tell me!"

"RaeLynn," Corrie began, then stopped. She wanted so badly to believe that RaeLynn's offer would be able to help, but surely she only had a few hundred dollars, nowhere near enough to make a dent in what she needed.... "It might be more than what you can offer...."

"Is fifteen thousand enough?"

Corrie grabbed hold of the counter as the blood rushed out of her head. Had she heard RaeLynn correctly? "What?"

RaeLynn's face fell. "Fifteen thousand dollars. It's all I have, Corrie. I'm sorry it's not more but will it help just a little?"

"Help a little?" Corrie laughed and wiped at the tears she couldn't hold back any longer. "A little? RaeLynn, that's more than enough! Where on earth did you get that much money? I didn't realize I was paying you THAT well!"

RaeLynn squealed with joy and clapped her hands. "Oh, I'm so glad! Listen, tell me what you need, I'll go to the bank right away and...."

"Whoa, slow down," Corrie said, catching RaeLynn's arm as she tried to dart away to grab her coat. "Sit down for a minute. We need to talk about this and work out details."

"What details?" RaeLynn frowned. Corrie laughed.

"Well, for one thing, I won't take your money until we make up a contract."

"For what?"

"For me to pay you back," Corrie said firmly. "Because I AM going to pay you back, RaeLynn, every penny...."

"You don't have to." RaeLynn shook her head. "Really, you don't. I don't need...."

"Yes, I do, and yes, you need me to pay you back," Corrie said, tapping on the counter for emphasis. "And we're going to do this right, so no one can ever say that I took advantage of you or our friendship."

"I think I've taken more advantage of you already," RaeLynn said softly. "And we'll do whatever you want to do. I just want to make sure the Black Horse is safe." She took a deep breath. "Okay, what do we do first?"

"First, we're going to write up a contract, saying how much you're loaning me," she said, emphasizing the word "loaning", "and then you're going to tell me where on earth you were able to get that much money," Corrie said. "I don't want to take your money if you need it for something else, something you've been saving for."

RaeLynn dropped her gaze to the floor and blushed. "I got it from Mama," she whispered. Corrie stared at her in shock.

"Your mother? When did you see her?"

"I didn't," RaeLynn said, tears welling in her eyes again. "She called one day... she said she was sorry she didn't come see me, said she hoped I'd understand if she never came back to Bonney again, not even to see me. But she wanted... to make up for a lot of things. But she didn't know how to start, so she said she and Teddy talked it over and they decided the best thing she could do was give me something to help me make a start on a new life. She said she was sending me a check to help me out. Fifteen thousand dollars. She said it wasn't much...."

"Wasn't much?" Corrie echoed. She shook her head. Where had Mrs. Shaffer gotten that kind of money? A cold hand clamped around her heart, knowing how the Shaffers had always acquired their money. "How...? Where...?"

RaeLynn understood. "The life insurance settlement from my... father's death," RaeLynn said, her face growing paler. "She was the sole beneficiary. I guess... I guess even my father didn't trust his own sons by making them beneficiaries. Of course, she only has Teddy now. And me. She says she won't use a penny to help Cliff or Johnny, they can serve out their prison sentences. She deserves a little peace and happiness in her life. I said I could take care of her, but," she drew a ragged breath, "she doesn't want to have anything to do with Bonney. Not even me. She wants a fresh start someplace else. But she wanted to help me because... because she's my mother...." The rest of her words were lost in a sob and Corrie caught her in her arms.

"It's okay, RaeLynn," she said soothingly. She understood now why the Black Horse meant so much to RaeLynn. It was the only thing she had left, the only thing that gave her stability and an anchor. No wonder she was frantic at the thought of the Black Horse closing. Where would she go? Her own mother hadn't even offered to take her in. "RaeLynn, you never have to worry about where you belong," she said, holding her friend at arm's length. "I promise you, you will always have a place as long as I'm around. And thank you, for saving the Black Horse. I think you understand how much it means to me."

"And to me," RaeLynn said, wiping her tears away. She

hugged Corrie tight again. "You saved me more than once, Corrie," she said. "The least I can do is save the campground, even if it is kind of selfish for me to do so."

"You can be selfish all you like," Corrie joked. She pointed to the pile of bills on the counter. "Let's sit down and figure this out. Maybe we can keep our heads above water until the weather and business improves." RaeLynn nodded happily.

"Let me grab us some coffee first," she said, turning toward the courtesy table.

"Good idea," Corrie said as she ripped Conrad Englewood's business card in half and threw it into the trash can.

Chapter 8

"You're not going to believe this."

"Try me," J.D. said. He and Sutton rarely bothered with conventional greetings anymore when they called each other, though he was surprised to hear from the sheriff again so soon. He figured he had better get used to hearing from him more frequently than he had in the last two months.

"I just got off the phone with my attorney." Judging from the slight echo and the sound of boots pacing on a hardwood floor, J.D. guessed that Sutton was calling from his family home in Tunstall, not far from Bonney but still within the county. He must have gotten tired of standing outside in the cold wind to call and he didn't feel comfortable calling from his own apartment in the village. Few people would think to track him down in his mother's home. J.D. had never seen the place, but his imagination painted a picture of a large, elegant home with a dark paneled study or library where business was discussed. That was where he imagined Sutton was at the moment. "He's got an army of investigators at his disposal and connections in Vegas."

"Let me guess—there's no record of Durán's and Meghan's marriage license being filed anywhere," J.D. said. In spite of himself, his interest was piqued. He got up and moved down the hall to a private conference room. Chief LaRue was gone for the day and there was no one else who would have any reason to be using that room. He would have privacy there. "Am I right?" he asked, as he shut the door behind him.

"Yes," Sutton said, a shimmer of anger in his voice. "But there's more."

"What's that?"

"They managed to track down a former employee of that wedding chapel, one of the 'ministers' that used to perform wedding ceremonies. He retired from 'active ministry' after the place went out of business, but he remembered Meghan and Durán. "

J.D.'s pulse quickened. "After ten years? How can he be sure it was them?"

"The investigator had a picture of Meghan from... back then," Sutton said. J.D. wondered if it was the sheriff and Meghan's wedding portrait, but he said nothing. The sheriff went on, "He immediately recognized her, said she paid for everything, refused the wedding portrait, the whole nine yards. 'Just the ceremony and certificate', he remembered her telling him. But what clinched it for him was that she called him from the airport, maybe an hour after the ceremony and told him not to file the certificate. That there was ten grand in it for him if he'd conveniently 'lose it'."

J.D. let out a low whistle. "They were still in Vegas when she called him? And Durán never found out about it?" He shook his head. "Wait a minute, so how did Durán get a copy of the certificate? He told you himself that she ripped it up the minute they were back in Cabo and she collected from her bridesmaids."

"The investigator asked the minister that," Sutton said. "He said that, since he had to wait for Meghan to wire him the money, he decided to hold onto the certificate until he had the money in hand. He had agreed to wait till she got back to New Mexico, which turned out to be a week later. But apparently, after Meghan pulled her stunt with Durán, ripping up the certificate, Durán called the chapel himself and requested a notarized copy. The minister figured he wasn't going to blow ten thousand dollars, so he played dumb and never told Durán that he had instructions not to file it. He hedged his bets, however, and charged a hefty sum, then sent Durán the notarized copy as requested and figured that maybe Meghan had changed her mind. But then he got the money from her with a note saying, 'Don't forget our deal', and he just filed the certificate in a random folder and the court never received it. Then, after the files were destroyed and the chapel closed down, he figured that was the end of it."

"So that means," J.D. said slowly, as his heart began to pound, "that Meghan was right; the so-called marriage didn't mean anything. It wasn't legal and she was free to marry you." He had been pacing, but now he sank into a chair, trying to get his chaotic thoughts in order.

"Not quite," Sutton said, before J.D. could get his hopes up. "Durán has proof that Meghan attempted to contract a marriage while she and I were engaged. It calls into question whether or not she was serious about marrying me... and the marriage tribunal might decide that that would invalidate our marriage."

"Even if it wasn't legally filed with the county clerk's office? She wouldn't need to divorce him in that case, would she?"

"It doesn't matter," Sutton said doggedly. "Her little stunt would be enough to call her intentions into question and that would call the validity of our marriage into question. If I'd known about all this, I'd have called off the wedding, and she knows it.

That's why she's kept it all under wraps, probably paid off her friends to never speak about it. Durán is the only person who has any kind of proof that all this happened. If he didn't have that notarized copy, she could have had him written off as some kind of crackpot without proof."

"Have you talked to Durán again?" J.D. asked. He felt numb. Was it possible that Sutton really did have an invalid marriage… another chance to start over with Corrie?

"Not yet," Sutton said. "I called the number he gave me and it went to voice mail. I don't know if he's still in Bonney or not. I left a message for him to call me or come see me."

"What about Meghan?"

"Not till I get Durán to sit down with my attorney and find out exactly what happened and what it is he wants. I still don't know why he waited ten years to try to contact Meghan. And I'm sure he's known how to get hold of her all these years… she doesn't exactly shun the spotlight. There's something he wants that she's not giving him and that's why he came to me."

J.D. said nothing, just tried to digest everything he was hearing without getting sick to his stomach. What the sheriff was telling him made perfect sense, regardless of how crazy it sounded. He cleared his throat, aware that Sutton had been waiting patiently for him to speak. "So now what? Is there something you need me to do?"

"Just let me know if you happen to hear of Durán still being in town. And if you see Corrie, don't tell her anything. Until I know for sure just where I stand…."

"Right," J.D. cut him off. He drew a deep, silent breath. "Listen, Sutton, I gotta run. LaRue's not here and I have to check on my officers."

"Thanks, Wilder," the sheriff said. He ended the call before J.D. could respond.

"Sure, Sheriff. Anytime," J.D. muttered.

"Yes, I understand," Corrie said, her patience wearing thinner by the second. RaeLynn sat close by, her eyes round as she listened to Corrie's end of the conversation. "It's a large amount, I get that, but I have the money in my account… an electronic check is all I can do… no, I can't use a credit card. Listen, I need the account paid up to date as soon as possible, my local insurance office is closed so I can't make the payment in person, and five business days to process the payment is going to be past the due

59

date." She blew her breath out and stared at the ceiling. She had been on the phone for over forty-five minutes, talking to one person after another, trying to catch up her insurance payments. The problem was that her payment wouldn't clear their system in time to keep her insurance from lapsing, unless she used a credit card, and her business and personal cards were already maxed out. She had suggested using Jerry and Jackie's card, knowing she could pay them off immediately with the loan RaeLynn was offering her, but the insurance company said they couldn't accept payment from an account that didn't have the insured's name on it. Company policy, they claimed. Corrie had no way of knowing if that was true; she'd never been in this situation before, and they weren't backing down. And even if she tried to pay off her own credit cards with the money RaeLynn was lending her, the credit line wouldn't be adjusted and available in time for her to make the insurance payment. It had taken her less time to get the money she needed than it was taking to actually make the payment and now it seemed like it wasn't going to make a difference.

The person on the other end of the line—she wasn't sure if it was the third or fourth person she'd talked to—seemed to be growing increasingly nervous. Corrie had followed the chain of command all the way to the top and the person she was talking to now was probably as far as she could go to get the situation resolved. "Can I at least get a grace period until the check clears?" she asked, feeling hopelessness begin to close in on her.

"Ma'am, I'm sorry," the woman stammered. "I've been here for twenty years and a year ago, we might have been able to work something out. But things have changed since the new owner of the agency took over last summer and the new rules and regulations are pretty much inflexible now."

New owner? Fleetingly, Corrie seemed to recall a notice that the agency's former owner had retired back in the fall, but she couldn't remember having seen anything about who the new owner was. Another casualty of her amnesia days, she thought gloomily. She winced, hating to be "that person", but.... "Well, is there any way I can speak to the owner? The former owner and I were on very good terms...."

"Oh, uh, she's not available now and she is not easy to reach at a moment's notice," the woman said hurriedly. *Of course not,* Corrie thought crossly. "I can give her a message to call you as soon as she can."

"When will that be?" Corrie snapped, feeling sorry for the

person on the phone but also reaching the limits of her patience. "You don't understand, I cannot afford to have my business go uninsured and I cannot afford to have to restart my policies again! I need to have this resolved immediately and if you can't help me, then please let me talk to someone who can!"

"All right, ma'am, let me see what I can do," the woman on the phone said, trying to sound soothing, which only served to irritate Corrie even further. "Please hold for a minute?"

"Yes," Corrie said, biting her tongue to keep from making any further comment. She shook her head as insurance ads, interspersed with supposedly calming music, came over the line. RaeLynn gave her an inquiring look and Corrie shrugged. "They're going to try to put me through to someone who's in charge and can take my payment," she whispered, even though there was no one on the line.

RaeLynn held up both hands with fingers crossed and gave an encouraging smile. "It's going to be fine," she whispered. Corrie wished she were as optimistic. Before she could say anything, a strident voice spoke in her ear.

"What can I do for you, Miss Black?"

Corrie nearly dropped the phone. The voice sounded vaguely familiar, but the speaker made no effort to identify herself. "Yes, um, I need to talk to someone about making my payment immediately, over the phone, to keep my policy from lapsing. To whom am I speaking?" she said, drawing herself up straight and striving to sound polite but uncompromising. She HAD to get this payment done right away.

The door opened and Meghan Stratham walked in with her cell phone to her ear. Great! The last thing Corrie needed was to have Rick's ex hanging around while she was trying to conduct business. She got up and motioned RaeLynn to come behind the counter and covered the phone with her hand. "I'm on a very important call," she said to Meghan in a low voice. "RaeLynn will be happy to help you."

"I think I'm the one who needs to be helping you," Meghan said, her voice loud and clear on the phone in Corrie's ear. Corrie stared as Meghan's lips curved into a smile. She slipped the phone into the pocket of her coat. "You can hang up now, Corrie."

"*You* own my insurance company?" Corrie stuttered. She prided herself on keeping her cool, but somehow Meghan always had a spectacular way of making her lose it. She managed to set

61

the phone down before it dropped from her shaking hands.

"Well, not the whole company, of course," Meghan drawled, pushing her scarf back from her face. How was it possible that, despite thirty-mile-per-hour wind gusts, not a strand of her golden hair was out of place? She smiled thinly. "But I do own the local agency and we do set our own rules about a lot of things. I understand that you have a problem."

"I just need to make a payment," Corrie said. She felt her cheeks burning and it was all she could do to keep tears of humiliation from leaking out of her eyes. For a split second, she was relieved that she hadn't asked Rick to help her out, although she was positive that he'd be hearing about this in very short order. Now all she had to do was remain calm and professional and get this situation taken care of so that her campground would have insurance. She'd go and have a good cry in her apartment later on.

"So I heard." Meghan smiled and shook her head pityingly. "I understand it's quite a large amount that your account is in arrears. I'm surprised, to be honest. I'd always heard what a terrific businesswoman you are. I guess some people's perceptions can be skewed to only see the best." She smirked and Corrie's rage boiled up inside her despite her resolution to keep her feelings hidden until she was alone.

"I've never been late or missed a payment in years. There were circumstances," she said through gritted teeth. No sense in explaining as she was sure Meghan probably knew what had happened; her boyfriend had been a prime suspect in Corrie's attack. "And I can pay the whole account up in full before the due date if your office will just let me."

"Well, if you've been talking to my office, then you know what the answer is… whatever they've told you."

"That's why I've been on the phone waiting to talk to you!" Corrie snapped. "They're putting me off till after the due date has passed and won't cut me any slack!"

Meghan tsked. "What a shame."

Corrie stared at her in disbelief. "You mean you won't authorize my payment immediately? I can give you a check right now! I can even get you cash if you prefer! I just need to run to the bank.…"

"I don't take payments. Do I look like a cashier to you?" Meghan sneered.

"Meghan, if my coverage lapses it's going to cost a fortune to get insured again, not to mention I could get slapped with a fine! I can't afford that!" The words slipped out before she could stop herself and she felt her face grow even redder.

"So the Black Horse is struggling a bit," Meghan mused. "What a shame," she repeated.

"As if you didn't know!" Corrie snarled. "You've been obsessed with finding that out for months! Why didn't you come to me if you wanted to know anything about my campground?"

Meghan shook her head. "I doubt you'd have told me what I wanted to know."

"I'd have told you what you deserved to hear!"

Meghan's ice-blue eyes widened and her mouth dropped open. She recovered quickly and narrowed her gaze. "I'm not sure you should be so disrespectful to someone you want a favor from," she said.

"A favor?" Corrie scoffed. "I don't want or need a favor from you! I just want you to be fair! You raised my rates when I was already behind on my payments. How many other businesses are you planning to take advantage of? You know it's fire season and none of us can afford to let our coverage lapse!"

"That's right, so you'd better not let that happen!" Meghan straightened up and yanked her scarf over her head. She turned toward the door, then paused and glanced at Corrie. "Your payment is due and needs to clear the main office in two days. Good luck."

The door slamming behind her elicited a whine from Renfro and jolted Corrie from the shock that had her frozen in disbelief. She began to tremble and she wasn't sure if it was rage or despair. RaeLynn reached out and touched her arm. "Are you all right?" she whispered.

Corrie started and looked bleakly at her. She felt the burn in her face and RaeLynn's face swam in and out of focus through her tears. "So help me, RaeLynn, I know it's wrong, but I wish she were dead and I feel like I could kill her myself!"

Chapter 9

J.D. finished up the day at the police station with no incidents and no further calls from the sheriff. He stopped by the front desk and spoke to Joanie Shanta, the new dispatcher who had been hired just after the beginning of the year. "I'm off for the day, Miss Shanta," he said. "Anything I need to know before I go?"

The attractive young woman had transferred to the Bonney P.D. from the Mescalero tribal police department after she started dating Officer Charlie White, who was Corrie's cousin. J.D. had learned, not long after he started working in Bonney, that if rules regarding nepotism and "fraternization" were enforced in rural New Mexico, very few people would be able to find jobs. However, Joanie was a far cry from the previous dispatcher, Connie Archuleta, who had been secretly engaged to Chief LaRue but freely pursued every man in a uniform—either village or county—as if she were single and available. Joanie was professional and extremely efficient and no one would suspect that she and one of the officers were in a relationship if Charlie hadn't come and admitted it to J.D. "I don't want there to be problems and I don't want to hide anything from you," Charlie had told J.D. He had come a long way since his partner and friend, Ray Herman, had gone down the wrong road and was now doing time in prison for kidnapping, assault, and various other charges stemming from his association with RaeLynn's brothers and their criminal activities. Charlie had been shaken up enough to start taking his law enforcement career seriously and had become an exemplary officer. Even better was that he had mended fences with Corrie, even though he was the only member of her father's side of the family that had done so. It was a start and J.D. knew that, for Corrie, that was enough.

Joanie rarely cracked a smile while she was on the clock, but she never seemed ruffled or lost her composure either, no matter how hectic the day might be. Today, her brow was furrowed and lines of concern edged the corners of her dark eyes. "I've gotten some red flag alerts from the forestry service," she said. "Winds are supposed to kick up to over forty miles an hour and forest conditions are extremely dry. My brother, Kyle, is a Mescalero Hotshot and he says his crew is being ordered to be on standby, just in case."

J.D. grimaced. He'd never had to deal with concerns about forest fires in his entire law enforcement career, but he knew it was something he was going to have to learn as he went. "What do you suggest?" he asked Joanie, knowing she had more experience dealing with the situation than he did.

She tugged on one of her silver concho earrings and thought for a moment. "It wouldn't hurt to make sure that the village fire department and all volunteers are on standby," she said. "And you might want to coordinate with the sheriff's department, the forestry service, and the other law enforcement agencies in the area. We might need to share resources and we definitely need to stay in contact with each other about any potential fires that might pop up. With high winds, it wouldn't take long for a fire to get out of control. Now is the time to double down on enforcing the restrictions regarding open fires and flames of any kind. Also, you might want to alert the residents to be on the lookout for any possible fires and to take precautions, have evacuation plans in place, be ready to get out at a moment's notice."

"This isn't your first rodeo with this kind of weather, is it?" J.D. said, raising a brow. The young woman shook her head.

"We almost lost our home in a forest fire when Kyle and I were kids. Ironically, our dad owned a woodlot and sold firewood. Some guy came to buy a cord and—we think—flicked a cigarette out the window when he left. The forest was pretty dry that year. Of course, because of all the firewood, we had plenty of fuel and it took our parents and family all they could to hold the fire away from the house until the fire department arrived. That was the day Dad resolved to quit smoking and Kyle was so impressed by the firefighters that he decided he would become one. And I resolved from that day forward to never have a woodstove or fireplace in my house. Charlie is still trying to get me to change my mind eventually... I think he's afraid I won't let him have a grill or firepit someday." A brief smile lit her features before she resumed her serious expression and J.D. kept his own smile under wraps. Apparently Charlie and Joanie were already getting serious. She went on, "You never know, this might be all overkill, but it's better to be prepared and not need these measures than to need them and not be prepared."

"Good advice," J.D. affirmed. "Don't hesitate to call me if anything comes up."

"I won't," she said, without a trace of humor.

"What's going on?" RaeLynn asked as Corrie hung up the phone, her face grim.

"That was J.D. There's a fire burning to the southeast of Bonney, between the county line and Ruidoso," Corrie told her. She shivered as the wind rattled the windows, even though she couldn't feel the cold. Fire season had started early. "They've already got crews on it, but with the wind gusting as bad as it is, they might need to pull Bonney's fire-fighting resources."

"Are we in danger?" RaeLynn breathed. Her face was drawn with concern ever since Meghan had left earlier. Corrie had finally stopped seeing red, but now she was fighting despair and trying not to worry RaeLynn more. She took a deep breath and forced a smile.

"Not really. It's easily fifteen miles away. Unless there's a drastic change in the direction of the wind, we won't have much to worry about." She knew RaeLynn couldn't be fooled; she'd lived through almost as many fire seasons as Corrie had and knew the potential for disaster. But Bonney had been lucky. Rarely had a wild fire truly threatened the village. "J.D. was calling to tell me that they're asking for volunteers to come to the fire station and help prepare meals for the firefighters and the other first responders and also help set up an emergency shelter if they have to evacuate people from the area near the fire. I thought we'd go help. It might get our minds off... everything," she said dryly.

"Are you sure?" RaeLynn said and Corrie let out a laugh that didn't quite camouflage the hysterical sob behind it.

"It's not like we've got a lot to do here," she pointed out. "It'll do us good to be doing something worthwhile instead of sitting around worrying."

"If you're sure," RaeLynn said, her brow still furrowed. "But what about Meghan?"

"I'm not going to think about her right now," Corrie said as she went to the closet to get their coats. "I need to clear my head first, do something with a purpose, and then... then we'll figure out some way to get that insurance paid. Somehow. Even if I end up having to re-start my policy...." She let the thought trail as she handed RaeLynn her winter jacket.

"That's going to cost a lot more," RaeLynn said as she pulled on her jacket. "And won't your rates go up because you defaulted?"

"Maybe, probably," Corrie said, shrugging. "But I can't do anything about it, so I'll just have to deal with it when it happens." She hated to think how much her rates would skyrocket, especially now that Meghan owned the company. Maybe she should start looking for another insurance company. "Come on, let's put that roast you made in the fridge for later and see if the Pages and the Myers want to help out, too."

He watched in near-disbelief as two vehicles pulled out of the campground: the Pages in their Bronco with Corrie and RaeLynn riding with them and the Myers in their sport Kia following them. He couldn't believe it; there was no one in the campground. His hands shook as he pulled his phone out of his pocket and punched in the number that had been calling him almost hourly. He was glad that he finally had something to report.

"They're gone," he blurted as soon as the person on the other end answered. "All of them. I don't know, they didn't take anything, so they're probably planning on coming back sometime soon." He listened as he made his way to his vehicle, parked back where it wouldn't be seen by passing cars, especially cops who might ticket him, but close enough where he could watch the campground easily. He was nodding as he listened to the instructions he was being given. "Sure, sure, yeah," he said. "I won't let them see me, don't worry. And then what?" He frowned. "Are you sure? I mean, with all that's going on...." He got into his car and started the engine. "Well, okay. Just make sure I get paid beforehand. Cash only, no checks. You know the deal." He grinned as he listened to the caller grumble. People sure hated to have to follow their own rules. "You don't like it, you can do it yourself," he added. By the time he hung up, he was assured of receiving payment as soon as he got back from seeing where Corrie and her friends were going and before he put the next part of the plan in action.

He pulled onto the highway and saw the two vehicles heading toward the village. He followed at a distance that wouldn't draw attention to himself, then he squinted as he watched a huge cloud billow into the sky far ahead. His mouth dropped open. A forest fire? An idea came to him... one that would earn him a significant bonus.

He grabbed his cell phone and dialed. "Have you seen the fire?" he asked as the person on the other end answered. "I think this might make things even better...."

Rick's coffee had long gone cold but he didn't bother to go to the kitchen to dump it out and pour a hot cup. He knew the fresh cup would go just as ignored as the first one he had poured. He was in his office in his apartment, poring over old documents regarding his marriage and subsequent divorce, unable to take off to his family home due to the fire burning near the county line. He needed to be close by in the event things took a turn for the worse. His phone vibrated and he glanced at the screen, expecting it to be an update on the fire between Ruidoso and Bonney. Instead, he recognized Meghan's number and his stomach clenched. As tempting as it was to ignore it, he knew that doing so would only make things worse in the long run. He repressed a sigh. "Hello?"

"Well?" she snapped.

"Well, what?" he asked sourly. "You still think I'm going to allow you to move Ava if you bug me long enough? After what I just learned about you and your REAL first husband?"

"Stop calling him that! I'm telling you, Alex and I were never legally married!"

"The fact that you pulled this stunt has pretty much invalidated our marriage, regardless of whether or not the certificate was actually filed at the county clerk's office. You know that, right? I'm drafting a petition to the diocese based on this to have our marriage declared null and void. And I'm talking to my attorney regarding the fact that you might be guilty of fraud."

"What? Are you out of your mind?"

"Don't worry, I'm not suing you," he said dryly. All he would be doing was getting his own money back. "Not for money, anyway. As long as you stop trying to take Ava away from Bonney. From me." He paused, letting his words sink in. "I won't touch your assets, your money, your properties, your businesses. I won't even make a move to have our marriage declared illegal, which it would be if you were married at the time. I have more than enough evidence to make a fraud charge stick, but I won't even push to prosecute. I can make this very easy for you, Meghan. Easier than you deserve." He took a deep breath, trying to calm his pounding heart and stay in control. "Ava stays in Bonney. You keep everything else you have. And you cooperate with the tribunal on my nullity petition. You admit to what you did in Vegas with Alex Durán. It goes no further than that and you get to keep your 'good name'," he added, tempering his sarcasm. "And I get my freedom to marry in the Church."

"Corrie put you up to this, didn't she?" Meghan hissed. "It's always been about her, hasn't it? You couldn't wait to tell her you were finally going to be free, so she's already coming crying to you about me."

"I don't know what you're talking about," Rick said. He hid his bafflement behind his usual stony voice. Meghan let out a laugh.

"Sure you don't. I don't believe that and no one else in Bonney will, either. I know the law. And I have attorneys, too, Rick. You might think I care about what will happen to my reputation if this whole thing goes public. But I know you, and especially your mother, really do care about your good name being dragged through the mud. You could have gotten your annulment just by admitting that you married me even though you were in love with someone else and you never loved me in the first place!"

"That's not true," Rick stammered. He had been leaning back in his chair but now he was bolt upright, and his heart was hammering again. "Meghan, I'd have never asked you to marry me if I hadn't loved you, and I won't lie and say I didn't love you. I married you and I took it seriously. I planned to stay with you forever. If anything, you're the one who lied."

"Prove it," she said sweetly. "I'll never say I didn't love you and I didn't take our marriage seriously."

"Alex Durán has all the proof I need," Rick snapped. He was on his feet now and pacing. How had things suddenly turned around? He ran a shaking hand over his head. "No matter what you think, you're not going to be able to deny that our marriage was invalid from the start because of YOUR actions, not mine."

"Alex isn't going to be a problem," she said dismissively. "At least, not to me. So you might as well get comfortable with the fact that, unless YOU tell the tribunal you lied about our marriage, WE are still married and always will be, at least, as far as your church is concerned. And that's all that matters to you, isn't it?"

Rick hadn't realized that his jaw had dropped until he heard the call disconnect.

Corrie didn't have time to think about her own problems once they arrived at the high school gym. They had been directed to go there to help out the volunteers who were setting up emergency lodging for the people who had been ordered to evacuate their homes in the path of the wildfire. She and RaeLynn, along with the Pages and the Myers, jumped right in to start helping prepare meals for the evacuees who were streaming into Bonney. Corrie's heart went out to the families, especially the ones with children, who were crying in fear and uncertainty. RaeLynn gathered the

70

younger children around her and took them aside to tell them stories while their parents tried to get settled. It wasn't long before she had three small girls crowded on her lap and a half dozen other children huddled close to her as she taught them a funny song and soon their little voices piped up, singing "On Top of Spaghetti" as they ate their dinner. The grateful looks the volunteers got from the evacuees as they were handed plates of spaghetti and meatballs which were being prepared in the gym kitchen made Corrie's heart hurt. She tried to offer encouragement, but she had seen the effects of wildfires; there was a very good chance these people wouldn't have homes to return to after the fire was put out. And while several had suitcases and boxes of whatever they could grab, many had only the clothes they were wearing. The fire must have come up on them so suddenly all they could do was flee.

It was well after seven p.m. before they had finished cleaning the kitchen and washing the dishes. Another group of volunteers had arrived to stay overnight in case more people showed up. They brought boxes of donated clothing in all sizes along with spare blankets and pillows that they had collected. The people of Bonney were never stingy whenever their help was needed, Corrie thought with some pride and gratitude. She and her friends agreed to come back early the next morning to help with breakfast and they wearily made their way home.

It was no surprise to find that J.D. wasn't at his cabin. Was it only this morning that they had made plans for him to join them for dinner this evening? Corrie shook her head. She was certain that he and Rick were both at their respective department stations, standing by to take action to help protect Bonney from the fire and aid those affected by it.

As Corrie made sure the campground store was securely locked for the night, she fought off a shiver. A glance in the direction of the fire showed an eerie red glow reflecting off the hazy smoke-filled sky. She took some comfort in the fact that it was still a long way away from the Black Horse and the village of Bonney, but still… a gust of wind rattled the windows and a chill touched her heart. All it would take was a shift in the wind and they could all be in danger. But for tonight, all she could do was pray that the firefighters stayed safe and contained the fire as best they could.

And pray for rain.

Chapter 10

The following morning welcomed them with a hazy sunrise from the smoke that was drifting toward Bonney. Even though he had no experience with wildfires, J.D. knew that was a sign that the wind had shifted direction and was blowing toward the county line and the village. His morning fire report stated that there was zero containment of the fire and the high winds had grounded any air support to the firefighters. So far there were no casualties, but several structures, including homes, had been destroyed. He grimaced at the thought of having to inform people that they had no home to return to when the fire was out.

He made his way to the high school gymnasium and his first smile in hours came when he saw that Corrie and most of the Black Horse Campground's staff were on hand to help prepare breakfast for the evacuees, whose number had nearly doubled overnight as the fire swept through the mountains. Not only were RaeLynn, the Pages, and the Myers there, but so were Myra Evans, her fourth month of pregnancy starting to show but not slow her down, and Buster who was showing an amazing burst of energy at such an early hour. J.D. knew that their respective partners had been hard at work all night, at the sheriff's department and the medical center, and they were not about to sit home when they could help out in some way.

He made his way through the crowd, snagging two Styrofoam cups of coffee as he went, and presented them to Corrie and RaeLynn who were filling plates of pancakes, scrambled eggs, hash browns, and bacon and passing them to other volunteers who were distributing them to the evacuees. "Need some caffeine?" he asked.

"Yes, and an extra pair of hands wouldn't hurt," Corrie said with a grateful smile. J.D. immediately slipped on a pair of food-handler's gloves and took over the hash browns station. After several minutes, the rush seemed to die down and they were able to prepare enough extra plates so that they could take a break to sip their coffee. Despite the early hour, the volunteers all seemed to be bright-eyed and wide awake.

"What time did you get here?" J.D. asked. Corrie glanced at RaeLynn, who shrugged.

"I know my alarm went off at five, and RaeLynn made us some breakfast before we left. We knew," she went on, sweeping her coffee cup to encompass the Myers and the Pages, "that once we got here, we wouldn't have time to eat. I don't even know what time it is now."

"It's after eight-thirty," J.D. told her, as a man with a couple days' worth of beard growth, a dirty denim jacket, and a knitted cap pulled down nearly over his eyes shuffled up and took a plate of food. "How long are you planning to stay today?"

She gave him a weak grin. "Probably all day. I don't have any guests at the campground, so there's no need for me to hurry back until the evening volunteers show up. All of us," she added, nodding toward RaeLynn and the rest of her employees, "would rather be here doing something useful than staring at empty campsites." The man was still standing there and she turned to ask him if he needed anything and he quickly turned away and headed toward the coffee station. She shrugged and turned around so that her back was to the line of people picking up breakfast plates. "What's the report on the fire?" Corrie asked him, keeping her voice low.

He grimaced. "I wish I could say things were under control," he said, and proceeded to fill her in on the morning report. Her brown eyes swam with tears and she took a deep breath and sipped her coffee. She glanced over her shoulder and J.D. followed her gaze. A family consisting of a young woman, an elderly couple, and five children, including an infant in the young woman's arms, sat with shocked, despairing expressions. J.D. felt his stomach clench and he looked at Corrie questioningly.

"Her husband is deployed overseas," she whispered. "They had just built a new house with a little apartment for her parents. They barely got out ahead of the fire. They lost everything they had... except each other."

J.D. said nothing. What could he say? This time, there was no way he could go and find justice for these people. For the first time in his life, he felt that his job was useless. He shook his head. "What are they going to do?" he asked, his throat tight.

"For now, they'll stay with family nearby," Corrie said. It amazed J.D. that she had a ready answer. "Members of the community are offering places to stay for the folks who have lost their homes or for those who are going to have to wait until it's safe to return to their homes." She looked at him directly. "Insurance only goes so far and it takes time to process. There are funds set up at the local banks for people to donate what they can." J.D. looked at her in surprise.

"Everyone is struggling because of the downturn in business

right now," he said. "How will people be able to help out?"

Corrie gave his arm a squeeze. "Because we're all family, J.D. And when people help when they're struggling, too, that's not help. That's love."

Rick was almost thankful that he had the fire to keep his mind occupied, although he was denied permission to assist in any operation that took him too close to the fire, due to his still-healing lungs. Even the smoke that drifted to Bonney was making it hard for him to draw a deep breath without coughing, so he focused his attention on monitoring the crisis from a distance and making plans in the event the fire threatened Bonney County. It was during lulls in activity that his thoughts turned to other matters.

He still hadn't been able to get hold of Alex Durán and he was starting to get more than annoyed. He was concerned. Durán had the only certified, physical proof that Meghan had attempted marriage before their wedding day. If Rick couldn't get that from him, it would be a case of "he said/she said", which might—or might not—be enough for the tribunal to accept his appeal. The fact that Durán hadn't been in contact since their initial meeting had him worried. Had Meghan approached him and made a deal that he'd get whatever it was he wanted from her in exchange for disappearing with the evidence Rick needed? Maybe approaching Meghan had been a mistake. He knew she could be vindictive when she didn't get what she wanted. And he was still puzzled over what it was that Durán wanted from her that made him approach Rick in the first place.

He found himself pacing his office and growing more impatient. He snatched his Stetson and heavy jacket from the rack in the corner and made his way to his Tahoe, informing his dispatcher, Laura Mays, to call him immediately if he was summoned for any reason. "I'm going to take a quick patrol around the area," he told her. The silent, appraising nod she gave him made him wonder if she knew it wasn't just anything to do with the fire but something personal he was going to be looking for.

He was just getting into the Tahoe when Wilder roared up on his Harley. Rick stopped and waited for him to dismount.

"You in a hurry, Sheriff?" Wilder asked. Rick shook his head, and Wilder went on, "I just came from the high school gym. They're going to be tied up over there for a long time."

"You mean Corrie?"

"Everyone from the Black Horse," J.D. confirmed. "There are still quite a few evacuees coming in from the fire. Another community near the area has been evacuated. The firefighters are having a hard time containing the fire."

"I was just going on patrol myself to see how things are," Rick said, not mentioning that he was also going to see if Alex Durán was still around. Wilder seemed to read his mind.

"You haven't seen or heard from Durán, have you?"

Rick shook his head. "Wish I'd asked him where he was staying," he said. "I got the impression he'd be checking in with me and he gave me his number, but he hasn't answered any of my calls."

"Could be the fire spooked him," Wilder said. "And he got out of Dodge."

Rick inclined his head. The thought had crossed his mind, but he was sure that Durán would have been in contact. He also wondered where Meghan was. Wilder went on, "On my way over here, I saw your ex. I thought she'd left town, as well."

Rick's head jerked up in surprise. "Where'd you see her?"

"Didn't actually see her," Wilder admitted. "But I did see her car. Silver Beemer, right? Parked at the local insurance company office." He cleared his throat and glanced down for a second before he looked directly at Rick. "I thought something seemed off, so I hope you don't mind that I swung by for a closer look."

Rick's attention was riveted on the detective. "And?"

"Well, her car was the only one there and there was a 'Closed' sign on the door. And it's after nine a.m. on a weekday and there's a wildfire raging close by." His steel-gray eyes bored into Rick's. "RaeLynn caught me as I was leaving the gym. She was nervous and told me she probably shouldn't be telling me anything but Corrie needed help and was too stubborn to admit it. Apparently, your ex is the new owner of the local insurance agency."

Rick stared at him. "What? Since when?"

"Since the previous owner retired last fall. For some reason, she's been keeping it quiet. Her name's not even on the sign or the door. But the thing is, RaeLynn says Corrie's fallen behind on her insurance payments because her rates skyrocketed after Meghan took over… which was when Corrie was recovering from amnesia. Now her policy is due to be paid and she managed to get the money, but she won't be able to make the payment in time and Meghan isn't being cooperative."

"She talked to Meghan?" Rick said, feeling a stab of pain that Corrie never told him. *Well, why should she? She believes you're still married to Meghan, so maybe she thinks that's where your loyalties should lie.*

Wilder went on, "Apparently, the local office has been closed all week and she was trying to make a payment over the phone to the main office all day yesterday and has been getting the runaround. RaeLynn says Meghan actually went to the campground and told Corrie she had to make the payment on time or her policy would lapse. And she also refused to take the payment. Corrie is livid and also on the brink of despair. It's going to cost her a fortune to restart her policies and she's going to have to find a new insurance company. I'm sure she's not satisfied with the customer service she's getting with this company anymore," he added dryly.

"But Meghan's at the office?" Rick said. Wilder nodded and then shook his head.

"I wouldn't go in there with guns a-blazing, Sheriff," he warned. "First off, Corrie didn't even want us to know about this and I don't want to get RaeLynn in trouble. She only told me because she's worried about Corrie and didn't know who else to talk to. Second, I'm not sure, with all that's going on, that your ex is going to be particularly thrilled that you're going to bat for Corrie." He took a deep breath. "And third...."

"I know Corrie doesn't want anyone fighting her battles for her," Rick said bluntly. "She never has. But in this case, her business and her home are at stake. She could be shut down for operating without insurance."

"She's not operating much at all, right now," Wilder pointed out. Rick shook his head.

"I need to talk to Meghan anyhow, see if she's talked to Durán."

"Do you think she'll tell you if she has?"

"I don't know and, even if she does, I'm not even sure she'll be telling me the truth," Rick muttered. "But it'll give me an opportunity to try to help Corrie." Wilder looked dubious.

"If you bring it up, I doubt she'll be cooperative."

Rick allowed a half-smile. "I won't have to. I'm willing to bet Meghan will be dying to gloat about it." He grew somber again. "The only question is if she's willing to negotiate."

Wilder's eyes narrowed. "And are you willing to meet her terms?" he asked quietly.

Rick turned away and got into the Tahoe. He started the engine before he spoke again. "Depends on her terms," he said as he put the vehicle in gear and drove off.

J.D. fought the temptation to cruise back by the insurance agency to see if smoke would actually be coming out of the windows. He told himself it was none of his business, but then he'd already involved himself when RaeLynn had come to him.

"I just don't know what to do, J.D.... I mean, Detective Wilder," she'd stammered. "You should have seen Corrie, she was so upset. She actually said she could kill Meghan and you know Corrie isn't like that!"

J.D.'s brows had risen at that. From his brief conversation with Corrie at the gym, she certainly seemed to have gotten control of herself since that conversation with Meghan. Of course, he knew she had an uncanny knack for not holding a grudge, but he suspected that she was most likely trying to ignore the whole episode and focus on something else in order not to completely fall apart. And while he knew she would be upset, he also knew that she wouldn't blame RaeLynn for seeking out someone to talk to.

He wasn't sure that she would be so understanding of him telling the sheriff about it, though.

He decided it wouldn't hurt for him to take a spin around the village and around the lesser-traveled county roads. Most of his officers and the sheriff's deputies were on stand-by in the event of fire-related issues, so he could do some patrolling and call in anything he couldn't handle on his own. Maybe by that time, the dust would clear and the sheriff would have some information on the whereabouts of Alex Durán and perhaps even fix the mess Corrie was in. He hated to admit it, but in this case, there wasn't anything he, as a relative newcomer to Bonney, could do. The sheriff actually was in a better position to help Corrie. The best thing he could do was to step back and let him handle this.

He noted with some amusement that he automatically steered his Harley in the direction of the Black Horse Campground. He knew that Corrie and her friends would be at the gym, helping out, for the better part of the day, but it wouldn't hurt to stop by his cabin and stash a fresh set of clothes in his saddlebags in the likely event that he'd be spending the night at the police station again. As usual, he cut the engine at the top of the ramp and coasted down toward the campground store.

To his surprise, a dark blue Ford Expedition was parked in front of the building, the driver's side door wide open. He stopped the bike behind the vehicle and dropped the kickstand as he dismounted. No one was in the vehicle. He squelched his initial impulse to call out to see if anyone was around; his gut told him to remain silent. He slipped his weapon out of his holster, and held it down by his side as he made his way as quietly as he could around the side of the building. Normally walking on the gravel would make enough noise to alert someone to his approach, but in this case, the wind in the trees camouflaged his footsteps. He keened his hearing, listening for anyone approaching him from in front or behind as he headed for the patio and pool area.

He was a few feet from the wooden gate that opened into the pool area when it swung open and a man carrying a propane tank emerged. He gasped when he saw J.D. with the gun in his hand.

"Stay where you are," J.D. said. "Bonney Police," he added as he flashed his badge at the man. "What are you doing here?"

"I, uh, stopped to see about renting a cabin," the man stammered. He flushed when J.D.'s eyes went to the tank in his hand. "Or else see if I can get my tank filled. I'm out of propane for my camper and it's too cold to not have heat in it."

"Let me see some I.D., please," J.D. said. The man set down the tank and fished a wallet out of his back pocket. He handed it to J.D. It was filled with cash and several credit cards with the same name as the driver's license: Ronald Brown, from Dallas, Texas. The license photo matched the clean-shaven, slightly balding man in front of him. "What brings you to Bonney, Mr. Brown?"

"Decided to take a few days off while things are slow at work," the man said. He seemed ill-at-ease, but so did most people who were caught unawares by the police. "I didn't know New Mexico got so cold in February. I wanted to see about renting a cabin or maybe getting a space for my camper, but no one's here. I didn't see a 'closed' sign so I thought I'd look around. I'm not trying to steal anything, Officer, honestly."

"Detective J.D. Wilder. I'm afraid the campground doesn't sell propane tanks or refill them, Mr. Brown." While it seemed like a godsend to have a potential guest right here at the campground, something about the man didn't set right with J.D., even though he was well-dressed and obviously had plenty of money. He still wasn't about to give him too much information regarding where Corrie and her staff were. "And the campground is closed for the time being, due to the high fire danger, so I'm afraid you'll have to leave." He made a mental note to tell Corrie to close and lock the gate whenever they left the campground unattended.

"Oh... oh, all right, Detective," the man said. He made his way to his SUV quickly. "I didn't mean to trespass. I'll be on my way. Thank you," he added. J.D. wasn't sure what the man was thanking him for, but he stood and watched until the man had pulled out of the parking area and onto the highway, making a mental note of the license plate. He shook his head and went to get his clothes out of his cabin, then decided it wouldn't hurt to make a sweep around the campground. He checked the doors and windows of all the cabins to make sure they were securely locked and around the store, as well as the storage closet and the shed where all the lawn care equipment was stored. Everything seemed to be in place. He took note of all the propane grills and tanks, which Corrie rented to her guests during their stay, chained up near the storage closet in the pool area. Since the fire restrictions forbade open flames of any kind, including gas grills, she'd had Red and Jerry round up all the grills and tanks and secure them where thoughtless guests wouldn't be able to help themselves. J.D. shook his head, telling himself he was overreacting. Ronald Brown was probably harmless, but J.D. filed the encounter away in his memory and planned to mention it to Corrie when he saw her. It would still be at least six hours before she and her crew would be done at the gym; he knew they would stay through the dinner hour and help with the cleanup before coming home.

He loaded his saddle bags and checked his watch. Plenty of time to patrol and be back before Corrie got home.

Rick waited outside the insurance agency office a good thirty minutes. When he had arrived, another vehicle was parked next to Meghan's car. It was a luxury sedan with a rental sticker in the window and he suspected it belonged to Alex Durán. He had parked the Tahoe down the street and made his way to the door of the building. He gave the door a gentle tug, being careful not to rattle it. It was locked and he went around the side to where the windows of the offices were located. He hadn't be able to hear much over the freezing wind that cut through his jacket, but he was able to make out two voices raised in anger—one male, one female—coming from the back office. Nothing he heard was intelligible, but he recognized the pitch and sound of Meghan's voice. For a moment, his law enforcement instincts kicked in and he listened for any sign that she might be in distress or danger. However, it soon became apparent that she was obviously the aggressor, even though Durán was on her turf. He tried to look through the windows but all the shades were pulled down securely. He went back around to the front to wait for them to emerge.

After a few minutes, Alex Durán strolled out the door, an expression of satisfaction on his face that changed to surprise when he saw Rick. "Sheriff Sutton," he said, and glanced back at the door. "This is a surprise. What brings you here?"

"Strangely enough, I was about to ask you the same question." Rick had been leaning against the wall, but he pushed away and straightened up, his hands in the pockets of his jacket. "I've been trying to get hold of you, Mr. Durán. Why haven't you answered my calls?"

To his credit, Durán didn't try to pretend he hadn't been ignoring Rick. He shrugged. "Let's just say there has been a great deal of competition for my attention."

"If I recall correctly, you're the one who came to me in the first place." Rick turned his back to the wind and stepped closer to Durán. "I have some questions for you but first, I want your copy of your marriage certificate."

Durán's eyes narrowed. "Why?"

"It proves my marriage is invalid, as far as the Catholic Church is concerned," Rick said. He was glad that Durán wasn't going to play word games. "At least, it's evidence that I need. Whatever deal you have with Meghan doesn't matter to me; whether or not your marriage was legal doesn't matter to me. That's for the two of you to work out and it doesn't concern me. All I need is the evidence that Meghan at least attempted a marriage a couple of weeks before our wedding and then we can all get on with our lives."

"That's an interesting way of putting it," Durán remarked. He tugged his expensive coat around him and adjusted his leather gloves. He shook his head. "So what is that certificate worth to you, Sheriff?"

Rick blinked as Durán looked at him steadily. He couldn't believe the man had the audacity to ask him that, but he had a feeling that he was about to enter a bidding war against Meghan. "Name your price, Durán," he said.

Durán's eyebrows shot upward. "Meghan was right," he murmured.

"About?"

"About what this is worth to you. I thought she was exaggerating," he said, shaking his head. "I may have to talk to her again."

"I'm not playing games with you, Durán," Rick snapped. "Regardless of what you or Meghan might believe or would like to believe, the fact is that your marriage only existed on paper... maybe not legally, but at least it proves there was intent. And you have that paper. I know that Meghan's afraid she's going to lose a lot of money and property if I take it to the tribunal, but our legal marriage isn't the issue here. As far as the court system goes, our marriage is over and she'll get to keep what she's got. I'm not after retribution, nor reparation, believe it or not. All I want is the truth... the truth that Meghan attempted marriage, even if it was just a joke, before our wedding in the Church."

Durán was staring at Rick with an expression that showed disbelief with a tinge of amusement. He shook his head slowly. "I can hardly believe it. You're serious."

"Yeah," Rick deadpanned. "So, what's it going to be?"

Durán chuckled. "Well, that might be a problem, Sheriff."

"Why?" Rick's stomach clenched with dread.

"Meghan already came to an agreement with me. She has the certificate." He gave Rick a pitying smile. "See, Sheriff, I only came to you because I needed to give Meghan a little... nudge, so to speak. When we parted ways, she made an arrangement with me to say nothing about our little trip to Las Vegas. For the last ten years, she's made it a point to pay me quite well for forgetting that we'd ever met, an arrangement that was supposed to last for another ten years. However," he went on as Rick stared at him, "a situation came up where I needed a lump sum payment of the remaining amount. Quite a sizable amount of money," he said. "Naturally, Meghan wasn't too keen about paying out quite that much all at once. She's been putting me off for several months until the situation has become quite critical... situations involving the Mexican police usually are," he said with a self-deprecating shrug. "So I had to come and deal with her personally and apply a little pressure. She wasn't happy that I had approached you and now I see why. You have a very, very strict moral code to which you adhere, a 'hunger and thirst' for justice, and, if that weren't enough, you're also a gentleman. Admirable, but I can see how you and Meghan were never really compatible in the first place."

"Meghan has the certificate?" Rick managed to say.

"Yes, I'm afraid so," Durán said. "So any further discussion or negotiations will have to be with her. Good luck is all I can say."

"We're not done, Durán," Rick said, recovering quickly and taking a step closer as Alex Durán made a move toward his car. Durán raised an eyebrow. "I'll take your testimony, as an eyewitness and participant, instead of the certificate." He wasn't sure it would be enough, but he could only pray it was. "Just write out an affidavit that I can present to the tribunal. You won't even have to appear," he added doggedly, hoping he was right. Durán pursed his lips and shook his head regretfully.

"I'm not sure that would be right, Sheriff," he said. "After all, I essentially gave my word to Meghan that she held all the information that I had. I'm sure that effectively prevents me from using that information against her."

Rick barely managed to bite back an oath. "I'm not trying to get her thrown in jail!" he snapped. "I'm not trying to sue her or take any kind of legal action against her! I just want the proof that our marriage wasn't valid so I can…." He stopped but not before Durán caught the drift of what he was going to say.

"Meghan did mention that there was a possibility of another woman you wanted to marry. And the validity of your marriage to Meghan was the only thing that stood in your way." Durán sighed and shook his head. "You're going to have to talk to Meghan, Sheriff," he said apologetically. "I'm afraid she holds all the cards right now. After all, if you're not taking legal action against her, you can hardly subpoena me to appear before the church tribunal." He shrugged again. "As I said, good luck, Sheriff."

Rick stood by helplessly as Durán got into his car. There was nothing he could do; Durán was right. The only thing he could do was appeal to Meghan's sense of fairness and decency.

He'd never felt so hopeless in his life.

Chapter 11

J.D. finished his patrol around the county shortly before three in the afternoon. He hadn't encountered anything of concern. He'd made sure to stop at a few isolated homes, far from the villages, to make sure they were aware of the fire and of the restrictions that were in place. The curling columns of smoke from chimneys had quickened his heartbeat a few times until he became accustomed to them. He realized that many of the residents in the outlying rural areas depended on fireplaces and woodstoves for heat, especially now that this area of New Mexico had entered what was usually the coldest month of the year. He'd politely turned down repeated offers of hot coffee or tea from the residents who expressed concern and appreciation for his visit. He began to understand how the victims of the wildfire would be able to find support when it came time to recover and rebuild.

After calling to check in to the village police station, he decided to cruise by the sheriff's department. Seeing the sheriff's Tahoe in its usual spot, he pulled in to see how Sutton had fared with his ex-wife.

Laura, the dispatcher, was on the phone when he walked in. She tipped her head in the direction of the sheriff's office and made a grimace. J.D. understood; things must not have gone as well as Sutton had hoped. He made his way down the hallway and knocked on the sheriff's door. "Come in," came the wooden sound of Sutton's voice.

Steeling himself, J.D. entered the office. The sheriff was in his chair, staring out the window with a stony expression. J.D. felt his gut twist; he'd never seen that expression on the sheriff's face before. "Not good, I take it." He closed the door behind him and stood at the desk.

Sutton swiveled his chair around. The despairing look in his dark blue eyes was something J.D. had ever expected to see. "She wants Ava," he said, his voice tight with emotion.

"What?" J.D. wasn't sure he'd heard correctly. Sutton rested his elbows on his desk, his hands cupped around his mouth. "Start from the beginning," J.D. snapped as he dropped into the chair in front of the desk.

Sutton leaned back. "Meghan has been paying Durán to keep quiet about their 'wedding'. She's paying him fifty thousand dollars a year, for twenty years." He paused.

J.D.'s mouth had dropped open. "A million dollars to win a

forty thousand dollar bet?"

"It was much more than that," Sutton said, pushing away from his desk. He stood up and rubbed the back of his neck. "Meghan's friends had money. Ten thousand dollars was nothing to them; they'd pay that much for a pair of shoes and matching handbag. The bet was for one million apiece, but she didn't tell Durán that. She told him it was for ten grand so he would be content with the amount she gave him." He blew out his breath. "Durán found out about it, of course. He threatened to come tell me about the wedding. Since Meghan knew I'd call off our wedding if I knew, she offered him the hush money, but in yearly payments. Durán accepted and had been happy to take the payments and live his life pretty extravagantly. Fifty thousand a year goes way further in Mexico than it does here. Well, he took up gambling and found himself in pretty hot water, with his debtors and the *federales* as well. He needed the balance of what she promised him to make good on his debts. She figured if he reneged, his debtors would take care of him and this would be a good way to make the rest of what she owed him go away, so she refused. He threatened to come tell me, thinking that I would probably try to sue Meghan for fraud and an illegal marriage and try to take back everything she got from our divorce settlement... which was a lot more than half a million dollars. Of course, I couldn't care less about all that, as long as I had the evidence needed to prove my marriage to Meghan wasn't valid. But Meghan wouldn't believe that; she wanted to get the only physical proof there was, so she gave in to Durán's demands. She gave him the balance of what she promised him in exchange for the certificate." He took a deep quivering breath. J.D. stayed silent; he knew there was more. "She said if I wanted the certificate, if I wanted to be free to marry in the Church, if I wanted to make sure Corrie didn't lose the campground because of her insurance lapse, then all I had to do was agree to let her move our daughter to a cemetery in Dallas."

J.D. let out his breath, unaware that he'd been holding it. "My God, that's low," he managed to say. All rivalry aside, all animosity that there might have been between the two men, none of it mattered. J.D. had never been a father; he'd never lost a child. So he couldn't begin to imagine how Meghan's ultimatum was tearing the sheriff apart. To give up his child for the woman he loved? What kind of monster had the sheriff married ten years earlier that would make such a demand? J.D. got to his feet, but he was still at a loss for words. "I don't know what to say, Sutton." His mind scrambled for a solution that the sheriff might not have thought of yet. "Would Durán agree to testify to the tribunal on your behalf?"

"He won't because he's afraid Meghan will take back his half million," Sutton said, his voice devoid of emotion. Of course, J.D. thought. His neck was on the line with both his debtors and the Mexican police. He wouldn't do anything that would make Meghan take back the money he needed.

Before J.D. could say another word, Laura Mays burst through the door of the sheriff's office, her eyes wide with horror. "There's a fire at the Black Horse Campground!"

The next hour was a blur.

J.D. and the sheriff had run for the sheriff's Tahoe, while Laura, having regained her composure, called in all first responders and volunteer firefighters that weren't tending to the wildfire near Ruidoso to tend to the fire near the Black Horse. Information was sketchy; at first, it seemed that the fire was along the highway near the campground, probably caused by a careless motorist. But as soon as J.D. and the sheriff were less than a half mile away, it became apparent that the campground itself was the epicenter of the blaze.

Firefighting crews rushed to set a perimeter around the campground, trying to contain the fire before it spread to the trees along the river and to the neighborhoods close to the campground. The winds seemed to have increased, sending sheets of flames across the dry grass and brush on both sides of the highway. Sutton was on the radio, ordering his deputies to start evacuating people from their homes. He looked at J.D. "You're sure no one is at the Black Horse? Corrie and everyone are at the high school gym? What about guests?"

"She doesn't have any guests right now," J.D. said, relief washing over him. "She and RaeLynn and the Pages and the Myers are all in town. They're safe. Everyone here is safe." His voice trailed away and he and Sutton looked at each other, their eyes widening in horror.

"Renfro and Oliver!"

They dashed for the campground, running past the firefighters who shouted at them to stay back. The heat from the fire made the icy wind feel like it was blowing from the Sahara Desert. They paused halfway down the ramp and stared in disbelief at the campground store. The back of the building was engulfed in flames, fed by the wind and the dry trees that dotted the campground. And the propane tanks that had been stored behind the building. J.D. didn't dare look at the cabins; he knew they were already destroyed. Sutton grabbed his arm. "Come on, before the fire gets to the front of the building!"

J.D. sprinted past the sheriff, who was having trouble catching his breath. He hardly paused before he kicked the front door in. Smoke was billowing through the building. Where were the dog and cat? Then he looked up the stairwell and saw the door to Corrie's apartment was closed and his heart leaped with dread. He took the stairs two at a time, the sheriff on his heels, and yanked the door open.

Oliver flew out the door, a yowling blur of black and gray fur that hit the sheriff square in the chest. "Renfro!" Sutton yelled. "Come on, boy! Here, Renfro!"

A mournful howl came from the direction of the kitchen. J.D. charged through the smoke, noting with dismay that the flames had reached the roof outside the second floor. He could see them through the windows of the apartment. He pushed open the swinging door of the kitchen and saw the big black Lab, circling anxiously in the kitchen, whining and sniffing and occasionally letting out a howl. J.D. understood. "Come on, Renfro!" he said, reaching for the dog's collar. Renfro growled and pulled away, resuming his prowling. "Come here, you big dummy!" J.D. yelled. "Corrie's not here! She's safe! Let's get out of here!" He grabbed the dog by the scruff of the neck, thwarting his attempts to snap at J.D. Sutton stepped into the doorway, partially obscured by the smoke, one hand clutching a black fire safe, the other trying to hold on to a frantic Oliver.

"Let's go, Wilder!" the sheriff said, and dissolved into a fit of coughing. "We don't have much time!" The glass panes shattered and flames billowed into the apartment. Renfro howled again and jerked out of J.D.'s grasp.

J.D. set his jaw. There was only one thing they could do....

"What do you mean my campground is on fire???"

Corrie hardly recognized the shrill screech as her own voice. Deputy Mike Ramirez had apparently been tasked with notifying her and she almost had the presence of mind to feel sorry for him. She had noticed a change in the atmosphere in the gym as word of the fire spread through the evacuees, one of whom had a police scanner and heard the call come in. At first she had thought it was an update, perhaps reporting a shift in the wind of the bigger fire near Ruidoso until she heard people gasp and say, "The Black Horse Campground?" She had nearly dropped a pan of enchiladas that she was transporting to the oven for the dinner hour. She dashed out of the kitchen and almost ran into Deputy Ramirez as he was making his way toward her, slipping his cell phone back into its holster. He winced and backed away a bit, but had no choice but to catch her by the upper arms when she tried to bolt for Jerry and Jackie's Bronco.

"Miss Black... Corrie," he stammered. "You can't go out there. The road is closed off to everyone but first responders and I'm sure the sheriff will get word to you as soon as he can. You can trust us to do everything we can...."

"My dog and cat are at the campground store!" Corrie wailed, trying to twist free of Mike's grip. His bronzed face paled, but he cleared his throat.

"The sheriff and Detective Wilder are out there," he said soothingly, although she could tell by his expression of uncertainty that he didn't know whether or not they had been able to save her pets. Jerry came up behind her and gripped her shoulders, gently pulling her away from the deputy.

"Come on, honey," he said gruffly, steering her toward Jackie. "There's nothing any of us can do. We have to let Rick and J.D. do their jobs." *Rick and J.D.* They were both on site of the fire. How much danger were they in? Corrie tried to speak but all she could manage was a hiccupping sob and she collapsed on Jackie's shoulder in tears. RaeLynn stood by, her eyes wide with horror and her hands over her mouth. Never had Corrie ever felt so helpless. If it weren't for Jackie's motherly embrace, she felt that her legs would buckle under her. Suddenly all she could think of was her father, Billy Chee Black Horse, and how much work and time he had invested in the campground. Her fear of losing the campground to Conrad Englewood seemed a distant memory. Now she faced an even greater threat to her campground. She swallowed her sobs and pulled out of Jackie's arms. She had to be strong. Maybe things weren't as bad as she was imagining. She swiped her hands over her cheeks and turned to Mike again.

"I need to know what's happening," she said, trying to keep her voice from trembling. "No matter what's going on, no matter how bad it is, I need to know. Don't try to protect me from the truth." Deputy Ramirez nodded solemnly as she took a deep breath. "Tell me exactly what Rick said." She braced herself for whatever he might say next.

He grimaced, his handlebar mustache drooping slightly. "Well, he didn't say much," he admitted. "Just said there was a fire at the Black Horse...."

"He said it was 'at' the Black Horse, not 'near' it?" she asked. He frowned.

"Pretty sure he said 'at', Miss Corrie," he said after a moment's thought. "He didn't say how bad or anything like that. Just that there was a fire and he and Wilder were on their way over there." He cleared his throat. "He didn't want me to create a panic, but he said he was sure you'd find out. He just asked me to keep you—all of you," he added, nodding at the Pages, the Myers, and RaeLynn, "away from the area. That there wasn't anything any of you could do and you'd only be putting yourselves in danger and making it harder for the firefighters to do their jobs." He stopped and shrugged. "I know what you're asking, but he didn't say anything about your pets, ma'am," he said softly.

"Corrie, you know good and well that Rick and J.D. will do anything they can that's possible," Jackie said. "If there's any way they can...."

"I know," Corrie said brusquely, her tears threatening to burst from her again. Of course, she knew Rick and J.D. would save Renfro and Oliver—and her campground—if they could.

But if they couldn't....

She moved apart from everyone else and wrapped her arms tightly around herself and fought off a shiver. Oliver... she remembered the tiny gray ball of fluff with the black tiger stripes that her father's black Lab, Renfro, had found huddled near the gate to the campground. Was that six years ago already? Renfro was already nine years old at the time... he was fifteen now and moved slowly, his legs stiff with arthritis but stubbornly insisting on going up and down the stairs from the campground store to the apartment every day, with Oliver urging him along. They were inseparable and as much a part of her as the Black Horse.

She couldn't bear the thought of losing them, but she was certain that, no matter what happened, they would be together.

"Corrie?"

She turned with a start and RaeLynn jumped back. "Oh, sorry," Corrie breathed, willing herself to put on a strong, calm demeanor. She sniffed and took note of RaeLynn's face. Her heart dropped. "What happened? Are Rick and J.D. back?"

"No, not yet," RaeLynn said. Her lower lip was quivering and she was fighting hard to keep the tears locked away. "I just wanted to see if you were okay. I mean, I know you can't possibly be all right, but if there's anything I can do...."

Corrie drew a deep breath, willing herself to stop shaking. "I'll be all right," she said and she could tell that RaeLynn didn't believe it anymore than she did. "Really, I will. Thanks," she said but RaeLynn was shaking her head.

"How?" she cried softly, tears running down her face. "How can you be okay? The campground... Renfro and Oliver... what if...?"

"RaeLynn, I won't think the worst!" Corrie snapped. "We don't know what's going on, we won't know until Rick and J.D. report in! Everything... everything will be okay. It has to be," she finished in a whisper. RaeLynn let out a small cry and wrapped her arms around Corrie and the two women clung together.

"Corrie!" Jackie cried, rushing toward her. "Rick and J.D. just pulled up outside!"

Corrie broke into a run, weaving around the people huddled in groups in the gymnasium who were also awaiting news. She burst through the double doors that led into the parking lot with RaeLynn and the Pages right behind her. J.D. was getting out of the passenger side of Rick's Tahoe and hurrying around to the driver's side. Corrie ran up to the door as Rick swung it open and before she could say a word, Oliver shot out of the door and latched himself onto Corrie's shirt, meowing piteously. She hadn't bothered to grab her coat and the freezing wind nearly took her breath away, but what sent icy chill through her veins was the look on J.D.'s and Rick's faces. "Where's Renfro?" she cried.

"That stupid mutt," J.D. grumbled hoarsely. He broke into a coughing fit that mirrored Rick's. Rick was moving slowly, easing himself out of the driver's seat, his own body racked with coughs. It was then that Corrie noticed that they were covered in ash and soot, the smell of smoke overpowering every other scent in the area. "He didn't want to leave the apartment," J.D. said and Corrie felt her heart stop. "I kept trying to drag him down the stairs but he snapped at me and growled. He kept thinking you were there and he didn't want to leave without you." He opened the back door of the Tahoe and reached in. "Come on," he muttered as a whine reached Corrie's ears.

"Renfro?" she cried. J.D. turned with the dog in his arms. Renfro let out a joyous bark at the sight of Corrie and squirmed until J.D. set him down before he dropped him. Corrie went down on her knees and threw her arms around the black Lab. "Oh, Renfro! Oliver! You're safe!" The old dog barked and whined, licking Corrie's face, as Oliver nestled himself tightly on Corrie's shoulder, his claws embedded in her shirt as if he'd never let go. She looked up at J.D. and Rick, both of whom were leaning against the Tahoe, their images blurry through the tears in her eyes. "Thank you," she whispered.

"You want to thank me, put that dog on a diet," J.D. said, half-jokingly. "I almost got a hernia carrying him downstairs."

She laughed and then jumped up and threw her arms around J.D. and hugged him fiercely, then Rick, nearly knocking him over. "Thank you, thank you, both. Oh, my gosh, I don't know how to thank you for saving them!" Her words came out in laughter-choked sobs and she nearly fell over the dog and cat as they circled around her feet. Dana and Red came out of the gym to join them and Dana draped Corrie's coat over her shoulders. She stepped back, drawing a shaky breath, and took a closer look at Rick and J.D. Her smile faded as she realized that their faces were sober, their expressions pained. "What is it?" she whispered. Even though she already knew what they were going to say.

The two men exchanged a glance and Corrie's heart plummeted to her shoes. J.D. shook his head and looked away. Rick chewed on his lip and cleared his throat. "Corrie," he said and hesitated. She wanted to yell at him to spit it out but the words were frozen deep inside her. He didn't have to say anything, but she still had to hear it. "Corrie, the Black Horse...."

"How bad?" She wasn't sure if he heard her. She hardly recognized her own voice.

He blew out his breath and looked her square in the eyes. "The firefighters were doing their best. The wind wasn't helping matters. The fire was spreading faster than they could keep up." He removed his Stetson and raked his fingers through his hair. "We didn't stay around... we would only be in the way and we had to get these two," he added, patting Renfro's flank, "over here to you." He paused. "The whole building was in flames when we left."

She felt her face go completely white and her head swam. She picked up Oliver and buried her face in his black and gray striped coat, trying to process what Rick was saying. The smell of smoke pierced her consciousness and she was aware of her tears soaking his fur. She felt hands on her shoulders, heard low comforting voices murmuring words she couldn't process. She drew a shuddering breath and looked up again, hardly able to stand the looks in J.D.'s silver eyes and Rick's blue ones. She opened her mouth, but she had no idea what to say. She felt a crowd of people, friends and strangers from the village and the whole county, clustering around her, and all she wanted to do was go far, far away, someplace where she wouldn't see her own pain and horror mirrored in their faces.

"Come on," Rick said gruffly, taking her arm and steering her toward the Tahoe. He helped her into the backseat, then turned toward the Pages and Myers and RaeLynn. "All of you, follow me." Corrie stared numbly at her friends—her family—and realized that they were in the same position she was in. Jerry and Jackie led RaeLynn to their Bronco and Red escorted a sobbing Dana to their Kia. J.D. lifted a now-docile Renfro into the backseat along with Corrie and Oliver. His eyes met hers briefly and he gripped her hand for a second before he shut the door and climbed into the passenger seat beside Rick.

Renfro let out a soft whimper and laid his head across Corrie's lap as Oliver huddled close to his buddy and kept his paw on Corrie's arm. Corrie leaned her head back against the seat and closed her eyes.

And prayed she'd wake up from this nightmare soon.

Chapter 12

J.D. noted with keen interest as the sheriff took the roundabout way out of Bonney that didn't follow the highway past the Black Horse. He knew that route would be blocked for hours as the firefighters battled to put out the fire at the campground and it wouldn't be a good idea to have Corrie see what was going on at her home at the moment. She had already had enough of a shock for one day.

He didn't ask Sutton where they were going, but it didn't take him long to figure it out as he saw the sign indicating the distance to the village of Tunstall. He recalled during his first few days in Bonney that he'd traveled that road from a different direction. Before long, a large house loomed ahead of them in the fading light of day and it took all of J.D.'s discipline to keep his jaw from dropping. Lights blazed from several windows on the ground and second floors. A large bronze-colored metal gate, set into a stone wall that seemed to run for miles across the plains, was decorated with a large circle that was etched with an ornate letter "S" and it swung open slowly as the sheriff approached and touched a button on a box attached to the driver's side visor. After making their way up the winding drive, J.D. was able to see just how big the house was—two stories in the front and a third story that was apparent from the row of four dormers that jutted from the copper roof. A wraparound porch was furnished with various sets of outdoor furniture but J.D. didn't have time to look at all the details as the sheriff parked the Tahoe at the bottom of the front steps, the Pages and Myers pulling in behind him. Before J.D. had his seatbelt off, he saw a couple standing in the doorway, impeccably dressed in black and white. Sutton got out and went around to open Corrie's door.

"Come on," he said, glancing at J.D. and jerking his head toward the house. J.D. couldn't help but notice that Corrie seemed to shrink back for a second until Sutton offered her his hand to help her out of the vehicle. She stood staring up at the huge house for a second until J.D. had helped Renfro out of the backseat and her friends had joined them. "Mother's out of town for a couple weeks. Let's go inside. Luz has dinner ready. Just follow Manuel," Sutton said.

They climbed the steps and the couple at the door inclined their heads and welcomed them. Both of them were Hispanic with dark hair shot through with silver, although their faces were unlined except for laugh crinkles at the corners of their eyes. Their faces softened when they looked at the sheriff and J.D. realized that they might have had a hand in raising Sutton.

J.D. managed to hide his shock as they walked into the front room, which was as large as a hotel lobby. Hardwood floors were covered with Native American rugs and there were separate sitting areas with leather couches and chairs around low wooden tables that had Native American pottery and vases with floral arrangements on them. Manuel stepped forward and ushered them through an arched doorway toward the dining room. J.D. was relieved when the man led them past the vast oak table with a dozen chairs and into the kitchen. Despite the howling wind and cold weather, there was a warmth in the kitchen that came more from the hospitality than from the double wall ovens and the fireplace. Several tall stools had been set around the butcher-block kitchen island and each place setting included a tall glass of ice water, a cup of coffee, and a steaming crock of chicken tortilla soup, with bowls of toppings set on a lazy-Susan serving tray in the center of the table. Luz bustled about, urging them all to seat themselves and eat, while Manuel collected their coats and jackets. No one said much as they all dug in to the food. J.D. hadn't realized how hungry they all were, but it had been early morning since Corrie and her friends had all gone to the gym to help out. A glance at the clock on the wall revealed that it was almost six in the evening. Sutton had excused himself to make a phone call. And while J.D. itched to go with him and find out what he was being told, he didn't want to be too far away from Corrie. She hadn't said a word since they'd left the gym. Shock, he knew, but there really hadn't been any way to break the news about the campground easily. He had no idea how bad the fire had affected the rest of the campground, but he suspected that, as far as the campground store building—and her apartment—went, it was a total loss. She stared at the table in front of her, not seeing anything, not reaching for her spoon or anything else. J.D. took her hand. "Corrie, you need to eat something," he said.

"I'm not hungry," she whispered. She didn't pull away and he squeezed her hand.

"You haven't eaten all day," he said. He nudged the soup crock closer to her. "You're going to need to stay strong and healthy." Her head jerked up and she looked at him, her eyes wide with dismay, and he looked back at her steadily.

"It's that bad?" she managed to say. J.D. was aware of

everyone else's eyes on him, and every spoon around the table had been set down. He drew a deep breath.

"It looked pretty bad when we were getting Oliver and Renfro out," he said. He knew that there was no point in trying to downplay what he and the sheriff saw. Better for her to expect the worst and hope that it wasn't as bad after all. "You need to prepare yourself. All of you," he added, looking at the strained faces of Corrie's friends. "I don't know if your homes will be saved or not." He took a deep breath. "The only thing I know for sure is that the cabins were completely destroyed."

Gasps went around the table and RaeLynn cried out in dismay. Corrie stared at him and clutched his hand tighter. "Oh, J.D., no! I'm sorry!"

"Hey, it's not your fault and it's not like I had a lot of stuff there," he said, mentally taking inventory of what meager possessions he had in his cabin. Mostly clothing; he didn't have much except his Harley and his firearm, both of which he had with him at all times. But Corrie's home... and the Pages and the Myers... and RaeLynn....

He looked up across the table, right into her tawny eyes, and his gut wrenched. Tears streamed down her face and he could see her tears were more for Corrie than for herself. As far as possessions went, the poor kid couldn't have had much more than he, himself, had and now it was probably all gone, lost in the fire. At least he had a spare set of clothes that he'd grabbed earlier... he sat bolt upright as the memory of Ronald Brown, wandering around outside the campground store, suddenly snapped into his mind.

"What is it?" Corrie asked as he pushed his stool back and stood up.

"I need to talk to Sutton," he said as he rushed from the kitchen and through the door into the large entry area. He spotted the sheriff across the room, looking out the vast picture window into the dark night. Sutton turned and raised a brow at J.D. as he holstered his phone. He motioned him to approach.

"Something wrong?"

"Besides the obvious? You could say so. I just remembered something." He proceeded to fill the sheriff in on the man, Ronald Brown, that he'd found lurking around the campground store earlier in the day. Sutton listened, his face darkening.

"He was carrying a propane tank?"

"Claiming he needed to have it refilled to warm up his RV or else wanting to rent a space in the campground because of the cold weather. He seemed legit—a wallet full of money and credit cards, showed his I.D. when I asked him for it. Apologized and left when I told him the campground was closed down due to the fire. Didn't even ask where he could get his propane tank filled." J.D. shrugged. "Sutton, I went around the whole campground store and checked to make sure nothing was missing, that the doors were locked, and nothing looked tampered with. Everything seemed secure. Yeah, it seemed odd and gave me a funny feeling, but I thought I was overreacting. I was going to mention it to Corrie, tell her to keep her gate closed and locked when they were all gone, but I didn't think it warranted me calling her right then and there because she was busy at the gym. Then a lot of other stuff came up...." The sheriff was shaking his head.

"It may or may not have something to do with the fire. Might be a coincidence."

"Which you don't believe in."

"Could you identify him if you saw him again?"

"Yeah," J.D. said. "I got a good look at him and his I.D."

Sutton nodded. "Okay, I was just talking to Jack Dolan, the fire chief. He says they're getting a handle on the fire at the Black Horse. It seemed like it flared up and then almost immediately died down. The weather is finally cooperating, the wind is calming down, and he thinks they'll be able to contain it quickly." His cell phone buzzed and he glanced at the screen. "It's the fire chief," he informed J.D. "What do you have, Jack?" he answered. After a second or two, his face paled briefly and J.D. straightened up in alarm. "Are you sure?" Sutton asked, his tone clipped. "Okay, don't tell anyone else until we have a chance to see what's going on. I'll notify the M.E. right away. Wilder and I will be there shortly."

"Be where shortly? And why notify the medical examiner?" J.D. said although he was almost positive he knew the answer.

"The campground. They found a body."

"What?" J.D. asked sharply. Sutton shook his head.

"I don't have all the details. Just that the body of what looks like an adult male was found at the site of the fire. We have to go now. They have the fire almost completely out, or at least contained, but we can't let Corrie and the rest go out there until we find out what's going on."

"Are you going to tell Corrie?"

"He'd better."

The two men spun around. Corrie was standing a few feet away, her arms folded across her chest, her expression stony. She looked from one to the other and waited.

For once, the sheriff didn't hedge or tell her that he couldn't talk about it. "We have to go to the Black Horse. The firefighters found a body."

She blinked. A hand went up to cover her mouth and she took a step back. J.D. moved toward her, afraid she was going to be sick, but she waved him away. "I'm going with you, Rick." Her voice shook for a second, but she cleared her throat and got the trembling under control. "Whether you want me to or not, that's my home. I'm going to see what's left of it...."

Sutton took a deep breath. "Corrie, you've already had a shock—"

"So what's one more? For once, Rick, neither you nor J.D. are going to stop me. I'm going with you." She spun and headed toward the door. "Are you coming or not?"

There was complete silence in the Tahoe, broken by occasional radio calls, but neither Corrie, nor Rick, nor J.D. spoke the whole way into Bonney. Corrie knew she had to brace herself; no matter how much she tried to convince herself that she could handle what she was going to see, she knew it was probably far worse than she could imagine. Added to that was the knowledge that someone had died out there. Who could it be? Mentally, she ran over the list of guests that were still registered at the campground. They were all year-rounders and she knew that every one of them was scheduled to be gone until after spring break. The Westlakes, her oldest "tenants" weren't planning to be back until just before summer. The other two had homes in Arizona and wouldn't leave the warmer climes of Phoenix and Tucson until the middle of April. There was no reason to think any of them had returned early for some reason. So who could it be that was found dead at the campground? A transient? It was possible... someone seeking shelter from the cold winds. She felt a hitch in her stomach. Was it also possible that person had started the fire trying to stay warm? Or was it possible that someone started the fire on purpose? She shook her head and looked up, meeting Rick's eyes in the rearview mirror.

"What is it?" he asked.

"It's bad enough that my home caught fire," she said. "And now there's a dead body there. I'm just wondering how that could have happened."

"I should have told you right away about that Ronald Brown I saw around the campground store earlier," J.D. said. Corrie shook her head.

"I don't think that would have made a difference. You handled it the way Jerry or Red would have handled it, the way I would have handled it."

"You're sure the name doesn't ring a bell?" Rick asked, for probably the fourth time. Corrie had stopped counting.

"Maybe. I'm kind of foggy right now. Ronald Brown is a pretty generic name and I haven't exactly had hordes of people staying at the campground recently. And you said it was a Texas license plate on his vehicle, right?" she asked J.D. He nodded. She went on, "The majority of my guests that come from out-of-state are from Texas, so that doesn't help. And a dark blue SUV? I see a lot of those, too. In fact, the last three guests I've had have all had an SUV, all of them dark colors—blue, or black, or charcoal gray." She stopped talking and her heart leaped into her throat as flashing lights loomed ahead on the highway. Rick slowed down until he came up next to Deputy Andy Garcia, who waved him on through the roadblock. Corrie sat bolt upright as Rick drove across the oncoming lanes of the highway and pulled onto the shoulder of the road, about fifty yards from the campground entrance. Thick smoke hung heavily on the night air without the earlier high winds to blow it away. He put the Tahoe in park and turned and looked over the back seat.

"You okay?" he asked, his blue eyes grim, studying her face to make sure she was being honest with him. She gave him one firm nod. "Are you sure you want to do this?" he persisted.

No, I don't, she almost blurted. For a brief moment, it occurred to her that he might have said that to someone who was being asked to identify a body and she fought back a shudder. "It's never going to be easy," she said. "Let's just get it over with." Rick nodded.

J.D. got out of the passenger side door and opened the back door for her. Rick waited for them at the front of the vehicle and the three of them walked toward the ramp that led down to the campground. Corrie kept her eyes trained ahead of her. Despite the fact that it was only seven in the evening, it was dark as night, as it usually was in February at this hour, but the blazing, bright-colored lights of all the emergency vehicles in the area and the lingering smoke gave the impression of being in a nightclub or funhouse. She tried not to look at the faces of the first responders who no doubt recognized her: locals, friends, acquaintances. It seemed like Rick and J.D. moved closer on either side of her, flanking her for support or protection. If they expected her to reach for their arms, they were disappointed. She held her head higher and grit her teeth as they rounded the bend.

She stopped in her tracks and stared down at the smoldering hulk of what used to be her home and campground store. Wisps of smoke and glowing embers dotted the crumbling remnants of the building. She blinked, praying that she was seeing things, that the blue and red bubble lights from the emergency vehicles and the spotlights set up to aid the first responders were playing tricks on her, but when she opened her eyes, the blackened timbers of the building's framework shimmered through her tears. Part of the wooden fence that encircled the patio area and pool was gone; twisted metal was all that remained of the picnic tables; the pool water looked murky, soot and ash floating on top of the pool cover. A glance to the right showed that only two of her cabins were still intact, both of them the furthest away from the campground store. She couldn't bring herself to look at the spot where J.D.'s cabin had stood. Not much remained but part of the roof.

Her vision wavered and her legs crumpled under her. "No," she breathed. One knee hit the ground and both Rick and J.D. reached for her arms to catch her. "No!" She forced herself to her feet and lunged forward, avoiding their hands. The chill from the winter cold froze her tears on her cheeks and the heat from the fire along with her own grief propelled her down the ramp so quickly that the two men had to practically run to catch up to her.

"That's close enough," Rick said sharply, catching her arm at the bottom of the drive. J.D. took another step ahead of her, as if to head her off if she broke free from Rick's grasp. But she didn't have the heart or energy to move any closer or even shake Rick's hand off. Her breath came in gasps and, from the expression on J.D.'s face, she must have looked like she was on the verge of hysteria.

"How?" she whispered. "How can it all be gone like this?" She wasn't sure if Rick and J.D. had heard her, but they exchanged a glance that drew her attention away from the ruins of her home. "What? What is it?" she demanded.

"Stay here," Rick ordered as the fire chief, Jack Dolan, approached them. Rick and J.D. stepped away from her, trusting that she would remain in place, and met him a few yards away. She didn't argue or respond; the truth was she didn't trust her legs to carry her anywhere without collapsing. Numbly, she watched as the three men talked, the fire chief gesturing toward what was left of the building. He motioned for Rick and J.D. to follow him and, after they cast a glance back toward her, they did, heading toward the back of the building.

She turned and looked around, drawing her jacket tighter around herself. The previously howling wind had died down to a gentle breeze that blew the heat from the smoldering remnants of the fire toward her, warming her body but failing to touch the freezing lump that sat in her stomach and heart. She watched the firefighters work, keeping their voices low out of deference to her. It reminded her of sitting in the funeral home at Billy's wake two years ago, people tiptoeing around her, as if by maintaining silence she would forget that her life had been torn apart. A lump rose in her throat.

"Billy," she whispered, as her father's image filled her mind. "Oh, Billy... Dad. I'm sorry. I'm so, so sorry. What am I going to do?"

She hiccupped and the breeze stirred the dead limbs of the trees, a dry sigh coming from them as if they, too, were lamenting the loss of the Black Horse along with her. She bit her lip and tried to stifle her sobs. She had to hold it together.

She was positive she hadn't learned the worst yet.

"Arson? You're sure?" Sutton asked sharply.

J.D. knew that the sheriff was just as positive of the fire chief's pronouncement as he was. A whiff of gasoline or some other accelerant tainted the cold night air. Jack Dolan nodded, his face grim.

"Of course, we don't have all the details yet and can't make an official pronouncement, but it's pretty clear the cause wasn't the weather. And it wasn't an accident. As far as the body goes," he went on, nodding toward the blackened form lying amid the ashes of the patio area, "I'm not sure if that was accidental—the arsonist miscalculated how fast the fire would spread and didn't get out in time—or if someone left him there, hoping to eliminate any evidence."

J.D. grimaced. "Him? So you think he can be identified?"

"Depends," Jack said, shrugging. He led them toward the body, cautioning them to watch their steps and calling for someone to direct a spotlight in that direction. "We're just now able to get close enough to see him clearly. I say 'him' because... well, it just seems more likely that it would be a man setting a fire." He pointed to a twisted lump of metal near the body. "Looks like a gas can. Might be he did start the fire, but then it reached the propane tanks near the grills, and then the tank that serves the building. So far no one has mentioned hearing anything, so it's hard to tell when all this got started." By now they had reached the body, careful not to get too close although any evidence or clues around it were no doubt destroyed. Jack stood back and let J.D. and the sheriff begin their investigation.

"Well?" Sutton asked as they looked down at the crumpled, blackened remains of what had been a living, breathing person just a few hours earlier. "What do you think? Think it might be Ronald Brown?"

"Hard to say," J.D. murmured. "Doesn't quite look tall enough, but there's not much left to go on. We'll have to see what the medical examiner says."

"He'll probably say they'll need to pull dental records to identify him."

"That's going to take time," J.D. sighed. He looked around at the devastation that marked the end of the Black Horse. "I just wonder if he was the one who did all this."

"I don't think so," Sutton said. He squatted down and aimed a strong flashlight beam at the charred remains and swept over to the gas can. "He must have poured out the gasoline near where the can is, dropped the can, and lit the gas to start the fire." He aimed the beam at the area where the grills and propane tanks had been secured. "Propane tanks don't explode. If they get hot enough, a relief valve would release propane and cause the fire to flare up. But it would take a while for the tanks to get hot enough for that to happen." He paused and looked up at J.D.

J.D. caught on. "Not likely that it happened so quickly that he couldn't get away... unless someone stopped him." The sheriff straightened up.

"We're looking at possibly two arsonists. But it's going to take time to identify this one," he said, nodding at the body in front of them, "so we need to find out who might have wanted to torch the Black Horse. Someone who might have had a grudge against Corrie," he added, his voice hardening as he glanced back to where Corrie stood, watching them from a distance. J.D. raised a brow.

"Interesting. They didn't even try to make it look like a wildfire," J.D. said. He looked around the darkness that surrounded the perimeter of the fire. "Only the campground store building, the attached patio and pool, and the closest cabins caught fire. Nothing else, not the Pages' or the Myers' RVs or any of the year rounders' RVs, not even the trees around the campground, except those in the immediate vicinity of the store, got more than singed." He followed the sheriff's gaze toward Corrie and he felt a chill spiral down his back. Had she been targeted? "No," he whispered. Sutton turned toward him and raised a brow.

"No, what?"

J.D. shook himself and looked at Sutton. "Corrie wasn't the target. Whoever this is," he gestured toward the body lying in the ashes, "and whoever put him up to this knew Corrie wasn't home. He knew the campground was empty. Corrie wasn't the target. The Black Horse was."

Chapter 13

Corrie stared numbly out the window of the bedroom she had been given at Rick's mother's home. The House, they called it when they were kids. Here in Tunstall, they were too far away from the scene of the wildfire near Ruidoso and the red glow that could be seen from Bonney couldn't be seen here. It should have given her some sense of security. But not when her home was destroyed.

Rick had made arrangements for one of his deputies—she wasn't even sure which one—to drive her back to the house. He and J.D. had to stay to continue their investigation. She didn't bother to argue because she knew it would be futile... and she had nowhere else to go. She could still see the anguish in his eyes and J.D.'s. She had dreaded to see pity, and she kept them both at arm's length. Despite the temptation to collapse into a pair of loving arms, she knew that if she gave in to tears, she might not stop. Her repeated assurance that she was fine wasn't believed by either man and she couldn't blame them; she didn't believe it herself.

She shivered in spite of the warmth of the room which included a gas fireplace. Luz had thoughtfully turned down the bed and provided her with a clean set of sleep clothes along with towels and toiletries. She had also instructed Corrie to leave her clothes in a laundry bag, right outside the bedroom door. She had tried to argue with Luz that she didn't have to wash her clothes, and certainly not tonight, but the realization that those were the only clothes she now owned killed her argument. The warm look of sympathy that Luz gave her nearly brought her to tears, but she swallowed them and thanked Luz. She knew the housekeeper would be collecting everyone's clothes from the Black Horse and doing their laundry tonight.

A soft whimper from the bedside drew her attention. She smiled through tear-filmed eyes. Renfro, freshly bathed to rid his fur of the scent of smoke, watched her from the large makeshift dog bed that Manuel had cobbled up from several pillows and a quilt. Oliver, having gotten over his own freshening up, was curled up on Renfro's back. Both animals watched her closely to make sure she didn't leave them again.

"I should probably shower so you guys don't kick me out to sleep in the hallway tonight," she murmured. She could still smell the smoke from the campground on her clothes and in her hair.

She made her way into the bathroom, stopping to drop the laundry bag outside the door as instructed by Luz, and allowed her tears to flow along with the shower.

When she emerged from the bathroom, with her hair dried by an Egyptian cotton towel and wearing pajamas that probably cost more than her entire wardrobe, the magnitude of what had happened finally hit her. She made her way across the vast room and sat on the edge of the king-size bed, staring around in disbelief, hugging herself. Here she was, in the most opulent room she'd ever set foot in, with hardwood floors and hand-woven rugs, expensive furnishings, artwork, and bed linens, out of charity. Nothing in the room, except her dog and cat, belonged to her. What few possessions she had left in the world were in the laundry room, somewhere in this vast house. She began to tremble and she bit her lip hard to keep her sobs locked in. Oliver jumped up onto the bed and rubbed his head against her chin, while Renfro sat up and laid his head on the edge of the bed… the best he could do since his arthritic legs wouldn't allow him to jump up onto the mattress. She curled herself into a tight ball, hugging her pets to her, her tears soaking the bedding until she fell asleep.

It was still dark when she opened her eyes, her inner alarm clock waking her at precisely five a.m. like it had for most of her life. She sat up, pushing the down comforter away, sending Oliver jumping off to join Renfro on the makeshift dog bed. She slipped out of bed and went to the bathroom to wash her face and pull a brush through her hair, then made her way to the door, trying not to step too heavily on the hardwood planks, though she doubted her footsteps would have been heard outside of the room. Opening the door a crack, she found a small table set up outside the room with her clothes clean and neatly folded on it. Even her sneakers had been cleaned until they almost looked new, a remarkable feat considering they were over a year old. She took the clothes into the bathroom and got dressed, grimacing at her reflection. Had she cried in her sleep all night? She quickly braided her hair and went to the door, hoping she wouldn't wake everyone by letting her dog and cat out.

She was surprised to see a dim light in the dining room, spilling out from the kitchen beyond, and the smell of coffee wafting out to the entry way. She opened the front door for Renfro and Oliver then turned as Luz came out of the dining room. "Oh, Corrie, it's you," she said. "I was thinking Rick might be back," she added, her voice carrying only a trace of a Spanish accent, her brow furrowed with concern and her hands wringing her apron.

"He hasn't called or anything?" Corrie asked. Her own stomach knotted in fear as Luz shook her head.

"No, he told Manuel to call him if we needed him here, but that otherwise he and Detective Wilder would be tied up for several hours."

"I'm sorry if I woke you," Corrie said. She opened the door and Oliver and Renfro scooted inside immediately, the cold wind following them in. They shook themselves and Corrie shivered. "I had to make sure these guys got outside first thing," she added as she shut the door. The two animals made a beeline for the large braided rug in front of the fireplace.

Luz nodded and beckoned Corrie to follow her. They made their way into the brightly lit kitchen, where it was obvious that Luz had already been up for some time. She slid a pan of cinnamon rolls into the oven and stirred a pot of beans that was bubbling on the stove. She glanced at Corrie. "Are you hungry, *mija?*"

"I think I'll just have coffee for now. I'll wait for everyone else to wake up," she said, making her way to the coffee pot. Luz nodded and turned her attention to chopping up green chiles and onions and tomatoes. "Can I help you with anything?" Corrie asked.

The older woman smiled. "You can peel and cube some potatoes for me if you like," she said, indicating a cutting board with several potatoes lying on it. Happy to have something to keep her hands, if not her mind, occupied, Corrie started on the task. They worked in companionable silence for several moments until they heard footsteps out in the dining room. "We're in the kitchen," Luz called out softly. The door swung open and RaeLynn walked in, stopping in surprise when she saw Corrie.

"Oh, I was afraid I was going to wake everyone up!" she said. Corrie smiled and nodded toward the coffee pot.

"I thought I was an early riser," she commented as RaeLynn filled a cup for herself and then topped off Corrie's and Luz's cups. RaeLynn studied her closely.

"How are you doing?" she asked softly.

"As well as can be expected," Corrie said, not meeting her eyes. She dumped the cubed potatoes into a large bowl with water and then took the cutting board and knife to the sink. "I haven't heard from Rick or J.D. so I don't know how bad things are officially."

"You said the whole building was... destroyed," RaeLynn said hesitantly. The word "destroyed" felt like a knife through Corrie's heart, but she swallowed hard and forced herself to respond calmly.

"Yes," she said. "The whole campground store is gone, and that includes our apartment and... everything in it," she said. RaeLynn looked into her coffee cup and, with a pang, Corrie realized that she was probably thinking about how little she owned in comparison to what Corrie had lost in the fire. Corrie couldn't bear to dwell on it herself. She knew Rick had managed to retrieve her fire security box—the "black box", as she had jokingly referred to it—but she hadn't been able to bring herself to open it and go through her paperwork. Not yet. She wasn't ready to deal with the finality of the loss of her home and business. "We were lucky, RaeLynn," she said, and her friend turned and stared at her as if she'd lost her mind. "It didn't happen while we were all at home, asleep. This could have been so much worse."

RaeLynn nodded, her face growing pale at the thought of what could have happened. Corrie motioned her to sit down. She took a seat at the kitchen island and looked around the kitchen, wide-eyed and awed, and Corrie couldn't help but smile. RaeLynn had taken to doing most of the cooking since she moved in with Corrie and watching cooking shows in her spare time. She was sure that this huge kitchen that effortlessly blended a professional chef's kitchen with farmhouse style was the stuff of fantasy to RaeLynn. Luz seemed to notice her admiration, too. "Would you like me to show you how I make my sauce for *huevos rancheros*?" she asked, realizing that it might help RaeLynn for her to stay busy as well.

"Oh, yes, please! If it's not too much trouble," RaeLynn said, jumping up. Corrie smiled as RaeLynn scurried to stand next to Luz at the stove. The door opened again as the Pages and the Myers walked in, following Manuel.

"Corrie, honey, how are you this morning?" Jackie said, hurrying to her side. Corrie noted with a pang that all of them were wearing the exact same clothes they had worn the day before, freshly laundered—possibly the only clothes they had left right now.

"I'm okay," Corrie said. "We all are okay," she said, getting up and retrieving the coffee pot to pour cups for her friends. "No one was hurt and... well, we'll deal with everything else once

Rick and J.D. finish their investigation."

Dana slumped in her seat, running her fingers through her short, frosted hair, her eyes red-rimmed. Red patted her shoulder. "I just can't believe this," she said, her voice quivering. "I mean, how did that fire move so quickly from near Ruidoso, without touching the village of Bonney, to reach the campground?"

Corrie winced inwardly as the Pages and Red exchanged glances with each other. It was apparent that all of them, except Dana, realized that the fire at the Black Horse had nothing to do with the fire near Ruidoso. Corrie hadn't voiced the suspicion that it was arson but neither Rick nor J.D. had told her not to. She took a deep breath. "Dana, that's not what caused the fire at the Black Horse. They—that is, the fire chief and Rick and J.D.—have evidence that someone started the fire. On purpose," she added, in case Dana was still confused.

"Oh, how awful!" Dana cried, causing RaeLynn to look even more alarmed. Red tried to comfort her, but she shook her head. "Why would someone do that?"

"No one knows," Corrie said, trying not to make it sound like the obvious answer. "But Rick and J.D. are investigating. So far, they know it wasn't caused by nature or an accident." She didn't mention the body that had been found in the ashes. She wasn't sure if she was at liberty to talk about that just yet. "I'm sure they'll let us know as soon as they have some answers."

A friendly "woof" and "meow" from the main room announced the arrival of Rick and J.D. They came in, shrugging out of their heavy jackets, which Manuel rushed over to take for them. Luz stopped what she was doing to fill coffee cups for both men before Corrie could do it. She stood back while the older woman clucked and fussed over Rick in a motherly fashion, to which he responded with a quick hug and few murmured words in Spanish, evidently reassuring her that everything was fine. J.D. watched with barely-suppressed humor until Luz returned to her work and Rick shot him a glare. Corrie bit back her own smile and then her concern deepened as she studied the dark circles under both Rick's and J.D.'s eyes. They both looked exhausted, emotionally as well as physically, and though she didn't want to add to their burden, she had to ask, "Well?"

Rick sighed and looked around the room. For a moment, Corrie fully expected him to say that he couldn't talk about it, but every person in the room had his or her attention riveted on him and J.D. It took her a second or two to realize that he was steeling himself to tell them everything they knew. And it wasn't good.

He had removed his Stetson and hung it on a peg near the door. He ran a hand over his head as he searched for words. J.D. stood back, sipping his coffee, his gaze darting between Rick and Corrie. His own brow was furrowed with concern, but he let Rick take the lead. "I don't know how much Corrie has told you all," Rick began. "The fire at the Black Horse was arson. There's no question about it. Someone poured gasoline around the back of the building, near the storage area where the propane grills and tanks were chained up and started the fire there." He paused for a second and Jerry spoke up.

"Any idea who it might have been?" His walrus mustache was bristling and Corrie almost expected him to whip out a pad and pen and take notes for a newspaper story. Corrie was actually surprised that Rick didn't have his own ever-present notepad and pen.

Rick looked toward her and she detected a hint of gratitude that she hadn't told them about the body. "Actually, we know there were at least two people who were there. One of them," he paused and took a deep breath, "didn't walk away."

A stunned silence filled the room, with confused looks being exchanged all around. Finally Red spoke up, "You mean... someone died in the fire?" There were gasps and almost everyone looked at Corrie. She felt her face grow pale but she said nothing, just kept her eyes focused on Rick and J.D.

"Yes," Rick said. Out of the corner of her eye, Corrie saw Manuel and Luz cross themselves and bow their heads. Rick went on, "We're waiting on the medical examiner to tell us if the person we found died accidentally or if he was murdered." He paused when Jerry stood up, shaking his head in confusion.

"What do you mean, 'died accidentally'?" he barked. "If he set the fire...."

This time, J.D. answered. "We assume whoever set the fire didn't mean to get caught and die in it," he explained. "We don't know if he was trying to get away and something happened to prevent him—like he tripped or passed out from fumes—or if someone made sure he didn't get away." He, too, ran a hand over his disheveled hair and tugged on his ponytail. "So we're looking at a possible homicide here and we're waiting on dental records to see if we can identify the victim."

"Any suspects?"

Rick patiently addressed Jerry. "Not yet, but we need to know if any of you have noted anyone or anything suspicious recently. Any guests or…?"

Corrie couldn't help herself; a near-hysterical laugh escaped her lips. "I've only had one guest in the last week," she said. "He didn't even stay an entire week and I only saw him in the store maybe once a day. He came in a standard rental RV, no car. That's the most I can tell you. I can't even remember his name!"

"Did you talk to him much?" Rick turned his attention to her.

"Good morning, how's it going, is there anything you need, that kind of thing," she said. She thought for a second and shook her head. "He never said much, just got coffee and a muffin, wandered around the store for a bit, sometimes he bought something, most of the time he didn't. He might have been bored or just killing time. He never really said what the purpose of his visit was, either."

"Can you describe him?" Rick said. Corrie stared at him.

"Do you really consider him a suspect?" she asked.

"He's the only one we've got," J.D. answered dryly.

"Great," she muttered. She turned to Jackie and RaeLynn. "Help me out," she said. "He was, what? Late fifties, thinning brown hair, not particularly thin or fat…."

"That's the best you can do?" Rick said incredulously. Corrie shot him a poisonous look.

"Is the word 'non-descript' better?" she snapped. "I suppose I should have had surveillance cameras in the store in case someone tried to shoplift a postcard!"

"Wait!" Jackie said, jumping up and patting the pockets of her slacks. "Jerry, where's my purse? I need my cell phone!"

Jerry gave her a mystified look. "In the bedroom. I'll get it. But what…?"

Jackie turned to Rick. "Corrie hates when I do this, but I was getting material to post some ads to the campground's social media page, you know, to try to drum up business. Anyway, I took some pictures in the store to add to the post and even took some video!" Rick and J.D. straightened up and exchanged a glance.

"Did you catch this guest on camera?" J.D. asked sharply as Jerry hurried out of the room. Jackie shrugged helplessly.

"I think so. He was in the store when I took pictures because… well, I didn't want the campground to look like it was deserted. I wanted it to look like we had guests. I took pictures on different days, when the man was wearing different clothes, giving the impression we had more than one guest. And I tried not to get his face," she admitted. "But when I was taking video, he may have turned to face the camera. I don't know how clear the images might be...."

"We'll take what we can," Rick said as Jerry returned, Jackie's cell phone in hand. She took it from him and opened the camera app and began scrolling through her pictures, with everyone except Luz and Manuel crowding around to look over her shoulder.

"Here!" Jackie said triumphantly. She handed the phone to Rick. "In the video I posted online, I edited out his face, but the entire video is here. I hope it's clear enough."

Rick started the video and zoomed in on the lone man who was prowling among the displays in the campground store. Jackie had done an admirable job of keeping him in focus until he turned toward her and the image blurred as she changed position so he wouldn't notice her filming him. However, in the brief moment that his face was clear....

"That's him!" J.D. said. "That's Ronald Brown. He's a little scruffier than when I saw him yesterday." He frowned, then his brow cleared and his eyes widened. "Corrie, that's the guy that was at the gym yesterday! Remember? He came through the food line and was standing there listening to us!"

"You're right!" Corrie gasped. "I didn't remember his name, but now I do! He was clean-shaven and neatly dressed when he checked into the campground, and I never saw him wearing a hat of any kind. Yesterday, he had a knitted cap on and looked like he hadn't shaved in days! I thought he was one of the people who had lost their homes in the fire!"

"He must have shaved before I saw him at the campground later on," J.D. muttered. He looked at Rick. "He was there when Corrie and I were talking. He heard her say that she was going to be working at the gym all day. He knew no one would be at the campground!"

"So it IS the campground that's being targeted!" Rick forwarded the photos and video to himself and handed Jackie's phone back to her. "He made sure that no one was there before he set the fire."

"So who's the body that you found?" Red asked. "Did this guy have an accomplice?"

"Looks like it," J.D. said. "And it looks like he wanted to make sure he didn't talk."

"You're sure that it wasn't Ronald Brown's body you

112

found?" Corrie asked. Rick shook his head.

"Not one hundred percent, no," he admitted. "Preliminary investigation seems to indicate it's someone else—shorter, not as heavy, but the remains were… well, I'm sure I don't need to go into detail. Suffice it to say, we're going to have to rely on dental records, DNA, missing person reports, whatever forensics can find on the body, to make a positive identification."

Corrie fought back a shudder. "So now what?"

"We have an APB out for Ronald Brown," J.D. said before Rick could say anything. "He was driving a dark blue Ford Expedition when he was at the campground yesterday and I managed to remember the license plate number, in spite of everything that's been going on. Jackie's photos of him will be sent to every law enforcement agency in the region, including the Border Patrol. Hopefully, he didn't get too far…."

"But why?" Corrie broke in. Everyone turned to look at her. She shook her head. "Why me? Why my campground? He was here for a week, so why did he wait till after he left to burn my campground? And for what reason?" She looked around the room. "There has to be a reason. Who is he? What did I ever do to him that he would want to destroy my home and business?" The room remained silent and Corrie turned to Rick and J.D. "I can only think of two people who either didn't like me or had an interest in the Black Horse—Conrad Englewood and," she paused for a second and swallowed hard, "Meghan."

Rick closed his eyes for a second and Corrie noticed how exhausted and deeply pained he was. J.D. didn't look much better, but it wasn't his ex-wife who had been threatening the existence of the Black Horse. She hadn't meant to make it sound like Rick was responsible, but she knew he would still blame himself. He didn't argue with her. "I'll start looking to see what possible connection there could be between Meghan or Englewood—or both—and this Ronald Brown," he said. "It might help us identify the body that was in the fire." J.D. unholstered his cell phone.

"I'll get Aaron Camacho on it. He's the best officer I have at doing research. And he's discreet," he added, probably for Rick's benefit. Before he could make the call, his phone buzzed and his face showed surprise. "And that's him calling," he said. "Wilder," he answered. "What's up, Camacho?" He listened and his lips hardened into a grim line. "Where? Okay, we'll be right there. Stay where you are and don't let anyone approach the vehicle." He ended the call, looked at Rick, and jerked his head toward the door. Rick responded with a raised brow but nodded.

"What's going on? He found Ronald Brown?" Corrie cried, stepping toward them. J.D. shook his head at her, then glanced at Rick once more before he answered.

"The sheriff and I need to check on something. We'll let you know as soon as we can." And with that, they left without another word.

Chapter 14

"Sure looks like the car Durán was driving."

"Camacho is running the plates. We'll know any minute." J.D. sighed and looked around. It was fortunate that Officer Camacho always patrolled on high alert and had sharp eyes. Although the sun wasn't even up yet, J.D. couldn't help but wonder how many people had passed the gray Lincoln Town Car that was neatly concealed in the dry shrubbery that lined the highway a half mile from the Black Horse Campground. The dead branches made a nearly impenetrable screen around the vehicle; a chance reflection of Camacho's headlights off a tail light in the early morning darkness aroused the young officer's suspicions. And now....

"It's registered to a rental agency at the El Paso International Airport," he confirmed to J.D. and the sheriff. "It was due to be returned today at four p.m. and the person who rented it is Alex Durán, who also has a flight booked to Mérida, leaving at eight p.m. That's at the southern end of Mexico, then a transfer to the Cayman Islands."

J.D. let out a low whistle. "Sounds like Durán was going to take the money and skip out on his creditors. He's either brave or incredibly stupid."

"Either way, it doesn't look like he's going to have to worry about being tracked down by the people he owes money to," Sutton said tonelessly.

"Meaning, you think that body at the campground was Durán."

The sheriff shrugged. "Why is his car hidden here? No signs of a struggle, so it looks like he left the car on his own." He reached a gloved hand into the console between the seats and found a wallet and cell phone. The wallet was empty; no identification, nor any cards with a name on them, no cash or photos. He tried to turn the phone on but it was immediately apparent that the battery was dead. He handed the phone to Camacho who had an evidence bag at the ready. "Let's see if there's anything there that will give us a clue to what happened. I don't see the connection, but it will give us a starting point for identifying the body." He seemed lost in thought. "Why leave his wallet and phone behind?" he muttered.

J.D. answered. "Maybe he didn't. The body at the campground didn't seem to have any I.D. or a phone. Maybe whoever left him there took his wallet and left it in the car after cleaning it out, trying to make it look like he was robbed."

"Except anyone who robbed him would have probably taken the car and just dumped his body." Sutton drew a deep breath. "I think someone is trying to frame Durán for the fire at the Black Horse." J.D. was silent for a long time. He knew he didn't have to say what he was thinking because he was pretty sure Sutton was thinking it, too.

The sheriff's cell phone buzzed. He glanced at the screen and raised a brow. "It's the M.E.," he told J.D. "Sheriff Sutton," he answered. He listened for a few seconds. "You're positive?" he asked, his voice tight. He nodded, thanked the caller, and reholstered his phone. "I was ready to have Meghan picked up for questioning, but now I'm not so sure."

"Why not?" J.D. asked.

"Durán, or whoever we found at the campground, wasn't just knocked unconscious and left there for the fire to take care of him. The medical examiner found a bullet wound in the victim's upper back. He's pretty sure that's the cause of death, not the fire or smoke inhalation or anything like that. He was dead before the fire even got started." He blew out his breath and rubbed the back of his neck. J.D. had never seen him under this much stress before. Sutton went on, "I can't swear to what's been going on for the last five years, but I know that for as long as I've known Meghan, she's never so much as fired a water pistol, let alone a real gun. And in spite of everything she's done, I can't picture her shooting a man in the back."

J.D. spoke up quietly. "She has a motive."

"Silencing Durán about their marriage? Murdering him seems extreme. She's got the only physical proof, the certificate, so his word wouldn't stand up in court without any corroboration, if this ever did go to court. And why at the Black Horse? She owns Corrie's insurance agency. Why set the campground on fire? In another day, Corrie's policy would have lapsed...." His voice trailed away and a look of horror crossed his face.

J.D. nodded grimly. "How much is the campground insured for?"

Sutton spun on him. "You're saying she's trying to frame Corrie for arson? But why?"

"Because Englewood keeps showing up, offering to buy the campground and Corrie won't budge." He looked at Sutton directly. "You think maybe *he's* capable of killing someone?"

"That's crazy!"

"I agree, but so is all this. Someone is trying to frame someone here," J.D. said. "Nothing makes sense otherwise." He shook his head, trying to understand it all: Englewood wanting to buy the campground, Meghan coming to Bonney to find out how the campground was doing, Durán wanting money, Sutton wanting to prove his marriage was invalid, Meghan wanting to move their daughter to Dallas. And where did Ronald Brown fit in all this mess? Did he have a connection to either Conrad Englewood or Meghan…. "How much do you want to bet that Corrie's insurance policy precludes payment if the fire was arson?" J.D. said suddenly.

"You mean, Corrie can't collect on the insurance if she's accused of starting the fire?" the sheriff sounded incredulous.

"That's too iffy. They'd have a hard time proving she had anything to do with it. She has a solid alibi for the time the fire was set. She was at the gym all day. And I doubt anyone can find a connection between her and Durán. The only thing that would raise suspicion is the fact that the fire started when everyone was gone from the campground. But that wouldn't be enough to convict her of arson. I'm willing to bet that during the time Corrie wasn't completely with it, mentally, and her policy was falling behind, Meghan slipped in a clause that precludes payment in the event of arson, regardless of whether or not the policy holder had anything to do with it. And that's all that she or her boyfriend would need. Just the fact that she can't get the insurance money means that she'll have to probably file bankruptcy and she'll lose the campground anyway. If Englewood couldn't get her to sell, he'll pick it up at auction for dirt cheap."

Sutton slammed a fist onto the hood of the Tahoe, cursing under his breath. "It comes back to the campground! What is it about the campground that Englewood and Meghan are so eager to get their hands on it?"

"That's what we have to find out. Camacho!" J.D. turned as the young officer hurried to his side and all but saluted.

"Sir?"

"I need you to look into anything you can find about the Black Horse Campground and the property surrounding it— inquiries, interested parties, past ownership of the land, the history of the area, everything." He didn't say to do it immediately; he knew Camacho wouldn't waste a second. "We'll finish this up," J.D. added as Charlie White's patrol car arrived.

"Yes, sir!" Officer Camacho said. He returned to his cruiser and left as Charlie approached, the tow truck right behind him.

"I think we can agree this is now a crime scene," J.D. said as he and Sutton watched the officer assist the tow truck driver. "They'll get the car to the village yard and I'll have my guys go over it with a fine-tooth comb for any clues. Let's get going."

"Where?"

J.D. couldn't remember a time when the sheriff wouldn't be the one taking the lead in an investigation. This whole situation was overwhelming him. "Let's go talk to Corrie, see what exactly her insurance policy says. I doubt she's got anything to do with Alex Durán, but she may have encountered him under a different name. And we're going to have to talk to Meghan, if she's still in Bonney. Whether or not she had something to do with Durán's murder doesn't matter, she might have been the last person to talk to him before he met up with whoever set him up and killed him."

Sutton nodded and they made their way back to the Tahoe in silence.

Corrie pushed away the paperwork, spread over the large mahogany desktop, her hands shaking and tears spilling down her cheeks. She bit her lip hard to keep her cries locked away. Jerry was muttering under his breath as he patted her shouder and Jackie drew her into an embrace as her own tears mingled with Corrie's.

They were in a small room off the main great room that was primarily used for an office, where she imagined that Rick's mother sat to conduct business and pay her household staff. Only she and Jerry and Jackie were present, along with Rick and J.D., to open the fire safe and examine her policies and other documents regarding the Black Horse. Billy's will, the deed to the property, everything was laid out, indicating just how much Corrie had lost in the fire… and how much more she would lose if the insurance company denied her claim. A very strong possibility, as she stared at the "revised policy concerning property loss due to arson"… with her signature on it.

"Billy, I'm sorry," she whispered. She could kick herself. Why hadn't she let Jerry and Jackie take over her business while she was incapacitated? Why had she let her stubborn, foolish pride convince her that she could manage everything without help? And now the business, the home that her father built with countless hours of work, sleepless nights of worry, and immeasurable love and dreams, with money scraped up wherever he could, was about to slip away from her, probably to a man and woman who had no desire to do anything with the campground other than wield it like a sword that would cut through Corrie's heart.

She looked up from the papers, swiping tears away, until she could make out Rick's and J.D.'s blurry faces. She was glad she couldn't see their expressions clearly; she couldn't take any more pity. "This isn't fair. Can she do this? Is this legal?" she whispered.

Rick's face was red—from anger or embarrassment, she couldn't tell. Probably both. He cleared his throat. "Meghan knows the law," he said. "It may not be fair or right, but I'm almost positive she made sure it was legal."

"How can it be legal? She took advantage of a customer who was mentally incapacitated!" J.D. snapped. Corrie winced at his words and started to protest but he cut her off. "Put your pride away, Corrie! There's no shame in admitting that you were injured and in no condition to sign legal documents! Meghan should have known that! In fact, it's pretty suspicious that she altered Corrie's policy in this one specific way. There's no way that this policy is legit, Sutton, and you know it!"

"It's not Rick's fault," Corrie said wearily. "If anything, it's mine. You're right, J.D. I *am* too proud and now I'm paying the price. I should have let Jerry and Jackie take over running the campground after I lost my memory." She looked up at Rick who stood silent and stone-faced, avoiding J.D.'s accusing glare. He probably knew the law as well as Meghan did, even if he didn't take advantage of his full scholarship to Yale. "Is there anything I can do?" she asked, hating the pleading tone of her voice.

Rick sighed and rubbed the back of his neck. "You'd have to get medical proof that you were injured and unable to make legal decisions. Like when you're given certain drugs and you're warned not to drive or sign important documents while under the influence. The problem is, you weren't taking any medications at the time these documents were signed and you were, for the most part, operating the campground as usual without any sign of being impaired. I know you had memory lapses from time to time, but I also know you probably didn't follow up with the doctor as much as you should have." It wasn't a question, so she didn't respond; she was sure the color in her cheeks was all the answer Rick needed. He went on, "You can ask Dr. White to testify to your condition but without medical documentation to show that you were having memory issues at the time the new policy changes were signed, I'm afraid there's a good chance that you won't be able to collect."

Corrie swallowed hard and blinked. She was determined not to shed anymore tears. "So just how bad was the damage? Is the whole campground gone? From what I saw last night...."

Rick's face softened a little, though J.D. still had storm clouds in his gray eyes. "The Pages and the Myers didn't lose their homes, though there might be some smoke damage. And your year rounders' RVs are safe. The fire was nowhere near them and they weren't affected. As far as the cabins go," he went on, glancing at J.D., "all but two were completely burned down. Those two had some damage, but...." He hesitated and Corrie knew what he was going to say.

"But the main building is a total loss," she finished. She took a deep breath, amazed that saying the words didn't cause her to burst into tears. That was a small victory; she was tired of crying. "Along with the pool and patio area, right?"

"And the storage shed and a lot of the trees and outdoor areas were damaged," Rick added. He took a deep breath. "Even if the insurance pays out, Corrie, you might want to rethink the idea of rebuilding the campground."

"Why?" she asked, her heart pounding. The thought of rebuilding the campground had hovered near the edges of her mind, but right now she was still processing the reality that her home and business were destroyed. Of course, there had been no question that she would rebuild—it's what her father would have expected of her—but Rick's words doused the tiny spark of hope that had kindled in her heart.

"It would take years for the trees to regrow," he said, softly. "You know how long it takes the forest to regenerate.

"Yes, but...." The words trailed away as she realized what Rick was saying. Building a new campground store and new cabins and fixing the pool and patio wouldn't be enough. Her campground had always been a place of escape for people who wanted to relax and have fun and get away from the rest of the world. The Black Horse had won numerous awards from various organizations that judged campgrounds on appearance, hospitality, amenities. Who wanted to camp where there were no trees to provide cooling shade? How long would it take for the grass and shrubs to regrow? For the burn scars to fade so that there weren't any constant reminders of what had happened? For that matter, how long would it take for all the repairs and replacements to be made? Even if, by some miracle, she received the insurance payout and managed to start work, how long would it be before she could open up again? A year or two? Three?

And would she have any guests when she finally reopened?

She slammed her fists down on the desk and stood up, her arms wrapped around herself as she paced the room. No one broke the silence; it was as if they knew there was nothing to be said that would make anything better. She forced herself to take slow, deep breaths. *I won't cry, I won't cry, I won't cry*, she repeated to herself. Her mind raced, the events of the last few days, weeks, months, tumbling over themselves in her memory. She knew she had to get them in some sort of order, but for now only one solution kept presenting itself to her. And it was the one she had never wanted to consider.

She stopped pacing and turned to face them. Jerry and Jackie had the same resigned expression on their faces. They already knew and had accepted what Corrie was finally going to have to acknowledge. Rick and J.D.... they looked both frustrated and angry, far from resigned. Her heart twisted as she realized that they weren't used to feeling helpless. To serve and protect was more than a motto to them—it was who they are. And right now there was nothing they could do. Her home was gone, along with all her possessions and her business. So were RaeLynn's, although she hardly owned more than a suitcase full of clothes and her beloved cookbooks. And J.D. had lost his home as well, humble and small though the cabin was. It had been his place of refuge for nearly a year. But the look in his eyes had more to do with her loss than his. She took a deep breath.

"I guess I'll have to bite the bullet and file a claim with the insurance company... and see if I'm just homeless or homeless and bankrupt as well."

The rest of the morning crawled by. The Pages and Myers were given the "all clear" to go and move their RVs from the campground. Rick invited them to move onto the Sutton property which had hookups available for whenever they had seasonal ranch hands working. Corrie had notified her year-rounders about the fire and told them they would have to find another place to move to. She appreciated their expressions of dismay at the news and their voiced hope that she would re-open soon, that they couldn't imagine having a better hostess and landlord, although she had no choice but to encourage them to find a more permanent place to move.

Rick and J.D. had left after a hasty breakfast that Luz insisted on feeding them. They had a lot of work to do and they had to be at their respective stations. RaeLynn, mirroring Corrie's stoicism, made herself useful in the kitchen, helping Luz prep meals for the rest of the day and other household chores. It was after nine a.m. before Corrie could call the insurance company. The local office still had its answering machine on, indicating it remained closed, and Corrie sighed with irritation. She'd have to call the main office and jump through hoops again.

She knew something was wrong as soon as she identified herself. "Oh, Miss Black... I'm afraid we can't take care of your claim at this time. We'll need to conduct an investigation...."

"Good news travels fast, I see," Corrie said dryly. "I haven't even said what my claim is for, but I'm sure you're already aware of what's happened."

"I'm afraid that we're waiting on an official police and fire marshal report," the voice on the other end of the line told her apologetically. "We really can't tell you anything until we get those reports. Is there a number we can reach you?"

She gave them Jackie's cell phone number. She could imagine Meghan's reaction if she saw the number for Rick's family home as her contact number.

As if it mattered, Corrie thought, on the verge of despair. *After all, Rick's still married to her as far as the Church is concerned. Meghan would probably gloat that I have to ask a man I love but can't marry for help with dealing with her.* Anger quickly replaced her despair. Why did she still feel that way about him? Why wasn't she angry enough to move past her feelings for him? Where was her stupid pride when she needed it?

"Miss Corrie?"

She looked up, startled. Manuel stood in the doorway, looking troubled. "Oh, sorry, I was thinking about something," she stammered, hoping her feelings weren't too obvious. "What is it?" she asked, suddenly realizing that very little bothered Manuel.

"There are some men at the door for you," he said, keeping his voice low. "They said they are from the police."

"Police?" Corrie stood up. What police? Surely, if it were Rick or J.D.... She followed Manuel out into the large room.

Two men in dark suits, accompanied by two state police officers stood near the door. "Corrie Black?" one of the men said. "We're Agents Simon Jackson and Eric Pinella from the

Fire/Arson Investigations Bureau. We need to speak to you."

"Okay," she said, her heart quivering. Manuel slipped away with a murmured excuse and she felt very much alone. Jerry and Jackie wouldn't be back for a while and both Rick and J.D. were miles away in Bonney. She wasn't sure if these people were here to give her information or ask her for some. "What is it?"

"We've been informed of the fire at the Black Horse Campground. We understand you're the owner?" She nodded. "We need to ask you some questions."

"I've already talked to both the Bonney sheriff's and police departments," she said. "They have reports...."

"We are now in charge of the investigation," Agent Jackson said. "We understand that there's a possibility that the fire at your campground was arson."

"All that is in the reports with the sheriff's department and the local police," she repeated, her heart thudding hard in her chest. She told herself to remain calm. She'd been friends with law enforcement officers almost her entire adult life. Why were these men making her nervous?

The two agents exchanged a glance and the two state police officers shifted uncomfortably. Agent Jackson cleared his throat. "We understand that you have personal connections to both local departments. The state police have taken over the investigation."

Corrie's mouth dropped open. She stopped herself from blurting out her initial reaction. She wanted to ask why, but the answer was obvious: having either Rick or J.D. or, by extension, their departments investigate was a conflict of interest. She should have known—for that matter, Rick and J.D. should have known—but now there was nothing to do about it, except cooperate with the men from the Bureau. "Um, where would you like to talk?" she asked, wondering if the fact that she was staying in Rick's home was going to create issues.

"Unless you mind, right here is just fine, Miss Black," the man said, reaching into his jacket pocket for a notebook and pen. With a jolt, she recognized Rick's familiar gesture and thought it should reassure her and make her feel better.

It didn't.

Chapter 15

J.D. had no idea what kind of pull the sheriff had with the medical examiner's office, but by mid-morning the body that was found at the Black Horse was positively identified as that of Alex Durán, the cause of death confirmed to be the single bullet wound between his shoulder blades that penetrated the heart. "Definitely a homicide," Sutton said flatly.

"Any definite suspects?" J.D. asked. They were at the sheriff's office, having stopped at Sutton's apartment in town where he had offered J.D. a chance to shower and put on fresh clothes. J.D. was thankful he had grabbed a set before his cabin burned down and tried not to think of what he had lost. He didn't have many personal effects, but there was still a sense of loss that was probably nothing compared to what Corrie was going through. He couldn't get the haunted look on her face out of his mind. It wasn't the sheriff's fault that his ex-wife was being vindictive, but J.D. hadn't been able to keep from lashing out at the man. Sutton hadn't batted an eye at J.D.'s reaction; he probably felt a measure of misplaced guilt as well.

The sheriff shook his head. "We're still looking for Ronald Brown. If nothing else, he was at the scene of the fire earlier in the day and we don't know if he has connections to Alex Durán. They both seem to have shown up in Bonney around the same time. But he seems to have vanished off the face of the earth. No one matching his description has been seen anywhere. Every blue Ford Taurus within three hundred miles has been checked and nothing's come up." He paused and tapped his pen on the desktop. "I called Meghan myself," he went on, his voice tight. "She's ignored both my calls and I had Laura try to reach her from the department phone. She still won't answer. I'll try again in a bit."

"That seems suspicious," J.D. said, tipping back in his chair. He folded his arms across his chest. "Don't you think?"

"Knowing Meghan, she's probably lawyering up," Sutton said. "She knows that when Corrie files her insurance claim, there are going to be lots of questions. She might even expect Corrie to threaten to sue her...."

"Corrie? Sue somebody? Not likely," J.D. scoffed.

"Meghan likes to assume the worst about everyone," the sheriff said dryly. He shook his head. "Anyway, the M.E. says that Durán was shot at close range. His fellow arsonist probably got him to pour the gasoline around the patio and, while his back was turned, came up behind him and shot him. He was probably dead before he hit the ground." He pushed the report across the desk for J.D. to look at.

J.D. grimaced. "Even without the fire, that bullet did a lot of damage to him. Kind of a big gun for your ex to be toting around, if she did get over her aversion to guns."

Sutton shook his head. "If Meghan had anything to do with this, it was someone she paid to do the dirty work. She'd make sure her hands were, literally, clean." He drew a deep breath. "I know what you're thinking, Wilder, but I still can't picture Meghan hiring someone to take out Alex Durán, regardless of what was going on between them, much less pull the trigger herself."

"Yeah? Did you picture her marrying some guy she didn't know two weeks before you two got married?" The sheriff flinched and J.D. almost felt bad for saying that. "I don't think you know your ex as well as you think you do," he added, not quite apologetically.

Sutton inclined his head but said nothing. The intercom buzzed, saving them both from speaking. "Yes, Laura?" the sheriff said.

"Sorry to interrupt, Sheriff, but there's an update on the fire near Ruidoso. The fire chief says it looks like they'll be able to start containment. The weather is cooperating and they're getting a little snow up there. I wasn't sure if you were still monitoring it," the dispatcher said.

"Thank God," Sutton said under his breath. "Thanks for the update, Laura," he said. "Keep me posted on any new developments." He clicked off the intercom. "That's one less thing to worry about," he commented. His cell phone buzzed and he glanced at the screen and froze. J.D. noticed and sat up straight, the front legs of the chair banging on the floor. Sutton quickly swiped open the phone. "Manuel? Is everything okay?" Sutton asked. He listened intently, his face registering shock. "What? When? Are they still there?" He motioned to J.D. to grab their jackets as he jumped to his feet. "We're on our way," he said.

"Who's still where?" J.D. asked as they made their way to the sheriff's Tahoe.

"State cops and investigators from the fire and arson bureau showed up at the house. They're talking to Corrie."

"What are they doing here?"

"Taking over the investigation."

"Are you sure there's nothing else you want to tell us, Miss Black?"

"I'm positive," Corrie said, her patience growing smaller as her concern grew bigger. So far, neither of the State Police officers had said a word, though they remained standing and alert behind the agents. Agent Pinella had taken a seat but he hadn't spoken either, just watched her carefully. Their silence only added to her nervousness. Why on earth would so many people have to come to ask her a few questions? "I've told you everything that I've told both the sheriff and the local police," she added.

"And there's nothing else that you might want to tell us about?" Jackson pressed.

"They know everything you know and there are probably things they know that I don't know!" she snapped. "They're the ones with all the experts to help them investigate what happened. All I know is, while I was in Bonney volunteering to help the people who were evacuated from another fire, someone set fire to my campground. If you don't believe me, there are at least fifty people who can vouch that I was at the high school gym preparing dinner for the evacuees. That's all I know!"

The man cleared his throat. "And you know the suspect, Ronald Brown," he said.

"I don't KNOW him," she clarified. "A man by the name of Ronald Brown spent five days as a guest at my campground. Police detective J.D. Wilder found him wandering around my campground store with a propane tank the morning that the fire started. As far as I know, no one has seen the man since."

"And you didn't know him prior to his stay at your campground?"

"What are you suggesting?" She half rose from her chair but quickly sat back down when the state cops stiffened. The agents raised their eyebrows and exchanged a glance and she told herself to stay calm. "What are you suggesting?" she repeated, keeping her voice low.

"We're just trying to see what connections there are among all the parties involved in this situation," Jackson said with a shrug. "For instance, you're close friends with the local sheriff."

"We've known each other since kindergarten," Corrie said through gritted teeth. "Bonney is a small town. Everybody knows each other."

"And the police detective," the man went on.

"J.D... I mean, Detective Wilder, was a guest at the campground when he first moved here a year ago," Corrie said, realizing her error too late.

"So you DO have personal relationships with your guests."

"With some guests who became friends. I don't have any friends who became guests," she explained, hoping the distinction made sense.

The investigator moved on to another question. "I understand you've been facing financial hardship," he said.

"Where did you hear that?" Corrie asked sharply. She was beginning to wonder whether she should be answering their questions or not. What did her financial status have to do with investigating the fire at her campground?

"Are you?" He ignored her question.

"Everyone in the village is," she retorted. "It's common at this time of year, especially when there's a drought."

"But no other business has quite the amount of fire insurance that you have," he countered. "Nor has any other business come just a few days shy of having their coverage lapse before filing a claim."

"Now, wait just one minute," Corrie said, unable to keep her voice from shaking. She gripped the arms of her chair to keep herself seated. "Are you suggesting that I was in such dire financial straits that I set my own campground on fire to collect the insurance money?"

Jackson cleared his throat. "It's not unheard of," he said.

"First off, if that's what you wanted to know, why did you spend the last half hour asking me the same questions the local law enforcement asked me over and over? Second, how dare you accuse me of burning my own home and business down! I don't know where you're getting your information from, but if anyone told you I would do such a thing...."

The front door flew open and Rick strode in, with J.D. right behind him, both men's boots pounding with authority across the hardwood floor. They flashed their badges at the State Police officers who had turned toward them with their hands on their weapons and the officers stepped back. "I'm Sheriff Rick Sutton, and this is my home, and this interview is over," Rick said, his tone leaving no room for argument. "Corrie, you don't have to answer any questions!"

Agent Jackson stood up and turned toward Rick then introduced himself and Agent Pinella. "Sheriff Sutton, this matter has been turned over to the State Police and our office. We have every right to interview Miss Black."

"And she has every right to refuse to answer your questions, as I'm sure you know." Rick said firmly. "And she has the right to consult an attorney if she feels that you're making accusations. She is the victim in this situation and I'm informing you now that both the Bonney County Sheriff's Department and the Bonney Police Department are more than willing to assist you in your investigation. So unless Miss Black wants to continue this interview, I'm asking you gentlemen to please leave at once and, if you wish to continue questioning Miss Black, I'm sure we can arrange a time and place that is convenient for both of you, once she has had time to consult with a legal advisor." Corrie did her best to hide her shock at the smooth Ivy League voice that Rick was using. She kept silent and marveled at the change in attitude of the investigators and the state police officers.

"If she hasn't done anything wrong, then why does she need legal counsel?" Agent Jackson snapped, his face turning red.

"Because she has a right to it, whether she's been arrested or not. You're not arresting Miss Black, are you?" Rick asked calmly. Behind him, J.D. stood with his arms folded across his chest, causing the other investigator, Pinella, to blanch. Corrie was sure that J.D.'s record with the Bonney and Houston police departments, as well as his military background, was well-known among most law enforcement officers in the area. None of them wanted to force a confrontation. Jackson cleared his throat.

"We will be contacting your office for any information regarding this matter," he said to Rick. "We expect your full cooperation, Sheriff."

"You'll have it."

"And we will be talking to Miss Black again."

"That's up to her," Rick said stonily.

The two investigators and the two state police officers headed for the door. "We'll be in touch, Miss Black," said Agent Jackson as they left.

Corrie hadn't even realized that she'd been holding her breath until she let it out as the heavy oak door shut behind the men and Rick turned to her. "What did you tell them?"

"Just what I know," Corrie responded. "I was at the gym when the fire started and that I've told you and J.D. everything I know. I never mentioned Ronald Brown or Meghan, although they seemed to know about him and my insurance claim. I also didn't tell them that I was aware that the insurance wouldn't pay in the event of arson. And I especially didn't mention that there was a dead body found in the fire," she said emphatically. "That was one thing they didn't seem to know about, but I'm sure they'll hear about it soon and then they'll want to know why I didn't mention it. And I can't lie about not knowing about it, so if it ever comes up, I'll just say they didn't ask. In short, I played as dumb as I could," she added, shrugging.

J.D. grinned. "Sounds like you played smart," he said. She rolled her eyes.

"Rick's always told me that just because someone flashes a badge at me, I don't have to answer their questions. I was as cooperative as I could be without giving him more information than he was asking for. Now I have a question for YOU," she added, turning to Rick. "Why are the State Police taking over the investigation? Is it really because of a conflict of interest?"

"Is that what they told you?" Rick asked, raising a brow.

"Not in so many words, but he said because I have 'personal connections' to both the sheriff's department and the Bonney P.D., they were taking over."

J.D. spoke up. "And how would they know that?"

Rick sighed. "I have a very good idea who tipped them off."

"I don't know what you're talking about, Rick."

"The hell you don't, Meghan," Rick snapped, trying to control his temper. "Was it really necessary to get the state police involved? Don't you think I can run an investigation involving a friend in a fair, honest, impartial manner?"

"A *friend*," Meghan sneered. Rick could almost hear drops of rage falling on the cell phone screen like drops of poison. "You've always had the interests of this particular *friend* close at heart, haven't you? Is marrying her the only thing you wouldn't do for her?"

Rick's fury propelled him to his feet. He'd been seated at the mahogany desk in his mother's office, glad he had insisted on making this call in complete privacy. Still, the walls weren't completely soundproof and he wasn't sure that Corrie and Wilder weren't standing just outside the door, so he put in a heroic effort to keep his voice down. "This has nothing to do with my relationship with Corrie... or with you, for that matter," he said coldly. "It has everything to do with you interfering with and complicating an ongoing investigation into arson!"

"How am I interfering? By reporting it to an impartial agency? Isn't that what you should have done from the beginning?" He could picture her shaking her head, probably with a devious smile on her face. "Besides, Corrie called to start filing her insurance claim almost before the fire was completely out. Of course, the company informs me whenever a claim is filed by one of my customers. They said she sounded quite calm and collected. Seems highly suspicious to me that the shock wore off that quickly. Unfortunately, her claim is going to be denied because there is a clause that precludes payment if the cause of the fire was arson. Naturally, I felt it was necessary to report any peculiar behavior to the proper authorities and," she paused for a few seconds, "well, Rick, what can I say? You have very personal connections to both Corrie and to me. I felt it would be best not to get you or your department involved."

Rick drew in a deep, silent breath. "There isn't another reason why you don't want me or the police department investigating this fire, is there?"

"I *told* you," Meghan snapped, "that all I did was inform the state police and arson investigators about your connection to the arson victim. They made the decision to take over the investigation, not me. Anyway, aren't you always saying that there are no such things as coincidences? Don't you think it's rather convenient that Corrie's business burned down just before her insurance lapsed?"

Rick bit his tongue to keep from snapping out his immediate response. He was positive that Meghan had strongly suggested to the investigators that it could be considered a conflict of interest for him and his department, along with Wilder and the police department, to investigate the fire. He was equally sure she had made it a point to notify them that Corrie's insurance was about to lapse and how SHE believed it was too coincidental to be an accident. But he couldn't prove any of it. "When was the last time you saw Alex Durán or talked to him?" he asked.

The change in subject made Meghan pause. Rick could almost see her ice-blue eyes narrowing as she answered slowly, "Alex? Why are you asking me about Alex?"

Rick smiled grimly. Nothing like two former law students asking and answering questions of each other. Fighters didn't dance around this much. "His rental car was found on the side of the road this morning near the Black Horse," he said, keeping his voice neutral. "A village police officer saw it and ran the plates.

Turns out Alex had rented it in El Paso at the airport. He's supposed to return it this afternoon, but he was nowhere around it. We thought maybe he'd been in an accident or something, but he hasn't turned up at the E.R. Just wondered if you'd heard from him or knew what might have happened to him."

"I haven't seen him since yesterday," she said, her voice just as bland as Rick's. "Once our business was completed, I didn't have any reason to see him or talk to him again. I don't know anything about his plans or when he was supposed to leave."

He detected a restrained note of curiosity and sensed that she wanted to ask for more information but wasn't about to give Rick the satisfaction. She'd probably have her family lawyers making inquiries for her as soon as he hung up, if she wasn't already sending them an email while she spoke to him. He decided to fuel the fires of her interest, so to speak, and went on, "There was a wallet and cell phone in the car, but there was nothing in the wallet. The P.D. has someone trying to get information from the phone but they haven't gotten back to me yet."

"Was he robbed?" Her voice was razor-sharp.

"Who?"

"Whoever was driving that car you found, of course!" Meghan snapped. "You said his wallet was empty...."

"Yes," Rick said. "No identification, no credit cards, no cash...."

He heard the faintest intake of breath and his pulse quickened as he sat up straighter. Meghan said nothing for several seconds and he waited her out. "I can call Alex's cell number," she said. "If the phone the police have rings, then you'll know...."

"The battery was dead," Rick said. "Not sure if they've had time to get it charged yet...."

She muttered something he didn't quite catch and he bit back a grin. He forced a casual note into his voice. "Well, since the state police have relieved my department and the police department of investigating the arson at the Black Horse, I guess we can focus on trying to find out what happened to Alex Durán. Let me know if you happen to hear from him...."

"*You* let me know if you hear from him!" Meghan snapped, surprising Rick. "And if you happen to find out that someone robbed him, I want to know about it, too!"

"Is there a reason for that?" Rick asked. She hesitated and he was sure she was about to tell him that it was none of his concern, but she surprised him.

132

"Alex said he needed some cash," she said. "He's heading home to Mexico and he asked for some money. He guaranteed he wouldn't bother me again, so I gave him a few thousand."

"What's a few thousand?" Rick asked.

"Fifteen."

"In *cash*?" Rick shook his head. Whoever had killed Alex Durán had made out like a bandit, quite literally.

"Small price to pay to keep him out of my hair," she said dismissively. "However, if he was robbed, I want to make sure that money comes back to me!"

"To you? What about Alex?" Rick was astonished at her coldness, although he shouldn't have been surprised by it. "Aren't you concerned about what might have happened to him?"

"Why should I be? All he's doing is taking advantage of me and this particular situation. He should have been happy with what he got from me ten years ago and he wouldn't be in whatever mess he's in now."

It was on the tip of Rick's tongue to tell her the whole truth: that Alex Durán was dead, that he was responsible, at least partly, for the arson at the Black Horse. If he'd had the money Meghan had given him in his possession when he died, then it was gone forever, unless they found out who had murdered him. So far, Meghan hadn't said anything that implicated her in Durán's death—she even kept referring to him in the present tense—but her cavalier attitude toward his fate and her concern about locating the money she had given him certainly made her look suspicious. He decided he'd poked the bear long enough; if she was involved in some way, best not to show his hand too soon. "I'll be in touch again, Meghan. You don't have any plans to leave town any time soon, do you?"

The question would have normally sparked an angry retort that she could go wherever she pleased and it wouldn't have been any of his business, but she responded with an overly cheery tone. "I have an insurance fraud investigation to conduct," she said. "I assure you, I won't be going anywhere until it's resolved." Before Rick could respond, she ended the call.

Chapter 16

J.D. had retreated to the guestroom Manuel had shown him the night before and fired up the desktop computer that the sheriff told him he could use, after assuring him that the network was probably more secure than the one the police department used. "Not to brag, but my family's budget is a little bigger than the village's," Sutton deadpanned before leaving J.D. to get to work.

After listening to Sutton recount his conversation with his ex-wife, J.D. decided that they had to figure out what connections Meghan might have that could possibly lead to Alex Durán's demise. After researching all he could about Alex Durán and Ronald Brown, he called in a favor from a friend who had been a federal plainclothes criminal investigator in Mexico and asked him to pull any information that might be floating around for Alex Durán, Meghan Stratham, and Ronald Brown for the last ten to twelve years. He sent recent photos and gave him all the information he currently had. "I need connections, to each other, or anyone else of interest, and any information that seems suspicious or coincidental." He added that Durán had had a gambling problem and had been in trouble with people both inside and outside the police department.

"You're not asking for much," his friend said dryly.

J.D. grinned. "There's a bottle of Don Julio 1942 in it for you, my friend. How's your son doing, by the way?"

The son in question had nearly gotten himself locked away for twenty years in federal prison for being in the wrong place with the wrong people at the wrong time. J.D. had still been in Houston, working narcotics, when he had made the bust but, after finding out who the young man's father was, decided that it would be beneficial to have someone with inside knowledge of what was going on with drug investigations in Mexico in exchange for community service and probation. So far, the arrangement had worked well for both of them. "He's graduating college in May with a degree in rehabilitation science," J.D.'s friend said, with a well-deserved note of pride in his voice. "You scared him straight, Wilder, and for that I'm grateful. You don't have to sweeten the pot with good tequila."

"Your info made me look good to the department, so we're square on that. If you can get this information to me by the end of the day, I'll make it two bottles."

"Ah, you spoke too soon," his friend said. "Got a hit already."

"That was fast. On who?"

"Durán and Ronald Brown."

"Ronald Brown has a police record in Mexico? He and Durán knew each other?"

"Not directly. Apparently, they were both working at different times for a real estate developer who picked up prime real estate at, excuse the expression, 'fire sale' prices. And they weren't buying them to flip or use as vacation rentals, either."

J.D. sat up straighter. Could it be that Sutton's ex had a more sinister reason for having her bachelorette trip in Mexico? In the back of his mind, he seemed to recall that Meghan Stratham had always been involved in real estate, had even studied real estate law when she was in college. "Who's the developer?"

"Well, that's where it gets weird," J.D.'s friend admitted. "The developer's name is José Hernandez, which would be about as common a name as John Smith in the U.S. and, get ready for this, there doesn't seem to be any information about this particular José Hernandez. Probably fake. I assume you want me to start digging?"

"Get a steam shovel if you need it," J.D. said. He looked up when he heard a tap on the door and the sheriff poked his head in, motioning to J.D. that they had to get going. "I gotta run. You've got my number. Call me the minute you find anything and email me whatever you get." He ended the call and met Sutton in the hallway. "What's up?"

"I just heard from Dudley. He said a couple of people have shown up at the department and want to talk about what they witnessed in connection with the fire at the Black Horse."

"Witnesses?" J.D. raised a brow. "Shouldn't we be referring them to the state police?"

"We will," the sheriff said. "After we talk to them."

Corrie felt restless. Rick and J.D. had gone back into Bonney and neither one had told her much about what was going on. The Pages and Myers had returned from getting their RVs from the campground and Jerry and Red, assisted by Manuel, were doing minor cleanup and getting their homes settled on the Sutton property for the time being. Jackie and Dana had persuaded RaeLynn to go shopping for clothes and tried to get Corrie to go with them. She appreciated the concern, but the thought of going into town and facing the residents held no appeal for her. "You know my sizes," she'd told Jackie and RaeLynn. "Just get me a few things to hold me over until I feel up to going myself. And save me the receipts!" she added, wagging a finger at Jackie.

After they left, she paced the main room, glancing out the windows from time to time. She didn't expect the state police and the fire investigators to come back so soon, but she kept getting an inexplicable sense of something about to happen. What she didn't know was if it was a good thing or a bad thing.

Rick hadn't said much after he had his talk with Meghan. To Corrie's chagrin, it seemed Meghan was intent on placing the blame for the fire at the Black Horse squarely on Corrie, despite the fact that Corrie had plenty of witnesses who could vouch for her being nowhere near the campground when the fire broke out. Rick offered to have his family's attorney meet with Corrie that afternoon to discuss the situation. "Isn't getting a lawyer, in effect, admitting that I did something wrong?" Corrie asked, balking at the idea of having to retain lawyers she was certain she couldn't afford.

"Trust me when I say you don't want to fight Meghan without an attorney in your corner," Rick warned her. "She knows the law and she's got an army of attorneys behind her as well. I don't want you to get caught by surprise." He said he and J.D. would try to be back before the lawyer showed up, but that she should feel free to tell him everything—EVERYTHING—she knew about the fire and the events leading up to it, including Meghan's interest in the campground.

She shivered and wrapped her arms around herself, despite the fire roaring in the huge stone fireplace. Her gaze traveled around, taking in the staircase that led to the second floor landing and a gathering area almost as big as the main room. She hadn't set foot in Rick's house since she and Rick were both twelve years old.

The first year Rick's father wasn't around for his birthday.

Rick's father had always been a bit of an enigma, rarely seen around Bonney, and only mentioned in whispers. Even Rick didn't talk about him very much. Corrie had never understood why and, to be truthful, it hadn't mattered. Rick had spent more time at the Black Horse around Corrie's parents than with his own parents and he never had friends visit him at his home. Still, it had been a long-standing tradition that, every year on his birthday, Rick's dad would take him on a two-week long trip, just the two of them. When they'd get back, his dad would once again melt into the background and Rick would regale Corrie with stories of where they went and what they did: hiking and rafting in the Grand Canyon, visiting Washington D.C. and spending hours at the Smithsonian Institution galleries, museums, and zoo, or camping and fly-fishing in Yellowstone. To say that he lived for those two weeks every year was an understatement. And it all ended when, without warning, his father suddenly left a month before Rick's twelfth birthday.

Rick had been devastated. He didn't know why his father suddenly decided to leave. But, being Rick, he decided he wasn't going to mope about it. His mother had agreed, reluctantly, to allow him to have a party for his birthday, the first one he'd ever had.

Because he couldn't stand to leave anyone out, he'd prevailed on his mother to allow a party for his whole class and a few extra kids who were on his Little League team. All told, a total of twenty-six kids. Corrie couldn't help but smile as she recalled the dazed look in Cassandra Waverly-Sutton's eyes when all these kids showed up at her house, although every one of them showed up dressed in their Sunday best—the girls in dresses or skirts and the boys in khakis or their dress jeans—and every one of them on their best behavior. Of course, Luz and Manuel had pretty much done all the work of preparing the food and hosting and supervising the gathering, which had been restricted to the second floor landing and the main room. At one point, Rick and his friends were allowed the run of the basement area, which not only included several storage rooms, but also a wine cellar. A game of hide-and-seek had ensued, with all the kids pairing off and dashing for the best hiding places. Corrie and Rick had ended up being paired together—the only boy-girl team. No one had batted an eye; they had been the best of friends since they met on the first day of kindergarten. With Rick leading the way through the maze of rooms and closets, they found the perfect place to hide from the others inside the wine cellar. They had listened without making a sound as the other teams were found, the cheers and groans indicating, one by one, how many teams were left. With only themselves and another team left to be found, Rick surprised Corrie by breaking the silence. "I really like you, Corrie. A lot," he'd said, without preamble and without a bit of awkwardness. He left that for Corrie.

"Really?" She had stared at him, while he listened calmly at the door. "Why?" was the only thing she could think to say in response.

He had turned to look at her, his deep blue eyes intense in the small, dimly lit room. He didn't answer immediately. He studied her for several seconds, making her feel hot and uncomfortable even in the coolness of the wine cellar, before he shrugged and turned away to listen for the other kids who were still looking for them. "Because you always make me smile even when I feel sad. Because when we're together, everything is okay, even when it's not. And because I'm never bored when I'm with you."

Corrie hadn't found the words to respond back then before the rest of the party had found them. They never spoke about it again, either, not even while they were dating. But now, thinking back on the events of the last year, to say nothing of the last few days, she found herself smiling. Surely, Rick would have to admit that, lately, a little boredom around her wouldn't be a bad thing.

She wandered from window to window, trying to keep her mind from going back to thinking about Rick and what might have been, trying not to be impatient with him and J.D. for not reporting to her what was going on minute by minute. It occurred to her that it might not be a bad idea to jot down everything she could think of regarding Ronald Brown and the events leading up to the fire. It would be something constructive she could do and hopefully keep her from dwelling on things that couldn't be changed.

She went to the small telephone table that stood at the foot of the stairs. Even though it seemed that everyone had a cell phone these days, she had noticed that almost every room in the house, except the dining room, had a telephone in it. Years ago, that might have seemed more opulent than archaic, but now it gave her a perfect spot to search for a pad and pen to write down a few notes. She found a small notepad but no pens and she sighed in frustration. She thought about going into the kitchen where Luz was preparing lunch and dinner, but she didn't want to bother her to ask her for something to write with.

The office. What better place to find a pen? She crossed the room, surprised that her footsteps didn't echo off the walls and ceiling. The door to the office was ajar and Corrie hesitated; surely there was no problem with her just walking in. Rick hadn't said any rooms in the house were off limits and it was just as much his home as it was his mother's and she wasn't here anyway and besides, Corrie had been in the room earlier to look through her papers, although Rick had been there when she.... she told herself she wasn't a twelve-year-old anymore and she needed to stop trying to talk herself into taking action and just DO it.

She pushed the door open and walked to the desk and sat down in the plush office chair marveling at how comfortable it was. She'd been so distraught earlier when she sat in it to go over her paperwork that she hadn't really appreciated the buttery leather and the way it rolled so smoothly. She tugged the drawer open.

To her surprise the first thing she saw, besides a tray full of pens, was a bundle of mail, held together by a rubber band. Her first instinct was to forget about grabbing a pen and shut the drawer immediately, but a name on the topmost envelope caught her eye and she sucked her breath in sharply. As if on their own accord, her fingers picked up the bundle and she stared at the name on the return address: Patrick X. Sutton II. Rick's father. With a post office box in Columbia Falls, Montana. Unable to stop herself, she slowly thumbed through the letters, several dozen, postmarked in the last two years. The one on top was postmarked just a week earlier.

What shocked her the most, however, was that they were all addressed to Rick—formally Patrick X. Sutton III—at his mother's home address. She stared and stared at the envelopes, trying to make sense of what they meant. Rick hadn't spoken about his father since that twelfth birthday party. Only once did Rick make any reference to him, and that was when they were both thirteen and Corrie had asked him, straight out, what had happened to his father. Rick's cryptic answer was that he didn't care and he didn't want to talk about him. Ever again. The look in his eyes had effectively suppressed her questions, though not her curiosity, but she knew Rick well enough to know that he wouldn't talk about anything if he didn't want to. As far as she knew, Rick hadn't had any contact with his father in over twenty years. But now these letters told a different story.

To her horror, she suddenly realized that she had slipped the rubber band off the bundle and was dangerously close to pulling the letter out of the topmost envelope. As badly as she wanted to know what Rick's father had been writing him about, it was none of her business and she needed to put the letters down, grab the pen, and get out of the office before anyone found her there. Quickly she straightened the letters, put the rubber band back in place, and agonized for a full thirty seconds about where exactly the bundle had been in the drawer. Would it draw attention if it wasn't precisely where she'd found it? She had just made up her mind on where to place it when she heard Renfro's welcome "woof" echo in the main room and her heart leaped into her throat. She didn't know if it was Jackie, Dana, and RaeLynn who had arrived, or if Jerry, Red, and Manuel had come in from cleaning the RVs, but she knew it might possibly be Rick and she jumped up from the desk, remembering just in time not to slam the drawer shut, pushed the chair back in place, and rushed to the door, forgetting all about grabbing a pen. She slipped out the door and pulled it almost all the way shut before she realized she still didn't have a pen. But it was too late; she couldn't go back in. She turned around, hoping that no one would question what she was doing near the office door.

And stared in shock as Cassandra Waverly-Sutton turned from looking at Renfro and Oliver and her gaze locked with Corrie's.

Chapter 17

"Oh!" Corrie blurted. She bit her tongue hard to keep from following up with, "What are you doing here?"

"Corrie, I haven't seen you in a while," Cassandra said, as if they were long-lost acquaintances. She removed her silk scarf from around her neck and head, folded it neatly and stashed it in the pocket of her designer wool coat. She glanced around as she shrugged out of it, then frowned. "Are you here alone? Where is everyone?"

"I think Luz is in the kitchen," Corrie stammered. "Manuel is helping...." She stopped. Did Rick's mother even know who was staying in her house?

Cassandra nodded as she took her coat and hung it on the rack near the door. "Patrick told me what happened at the campground and that you and your friends would be staying here for a while." It took Corrie a few seconds to remember that Rick's mother always called him by his given name. Cassandra went on, "I'm so sorry to hear about the fire. If there's anything I can do to help, please tell me."

"Um, well, you're already doing plenty for me and my friends, letting us stay here," Corrie managed to say. She was shocked at the civility of Cassandra's tone, even if she did seem aloof. After their last meeting at Wendell's several months ago, she didn't think Rick's mother would be overjoyed to have Corrie staying in her home. Cassandra waved a hand.

"This is Patrick's home as well. He's certainly free to ask anyone to stay here that he wishes." She arched a brow, looking amazingly like her son, and tilted her head to one side. "Did you need something from the office?"

Corrie cringed inwardly. There was no way she could hide the fact that she'd been in the office; it was the only other door in that corner of the main room. She forced a weak smile. "Oh, I was going to write down some information for Rick and I needed a pen...."

Rick's mother nodded. "There are some in the desk. I'll get one for you," she added, leaving no room for argument as she made her way across the room. Corrie was astounded at how natural and casual she seemed to be. Was it possible she didn't know about the letters? She had to know... maybe she didn't think Corrie had seen them. She moved aside as Cassandra opened the door to the office, keeping her fingers crossed behind her back.

Waiting outside the office seemed to be the most prudent thing to do, but she peeked in and watched as Rick's mother opened the drawer, fished out a pen, and shut it without seeming to have cast a glance at the letters. The heels of Cassandra's boots clicked on the hardwood floor as she walked over to Corrie and handed her the pen. She raised an eyebrow. "Do you need paper as well?" she asked.

"Uh, no, I found some in the telephone table," Corrie said, nodding toward the table near the stairs. Cassandra inclined her head then glanced up as Luz came in from the dining area, wiping her hands on her apron.

"Oh, Mrs. Sutton, Manuel told me he saw your car out front. We didn't expect you back for another week," she said, seeming not the least bit flustered. Corrie was surprised; for some reason she had believed that Cassandra Waverly-Sutton would be a very demanding employer and her staff would be falling over themselves in a panic that they hadn't been prepared for her arrival. "It won't take me long to make you some tea and a bite to eat," the housekeeper added. Cassandra nodded, giving Luz a warm smile, and shrugged her elegant shoulders.

"I cut my trip short. It seemed I might be needed here at home," she said. She looked at Corrie. "Why don't you join me? Luz makes a wonderful tea with lavender, honey, and a touch of cream. You look like you could use something soothing," she added, following Luz toward the dining room. It took Corrie a second or two to recover from her shock before she hurried to catch up to the two women.

Luz directed Corrie to a small breakfast nook just off the main kitchen. Cassandra had settled herself in a chair by the window where she could look out toward the long driveway. Corrie slipped into a chair opposite of her, feeling extremely self-conscious. She had no idea where Rick's mother had been, but she was wearing a deceptively simple sweater and skirt set of cashmere and wool, the hem of her skirt swishing against her high-heeled leather boots, making Corrie feel severely underdressed in her t-shirt and jeans. Cassandra's brown hair had golden highlights in it, just like Rick's, and her face was expertly made up, showing no tell-tale signs of aging. Corrie wondered if that was due to surgery or good genetics and expensive cosmetics. For a fleeting moment, she wondered how much of Rick's good looks came from his mother—for sure, he had her dark blue eyes and her well-bred, no-nonsense bearing—and how much from his father. Try as

144

she might, she couldn't conjure up an image of Rick's dad from her memory. Had she ever really seen the man? And when was the last time Rick had laid eyes on him? A corner of Cassandra's mouth quirked up in a half-smile. Ah, that was where Rick got that. She realized with a start that she had been staring at Rick's mother and she felt color flood her face.

"Patrick told me about the fires—the one near Ruidoso and the one at the campground," Cassandra said, pretending not to notice Corrie's embarrassment. "He told me I should stay in Sanibel Island with my friends, even though there's really no danger here. We were having an unofficial college reunion, but after four days of listening to everyone either lie about how great their lives are or cry about how terrible they are, I was ready to come home. Besides, I didn't want to leave Patrick alone right now."

"Right now?" Corrie echoed. It couldn't be the fires; surely Rick wouldn't need anyone to stand by him for something that was a routine part of his job. Was she referring to his recovery after his surgery in December? But he was doing quite well and Corrie knew that Rick had stayed here, at the house, for the first few weeks after he was released from the hospital. Why right now? A startled look came into Cassandra's eyes and a slight flush tinged her cheeks. Corrie's heart began to race. Apparently there was another reason... one she didn't know about.

Just then, Luz came in with a tray bearing a pot of tea, tea cups, and two plates of chicken salad sandwiches on croissants, saving Cassandra from answering. She asked Luz if she knew when Rick—Patrick—would be returning and Luz said she had already had Manuel call to let him know that his mother was home. Luz poured the tea as she explained that he was busy at the sheriff's department but would return home as soon as possible. Cassandra nodded and glanced toward Corrie, who had remained silent the whole time.

"Anything else, Mrs. Sutton?" Luz asked. She, too, glanced at Corrie and gave her what seemed to be a sympathic look. What was that all about?

"Everything is wonderful, Luz, and I'll let you know if there's anything else we need," she said, a subtle dismissal. Luz flitted away to the kitchen and Cassandra picked up her tea cup. "Please help yourself, Corrie. I daresay you haven't eaten much these last couple of days.

Corrie hardly believed she looked like she was wasting away

after two days with little appetite, but the sandwiches looked delicious and the warm, sweet aroma of the tea tempted her to abandon her desire for a cup of piñon coffee. And she probably should eat something. Cassandra didn't smile, but she looked pleased when Corrie complimented her on the sandwiches and tea.

"The credit all goes to Luz," she said, waving away the words of praise. "I've hardly ever set foot in the kitchen since she came to work for me over thirty years ago. She was barely eighteen, but could cook like a professional chef. I understand she taught Patrick how to cook and bake as well. I'm sure that's served him well over the years. I don't know how I'd manage without her, although I had insisted that she go when Patrick said that, er, they needed some help at home...." Her voice trailed away and she turned toward the window, the color rising in her face. Corrie felt her stomach twist.

Years ago, she had heard through Bonney's notoriously accurate grapevine that Meghan had demanded a full-time, live-in housekeeper that also cooked shortly after she and Rick got married. Though the apartments they had lived in, both in Bonney and Albuquerque, were nowhere near the size of the Sutton family home, Meghan didn't want to have to deal with the daily drudgery of keeping house, doing laundry, and cooking meals for two... even though she had immediately given up school and work to be a full-time wife. She had subsequently hired—and fired—no fewer than ten housekeepers in the first four years of her marriage to Rick. It wasn't until they were back in Bonney and Meghan was pregnant that Luz had left the Sutton home to be Rick and Meghan's housekeeper... supposedly at Rick's request and upon Cassandra's insistence. Surely Rick's mother wasn't about to start talking about Rick's marriage to Meghan and the subsequent events? She thought about the letters in the drawer and the knots inside her grew tighter. Were the letters the reason Cassandra thought she needed to be here for Rick? What WAS in those letters? Corrie took a bite of her sandwich to keep her mouth full, before she blurted out questions that were none of her business.

Cassandra made small talk about her trip, the dry cold weather in New Mexico, and how dismal a month February could be. Corrie tried to respond politely, but it was getting harder the longer they sat at the table. She had hardly exchanged more than a couple of words with Rick's mother over the years and, despite Cassandra's polished manners, it was evident that she was feeling just as awkward as Corrie. She expressed dismay over the fire at the Black Horse, but didn't ask any questions, for which Corrie was grateful. "I'm sure Patrick will get to the bottom of that sooner than later," was all she said about the investigation. Corrie couldn't find much to say in response. She had always believed that Rick's mother had never liked her and she wasn't quite sure why, and perhaps had, in some strange way, blamed her for Meghan leaving Rick. Yet here she was making small talk instead of excusing herself and ignoring Corrie. Cassandra's behavior was disconcerting; her gaze would fix on Corrie and then flit away, her color fluctuating from ghost-white to deep crimson.

Finally, Corrie had had enough. She had been looking out the window toward the driveway, praying that Rick or someone would show up to distract them both, when she turned and was startled to see Cassandra staring at her and the look in her eyes made Corrie's heart pound. Little sparks of anger seemed to crackle in the dark blue eyes that were so much like Rick's but, even more, there was a look of deep, heavy sadness that jolted Corrie so much she almost dropped her teacup. She set it down, hoping her hands weren't visibly shaking. "Is there something wrong?" she asked, unable to keep the bafflement out of her voice.

Cassandra blinked, her eyes turning glassy for a split second before she looked away. She took a deep breath and then turned back to Corrie. "I'm sorry," she said, her voice husky. She cleared her throat. "I didn't mean to stare. It's just that… you remind me so much of… her."

Corrie's jaw dropped. She felt the blood drain out of her face and a ball of fire burst to life in her stomach and shot up through her spine, making her whole head feel like a volcano about to erupt. Had she heard right? How dare she? How *dare* Rick's mother compare her to Meghan? Did she have no idea what Meghan had done to Rick, her only son? Was she so blind that she couldn't see that, despite everything that had happened in the past, despite the fact that Rick had shattered Corrie's heart and dreams, that Corrie had always been there for him? How could she possibly have the sheer audacity to say that Corrie reminded her of that… that….

"Your cousin, Natalie."

Corrie blinked.

Cassandra's gaze dropped to her lap. She picked up her teacup and set it down again, still avoiding Corrie's eyes. "I'm sorry. You probably hardly even remember her. You and Patrick… you were both mere children when she… left."

Corrie snapped her lips shut when she realized she was still staring at Rick's mother. Her mind had gone blank but now she scrambled frantically to try to connect the name "Natalie" to a memory. *Natalie... Natalie... Natalie....*

"Oh!" Corrie said as the image came to her mind of a pretty teenage girl with long dark hair and sparkling, coffee-brown eyes, laughing and singing with her and Rick when they were... how old? Seven? She was the daughter of Corrie's father's oldest sister and she had been the teacher's assistant in their Sunday school classes when she and Rick were preparing for their First Holy Communion. She was a favorite among the children and the staff, always seeming so happy and full of life. It seemed like a dream-come-true when Rick's father, in a rare moment when he appeared in public with his wife and son at the First Communion Mass, saw Natalie and immediately offered her a job as a nanny, of sorts, to Rick, promising a salary that was more money than the seventeen-year-old ever expected to earn. Immediately, there was suspicion among the Black Horse family members—why would one of the wealthiest men in the entire state offer a job to a girl he had just met? Tongues had wagged even harder when it was discovered that job entailed very little work—Luz and Manuel were already established in the Sutton household—and Rick's father had a habit of gifting the young woman with expensive jewelry and clothing.

A few years later, she mysteriously disappeared. Shortly before Rick's dad left.

Corrie remembered Rick's heartbreak when his beloved nanny left, although she didn't do much more than make sure Rick did his homework and keep him entertained and out of the way when his mother hosted gatherings at the house—not that Rick had ever been a troublesome kid. But she had been fun, always willing to drive Rick and his friends to the movies or to wherever they wanted to go and joining in the fun while being the responsible adult she needed to be. The only times she didn't hang around with him and his friends was when he went to spend time with Corrie at the Black Horse Campground. The first and only time she did stay, Corrie's father, Billy, took her aside and had a serious, hushed conversation with his young niece, which resulted in Rick's visit being cut short by a red-faced, angry Natalie who insisted on taking him home immediately. All future visits involved her merely dropping him off at the campground store and disappearing for several hours until it was time to pick him up. Corrie couldn't understand why her cousin wouldn't come in to see her or why Billy always looked so solemn and sad whenever Rick would come over and he'd see Natalie dropping Rick off, studiously averting her gaze so as to avoid eye-contact with Billy.

She and Rick had been too young, too innocent to understand... any of it. And Corrie had pretty much forgotten about it all, especially since Billy had never talked about it and his family was estranged from him anyway.

Now things—a lot of things—had become uncomfortably clear.

She wasn't sure what she was supposed to say to Cassandra. Apologize? For what? It wasn't her fault that she bore a strong resemblance to a young woman who had, apparently, created a rift in Cassandra's family. However, she couldn't help but feel a stab of pain in her heart. She'd always wondered what she had done to have Rick's mother treat her so coldly over the years and she'd always suspected that Cassandra hadn't been happy to see her dating Rick. Now she knew why.

Before either of them could say anything, Renfro's friendly "woof" sounded in the great room, along with Rick's voice. "Mother? Corrie?"

"I'll get him," Luz said, materializing in the doorway, as Corrie and Cassandra stood up. Corrie wasn't sure if Rick's mother was as relieved as she was at the interruption but, judging from the way she avoided Corrie's eyes, it was obvious she welcomed it.

Rick and J.D. came through the door, shedding their jackets as they came in. Rick frowned even as he walked over and kissed his mother on her cheek. "What are you doing here? I told you there was no need to cut your trip short."

"I don't need anyone, especially my son, to tell me when I can and can't come back home," Cassandra said tartly. "And it's wonderful to see you as well, Patrick."

J.D. had just handed his and Rick's jackets to Luz, when he paused and shot Corrie a puzzled glance. "Patrick?" he mouthed silently. Corrie shook her head at him and waved his question away. Cassandra looked at him and raised her brow.

"You must be Detective Wilder," she said, extending a hand to J.D. "I've heard a lot about you."

"I'm sure you have," J.D. said dryly, taking her hand. Rick cleared his throat.

"Corrie, I need to talk to you for a minute," he said, tilting his head ever so slightly toward the door to the dining room.

"Go ahead," Corrie said, crossing her arms and leaning her hip against the table. To her amusement, Cassandra didn't excuse herself even though it was obvious Rick didn't want to talk in front of her. He gave Corrie an incredulous look and J.D. seemed to be fighting to keep a serious look on his face.

Rick cleared his throat again. "This is official police business. Regarding the investigation," he added, the dark clouds in his eyes warning her that this was not the time for her to challenge him to a battle of wills, even if his mother appeared to be on her side.

She repressed a sigh and took pity on him. "All right," she said, following him out of the breakfast nook. J.D. made a slight bow to Mrs. Sutton, who also seemed to resign herself to being excluded, and headed after them.

"I'll have Luz make you some lunch," Cassandra called after them.

Rick led the way through the dining room and into the great room, to the far side near the fireplace where they could talk in private and, at the same time, see anyone who came into the room. He removed his Stetson, blowing out his breath. "Sorry about that," he muttered.

Corrie wasn't sure what he was apologizing for but she nodded. "What's up?" she asked.

"We talked to two residents who live near the campground," he said. "The Morenos."

She nodded. "I know them. They're a retired couple who have lived there for almost twenty years. What about them?"

"They came in to tell us that they had seen a vehicle near the campground on the day that the fire started," J.D. said. "Mr. Moreno was out, cutting down weeds and clearing brush around their house and he shut down the weed trimmer when Mrs. Moreno came out with a bottle of water for him. They heard a vehicle idling near the edge of their property so they went over to see who it was. As they got closer, they heard the car doors slam and the vehicle pulled out and turned onto the highway."

Corrie felt her heart pound. "Did they see the car and who was in it?"

Rick shook his head. "They only caught a glimpse of it through the trees and brush and said it was grayish. Maybe light metallic blue. They couldn't agree on whether they heard one or two doors slam, so they aren't sure if it there was only one person or more. They weren't even sure which direction the car went on the highway."

"That's helpful," Corrie said with a sigh. "There must be a lot of cars out there that color, whatever it was. And maybe the driver just pulled over to, uh, you know...."

"They'd have had to pull way off the highway to get close to the Moreno's property just to make a pit stop," Rick said shortly. "If the car had been dark blue, it might point to Ronald Brown, but a gray car...."

"It might have been silver," J.D. said. "Like Alex Durán's rental car, or...." He let his voice trail away and Rick's jaw tightened.

"Or Meghan's BMW," Rick finished. "Though I can't see her sneaking through trees and brush where she might mess up her clothes or hair."

"But she might get someone to do it for her," Corrie put in. She almost regretted saying it when she saw Rick's face grow darker.

"That's a possibility," he admitted. "But I still don't see how it would benefit her." A muffled buzz came from J.D.'s cell phone. He checked the screen and gave a nod.

"That's my contact in Mexico. Maybe he has something. Let me take this in the office and then I'll talk to you both," he said as he strode away, answering the call in a low voice.

Corrie watched him walk away and turned back to Rick. She jumped when she saw him staring at her intently. "What is it? What's wrong?"

"Are you all right?"

"All things considered, yeah, I'm fine," she said dryly. "Why do you ask?"

He nodded in the direction of the kitchen and breakfast nook. "You looked a little disturbed when I walked in there. Did Mother say something to upset you?" His gaze bored into her face and she hesitated for a second. Just long enough to confirm his suspicions. "What happened?" he asked.

"Nothing," she replied with a shrug.

"Why did you look upset?"

"I wasn't upset," she said, straight-faced. He raised a brow and she shook her head. "Oh, come on, Rick, it's not like your mom and I have lunch together every week. It was just a little... awkward," she finished with a weak grin.

"Awkward," he repeated. He sighed. "You're being very gracious, Corrie, but I know how Mother can be sometimes. What did she say that upset you? Don't think I can't tell."

151

"Yeah, you've seen me that way more than anyone else ever has," she said dryly. He flinched slightly and she felt a twinge of guilt. But wasn't that part of the problem? Keeping things from each other? And who was this Alex Durán that J.D. had mentioned? She thought about asking Rick, but she was afraid it would look like she was avoiding his questions. She blew out her breath. "She said I reminded her of my cousin, Natalie."

Rick blinked. "She said what?"

"Pretty much what I said."

"Why would she...?" Rick shook his head and ran a hand over his hair. "I can't believe she said that."

"Do you think it's true?" Corrie asked, her voice low. Rick stared at her for a long minute until she began to feel like she would suffocate.

He sighed. "Yeah, kind of. She was very pretty, but you're...." He let his voice trail away and the look in his eyes intensified.

"At least ten years younger?" she offered, hoping to break the uncomfortable silence. He looked away and swallowed hard. "It's unbelievable that it took me this long to figure out what happened to your dad," she said softly.

"I figured it out a long time ago," he said, his voice gruff. "I just never wanted to talk about it."

"Even with me?"

"With anyone," he retorted. "It made things difficult for everyone. Especially Mother."

"I think I understand her a little better... along with other things," she added, swallowing the painful lump in her throat. Rick looked at her in confusion but before he could say anything, J.D. emerged from the office and came toward them, his face grim.

"We have problems," he said. "First off, my contact found out a lot more about Alex Durán than we expected, but I'll get to that in a moment. It turns out that you've met Ronald Brown before, Sheriff. Five years ago. He was in Bonney, working under another name, as an assistant funeral director. He helped arrange your daughter's funeral."

Chapter 18

J.D. had seen the sheriff shot once before, had seen him lying in a hospital bed on the verge of death from blood loss... but he had never seen the sheriff's face as white as it was at this moment.

"Are you sure?" Corrie whispered when it seemed that Sutton had lost all power of speech. She looked at the sheriff in alarm as he remained frozen in place and she gently touched his shoulder, easing him down into a nearby chair. For once he didn't resist and J.D. wondered if the man was having a stroke.

"I know it sounds crazy," J.D. said as he sat in an adjacent chair, deciding that it might be better if he wasn't standing over the sheriff while he told him all the details. Corrie perched on the arm of Sutton's chair, her hand still on his shoulder but her attention riveted on J.D. "Let me start from the beginning," J.D. said, taking a deep breath. "First off, Alex Durán was married and he and his wife had a very lucrative gig going on, namely they'd been stealing from the resort guests—jewelry, money, whatever was easy to take and sell. Durán, being a bartender, could feel out who the easiest marks were... people who weren't as careful about their money and belongings, who bragged about their wealth, who were careless about their credit card information, and so on. He'd get their room numbers and their credit card numbers and pass that on to his wife, who worked in housekeeping and had access to their rooms and belongings, without raising any questions. They kept the fact they were married a secret and had forged references that were glowing about their honesty, so the places that hired them never questioned them when it came to missing property... and most of the time, the guests themselves took the blame when money went missing from their wallets or jewelry and other belongings went missing. Durán would spike their drinks a little stronger so they would blame their losses on overindulging on alcohol." He stopped for a moment to catch his breath and see if Sutton had any questions or comments, but the sheriff seemed dazed and, for once, patient for J.D. to get to the part about Ronald Brown's involvement with his daughter's funeral. Or maybe he was just wanting to put it off as long as he could. J.D. went on, "Finally one person too many questioned the losses and the fact that the same housekeeper was involved, so Durán's wife decided to quit before the resort management got the police involved. This happened just before he met Meghan at her bachelorette weekend. He was planning to quit his job a few weeks later, so as not to make it look suspicious that he and his wife both bounced at the same time and tie him to her, but when Meghan came along and made her offer...well, he figured it would be easy money. He told his wife about it and, even though she wasn't thrilled at the idea— she probably figured he'd skip out on her—she was too greedy to tell him to turn it down. He had hoped to stick with your ex for a while and try to get as much money, jewelry, and property from her before he skipped out on her as well, but as we all know, that didn't happen. He and Meghan took off to Vegas and got married...."

J.D. stopped when he saw the sheriff's eyes widen and his face turn brick-red and he suddenly realized what he'd done. For a few seconds there was dead silence in the room, and then....

"WHAT?" Corrie stood bolt upright from Sutton's chair, her eyes wide and her face going almost as pale as the sheriff's had been.

"Oh, my God," J.D. breathed, just stopping himself from clapping his hand over his mouth. Not that it would have done any good. Corrie wheeled around and stared at Sutton.

"What's going on? What is he saying? Meghan was married to someone else before you married her? Is that who this mysterious Alex Durán is that you keep mentioning? Why didn't you tell me?"

The sheriff stood up and put his hands on Corrie's shoulders but she fiercely shook them off and stepped back. "Corrie, this isn't how I wanted to tell you...."

"Oh, you *wanted* to tell me this? Really? I find that hard to believe, Rick! What's so hard about saying, 'Hey, Corrie, guess what? My ex-wife was married to someone else before we...." She stopped and swallowed hard, realization dawning in her eyes. She took another step back, looking from the sheriff to J.D. and back again. Her lips trembled and her eyes glazed with tears. She shook her head, blinking. "How could you not tell me... either of you?" she whispered.

"Corrie... Sutton... damn it, I'm so sorry," J.D. said hoarsely. The look on Corrie's face... was it hurt or anger? No, it was betrayal. And it was directed at him, J.D., just as much as it was directed at the sheriff.

"Corrie, let me explain," Sutton said, reaching a hand toward her. She backed away even further and shook her head.

"No, Rick," she said, her voice quiet and achingly in control. "There is no way, *no way*, you can explain this."

154

Before another word was said, with epic bad timing, the sheriff's cell phone rang. J.D. winced; he knew there was no way that Sutton wouldn't answer his phone, not with everything that was going on all around them in the village and the county, even though nothing mattered more to any of them than what was going on in this room right at this moment. They all knew it; Sutton would not ignore the call of duty, no matter how little he might care about it at the moment. The sheriff's fists clenched and, for a second, J.D. almost believed he would snatch the phone out of its holster and fling it across the room.

Instead, keeping his eyes fixed on Corrie, he answered as calmly as he could. "Sutton," he said through gritted teeth. His eyes closed briefly, as if in pain. "What do you want now?" he snapped.

It had to be Meghan.

It was evident that Corrie had reached the same conclusion. She stiffened and her head went up as she threw the sheriff a challenging stare. He met her gaze steadily, even as his jaw clenched. "This isn't a good time, so unless you have something important to tell me.... What?" His eyes narrowed, but still stayed focused on Corrie. "You've lost your mind, Meghan. There is no way that I... yeah, I doubt he will, either. You have no evidence for your accusations and no one is going to take you seriously." Whatever else she said next made the sheriff's expression freeze. "I'm not discussing this with you anymore," he said, his voice quiet and tightly controlled. "It's out of the question...." He blinked and finally broke eye contact with Corrie. Before he said another word, he turned and strode across the room and went into the office, the phone still to his ear. The door slammed shut behind him.

Corrie had turned to watch him leave, tears still standing in her eyes and her lips trembling. J.D. moved toward her silently, not sure what he was going to say. He wanted so badly to reach for her, to take her in his arms, but he knew she wasn't just angry at Sutton. He cleared his throat. "Corrie, he didn't want you to know until he knew for sure...." He stopped as she turned and looked at him, her tears still locked away.

"Why didn't you tell me what was going on?" she whispered.

"It wasn't for me to tell you," he said, using the same words he'd heard so many times since he'd arrived in Bonney. "Corrie, I told him you needed to know, that he needed to tell you. But he wanted to be sure it was true. He'd already been disappointed before, when the tribunal found his marriage valid, and...," he took a deep breath. His chest hurt as he watched Corrie's tears spill down her cheeks, "...he didn't want to get his hopes up—or yours—until he knew it was true. He wanted to make sure there was actually a chance that you and he could...." He couldn't bring himself to say it. And he couldn't bear to see the anguish in her eyes any longer. He shook his head and looked away, rubbing the back of his neck. "You're right, I should have told you, or at least insisted that he tell you himself," he muttered. "This involves you and you should have known what was going on. Even if Meghan's marriage to Alex Durán had been invalid or illegal or whatever, it still would have made the sheriff's marriage to her invalid and... well, you know." He blew out his breath but his chest still felt as if it were being crushed under a ton of sand. If he were honest with himself, he'd admit that he'd been putting off the truth for as long as he could, trying to hold on to the tiniest sliver of a dream he'd had almost from the moment he'd laid eyes on Corrie nearly a year ago. But now the truth was known; he could easily see that as soon as Corrie recovered from her shock, she and Sutton would make up and then.... His thoughts trailed away and he turned back to look at Corrie. Tears were still streaming down her face and she was staring at him with a look of bewilderment and hurt. Baffled at her expression, he tried to smile, but feared it came out as a grimace.

"It's okay, Corrie. I'll be fine," he said. "Everything's fine." He didn't believe it right then, but he hoped maybe someday everything really would be fine.

"No, it's not fine, J.D.," she said, her voice cracking. She turned away from him, wrapping her arms around herself, her shoulders heaving with silent sobs.

J.D. moved toward her. "Hey," he said, touching her shoulder. He gently turned her around, made her face him. "What are you talking about? Everything will be back on track, you and he can...." He swallowed hard and forced a smile. "You know he's always loved you, right? He never stopped loving you."

She looked at him and her next words were so full of pain that they stabbed into his heart. "Then why did he leave me... and marry Meghan?" She shook her head and stepped away. "No, J.D., nothing has changed. Rick still chose to end our relationship, even before he met Meghan, and he never told me why. Until he can explain that, there's no way—no way at all—that I'll let myself be in a position to get hurt again." She turned and hurried up the stairs, leaving J.D. stunned into silence.

Rick stood in the office, staring at the phone in his hand. Meghan had ended the call minutes earlier but he could still hear her voice echoing in his head:

"It's simple, Rick. I want Ava. Sign the release to have her moved to Dallas. I already have a mausoleum picked out for her. I can't stand the thought of my baby girl underground, especially in Bonney, that godforsaken hick town you've always insisted on calling home. And you'll be paying all the expenses connected with moving her and her new burial place and, believe me, I'll make sure they're worthy of my daughter. Then, after you sign the release and the agreement to pay for everything, I'll give you the evidence you need to present to the tribunal so you can get your precious annulment AND I'll call off the state police and fire investigators AND I'll authorize Corrie's insurance claim to be paid immediately. Otherwise, I'll have her arrested and charged with arson and insurance fraud and I'll sue her for everything she has. Don't think I can't and won't do it. She'll lose everything she's ever cared about. I'll take it all, just like I took you from her. I want that release signed by the end of TODAY."

He took a deep breath and closed his eyes. He knew, in the far corner of the office, stood an unobtrusive small cabinet that contained expensive crystal glassware and a bottle of his mother's favorite sherry, a bottle of expensive Bordeaux… and a bottle of Crown Royal Reserve. She kept it on hand because Manuel and Luz sometimes joined her for a drink after she took care of payroll and Manuel had a fondness for Canadian whiskey.

Right now, Rick had never felt the pull of alcohol so strongly as he did at the moment. Something to numb him, something to calm him, something to encourage him….

"Sutton?"

He turned with a start, shocked to realize he was standing in front of the cabinet. Wilder stood in the doorway, looking at him with cautious concern. "I knocked twice. Just wanted to see if you were okay."

"Yeah," Rick said automatically. He shook his head and wiped his hand over his face. Taking a deep breath, he turned toward Wilder, away from the liquor cabinet. "How's Corrie?"

"How do you think?" Wilder stepped into the room and shut the door behind him. He stood with his feet apart, his hands shoved into the pockets of his jeans, and shrugged. "You should have told her. We both should have told her."

"I know." Rick let out his breath in a weary sigh. "I'm sorry I dragged you into this, Wilder. Now Corrie's upset with you and blaming you for something that isn't your fault. It's all my fault... all of it," he added in a whisper. He wasn't sure if Wilder heard him.

"She's hurt. She trusted us," Wilder said. "We both betrayed that trust. I had a choice—her trust or yours. Guess I chose wrong."

Rick felt his gut twist. Corrie would understand and respect the fact that Wilder had kept silent because Rick had asked him to... but how could she understand why Rick hadn't told her? He drew a shaky breath. He'd have to tell her. Someday. Somehow. He'd have to find a way to explain... everything.

Meghan's voice echoed in his head: *I'll have her arrested for arson and insurance fraud... she'll lose everything... I'll take it all, just like I took you from her....*

I want Ava.

"Sutton!"

Rick blinked, Wilder's grim face coming into sharp focus. He had to do something to get himself together. Wilder's penetrating gaze unnerved him. He shook his head to clear it. "I'm sorry, what...?"

Wilder's voice and eyes were like stone. "You're not listening to anything I'm saying. You're a million miles away. What's on your mind, Sheriff?"

Too much to mention. "You never told me about... Ronald Brown," Rick said, hoping to divert Wilder's attention but wincing as the mention of the man's name brought back an avalanche of memories of making his infant daughter's final arrangements.

Wilder nodded slowly. "Yeah, that subject got derailed a little," he said dryly. "But that's what my source told me. Brown dabbled in real estate deals in Mexico, but he also had several sidelines—car dealerships, jewelry stores, employment agencies, to name a few. And funeral homes. Apparently, he's worked all over the southwestern U.S. and down into Mexico in all of these lines of work. He ended up in Bonney when things got a little too warm for him in Mexico and he figured a town this small would be the last place anyone would look for him...."

...that godforsaken hick town you've always insisted on calling home....

"... and the local funeral home happened to be looking for an assistant funeral director right about the time Brown arrived here. On the surface, it doesn't look like he's done anything illegal... but he was with the agency that placed Durán and his wife at the resort where he met Meghan, and other resorts where there were thefts. Coincidence? Maybe. But I know how you feel about that...."

Rick tried to process everything Wilder was telling him, but his mind kept dragging him back to Meghan's threats.

I want Ava.

Corrie will lose everything.

It's simple, Rick.

If only it were....

He shook his head, his mind coming into clear focus. He'd made many mistakes in his life, made many choices he'd come to regret, let himself get pushed into making decisions that went against his better judgment in order to spare the feelings of others. As a result, he'd ended up compromising his conscience and gaining nothing but heartache—for himself and the people he cared about the most—for his efforts.

It wouldn't happen again.

He became aware of Wilder's penetrating stare. The detective knew he wasn't thinking about Ronald Brown or what his connections to Alex Durán might be. But Rick couldn't talk about any of it. Not now. He needed to take action. He had to clear up one thing before he could focus on Alex Durán's death, the fire at the Black Horse, anything else. He straightened up and avoided Wilder's gaze.

"There's something I need to do, Wilder. Once I take care of this...I'll get back to you."

"I'm coming with you."

"No," Rick said sharply. "You can't."

"Wanna bet?" Wilder's eyes narrowed. He folded his arms across his chest. "Whatever it is you need to do, you might need backup."

"It's got nothing to do with the case."

"Which one?"

Rick shook his head in exasperation. "We're off the case of the fire at the Black Horse. Alex Durán's death is connected to the fire. What other case is there?"

"A personal one," Wilder said pointedly. Rick forced himself to meet his gaze.

"It's my business. I'll handle it. Alone."

"Not sure that's a good idea, Sheriff."

"Wilder, if I needed your help, I'd ask for it!" Rick snapped.

"No, you wouldn't." The detective shook his head. "You're wound so tight right now, it's a wonder you haven't snapped. I won't interfere, Sutton, but I can't let you go alone. I don't know what's going on, but I guarantee you need my backup."

"What about Corrie?" Rick asked, suddenly feeling the crushing weight of her accusing glare settling on his heart. As much as he hated to do it, he didn't want her to be alone. Even if it meant that J.D. Wilder would be the one on hand to support her.

Wilder snorted. "Come on, Sheriff, you know she doesn't need or want either of us right now. She's stronger than you or I give her credit for. Now, let's go take care of whatever business it is you need to do."

Rick sighed. He didn't need this fight right now. "Wilder, I have to deal with Meghan. Really, this is my problem to handle, not yours, not anyone else's."

"So you'll handle it. I'm just going along for the ride in case things go sideways. She won't even know I'm there." He cocked his head toward the door. "Let's get going before your ex loses her patience and sics those state cops and fire bureau agents on Corrie again. And before you take another step closer to that bottle of Crown."

Chapter 19

Corrie paced the bedroom, feeling trapped, even though nothing could stop her from walking out the front door and right back to the Black Horse. Or what was left of it. She forced herself to stop, took several deep breaths, and ordered her tears to stop falling. They refused to obey and she couldn't blame them.

She sat on the edge of the bed, trying to get her thoughts in order. Meghan had attempted marriage before her and Rick's wedding. Their marriage wasn't valid in the eyes of the Church. There's no way it could be, or had ever been.. Rick had to know that. So why hadn't he told Corrie when he found out? If he really wanted to rekindle their relationship....

But he also hadn't told her that he'd petitioned for a decree of nullity. Three times. Despite that, the tribunal had found his marriage valid. A part of her she tried to stifle reminded her that he'd already been disappointed three times. Even J.D. had told her that. Could she blame him for not telling her? He'd obviously gotten his hopes up repeatedly only to have them dashed. She could see him not wanting to do the same to her. But still....

She shook her head and jumped up to pace again. Her words to J.D. echoed in her ears: *Why did he leave me...?* Full stop. For years, she had ignored that fact. Her wounded pride and broken heart had conveniently placed the blame on Meghan, but the truth was that Rick hadn't even met Meghan until nearly two years after he had ended their relationship. Meghan couldn't be blamed for their breakup; she couldn't really even be blamed for Rick being unable to remarry. He had chosen to break up with Corrie, he had chosen to start a relationship with Meghan, he had chosen to marry Meghan.... She stopped again and her tears began to fall.

Why had she held on all these years? What had she been holding on to? Memories of a love she thought she'd never find again? False hope? Mere friendship? Her thoughts flew to J.D. and her heart constricted. He'd been patient, so patient. She'd felt a connection, almost from the moment they had met. She knew he had, too. Yet she had kept him at arm's length. Why? He was a good man, handsome and strong, yet gentle and kind, a man who believed in doing what was right, who tried to protect and defend, who cared about others despite the fact that he had suffered pain and loss....

"Like Rick," she found herself saying out loud and then shook her head in exasperation. Was that why she'd hesitated to get involved with him... and was that the reason she'd been attracted to him in the first place? And now she had no choice but to accept both their help, stand by and let them do their jobs, let them help her navigate the nightmare she was living in.

And after it was all over?

She jumped when she heard a knock on the door. "Corrie?" It was Luz. She swallowed hard, but before she could speak, Luz went on, her voice low but urgent, "Corrie, there are some men here to see you from the state fire marshal's office. They said they spoke to you before...."

Corrie crossed the room and yanked the door open. Luz looked perturbed, her brow furrowed with concern. "Mrs. Sutton is downstairs talking to them. She didn't know that they'd been here earlier and she's upset."

"I'll bet," Corrie murmured, as she hurried past Luz and down the stairs. She could hear Cassandra's strident voice drifting up the stairs.

"This is ridiculous and I won't have you harassing a guest in my own home! My son is the local sheriff and he will not tolerate this...."

"Cassandra, it's all right, I knew they'd be coming back to talk to me," Corrie interrupted, as she reached the bottom of the stairs. This time the state police hadn't showed up, for which Corrie was grateful. The two men and Rick's mother turned to look at her and she felt heat rise to her cheeks, in spite of the iciness in Cassandra's blue eyes. Just like Rick's eyes.

"Agents Jackson and Pinella, what are you doing here?" she asked. "I believe Sheriff Sutton told you that I'd be consulting with an attorney before I spoke with you again. I've hardly had time to do that, so you're wasting your time." She stopped and folded her arms across her chest, hoping to keep her voice from trembling as her heart hammered away in her chest.

The agents frowned. "Miss Black, were you aware that a dead body was discovered at your campground?" Agent Jackson said.

Cassandra drew her breath in sharply and Corrie's heart skipped a beat. "So I've heard." She hoped they wouldn't ask her *when*, exactly, she'd heard.

"A dead body? At the Black Horse?" Cassandra said sharply. Corrie cringed; she half expected Rick's mother to add, "Again?"

"Miss Black, who told you that a dead body was found at the campground? To our knowledge, it hasn't been announced on any media and you haven't left this house."

"Are you spying on me?" Corrie asked, raising a brow at the agents. Pinella had the grace to turn red and look away. Jackson drew himself up stiffly.

"Did Sheriff Sutton tell you about the dead body?" he snapped.

"And if he did?" Corrie retorted. "It's my campground, my property, we're talking about here! I believe I have a right to know what happened at my home! Were you planning to keep it under wraps? I'm sure that the local law enforcement would have released that information by now if you all hadn't taken over their investigation!"

Agent Jackson's face turned a bright shade of red. "We're going to have to talk to you at our office, Miss Black."

"I haven't had time to consult with an attorney. Are you arresting me? If not, then let me remind you that Sheriff Sutton told you I had a right to legal counsel before I speak to you or anyone else." It occurred to her that the agents might have come back in order to arrest her and it was all she could do to remain calm when all she wanted to do was burst into hysterical tears.

Agent Jackson sighed irritably. "No, we have no reason to arrest you, Miss Black. Not yet," he added. "We were hoping you would cooperate in this investigation without having to go to that extreme."

"Then I'm going to ask you to leave my home and stop bothering my guests," Cassandra said coldly. She stepped forward and, to Corrie's shock, the two agents actually took a step back. "Miss Black has already told you that she would be talking to a lawyer and then she would speak to you. You can trust her to keep her word. Therefore, you have no business being here. Good day, gentlemen."

Muttering under their breath, the two men retreated toward the door. Manuel appeared discreetly and let them out. As the door shut behind them, Corrie realized she'd been holding her breath and she let it out shakily. "Thank you, Cassandra."

Rick's mother waved a hand dismissively. "I presume I'll learn all the details of what's going on soon enough. In the meantime, let me call Mr. DiMarco, our family attorney. You can use the office to talk to him in private. I'm sure he'll agree to come immediately to help you."

"Cassandra, I appreciate that very much, but I can't afford...." Corrie stammered. She stopped when Cassandra shot her a sharp glance.

"I'll leave it up to Mr. DiMarco to decide if he wants to take your case *pro bono*. He often does if he feels a client is being unjustly persecuted." Corrie suspected that the Sutton family paid their attorney handsomely enough to make *pro bono* cases no real financial hardship for him or his firm. She beckoned Corrie to follow her as she made her way across the room toward the office.

It only took a half hour for Corrie to explain her situation to Anthony DiMarco, the Sutton family attorney, and he agreed to come immediately to the Sutton home to speak with her. He advised her not to speak to anyone, not the insurance adjusters or the police and especially not Meghan, until he had gone over everything with her in depth. No, she was not admitting that she was guilty of any wrongdoing, but he was going to make sure that nothing she said or did was misconstrued by anyone. And he dismissed any talk of his fees. "You can discuss that with Mrs. Sutton," he said, before assuring her he would be there as soon as he could.

"Nothing to discuss," Cassandra said when Corrie approached her. She was seated on one of the rich, leather couches in the main room, having excused herself from the office once she'd briefed her attorney on the situation and then left Corrie to discuss it with him in private. She set down the magazine she'd been reading and sat up briskly. "I'm well aware of the pitfalls of dealing with attorneys when one isn't well-versed in legalese. Even Patrick prefers to let lawyers deal with other lawyers whenever necessary, despite his background."

"You didn't have to go to all this trouble, though," Corrie said. "I didn't mean for this whole mess to be dumped on your doorstep. I don't know how to thank you or how to repay you for all you've done... you and Rick," she added.

Cassandra remained quiet for several moments, staring into the fireplace. She didn't look at Corrie and when she spoke, her voice was so quiet that Corrie thought she'd imagined what she said: "There isn't anything Rick wouldn't do for you."

Corrie blinked; she wasn't sure if she'd heard correctly, either what Cassandra said or the fact that she hadn't called Rick "Patrick". She sat down across from Rick's mother, not sure how to respond. Cassandra looked up at her and the kaleidoscope of emotions in her face stunned Corrie. Sadness, confusion, but mostly a shimmering thread of anger seemed to run through every fiber of Cassandra Waverly-Sutton's being and Corrie had no idea

164

why. "Cassandra?" she asked tentatively.

"I'm sorry," Rick's mother said, glancing away and blinking. "I just... I know this isn't the time or the place, but I just can't understand why...." Her voice trailed away and she cleared her throat, straightening up in her seat. "I'm sure you had your reasons, Corrie, but it's taken me a long time to... get over my own anger in the matter. Sometimes I'm not sure that I am over it."

"In what matter? Get over what?" Corrie stammered. She was confused and alarmed. One moment Cassandra looked like she would faint, then the next minute as if she would explode. Her elegantly manicured hands clenched and unclenched. She stood up and began to pace.

"This probably isn't the best time to bring this up, if there ever would be a good time, and I know that there are probably far more pressing concerns on your mind at this moment." She stopped and her eyes seemed to bore right into Corrie's heart and soul. "However, I can't help how I feel and I'm sorry that time hasn't erased my feelings of... well, I'm not sure how to articulate what a mother feels when her son is hurt so badly by someone he loved and trusted."

"Excuse me?" Corrie stood up and stared at Cassandra. She felt her stomach churn and her heart twisted at what the implications of what Rick's mother was saying. Cassandra's chin lifted and she looked at Corrie with barely-concealed disdain.

"I know Patrick never wanted to discuss it and I'm sure he'd be furious at me for bringing it up to you. I know that, in spite of everything, he still has feelings for you. He's also far more forgiving than I could ever be. But I can't help but wonder if all of this could have been avoided if only...." She took a deep breath. "Why did you do it, Corrie? What did Patrick do that made you want to end your relationship with him?"

Corrie's mouth dropped open and any words she might have said seemed to freeze in her throat. It seemed like hours passed before she could speak. "What are you talking about? You think *I* broke up with Rick?" She shook her head. "Did Rick tell you I broke up with him?"

Cassandra shrugged. "He didn't have to tell me," she said, her cultured voice thick with emotion. "I saw his face, the look in his eyes, that night he came home...the night he said you wouldn't be seeing each other anymore. He was destroyed, Corrie. He's never really been happy since. I thought maybe Meghan... but I could tell she wasn't right for him. He'd have never given her a second glance if only you had...."

"Cassandra," Corrie said, as fury rose in her chest. "I don't know what Rick told you but I wasn't the one who broke up with him. *He* broke up with me. It was *his* decision, not mine." She bit her lip hard to keep from breaking down into sobs. What on earth had Rick told his mother about her? Was this the reason Cassandra never liked her? She drew a quivering breath. "He told me that it would be better for us, for me, if we didn't see each other again... but he never told me why. I thought it was because of you. And what you said earlier about my reminding you of my cousin, Natalie," she went on, nodding toward the breakfast nook, "that just confirmed that you blamed me and my family for what happened between you and Rick's dad. And why you didn't want me and Rick to be together. I'm sure he made his decision to prevent you from further pain of having to be reminded of her... every time you saw me."

Cassandra Waverly-Sutton stood with her mouth open, her face going ghostly pale. She licked her lips. "You say *Patrick* broke up with you? It wasn't... your decision?"

Corrie crossed her arms in front of her and shook her head. "I loved Rick," she said. She didn't say she still did; let Cassandra draw her own conclusions. "I was devastated, Cassandra. My life was pulled out from under me, without warning. He never told me why, even though I begged for an explanation. He just kept saying it was for the best, that he hoped someday I'd understand. Well, it's been over fifteen years and I still don't understand and he still hasn't explained why he ended it. But if he told you that I was the one who broke it off... well, it's not true. I don't know why he let you think that. I don't know... anything," she finished weakly.

Cassandra's hands flew to cover her mouth. She slowly shook her head. "Patrick broke up with you," she whispered. "I thought it was you. The way he acted... I was so sure you were the one who broke his heart. Not the other way around." She sighed and dropped her hands. "I can still see his face. That night, he came home early and I remember I was surprised. He'd been acting strange all day... in fact, he'd seemed a little distracted, moody in the weeks leading up to it. You had been in Albuquerque with your father while he was undergoing his treatments and I just figured that Patrick felt antsy because he was worried about your father and he wasn't able to see you. I know he was happy, relieved that your father was going to recover. So it was a shock

166

when he went to go see you after you got back, that he didn't seem as excited and thrilled as he should have been. And then he was back, after only an hour, and he looked... I don't know how to describe it. Furious, horrified, sick to his stomach. But most of all, he looked devastated. All he said was, 'Corrie and I won't be seeing each other anymore. And I don't want to talk about it.' That was all he said," she added, her eyes coming into focus. "The only explanation I could think of was that you had decided to end the relationship. He was so miserable."

"You should have seen me," Corrie snapped. She tried to feel bad when Rick's mother flinched, but she couldn't. "The only thing that I could possibly find to be glad about is that he waited until my dad was in remission from cancer before he broke up with me. I had that to be thankful for, I had that to keep my sanity and give me a reason to be happy." She bit her lip. "I always wondered... why, what I did that made him decide to end it. When you said I reminded you of Natalie, I thought maybe that was the reason. He felt guilty, like he was rubbing it in your face about his dad leaving, or maybe you told him you didn't want me around as a reminder...."

"I thought you were the best thing that ever happened to Patrick," Cassandra said with a hitch in her voice. "What Patrick's father did, what your cousin did, is strictly theirs to own. I never blamed you or your father or your family for what they did. I'm so sorry," she said. "I assumed the worst. If I had asked him...." She sighed again. "He probably still wouldn't have told me why, but he would have at least set me straight about who ended it. He would never have let you take the blame for what he'd done, if he'd known that I thought you were at fault. I should have insisted he talk to me about it. Maybe... maybe all this could have been avoided if *I* had done something, said something. All these years I've been blaming you. I'm sorry."

Corrie didn't know what to say. A very small part of her was glad that Rick's mother had never hated her or blamed her and her family for Rick's father leaving them. But that left even more questions, painful ones. Why HAD Rick broken up with her? It hadn't made her feel better to think that it was because his mother had demanded that he break up with her... but at least it would have made sense.

Nothing made sense.

Chapter 20

J.D. watched the sheriff closely as they drove into Bonney. Sutton was in no hurry to face his ex, but he was also tired of putting off something he should have dealt with a long time ago. Sutton's grim jaw told J.D. that, whatever he had to talk to Meghan about, he wasn't going to be pleased about the outcome. He had made a hard decision and he was going to follow through on it. Finally, J.D. broke the silence. "Does she know about Durán?"

"I don't know. She didn't mention him."

"Does this have to do with you meeting her demands?"

Sutton never took his eyes off the road. He gave one nod so slight that J.D. would have missed it if he hadn't had his gaze trained on the sheriff. He shook his head. "Where are you meeting with her?"

"The insurance office. She has papers for me to sign, then she'll hand over her wedding certificate and call her main office to authorize Corrie's insurance claim. She'll also call off the state cops and fire investigation bureau."

"She can't do that...."

"Apparently, she can," Sutton said. He rubbed the back of his neck as the sign for the village of Bonney came into view. "She's got money and connections."

"So do you."

"I'm not Meghan!" Sutton snapped. His face reddened but he said nothing for several seconds. Then, "I won't let her hurt Corrie anymore."

Before J.D. could say another word, his cell phone buzzed. He glanced at the screen and groaned, letting a mumbled curse slip out. He swiped it open with an irritable sigh. "Wilder," he said. He glanced at Sutton. "LaRue," he mouthed. He cleared his throat. "Yeah, Chief, I'm heading back into town right now." He grimaced as LaRue reminded him that they had paperwork that had been neglected for far too long that needed to be taken care of. "Right now?" He winced as LaRue's raised voice left no question. He sighed. "I'll be there shortly."

"I'll drop you off," the sheriff said. J.D. shook his head.

"No, LaRue can wait. Those reports and evals have waited this long, another hour won't hurt. I'm going with you."

"Wilder," Sutton said, his voice shaking slightly, "please, let me deal with Meghan. Trust me, she's easier to deal with when

169

she's not playing to an audience. If it's just me...." He took his eyes from the road and looked at J.D. Raw anguish was all J.D. could see. Sutton drew a deep breath. "I know what I need to do and I need to do it alone. Thanks for everything."

J.D. didn't like the sounds of that. He raised a brow as the sheriff pulled the Tahoe up in front of the police department and he slowly got out. He turned and leaned in the door. "You call me when you're done. Hear?"

"I don't...."

"Yeah, you do," J.D. said shortly. "I don't hear from you in an hour, I'm coming to look for you and I won't be discreet about it." He shut the door, stepped back, and slapped a hand on the hood. His eyes met with Sutton's for a brief second before the sheriff put the Tahoe in gear and drove away.

J.D. watched him drive away with a heavy feeling of dread settling in his chest.

The next two hours crept by.

J.D. knew that Chief LaRue was getting more annoyed by the minute as he caught J.D. checking the time more frequently the longer their meeting went on. Finally, in exasperation, the chief slapped the folders on the desk. "What is it with you, Wilder? Am I boring you?"

"Sorry, Chief, I've got more pressing matters at hand," J.D. said curtly. "Anyway, I don't know what the purpose of this meeting is. I was only acting chief for a few months, I gave you detailed written evals on every officer in the department, most of whom have been here longer than I have, so I don't know how you expect me to judge their performance. Same goes for the budget report. Anything you don't understand, I'll clarify, but there's no sense in going over everything I turned in, line by line." He forced himself to stay seated until LaRue let him go. Standing up would only incense the chief and he would insist on J.D. staying even longer out of spite. LaRue's eyes narrowed and he pushed the folders to the side.

"What's going on, Detective? You've been spending a lot of time helping out the county. I get that you and Sutton are buddies, but you need to focus your energy and attention on the village. The county's got plenty of deputies to tend to things."

"I've been tending to the village, in cooperation with the county," J.D. said tartly. "In addition to the fire near Ruidoso, we also had a fire threatening the village...."

"Which, I understand, is now under the jurisdiction of the state police and fire investigation bureau, and no longer ours nor the county's responsibility," LaRue said, tapping a finger on the desk. "So let's just let them do their jobs and we can focus on ours." He paused and when he spoke again, he sounded almost apologetic. "I know it's hard for you to step back when it's Corrie who's involved, Wilder, but I'm sure you've done all you can— you and Rick both—and now the best thing for you to do is stay in your own lane and…."

"This isn't about Corrie!" J.D. snapped, and this time he did stand up. LaRue stared at him. "Look, Chief, I'm not trying to avoid my responsibility to the department and I'm not trying to prove anything to the state cops or the fire bureau. I just know that this whole thing has taken a toll on the sheriff and all I'm trying to do is be a support to him and his department." LaRue raised a brow and J.D. went on, "You've got great officers on the force and you don't need me to tell you that. And the sheriff has top-notch deputies. But what's happened at the Black Horse… it's affecting certain people on a personal level."

"You mean you and Rick."

J.D. blew out his breath. "Yeah, it is. I mean, I lost my home, too, but it's nothing compared to what happened to Corrie. Her home, her livelihood." He noticed LaRue looking distant and he leaned closer. "It bugs you, too, doesn't it?"

Eldon LaRue didn't hesitate. "Yeah. What happened was awful. I mean, I kinda envy you and Rick, you know? You guys are closer to Corrie, I know she comes to you both when she needs help or just a friend. I messed up my chance with that—not that I'm jealous or anything," he added, his face reddening slightly. "And I never told you, but thanks for stepping up when that whole thing with Connie went down." He cleared his throat. "Look, we'll take care of all this later, once things calm down a little. Go, do what you have to do, I know you're still on duty even when you're not here. If Rick needs you…."

"I didn't say it had anything to do with the sheriff." J.D. looked at Chief LaRue and the chief looked back at him just as steadily.

"You didn't have to," he said. "People talk in this town, Wilder. Not to newcomers and, even though you've been here almost a year, you'll be a newcomer when you're seventy years old," he said without a trace of a smile. "So… I heard Rick's been having a tough time. I mean, I don't know all the details, just that

171

his ex is being, um, difficult. He needs a friend," LaRue said as he stood up. He began to gather up the papers on the table. "Go ahead, Wilder. And if you need help, you can call me. Tell Rick I said so."

J.D. hurried out to his Harley, thankful he'd left it at the police station instead of at the sheriff's home. He checked his phone and frowned. Sutton hadn't called, nor had he responded to the half-dozen texts J.D. had sent him or the two calls he had made. For the third time, J.D. punched in the sheriff's number only to have the call go straight to voice mail. Had the sheriff's phone battery died? A month ago, J.D. would have scoffed at the idea that Sutton wouldn't be completely prepared for anything, but after the last week....

He rode past the insurance agency, surprised to see that Meghan Stratham's BMW was still parked in front of the building, but no sign of the sheriff's Tahoe. He really hadn't expected that Sutton and his ex were still talking after over two hours, but he didn't think that Meghan would have stuck around once she got what she wanted.

It was mid-afternoon and the smoke drifting in from the fire near Ruidoso made the afternoon appear overcast. The latest fire report said there was some containment, but progress was slow. Still no moisture in the forecast and the wind seemed to slice right through J.D.'s leather jacket. A shiver ran down his back and it wasn't completely from the weather. In his gut, he felt that something was off. He was sure that Sutton wouldn't have headed back to his home without letting J.D. know, so there was only one other place he could be.

He pulled up to the sheriff's apartment building, the Tahoe parked in Sutton's usual spot. He climbed the stairs to the sheriff's unit and hesitated before he knocked. He wasn't sure if he was welcome right now, but his concern was greater than his manners. He reached for the doorknob and was only a little surprised to find the door unlocked. He resisted the impulse to barge in. "Sutton?" he called through the crack in the door.

"Yeah," came the toneless response. J.D. pushed the door open and found the sheriff sitting in one of the chocolate brown leather recliners. He was hunched forward, his elbows on his knees and his chin in his hands with a thousand-yard stare that J.D. had seen far too many times on Marines who had been traumatized by what they had been through. On the glass coffee table in front of him was a long white envelope. He looked up as J.D. shut the door behind him.

"You okay?" J.D. said, hating how dumb the question sounded. He sat down on the matching leather sofa and his eyes strayed to the envelope. Sutton let out a heavy sigh.

"No," he said with surprising candor. He glanced at the envelope and looked away quickly as if the mere sight of it caused him pain. "She's made arrangements to have Ava moved first thing tomorrow morning."

J.D. blinked. "That soon?"

Sutton leaned back in the recliner and stared at the ceiling. "I... tried to get her to wait a few weeks," he said, a slight tremor in his voice. "I told her that I can't leave Bonney right now, not with everything that's going on, to... be there, when Ava is entombed in Dallas. Meghan said it didn't matter, that I wasn't welcome there. She said she wasn't here when I had Ava buried, so it was my turn to be left out. I... I lost it, Wilder. I told her it was her choice to leave Bonney before Ava's funeral, that I had wanted her to be here, but she wouldn't even speak to me and left everything for me to arrange. I said a lot of stuff I've been holding in for a long time," he added, his voice cracking. "And she just laughed. She pulled out the copy of the marriage certificate and threw it at me," he said, glancing at the envelope on the table. "She said we could have avoided all of this if I'd only agreed to let her take Ava when she first asked. She kept repeating that I was finally being honest about who mattered more to me—Corrie or Ava. I told her to just stop, she got what she wanted, and call her adjusters and get Corrie's claim paid and she'd never have to deal with me again. She pointed out that I could have easily taken care of Corrie's insurance problems if Corrie had only told me about it, but since she never told me, then maybe I'm not that important to her after all. She kept... harping on that, stalling on calling her office I...." He buried his face in his hands. "Everything went blank. I went into a rage. I don't even know what I said to her. For a minute, I thought...." He looked up at J.D. "I thought I'd actually hit her. I've never in my life ever remotely considered laying a hand on her, or any woman, not even a few female felons who have attacked me in the past."

"You didn't, did you?" J.D. asked and winced inwardly when the sheriff's face went completely white.

"No," he breathed. He shook his head, his blue eyes wide. "No! Wilder, are you serious?"

"You'd ask me the same thing," J.D. said, his voice level. "What happened next?"

Sutton stood up and rubbed the back of his neck. "I... I left."

"Just like that? The conversation just ended and you walked out of the office?"

The sheriff shook his head. "More or less." He shrugged, "I don't know what else I said to her. I was so angry. Even Meghan looked shocked. I guess she couldn't believe I could get that furious."

"Was she scared?"

Sutton's face darkened. "Why are you asking me all this? Do you really think I'm capable of...?"

"Your ex has pushed you to the brink of snapping," J.D. said. "You haven't been yourself in weeks since you got injured, even more so now that she's taking advantage of your situation. I'm not saying you would have done anything out of character like that, but I'm not sure that Meghan wouldn't accuse you of doing something just so she could twist the knife she's stuck in you. You need to be prepared in case Meghan rethinks her arrangement and decides to make your life even more miserable. I'm just looking out for you. I know how bad a domestic situation can get and you need to be prepared because, frankly, I don't trust Meghan. Now, did she seem afraid of you?"

Sutton shook his head. "Meghan never liked to show she was anything but in control. She looked surprised, but she recovered. She picked up her phone and called her adjuster, told them to proceed with Corrie's claim, then after she hung up, she gave me a furious look and told me to get out. She reminded me that I only had till tomorrow morning to say goodbye to Ava." The sheriff took a deep breath. "I managed to keep myself from saying anything else. I left. I didn't look back. I slammed the door behind me and I came straight home."

"How long ago was that?"

Sutton shrugged and shook his head. "I'm not sure. Over an hour ago. I thought about going by the cemetery, but... I was afraid that if I went, I wouldn't be able to make myself leave." He ran a shaking hand over his head. "Sorry I didn't call you, Wilder. I wasn't in any mood or condition to talk to anyone. I needed to cool down." He walked to the window and looked out into the parking lot. J.D. gave him a moment to collect himself. Finally the sheriff cleared his throat and turned around. "So, what have I missed out on? Have you talked to Corrie? Did she get hold of an attorney?"

J.D. stood up and shoved his hands in the pockets of his jacket. "I just wrapped up my meeting with the chief and, since I hadn't heard from you, I decided to see where you might be. I haven't talked to anyone else." He tilted his head to one side. "Meghan tell you what her plans might be?"

Sutton shook his head. "She mentioned she had a plane to catch this evening. Apparently she's letting the funeral home in Bonney handle the... arrangements she made for Ava's transfer." A spasm of pain shot across his face. "I should go to the cemetery today, before I head back to the house. I'm not sure I can handle watching when they...."

"Yeah," J.D. cut in. No sense in making the man say the words. "So she wasn't planning to stay for that?" Sutton shook his head, looking at J.D. curiously. J.D. went on, "I wonder why she was still at the insurance office, then."

Sutton stared. "She was still there? When?"

"Just before I got here, I drove by on my way over. Her car was still parked out front."

The sheriff shook his head. "Are you sure? She said she was leaving soon, she didn't want to miss her flight and she had to drive to El Paso. And she was parked in the back of the office, where her car wouldn't be seen from the road. She didn't want anyone to know she was there and possibly interrupt us while we were talking."

J.D. raised a brow but before he could say anything, his cell phone went off. He looked at the screen and frowned. "It's LaRue," he muttered. "Yeah, Chief?" he answered.

"Wilder, where are you? Where's Rick?" Eldon LaRue snapped. J.D. bit back a retort and glanced across the room at the sheriff.

"He's right here. Why?"

A muffled curse came over the line. "You're with him?" LaRue barked. "Where's 'here', Wilder? I've been trying to call him but he won't answer his cell!"

"It's probably off," J.D. said, gesturing to Sutton to check his phone. "And 'here' is his apartment, Eldon. What's going on?"

"Listen to me, Wilder," Eldon said, his voice unsteady. "There's a situation and I need you both to stay right where you are until I get there. Got that? Don't go anywhere until I get there with Deputy Evans and you make sure Rick doesn't go anywhere, either! You hear? Once Evans is there with Rick, I need you to come with me, okay?"

"Eldon, what's going on?" J.D. snapped. He'd never heard the police chief sound so distraught, not even when his former fiancée had been found murdered. "What's happened?" His heart leaped into his throat and he glanced over at Sutton who was scrolling through his phone, bewildered by the number of missed calls and texts he had. He looked up at J.D. with alarm in his eyes. "Did something happen to Corrie?" His heart started hammering in his chest and he half-expected the sheriff to rip his phone from his hands.

"Wilder, I'm less than a mile away. I'll tell you when I get there."

"You'll tell me now!" His tone left no room for argument.

"It's not about Corrie! She's fine! It's…. I'll tell you when I…."

"Chief!" Eldon was silent then….

"We got a call from the secretary at the insurance agency. She just found Meghan Stratham, shot to death in the office."

Chapter 21

There was no way that J.D. was going to convince Sutton to stay away once he heard what Chief LaRue had called about. "You don't need to be there, Sheriff," J.D. said, knowing that if he couldn't convince the sheriff to remain at home, neither Deputy Evans or the chief would be able to. "Anyway, it's in the village limits, so it's not the county's jurisdiction."

"You know damn good and well that neither of us is concerned about jurisdiction!" Sutton snapped. "I have a right to be there, Wilder! I need to know what happened!"

"You can't interfere with...."

"I won't be interfering!" Sutton had yanked his jacket off the hook on the wall and clapped his Stetson on his head. Except for his pale face and the dilated condition of his eyes, he looked calm and in control, almost like normal, until he surprised J.D. by handing him the keys to the Tahoe. "You drive," he said.

After explaining to a nearly apoplectic LaRue that the sheriff would be coming with J.D. to the crime scene, nothing else was said as the Tahoe screamed through the otherwise quiet streets of Bonney until they reached the insurance office. Sutton reached for the door handle and J.D. grabbed his shoulder. "Sorry, Sheriff," he said grimly. "You're staying right here. No arguments. LaRue called in Deputy Evans to assist, as a courtesy to you."

"Wilder, I'm the sheriff. I have the right...."

"This is the village police department's responsibility, not the sheriff's department. Not only that, you have a personal connection here to the victim. You know the protocol." The sheriff's face turned even whiter. "You stay here. I'll have Evans call you over when and if I can," he added, squeezing Sutton's shoulder and giving him a gentle shake. Sutton inclined his head, took a deep breath, and nodded.

J.D. made his way through the group of onlookers that had gathered near the insurance office. LaRue was barking orders at two of the officers to keep the crowd back. Aaron Camacho was talking to a middle-aged woman who was shivering uncontrollably in spite of her heavy winter coat. She was shaking her head, glassy-eyed with horror, as she spoke in monosyllables.

"No, I did not call first... no, no one knew I was here... no, I did not hear the shot... no, I did not see who else was here...." Camacho looked up when J.D. approached.

"This is Sheila Larsen. She's one of the agents who work in

this office." He straightened up. "She's the one who found, uh, Ms. Stratham. Ms. Larsen, this is Detective Wilder. He'll want to talk to you, too."

"Ms. Larsen, are you all right?" J.D. asked, looking at the woman closely. Her eyes were round with shock, but not red, as if she had been shedding tears. Her trembling lips murmured that she was fine, despite the expression on her face that said otherwise. J.D. knew that the chief was waiting for him to enter the office, but he felt it would be wise to talk to Ms. Larsen first. "I need to ask some questions."

"I told the officer," she said without prompting, "that I was so upset with Meghan. I've been calling her and calling her all week, telling her that we needed to open the office, that people wanted to know that they could file claims if they needed to, what with the fires and all that's going on, and she would tell me that all that could wait, that the office was staying closed till the end of the week. I told her that I couldn't even go grocery shopping or run errands without running into disgruntled customers, but she didn't care. So I decided that, whether she liked it or not, I was going to come in today and take care of some paperwork and return some calls. It was the least I could do for our customers." She drew in a shaky breath. "When I got here, I saw her car was parked in front and... I almost left. I was afraid that she'd get angry to see me here and that we'd end up exchanging words and I'd probably get fired. But then," she went on with a shrug, "I thought, maybe it would be best to at least check in, see if she was maybe willing to catch up on everything and would appreciate my help."

"How long ago did you get here, Ms. Larsen?"

She shook her head. "I'm not sure, Detective. Maybe a little over a half hour ago."

"Was the door locked?" J.D. asked her. She blinked and looked up at him.

"I... I think so," she said slowly. "I mean, the "Closed" sign was on the door, so I used my key but I'm not sure if it actually *was* locked."

"Then what happened once you walked in?"

She drew a long breath. "Well, I called out to Meghan. I was apologizing, because I figured she'd be mad. But there was no answer. I wondered where she could be... her office door was partially open. I knocked. She never liked it if I walked in without knocking. The door swung open and I saw her...." She swallowed hard and her face paled. "She was lying on the floor. There was blood. So much blood...."

"Okay, Ms. Larsen," J.D. said, stopping her as her voice broke and she dropped her face into her hands. He straightened up. "Officer Camacho will take your statement. He'll bring you some water," he added as Camacho materialized with a bottle of water. He nodded to the young officer as he turned toward the insurance office. Camacho stopped him.

"Detective?" he said, keeping his voice low. He glanced in the direction of the Tahoe, concern furrowing his brow. "Is the sheriff all right?" he asked.

"Hard to say," J.D. said dryly. Camacho nodded and turned his attention back to Ms. Larsen. J.D. headed toward the office where LaRue was standing in the doorway.

"This is a hell of a thing, Wilder," Chief LaRue said. "From what we've found out so far, no one heard the gunshots...."

"She was shot more than once?" He followed the chief across the lobby to Meghan's private office. The door was wide open and he could see her body, face down, on the floor. He stopped and frowned. "This is how she was found?"

"Ms. Larsen said she didn't even check to see if she was all right. She just backed out of the office and called 911 from the front office," LaRue said, stepping into the office and to the side to allow J.D. to approach the body. The medical examiner's assistant was taking photos and measurements and he also stepped out of the way. J.D. turned to the chief and LaRue nodded. "You can see two entrance wounds. We haven't turned her over to check for exit wounds yet."

"Yeah," J.D. said shortly. He shook his head. "This doesn't make sense."

"What doesn't?" LaRue asked.

"Why would she be shot in the back? If she had been confronting a thief, she wouldn't turn her back on him, would she?"

"Wouldn't think so. Anyway, it couldn't be robbery, they don't keep cash in the office. So it's not like she was shot as she was going for a safe or some other place where money would be kept." He glanced around the office as if to assure himself that there wasn't anything else of value that a thief would be interested in. Meghan's oversized leather purse sat on a chair near the door. He reached a gloved hand in and drew out a leather wallet. He opened it and thumbed through several credit cards. His brows rose and a low whistle escaped as he showed J.D. a large amount of cash. "If it had been a thief, she could have given him what she had in her purse to make him go away... but she doesn't seem to have been heading for her purse."

"It wasn't robbery," J.D. said, shaking his head, as Officer Camacho entered the office.

"Detective... I mean, Chief," Camacho said, correcting himself, his face reddening. "There's a man here who was walking his dog by the office earlier. He says he heard shouting coming from the office, like there was an altercation going on."

LaRue nodded to J.D. "Let's see if we can pin down the time of the crime a little more."

J.D.'s stomach lurched. What if the shouting that the man had heard was the sound of Sutton and his ex having an "altercation"? LaRue stared at him curiously. He nodded and followed the chief.

The man in question was talking to Camacho and another officer and anyone else who would listen to him. He was middle-aged and barely five feet tall, with a brown trench coat that was unbuttoned, exposing a pot belly in a Texas A&M sweatshirt. He wore a matching beanie that was pulled down over his ears. He was gesturing wildly toward the building, then the parking lot, then the sidewalk. His terrier stood shivering miserably in a tiny Aggies sweater, oblivious to the leash that jerked back and forth in sync with the man's flailing arms. He stopped when he noticed J.D. and LaRue watching him. "Are you the investigating officers?" he asked.

"Police Chief Eldon LaRue and Detective J.D. Wilder," LaRue made the introductions. Neither he nor J.D. offered their hands to the man. "And you are?"

"Oh, I'm Warren Bradley. I work at the funeral home." He gestured up the street in the general direction of his place of employment. J.D. started but quickly recovered and hoped that LaRue wouldn't notice. "I'm the custodian there," Bradley added.

"Okay, Mr. Bradley, tell us what you saw," LaRue said.

"Oh, I didn't actually *see* anything," the man said earnestly, shaking his head. "I was walking Roxy here," he said, unnecessarily indicating the whining dog, "and, well, she decided to stop right here to do her business... you know what I mean," he added, as he gestured to the curb. "Well, I had to stand here a few minutes and I heard some awful shouting coming from inside the insurance office." He jerked a thumb over his shoulder and shook his head. "I could tell it was a woman, the way she was screaming. But there was a man, too. At least, I'm guessing it was a man...

deeper voice but just as loud as the woman."

"Did you hear what they were saying?" LaRue asked. J.D. was glad that the chief was taking the lead in questioning the man. Mr. Bradley shrugged.

"Not really. I mean, they were loud but not clear. I couldn't make out any words. I could tell they were angry, both of them." He pointed to the window and J.D. knew it was the one in Meghan's private office. "I'm guessing the woman was standing right near that window, because I did hear her say that she never wanted to see the other person ever again. Just like that, 'You got what you wanted, now get out of here, I never want to see you again', or something close to that," he amended. "I mean, she was shrieking like a banshee, so it was hard to understand exactly what she said."

"And you didn't see the person she was talking to? Did you happen to recognize his voice?" LaRue pressed. He glanced at J.D. as if wondering why he wasn't asking questions. Warren Bradley shook his head.

"I didn't even recognize Ms. Stratham's voice, to be honest, Chief," he admitted. "I just figured it was her because, well, because she was the one that was murdered."

"You know Meghan Stratham?" J.D. finally managed to find his voice. He hoped the strangled tone would be attributed to the cold weather. Bradley shot him a look and shrugged.

"Gosh, Detective, I guess everyone does."

"Did you see a vehicle parked out here?"

Mr. Bradley paused and pursed his lips. He scratched his head. "Now let's see… there was a vehicle out here…."

"Ms. Stratham's car?" Chief LaRue suggested. Mr. Bradley looked at Meghan's Beemer and frowned, shaking his head.

"No, it wasn't this car," he said, nodding toward the silver sedan. "No, it was kind of an SUV thing. Gosh, Chief, I can't even tell you what color it was," he said apologetically and J.D. let out a slow breath of relief. Bradley continued, "Roxy was done with her business and wanted to get going. She doesn't like this cold weather and I don't, either. But we always walk two miles a day and we were still short of the point where we turn back to go home, so we kept on going."

"So you're coming back from your walk now?" J.D. asked. He tried not to glance in the direction of the sheriff's Tahoe.

"Oh, no, Detective," Bradley said. "No, we finished our walk at least an hour ago. I'm here because I heard the commotion with the sirens and all and, well, I have to admit, I was curious. I didn't realize that I might have been a witness to a murder!"

LaRue's brows rose. "So you passed by here on the way back from your walk an hour ago?" He glanced at J.D. "Did you hear or see anything at that time?"

Bradley shook his head. "No, just saw that this car was here. And that other vehicle was gone. It was quiet then. I figured that whoever was arguing either settled their dispute or took it elsewhere. Or maybe Ms. Stratham got a client or something and her argument was put on hold while she took care of them." He cleared his throat and his voice dropped to a whisper. "I never would have imagined that she was dead."

J.D. winced. How long would it be before someone found out that Sutton and his ex had had a loud and heated exchange in the insurance office? He mumbled an excuse to LaRue and stepped away, avoiding the chief's eyes, as he made his way toward the Tahoe. The sheriff straightened up as J.D. approached. He said nothing, but J.D. saw the questions in his eyes.

"Guy named Bradley who works at the funeral home heard Meghan having a loud, angry argument with someone earlier this afternoon," J.D. said. Sutton sat bolt upright and J.D. held up a hand. "It was over an hour ago. He didn't see her car, but he saw another vehicle parked in front. An SUV, he thinks, but that's all he can tell us. No color or make or model, certainly not a license plate. I would think he would have noticed if it was a law enforcement vehicle, but he's adamant he didn't pay attention." The sheriff's face had paled.

"Wilder, I swear I didn't...."

"You don't have to tell me that," J.D. said. "But right now, I'm the only one who knows that you were here earlier. And besides the murderer, you might be the last person to have seen Meghan alive." He took a deep breath. "You're going to have to tell LaRue."

"I was planning on it," Sutton said. His eyes drilled into J.D.'s and he drew a deep breath. "I didn't kill Meghan."

"I know that, Sutton, but he's going to start digging. You know he'll have to. He knows something's been bothering you for the last few weeks. Despite what you might believe, I'm pretty sure the whole town is aware of that. He'll find out that you had a motive. And opportunity." J.D. couldn't believe how much whiter the sheriff's face could get. "You need to pin down the exact time you were in the office with Meghan. You need to remember everything you can about your meeting with her… what was said, what you did, and especially if you saw anyone around the office who might have seen or heard you."

The sheriff shook his head slowly, despair tingeing his features. "I'm not sure. I… I don't… I can't…."

"You have to," J.D. said urgently, as he glanced over his shoulder and saw Eldon LaRue heading his way, his dark face grim.

Chapter 22

Corrie knew something was wrong when the sheriff's department Tahoe skidded to a stop in front of the house with J.D. at the wheel.

She had finished her meeting with the Sutton family lawyer, Anthony DiMarco, and she and Cassandra were walking him to his car when they all stopped in shock as the Tahoe, flinging gravel and kicking up a dust plume, roared up the driveway. J.D. flung the door open before the vehicle had stopped completely and sprinted up the front steps.

"What's wrong?" Corrie cried as J.D. reached the porch. Cassandra's face had gone completely white.

"Where's Patrick?" she snapped. J.D. held up his hands and Corrie reined in her impulse to grab him by the front of his jacket. Instead, she took hold of Cassandra's arm as Mr. DiMarco stepped to her side as well, as if to support her.

"He's all right, he's fine," J.D. said. The look on his face seemed to tell a different story. "He's... he's at the police department." He drew in a deep breath and he looked at each of them in turn. "Meghan's dead."

Corrie blinked. "What?"

"Let's go inside," Mr. DiMarco said, but J.D. stopped him.

"You're the attorney, right?" he said. When Mr. DiMarco nodded, J.D. went on, "The sheriff is asking for you. He thought you'd still be here. Can you go down to the police department to talk to him?" The man nodded and started toward the front steps. He stopped and turned to face J.D.

"The police department, Detective Wilder? Not the sheriff's department?" Mr. DiMarco asked, his brow furrowed. Corrie glanced at J.D. and her stomach twisted as he grimaced.

"No, sir. He's... he'll explain it all to you." The attorney nodded and hurried toward his Mercedes. J.D. gestured inside. "Come on," he said to Corrie and Rick's mother. "It's going to take a while to explain."

"What happened to Meghan?" Corrie asked, unable to wait another second. "Was she in an accident? When did this happen?" She and Cassandra both stopped inside the door, clearly not willing to wait any longer for information. "Why is Rick at the police department?" she demanded, her hands on her hips.

J.D. shook his head as he shut the door. "It wasn't an accident. She was shot to death at the insurance office."

"What?" Cassandra gasped. "She was shot?"

"Was it a robbery?" Corrie asked.

"No," J.D. said and Corrie noticed he was avoiding her gaze. "I can't give you many details but, from what we know, we're treating this as a homicide and we're continuing to investigate."

"Why is Rick at the police department? Is he assisting Eldon with the investigation?" Corrie asked. J.D.'s answer was a fraction of a second too long in coming. "Surely Rick isn't a suspect?" she demanded, her hands dropping to her sides as she noted the stricken look on J.D.'s face. "Has he been arrested?" she gasped.

"No," J.D. said emphatically, this time looking squarely in her eyes. "He's not being detained, either. He volunteered to go to the police department and talk to them. I just came here to let you know what was going on and see if his attorney could come down because I didn't want to tell you over the phone. I have to get back."

"I'm going with you," Corrie said, snatching her jacket off the rack near the door. J.D. caught her arm.

"He said that you and Mrs. Sutton were to stay here," he said firmly. "He said no arguments, he doesn't want you to come to the station. There's nothing you can do there so...."

"So the alternative is to do nothing here?" Corrie shook off his hand. "Sorry, J.D., but I've had enough of Rick—of BOTH of you—keeping me in the dark with everything that he's going through! You both should know by now, especially Rick, that whatever happens, I'm not going to just stand by and wait to see how things go. I'm coming with you whether Rick likes it or not!" She yanked her jacket on and glanced at Rick's mother. "What about you, Cassandra?" she asked.

Cassandra Waverly-Sutton stepped back and shook her head. "I know Patrick is trying to protect us and I think you're about all he's going to be able to manage right now. He doesn't need us both there." She pulled herself together and fixed her glacial eyes on J.D. "Detective Wilder, I suspect you're not being completely forthright with me about why Patrick is at the police station, and I understand why. However, Corrie has helped you both solve several crimes over the last year. You can't deny that," she added when it seemed that J.D. was about to say something, "so no matter what you and my son say, Detective, Corrie IS going with you and, if there is anything she can do, you will allow her to assist in your investigation."

"Mrs. Sutton... ma'am...."

"Do I make myself clear, Detective Wilder?"

Despite her concern, Corrie couldn't help but bite back a smile. She'd never seen J.D. so conflicted in all the time she'd known him. He glanced at her, perhaps hoping she would help him out, but she just stared back at him pointedly. He shook his head in defeat.

"Yes, ma'am," he muttered, his face reddening. He turned to Corrie and motioned her to toward the door. "Let's go."

J.D. still felt the sting from Mrs. Sutton's edict as if the icy wind was slicing across his face, although he felt his cheeks were on fire. He didn't look at Corrie, even though he figured she was too preoccupied to give him so much as an "I-told-you-so" look. Besides, it was starting to get dark and the road was too narrow and winding for him to take his eyes from it.

"So tell me the complete truth, J.D.," Corrie said tersely as she also kept her gaze focused on the road. "Rick's not arrested, or detained, but he's at the police department. Is the sheriff's office assisting in the investigation of Meghan's death?"

There was no point in not being completely honest. "No," J.D. said. "Eldon and I are in charge of the investigation. The sheriff went to the chief and offered his assistance." He paused, not sure how to proceed, but it was immediately clear that Corrie already suspected what he was going to tell her.

"Because he was one of the last people to see her alive? Because it's common knowledge that they'd been having problems lately? Because he probably has the most compelling motive to murder her?" She drew a deep breath. "When am I going to be asked to assist in the investigation as well?"

J.D. took his eyes off the road to look at her. "No one suspects you of killing her."

"Even after what she did with my insurance? Even though I said I could kill her? I know RaeLynn told you about that. Come on, J.D.," she said, shaking her head. "I've probably got the best motive of anyone in Bonney and you know it! Everyone in town knows it!"

He allowed himself to laugh. "Maybe, but you've also got a rock-solid alibi. You were nowhere near the insurance office. Heck, you haven't even been to Bonney since... good Lord, was it just yesterday that the Black Horse...." His voice trailed away and he grimaced. Corrie glanced out her window and she swallowed hard. "I'm sorry," he said, wincing at how inadequate the words

187

sounded. "That was insensitive of me."

"It's okay," she said, although her voice sounded strangled. "And I know you're right. I'm just... I don't know. Maybe trying to create reasonable doubt about Rick...."

"You're assuming he's a suspect," J.D. said, keeping his voice light even though his heart felt heavy. He didn't want to tell her, but he knew she would never forgive him if she went into this blind, without knowing everything. He took a deep breath. "Okay, listen, I'm going to tell you a few things, because I don't want you to be caught off-guard, but I also don't want you to jump to conclusions, okay?" She stared at him, but nodded, mutely. He went on, "The sheriff had a fight with Meghan earlier this afternoon."

Corrie drew in a sharp breath. "What were they fighting about?"

J.D. rubbed the back of his neck. "It's complicated," he began, then he told her everything that had happened, had been happening, between the sheriff and his ex, from their battle over their daughter's remains to his agreement to Meghan's terms in order to prevent Corrie from losing her insurance... and obtain the proof that his marriage to Meghan was invalid in the eyes of the Church. Corrie said nothing and he wasn't sure if it was because she didn't want to interrupt him or if she was too shocked to say anything—the way her face grew progressively whiter as he went on seemed to indicate she was stunned into silence. "Witnesses heard Meghan and a man engaged in a shouting match," J.D. said. "They couldn't identify him and they didn't really hear what was being said, but it was close to the time that Sutton admitted to being at her office."

"He told Eldon all this?" Corrie's voice was strained.

"Eldon was bound to find out. It would look bad if he kept quiet about it and someone else came forward later on. He told Eldon he needed to talk to him in private and then he sent me to come fetch his lawyer. *Just* his lawyer," he added, giving her a look. "So I don't know what's happened since I left him. He's not going to be thrilled that I'm bringing you along."

"Just tell him his mother got involved, he'll understand," she deadpanned. Some color had returned to her cheeks but she was still pale. "You don't believe he shot Meghan, do you?"

J.D. looked at her. "No, I don't," he said quietly. "She pushed him, hard, she knew how to rile him up, but the sheriff... I know everyone has a breaking point, Corrie, and maybe, if he'd done it in the heat of an argument, then I might think he was capable. But in cold blood... no, I don't believe he'd do anything like this."

"But you think Eldon might believe he would?" Her voice hardened and J.D. held up a hand.

"Corrie, don't go in thinking that Eldon's got something against Sutton," he warned her. "I'm telling you how a cop needs to think in a situation like this. Just because we all know Sutton doesn't mean we can automatically eliminate him as a possible suspect. At least not officially, until we thoroughly investigate...." He stopped as they pulled up in front of the Bonney police department and they saw the black and white State Police cruiser parked in front of the doors, along with a vehicle with the state fire investigator shield on the door. "Oh, that's not good," he muttered as he put the Tahoe in park.

He turned to Corrie but she was already out of the vehicle and heading for the doors.

The scene inside the police station was something out of a bizarre dream.

Eldon LaRue was squaring off with Agent Jackson, both men red-faced and all but bumping chests, their voices raised with outrage as they argued about jurisdiction, with the Sutton family attorney vainly stepping between them like a boxing referee. Agent Pinella stood aside, his arms folded across his chest as if he were waiting for a signal to step in. Several Bonney police officers, including Aaron Camacho and Charlie White, glowered menacingly at the two state police officers who glowered back. The state cops flanked the sheriff, who seemed to be the calmest person in the entire room despite his slightly disheveled appearance. He glanced toward J.D. when he saw him walk in, did a double-take at the sight of Corrie, then rolled his eyes heavenward and shrugged, apparently resigned.

Corrie had stopped short when she saw the pandemonium, but then seeing the two fire investigators and the state police officers sparked her outrage and she stomped in their direction, apparently having made up her mind that they had to be the ones to blame for what was going on. J.D. managed to catch her arm before she launched herself at Agent Jackson. "Easy there, Calamity Jane," he murmured, drawing her back from the melee. "Let me do the talking before you end up in cuffs." She threw him a sharp glare, but relented. J.D. put two fingers in his mouth and blew a piercing whistle that brought instant silence and wide-eyed stares. "Okay, now that I have everyone's attention, can we all act like the professionals we're supposed to be?" he said, his voice as razor-sharp as his gaze as he looked around the room.

Eldon LaRue spun toward him and pointed an accusing finger. "Wilder, what in the ever-loving HELL is going on here? What are these guys," he said, stabbing his thumb toward the agents and the state police, "doing here and why are they involved in this case? It's got nothing to do with the fire at the Black Horse!"

"It's got EVERYTHING to do with the fire, since the woman who was murdered owns the company that insures the campground!" Jackson retorted. "And that woman," he went on, jerking his thumb in Sutton's direction, "met with the sheriff shortly before she was killed. AND may I remind you that she was the sheriff's ex-wife, with whom she had a contentious relationship, and that a heated argument between Ms. Stratham and a man was heard by passers-by earlier this afternoon?"

"And no one has identified that man as Sheriff Sutton," J.D. pointed out before Eldon could respond. Agent Jackson threw him an irritated glance.

"In any event, the State Police and our agency have taken over this investigation and that includes anything related," Jackson snapped. "Therefore, Sheriff Sutton is a suspect in the murder of Meghan Stratham and that is now in the jurisdiction of the New Mexico State Police, not the local police department. And since that is the case...."

"You can't arrest him," Corrie spoke up, startling everyone. The sheriff threw J.D. a nervous glance and J.D. reached out and caught her arm again.

"Corrie, let me handle this," he warned her in a low voice. She shook off his hand and glared at him coldly.

"No, I will handle this," she hissed. J.D. shook his head at her but she turned away and stepped toward the chief and Agent Jackson. "Rick didn't do this. YOU, of all people, should know he'd never do such a thing," Corrie said to LaRue. "You've known Rick for far too long, Eldon! He's not capable of killing someone!"

"All cops are capable of killing someone, Miss Black," Jackson said sarcastically. "The possibility comes with the territory!" Corrie spun on him.

"I'm not talking about in the line of duty, Agent Jackson! I'm talking murder and that's a completely different thing!"

190

"Corrie," LaRue said, holding up his hands, as if to either calm her down or protect himself, "we have to suspect everyone... it's the way the law works... it's how we have to do our jobs. If anyone has a possible motive, then that makes them suspects and, well, we're talking about Rick's ex, so...."

"So?"

"Well, so," Eldon began, then looked helplessly around the room. DiMarco, the attorney, cleared his throat.

"Whatever motive the police want to attribute to Sheriff Sutton is not to be discussed by anyone until I've had time to talk to my client," he said forcefully. "And he is not going to answer any questions or make any comments until then! Not unless you're prepared to arrest him, in which case I suggest you consider that move very carefully, Agent Jackson," DiMarco added ominously.

"He had motive and opportunity!" Jackson thundered.

"And so did I!" Corrie said, stepping in front of the fire investigator and planting her fists on her hips. "You going to arrest me, too?" she challenged.

"Corrie!" It sounded like five different voices responded in unison, with varying degrees of disbelief. Mr. DiMarco stepped toward her.

"Miss Black, I think it's best that you step back and let us...."

"Let you what? Allow Rick to get railroaded into a murder charge?" she challenged. She turned to the state cops, who looked uncertain of what they were expected to do, and thrust her wrists towards them. "Go on! Arrest me, too! I probably had more of a motive to kill Meghan than Rick did and, what's more, I can even provide a witness who heard me say I wanted to kill her as well!" A stunned silence fell over the room, all the LEOs staring at Corrie in disbelief, except the sheriff, whose eyes were shooting daggers at J.D.

"Wilder, would you get her out of here?" Sutton growled, his face growing pale.

"Corrie, have you lost your mind?" J.D. hissed, grabbing her arm and pulling her toward him. "Do you have any idea what you're doing?"

"Creating reasonable doubt!" She jerked her arm free once again and the look in her eyes told J.D. he'd lose his hand if he touched her again. He sighed irritably.

"That's not your job," he said.

"I don't care!" she snapped. "They don't have any proof that Rick murdered Meghan and they can't arrest him just because he happens to be a convenient suspect!"

Mr. DiMarco let out a discreet cough. "Agent Jackson, I suggest that you proceed with your investigation before you take any steps to arrest Sheriff Sutton. It will eliminate a lot of headaches and unnecessary paperwork down the road. I guarantee that he is not a flight risk and will cooperate with the investigation in every way. And I suggest you might want to hold off on questioning him or anyone else," he added, giving Corrie a sideways glance, "until the crime scene investigation is completed."

"Meaning you'll have time to meet with them and get your stories straight!" Jackson snarled, folding his arms across his chest.

"The sheriff and Miss Black have a right to counsel, as you should well know," DiMarco said smoothly. The lawyer seemed to have gathered the reins of control of the situation. "We will therefore meet with you tomorrow, in court, if you wish, after you have conducted your investigation of the crime scene. Until then," he paused and cleared his throat, "I trust you have no issue with allowing my clients to leave."

Agent Jackson straightened up, his face red and his jaw quivering with rage. The state cops and Agent Pinella exchanged nervous looks; apparently they were familiar with Agent Jackson's temper. He took a deep breath and glared at the lawyer. "Fine," he spat. He spun to point at the sheriff. "Don't think you've gotten away with murder," he snapped. "You might have the money to pay for high-end legal defense, but we'll be keeping an eye on you... and your friends," he added, glancing at Corrie and J.D. He turned to Eldon LaRue. "I expect full cooperation from the local police."

"You'll get it," LaRue said stonily.

Not another word was said as Jackson looked at his partner and the two state police officers and jerked his head toward the door. They left and it seemed like everyone left in the room released a collective breath.

"Will someone tell me what the heck's going on?" LaRue thundered as he wheeled around, facing J.D. but looking from the sheriff, to the attorney, to Corrie, and back at J.D. The sheriff stepped forward, holding up both hands.

"Eldon, I'm sorry about all this," he said. "I should have kept you in the loop with all that's been going on, but," he sighed, "well, it's been so personal...."

"I get it," LaRue said. "But now I *need* to know what's going on. Everything. I don't like being blind-sided by the state fellows." He addressed Officers White and Camacho. "I don't expect them to accept your help, but I want you to stick around the crime scene and keep an eye on them." Both officers nodded. Charlie cast a worried look at Corrie.

"Cousin, are you okay?" he asked.

"Sure," she responded, folding her arms across her chest. Charlie raised a brow and, at J.D.'s nod, shrugged and followed Officer Camacho out of the room. The other officers returned to their duties. Chief LaRue motioned everyone else to follow him to his office.

Chapter 23

"Peace and quiet" was something that Corrie had always craved, especially during the crazy-busy times at the Black Horse, when it seemed like no matter how many staff members she had working, it was never enough to keep up with the demands of the guests, and weeks would pass before she ever got so much as an afternoon off. At this moment, she couldn't remember ever experiencing a quiet so complete and profound as what she was experiencing in the dim light of the office in the Sutton house.

However, she wondered if she'd ever experience peace again.

The Pages, the Myers, RaeLynn, Luz and Manuel, and Cassandra Sutton had all gathered in the main room, waiting for Rick, J.D. and Corrie to return, to find out what was going on with the investigation into the fire at the Black Horse and Meghan's murder. Rick had been tight-lipped for the most part, giving them only the bare minimum that they needed to know, with J.D. and Anthony DiMarco doing most of the talking... exactly like he had done in Eldon LaRue's office. Then they had all been dismissed while Rick spent an hour talking privately with his attorney in the office. Luz and Manuel had insisted on feeding them all a hearty dinner, for which none of them, especially Corrie and J.D., had an appetite. After DiMarco left, Rick had entered the dining room and signaled to both J.D. and Corrie to meet him in the office. His mother had half-risen from her seat, but then her eyes connected with Rick's and an unspoken message passed between them. She stood and quietly announced she was going to bed. There were murmured "good nights" as she went up the stairs and then everyone's gaze locked on Corrie as she followed Rick and J.D. from the dining room.

She sat in the cushioned chair in front of the desk and Rick sat behind the desk, as if using it as a shield to protect himself—or was he trying to protect Corrie?—from what he was going to say. J.D. opted to stand near the door, leaning against the wall, his arms folded across his chest. To Corrie's surprise, she was in no hurry to hear what Rick had to say. She grasped at the moment, realizing that once he started to speak nothing would ever be the same again, no matter what he said. Rick's hands were clasped together on the desktop, his knuckles white. It was several minutes before he took a deep breath.

"There's a lot I need to tell you," he said, not looking up. Corrie frowned and glanced at J.D., not sure which one of them

Rick was talking to. It became clear as he went on, "I've been wrong to keep you in the dark, but I did it because... because I thought I needed to protect you. That I needed to take care of my own business, without making you worry about it. And to be honest, I really thought it was the best for both of us. I shouldn't have tried to make that decision for you." He looked up, his blue eyes as dark as midnight. "I've always tried to handle everything on my own, never asking for help from anyone. Not even the person I trusted most."

J.D. straightened up. "Uh, hey," he said, and paused awkwardly for a moment. "I'm sure I'm not meant to be here for this conversation, so I'll just step out...."

"No," Rick said, standing up. "Wilder, I'd appreciate it if you'd stay. There's a lot I need to say and you need to hear it as well. Please," he added, when J.D. hesitated. He looked at Corrie and raised a brow. She merely nodded, not sure why Rick was so insistent that he stay but also grateful for J.D.'s comforting presence in the room. J.D. resumed his position near the door and gestured for Rick to continue.

Instead of taking his seat behind the desk, Rick began to pace, the sound of his boots on the hardwood floor echoing dully off the book-lined walls. Corrie knew that nothing she could say would prompt him to speak before he was ready, but she glanced toward J.D. and saw he was doing his best not to fidget. Apparently he was just as agitated as she was.

Finally Rick stopped and looked at them both. He squared his shoulders and sighed. "There are a few things Wilder doesn't know," he said. "And they're things that we've never really spoken out loud, Corrie. So I may as well lay it all out for clarity." Corrie's heart seemed to skip a beat, recalling her earlier conversation with Rick's mother about his father... and her cousin. She felt her face heat up and hoped it wasn't noticeable, but, to her chagrin, Rick grimaced and she could feel J.D.'s gaze fixed on her. She wished SHE could leave the room, not wanting to see J.D.'s reaction to such a shameful and tawdry family secret, but then she chided herself. The past was in the past; perhaps if they faced it once and for all, it could stay in the past and not mar the future. Hadn't her conversation with Cassandra proved that? So many years of misunderstanding that could have been avoided.... She sat up straighter and held her head up then gave Rick a slight nod.

He cleared his throat. "My father left my mother and me, just before my twelfth birthday, and ran off with a young woman who was hired to look after me when I was seven years old—run me to school and other activities, make sure I did my homework, you get the idea—even though I didn't really need a sitter or a nanny," he added dryly. His eyes met Corrie's and he glanced away, his face reddening.

"She was my cousin," Corrie spoke up, surprising herself with how clear and calm her voice sounded. "Her name was Natalie and she was just a teenager when she came to work for Rick's family. She was my dad's niece," she finished in a whisper.

The silence seemed to expand in the room, like a balloon being blown up far too big. The tension grew as both Corrie and Rick waited to see what J.D.'s reaction would be. Corrie was faintly surprised that saying it out loud hadn't affected her as much as she thought it should have—that family secret no one ever talked about because it was so embarrassing and disgraceful. Without it ever being said, it was understood that Natalie had been disowned by her family, probably much the same way that Rick's father had been. J.D. had no trouble coming to that conclusion.

"You haven't had contact with them since they... left?" he asked.

Corrie shook her head, then stopped and looked at Rick. His face had paled and she bit her lip to keep from blurting out that she had seen the letters from his father. Somehow, she managed to keep from glancing at the desk and waited to see what Rick would say.

"Neither of them ever contacted our families. At least, not personally," Rick said. "My father's communications came through attorneys and other legal representatives. As far as I know, Corrie's family never heard from Natalie directly," he added. J.D. shot her a glance and she shook her head; if her cousin had ever contacted anyone in the family, she hadn't heard about it. Rick took a deep breath. "My father reached out to me two years ago," he said. "It's the first time since...." He stopped and swallowed hard and looked away.

Moments ticked by as they waited for Rick to continue. Corrie had an uneasy feeling that he wasn't telling them everything but, unless she admitted to snooping in the desk drawer, there was no way to get him to admit it.

"Okay," J.D. said, when the silence stretched on, "so what, exactly, does that have to do with what just happened today? Or, for that matter, what's been going on with your ex for the last few months?"

"Probably nothing, could be everything," Rick deadpanned. "I just want to make sure that I've been completely transparent and truthful, so that when I tell you that I had nothing to do with Meghan's death, you have no reason to doubt me."

J.D.'s brows rose. "I thought it was pretty clear that I don't doubt for one minute that you had nothing to do with that. You'd never murder anyone. I'd stake my life on that," he added.

"Thanks for the vote of confidence," Rick said dryly. "Still, you know as well as I do that, as an officer of the law, a person's word of honor is pretty much meaningless in the face of actual evidence when it comes to a crime. And even though one is supposed to be innocent until proven guilty in a court of law, you and I both know that the opposite is usually the case. No matter how well everyone in this town knows me, there will always be some question...."

"That's ridiculous!" Corrie stood up, her chest heaving with suppressed sobs. Rick and J.D. both looked at her in alarm and she did her best to get her emotions in check. She couldn't explain why listening to Rick and J.D. discuss his situation calmly, as if they were talking about one of their cases involving a stranger, triggered a burst of annoyance and impatience. Perhaps it was the fact that what Rick had just said was probably true—everyone in Bonney was well aware of Rick and Meghan's history. And hers. No matter how discreet they were, how well they guarded their privacy, someone, somehow, would always think they knew something... and would wonder.... She shoved the thought viciously from her mind and planted her fists on her hips. "There's no way that anyone who knows you would believe you'd be capable of... of...."

"Corrie," Rick said softly, "if this were to go to court, it's likely the members of the jury wouldn't know me."

"Which is why we have to clear your name, Sheriff, before it gets to that point," J.D. said. "What did your attorney tell you?"

Rick shrugged. "What you'd expect. He wants me to tell the truth, the whole truth, and not hide anything, even if it's completely innocent though it might look incriminating. Which I did," he went on, "and now I'm going to tell you both, as well. I don't want there to be any surprises."

Corrie exchanged a look with J.D. She wasn't sure what to think, but she knew that what Rick was going to tell them was going to sound very bad for him. She thought back to her conversation with RaeLynn, when she had, in her distress, said she could kill Meghan. She had blurted it out in front of the fire inspectors and state police. Apparently, it hadn't made an impression on them; otherwise, she was sure she'd be in cuffs by now. But now, Meghan *was* dead, killed by someone, and if they decided to pursue it, and they questioned RaeLynn.... She could picture RaeLynn's horror if she were to be questioned by the authorities and she was asked about what Corrie had said, even if she hadn't—and would never have—acted upon it. She took a deep breath and understood why Rick wanted to prepare them.

He sat down, gesturing for them both to sit as well, and seemed to gather his thoughts before he spoke. "As you both know, I've been trying to have my marriage to Meghan declared null and void for some time," he said, staring at the desktop. Corrie shifted in her seat, biting back a scathing reminder that she had just recently learned that, and the fact that J.D. had found out before she had still rankled. Rick glanced at her and she managed to sit still. "I filed two appeals, both of which were dismissed, after the tribunal's initial declaration that we were validly married. I'll admit I was devastated, depressed... but I never was angry with Meghan. I had only myself to blame because I went to great lengths to make sure our marriage was valid and true. If anything, the tribunal only showed what a great job I did at taking marriage seriously." He shook his head. "I had more or less resigned myself to that fact when Alex Durán showed up, claiming to have married Meghan in a Las Vegas quickie wedding while she was gone for her bachelorette party. I don't have to tell you what that meant to me," he said, looking directly at Corrie.

She forced herself to meet his gaze, acutely aware that J.D.'s eyes were trained on her as well. *What did it mean to you, Rick?* she screamed in her mind. *What? All these years, I've been blaming Meghan for us being apart... it never occurred to me to wonder why you broke up with me in the first place! So why should it matter to me that your marriage proved to be invalid? It doesn't explain why you married someone else in the first place!* She gave a slight nod, fighting the urge to look away and praying she wouldn't start crying. She gestured for Rick to go on.

"Meghan blew off the whole Vegas wedding thing," he said. "She argued that it meant nothing and wouldn't change anything about our marriage status. She said she'd deny it if I appealed yet again, so I needed the proof that Alex Durán had. But she had already bought it from him...." He paused when J.D. shifted and seemed about to say something. Then he shook his head and nodded for Rick to go on. "And she offered me a deal," Rick continued. He looked squarely at Corrie. "She would give me the certificate so I could prove our marriage was invalid... and she would authorize immediate payment of your insurance claim," he took a deep breath, "if I would agree to let her transfer Ava to Dallas."

Corrie's eyes widened and her breath caught in her throat. She glanced at J.D. and was astounded to see that he wasn't surprised at the news. Apparently, Rick had told him. His eyes were clouded with an emotion she couldn't quite define and it unnerved her. She looked back at Rick. "You... agreed to do it?"

"Yeah," Rick said. He sat back and looked away from her. "You know she's been after me to do it for a while now. But now... I had to do it. I didn't have a choice."

"What are you talking about? Of course you had a choice!" Corrie cried, jumping to her feet. She fought back her tears and her hands clenched into fists. "You didn't have to bend to her will, Rick! I don't care what she said, she has no right to take Ava away from you! Why did you agree to let her do that?"

"You really have to ask?" Rick said incredulously.

"Because of me? You did it so Meghan would pay my insurance claim? I never asked you to do that, Rick! I'd never ask you to do that!"

"I know you wouldn't," Rick said tersely as he stood up as well. "You didn't even bother to tell me you were in trouble with your insurance or that Meghan was giving you a hard time!"

"Why should I tell you?" Corrie snapped. "It had nothing to do with you! It's...." She stopped and swallowed hard. Rick cocked an eye brow at her and his eyes darkened.

"It's what? It's none of my business? Is that what you were going to say?"

"Well, it isn't your business! And you know what I mean by that!"

"Yeah," he said, stone-faced. "I know exactly what you mean."

"Whoa, whoa," J.D. broke in, stepping forward with his hands up. "Time out, you two. This is not helping the situation at all. We need to stay focused on what the real problem is here. You can work out your personal issues after we make sure no one is going to prison for murder." He shot them both a warning glare, although Corrie felt he looked at her longer than he looked at

Rick. She pressed her lips together and blinked back her tears of fury. She spun around and just kept herself from stomping out the door. J.D. was right. As angry as she was at Rick, she knew he hadn't killed Meghan. She took a deep breath and turned back to face them.

"Okay," she said as calmly as she could, looking Rick square in the eyes, "so you're saying that, according to the law, you have a motive for having murdered Meghan. And that makes you a suspect. I could probably give you a page-long list of people in Bonney who'd love to have been the one to pull the trigger as well, so to speak. I mean, who knows how many other businesses were hurt when she took over our insurance company... besides the fact that not too many people liked her in general. That doesn't mean they had the means and opportunity, even if they had a motive, to kill her. So just having a motive shouldn't be enough to make you a suspect," she argued.

Rick and J.D. both grimaced and Rick shook his head. "You'd make a lousy attorney," he sighed. "The fact is, Corrie, I actually did have the means and opportunity. I'm a law enforcement officer; I carry a gun at all times. And...." He paused, chewing his lip. "...someone heard Meghan having a heated argument with someone earlier today... around the time that I had a heated argument with her...."

"But you didn't kill her," Corrie said emphatically, even as she felt a chill spiral down her back. She realized what Rick and J.D. were trying to tell her—it didn't matter what they knew about Rick. A jury would have a hard time believing he wasn't guilty. Her heart began to pound. "I mean, the evidence... the bullets...."

"We're waiting on all that," Rick said shortly. "It's going to take time...."

"You don't have time," Corrie snapped. She looked at J.D. "You saw the crime scene?"

"Yes," he said. He took a deep breath and told them every detail of the scene in Meghan's office. Corrie felt her stomach twist and she prayed she wouldn't have to excuse herself to be sick. J.D. looked at her. "You okay?"

"I'm not sure," she managed to say. She glanced away from the concern in his and Rick's eyes and let her gaze travel around the room. She hadn't set foot in the insurance company office since before Meghan had taken over, but she could picture the room clearly from previous visits with the former owner. Almost against her will, her mind conjured up the image of Meghan lying sprawled on the floor of the office…. She turned to J.D. "She was shot in the back?"

"Yeah," he said slowly. "She was lying face down on the floor and there were two entrance wounds in her back. Why?"

She turned to Rick. "When you and Meghan were arguing," she said, "did she ever turn her back on you in the midst of it?"

Rick frowned. "No… as a matter of fact, she didn't. She never backed down or walked away from a confrontation." Light dawned in his eyes. "You're right, Corrie. She would have waited for the person she was arguing with to turn around and leave, but she'd never turn her back on someone in the heat of a fight."

"Which means," J.D. said, straightening up, "that she wasn't shot in the middle of an argument. She was either shot in cold blood or her murder was planned. This wasn't a crime of passion."

"And Rick would never shoot anyone in back," Corrie said firmly. "We all know that! So that proves…."

"Nothing," J.D. said sharply. "Just because we know the sheriff wouldn't do this doesn't prove that he didn't."

"You're not listening," Corrie said in exasperation. "Forget about proving that Rick didn't do it. Let's focus on figuring out who WOULD do it. It wasn't a robbery so it has to be someone who knew Meghan personally and had an axe to grind with her."

Rick shook his head, looking defeated. "The only person I can think of is Alex Durán and he couldn't have done it… he was dead before my meeting with Meghan today."

J.D. had been pacing then he stopped and his eyes widened. "And we still don't know who killed him, but I'd bet everything I own that it's the same person who killed Meghan!"

Rick's head jerked up and a ghost of a smile flitted across his face. "No offense, Wilder, but that's not much of a stake. But you're right," he said, his smile fading. He turned to Corrie. "You're right. We're focusing on the wrong thing. We have to find out who killed Alex Durán and that will tell us who killed Meghan." He blew out his breath. "But we'll have to find out who is connected to both of them and why he'd want them dead."

"He?" J.D. asked and raised a brow. "Are you thinking Ronald Brown?"

"If it's not him, I don't know who else it could be," Rick said. "I don't know what his connection is, but there has to be one. If we can find the connection, then we can prove he killed Meghan and Durán… if he is the one who did it."

"Well, at least it will take the focus off of you," Corrie said.

"Then maybe those investigators and the state cops can actually try to catch the real guilty party." She turned to J.D. "I missed hearing what your contact in Mexico said about Ronald Brown and his connection to Rick." She fought back the rush of heat to her face and J.D. seemed to be surprised that she brought it up. He nodded and repeated what he'd learned about Ronald Brown. Corrie nodded silently. "So that was about five years ago?" She glanced at Rick, realizing that it was a sensitive topic for him, but also knowing that they had to go through every scrap of information.

Rick nodded. "When Ava died, I was just going through the motions. I don't remember a lot of what happened. You might ask Mother if she recognizes Ronald Brown," he said, looking at J.D. "She went with me when I had to make the arrangements. I have all the paperwork pertaining to her birth and death at my apartment," he added. "It might have his name on the contract with the funeral home, but I'll be honest, most of what went on back then is a blur."

J.D. nodded. "I suppose it wouldn't hurt to talk to Manuel and Luz as well. They were working for your family at the time, weren't they? They might have...."

Rick's head jerked up and he frowned. "Actually," he said slowly, "Luz had come to work for Meghan and me for a while around the time we were expecting Ava. Mother had to hire another housekeeper in the meantime. She really didn't want to," Rick said, shaking his head, "because she felt it would be disloyal to Luz, but Meghan insisted. For once, Meghan seemed sincerely solicitous, saying she hated to put my mother out by wanting to have Luz taking care of our home. She said she'd find a temporary replacement housekeeper and told me we should pay for it...what is it, Wilder?" Rick asked as J.D. held up his hands.

"Back up, Sheriff," J.D. said. "You're saying that, around the time that Ronald Brown was working for the local funeral home, your ex was hiring a temporary housekeeper for your mother?" He looked around the opulent office and waved a hand around. "Here?"

"Yes," Rick said, glancing at Corrie as if to ask her if she understood J.D.'s concern. "I mean, Luz was staying with Meghan and me in Bonney, but...."

"Why?" J.D. asked sharply. "Why didn't she hire a housekeeper for herself instead of having Luz come to work for you? What was her reason for taking your mother's long-time employee?"

Rick stared at him. "I... I don't know," he said slowly. "I was surprised, if that's what you're asking."

"That she wanted Luz, someone who had known you and your family for years, who probably knew how your marriage was struggling, who had a strong loyalty to you and your family? Why would she have wanted someone working for her who probably didn't like or trust her very much instead of someone who was totally unfamiliar with your family?"

Rick's face paled. "Mother was reluctant to let Luz go, even if she was coming to work for me," he said. "And she fought the idea of having another housekeeper, but Meghan insisted that she needed someone there since Luz would be gone...."

"When did the new housekeeper leave?" J.D. asked sharply. The expression of confusion on Rick's face mirrored what Corrie was feeling.

"I think Mother let her go around the time Ava... died," he said. "Meghan left right after Ava's birth, as soon as the hospital released her, so I didn't need Luz anymore and I ended up moving back here for a while after...." He shook his head to clear it. "Wilder, what are you getting at?"

"Look, Sutton, I know it's getting late and it's been a rough day on everyone, including your mother, but we need to talk to her right away," J.D. said urgently. "I need to know everything that happened when that new housekeeper was here."

Rick nodded in a daze and went to the door and summoned Luz, speaking to her in hushed tones. He returned and motioned to Corrie and J.D. "Let's go up to her room to talk to her. It'll be easier on her."

J.D. had the sudden urge to bow when he was shown into Mrs. Sutton's bedroom suite. She was seated in a plush velvet wingchair, wearing a silk dressing gown of midnight blue, looking regal and imperious, although an uncharacteristic sense of vulnerability permeated the atmosphere in the room. She set down the book she was reading and sat straighter in her chair. Her eyes met those of the sheriff, glancing a question at him, then turning to J.D. "How can I help you, Detective?" she asked.

"Ma'am, this is going to seem really intrusive and odd," he began as he seated himself in a matching wing chair beside her. "But I understand that about five years ago, you hired a temporary housekeeper...."

204

"Yes," she said crisply, her eyes growing cold and hard. "What about it? What does it have to do with Patrick's situation?"

"Would you mind telling me why you decided to let her go? I mean, I understand it was to give Luz her old job back...."

Cassandra shot her son a glance that was almost apologetic. "That's true, Detective," she answered. "However, I had other reasons—reasons I never told Patrick about because, well...." She cleared her throat. "It seemed like there was no point in telling him. Everything had been resolved and he had much more pressing matters on his mind. It all seemed rather petty when compared to what he was going through, so I felt it would serve no purpose to bring it up to him at that time. And after a while, well, it just really slipped my mind, I suppose. As I said, the situation had been rectified, there were no long term issues, so I never thought about it again."

"What situation?" the sheriff asked, his voice strained. One look at the bewilderment on his face told J.D. that Sutton was embarrassed to discover that his mother had, apparently, gone through some kind of difficulty during the time his marriage and life were falling apart, and he felt guilty for not having been aware of it. Corrie was staying back in the shadows of the dimly lit room and her face betrayed no knowledge of what Cassandra was talking about. Mrs. Sutton looked at the sheriff and cleared her throat.

"The young woman who came to work for me while Luz was helping you and Meghan had glowing recommendations and seemed to be very dedicated and hard-working," she began. "Naturally, I didn't confide in her, the way I did with Luz and Manuel, but she came from a reputable agency so I was satisfied with her. At first," she added dryly. "She seemed very conscientious, very meticulous about her job, always inquiring to make sure I approved of what she did. It became a little annoying after a while. Still, I had no reason to doubt her integrity. Then, shortly before Ava was born, things had gotten very, er, stressful for Patrick." She nodded toward him with a sympathetic look. "There wasn't much I could do, as he was adamant about keeping his problems to himself. However, I did have very strong feelings about how Meghan was treating him and, since I no longer believed she had any consideration for him, I decided that the one thing I could do was to make sure that my affairs were in order to protect Patrick's interests. So I went over my will, to make sure that only Patrick would be able to inherit, should anything happen to me, and also decided to take an inventory of personal items of value." She sighed and shook her head. "I can't tell you how many times Patrick, and even Luz and Manuel, told me I shouldn't keep valuables here at home, that I should put them in a safe deposit box at the bank. Well, there are times when I wish to wear a piece of jewelry and I don't want to have to make a trip all the way to the bank in Bonney to get the piece...."

"Mother, what happened?" Sutton asked sharply. "Are you telling me that this woman robbed you? She stole your jewelry while she was employed here?"

Mrs. Sutton raised a hand. "Essentially, yes. And, as you know, Patrick, I don't keep things locked up, simply because I feel that my belongings are quite safe here, with only people I trust coming and going." She nodded toward her bedroom. "I have an armoire where I keep my jewelry, right beside my dresser. Julia, the housekeeper, was well aware of it, as she was in my bedroom at least once a day, due to her chores. In the beginning, I did check the armoire every evening, just to make sure nothing had been touched, but as time went on and Julia seemed to be trustworthy, I stopped. It wasn't until Julia had been here nearly six months, when I decided to check the status of my affairs, that I found that several pieces of jewelry were missing. Rings, necklaces, bracelets... almost every one of my more expensive pieces were gone. I was frantic," she said, shaking her head. "I couldn't believe it. I was positive that Julia had taken the pieces and left, but then I was surprised to see her going about her normal duties. She was coming up the stairs with my clean laundry and I asked her if she knew what had happened to my jewelry." Cassandra's lips tightened into a firm line. "She expressed shock and dismay. She said she had removed the jewelry to clean it and had meant to return it earlier that morning, but had gotten distracted with other duties."

There was silence in the room for several seconds. J.D. weighed his words carefully. "And you believed her, ma'am?"

Cassandra's eyes frosted over. "Of course not, Detective, I'm not a complete fool," she said acidly. "I summoned Manuel immediately and Julia led us to her quarters. Sure enough, she had all my jewelry laid out on a table. I was relieved to see it was all there, no pieces were missing. However, I didn't like it one bit. I had Manuel gather it up and return it to my suite. Julia protested that she had done nothing wrong and she apologized profusely for not having told me what she was doing, she just thought I would appreciate it. I let her know, in no uncertain terms, that I did NOT appreciate her taking my belongings without my permission, no matter how well-intentioned her reasons were, and that she was dismissed from my service. I told her to be out of the house within an hour and I would make sure that she did not receive a glowing review and to forget about severance pay." She drew a deep breath and clasped her hands together to stop them from shaking. "Perhaps I acted hastily, but she didn't argue. I had Manuel and another employee supervise her leaving and they escorted her off the property while I made sure that all my jewelry was, indeed, returned."

"You didn't call the police?" Corrie spoke up. J.D. had almost forgotten she was there. She had apparently been so engrossed in Mrs. Sutton's story that she had crept forward and was now standing right behind J.D. Cassandra Sutton shook her head slowly.

"All my jewelry was there, intact, undamaged, and if I had involved the police... well, she hadn't actually taken the jewelry out of the house. I assumed that there wasn't much they were going to do that I hadn't already done," she added, looking at J.D., as if asking him to affirm what she'd said. He shrugged and nodded. She was right; there was no proof that there had been a theft. She went on, "So you can see why I said nothing to Patrick. He was going through hell, if I may say so, and since there was no damage done, I didn't want to add more to his burden."

"You still should have told me," the sheriff said, his voice pained. He moved toward his mother and took her hand. "I'm sorry I wasn't there for you."

"Nonsense," Cassandra said crisply, patting his forearm. "After all, nothing was lost or damaged. It's all over and done with. I hope you're not asking me to tell you where you might find this Julia, Detective Wilder," she added. "I can give you the name of the agency that recommended her, but I haven't heard from her nor seen her since the day she left."

J.D. stood up. "Mrs. Sutton, would you mind if we looked at your jewelry?" Cassandra Sutton stared at him. So did Corrie and the sheriff.

"Of course not," she said and rose from her chair. "But may I ask what you expect to find? It's been over five years since the incident and I have worn several of those pieces since then. I assure you nothing's missing."

"You haven't sent them out to be cleaned professionally,

have you?" J.D. asked as they stood by the armoire. It was made of dark cherry wood with gleaming brass handles. Cassandra reached into the bottom drawer of the nightstand and retrieved a small key from an envelope which she handed to J.D.

"Not since before they went missing five years ago," she said. "And I'm afraid my security measures aren't much more complex than they were back then," she said apologetically as he slipped the key out of the envelope. "But I haven't had so much as a pen go missing since Julia left."

J.D. nodded and unlocked the armoire. He pulled out the top drawer and sucked in a gasp, nearly drawing back in shock. He knew that the sheriff's family was wealthy; he knew the sheriff's mother was a socialite. What he didn't expect was the dazzling explosion of light reflecting off the vast number of diamonds and assorted jewels resting on a bed of black velvet. An opulent necklace of diamonds and rubies with matching earrings seemed to glow of its own accord. He pushed the drawer back in and pulled out the one below to find a similarly impressive jewelry set, this time with emeralds. He grew numb as he as checked drawer after drawer, seeing enough rings, bracelets, and necklaces to stock a jewelry store. Diamonds and gemstones of every kind, set in silver, gold, and platinum, worth an unimaginable amount of money, seemed to be safely stored away.

And yet....

He looked up. Neither Cassandra nor the sheriff seemed to be feeling anything but curiosity at his interest in the jewelry. Corrie seemed dazed, as if she had also been unaware of the magnitude of the sheriff's family's wealth. He gestured to the tray holding a necklace with a single large diamond. "Mind if I take a closer look?"

"Go ahead," Cassandra said, her head tilting to one side. J.D. held the stone up to the light, examining it from all angles, squinting as he studied the setting, and a heavy feeling settled in his gut. Mrs. Sutton shifted restlessly. "Is there anything wrong, Detective?"

"How often do you wear your jewelry, ma'am?"

She gave a short laugh. "Well, I certainly don't wear a different one every day just to go to lunch with my friends or go shopping. Most of these pieces are heirlooms and there are only a few I wear with any kind of regularity for special occasions. Perhaps once a year, for a formal fund-raising benefit."

He sighed. "How long would you say it was between the last

time you saw your jewelry and you discovered it missing?"

"Why?" This time it was the sheriff whose voice rang out. J.D. looked up at him grimly.

"I'm no expert, Sheriff, but I think you need to have someone more knowledgeable take a close look at these stones. Because I can almost guarantee they're fake."

Chapter 24

"That can't be!" Cassandra cried out in horror. She snatched up the large necklace in the top tray and brushed past Corrie as she strode toward the lamp in the sitting room. She turned it on as bright as it would go and rummaged in the small drawer of table until she found a jeweler's loupe. Somehow, it didn't surprise Corrie that she had one. Cassandra studied the stone in the setting and then the clasp and the setting itself. Her face paled and she glanced up at Rick.

"Let me see it, Mother," he said grimly. She handed him the loupe and the necklace and her hands were shaking. He took a minute to look closely at the stone and setting then he looked at J.D. and shook his head.

"Are you sure, Rick?" Corrie asked. He shrugged and shook his head.

"Not one hundred percent, no," he said. "But I think Wilder's right. Mother's family had some of the larger stones inscribed with serial numbers. Not all of them, but for sure this one would have had one. We'll have to get them examined by a jeweler to make sure."

"What happened? How can my jewels be fake?" Cassandra cried in bewilderment.

J.D. held up a hand. "Ma'am, let me ask you some questions and please don't take offense. You're sure that your jewelry was genuine, it wasn't ever duplicated for security reasons and the real jewels are stored elsewhere?"

"Detective, I assure you, I have always kept my jewelry here in my home and have never knowingly worn anything counterfeit for any reason," she said icily. Rick put an arm around his mother and rolled his eyes, careful not to let her see.

"No, ma'am, I'm sure of that, but your jewelry is a close enough duplicate that you haven't detected that it wasn't real. Someone had to switch out your genuine pieces and had them copied so professionally that you didn't notice right away, but it would take time to make counterfeit jewelry of that quality. How long did you say that Julia worked here?"

"Roughly about six months," Rick said.

"You're saying that she took the jewelry and had copies made? But why?" Corrie asked.

J.D. rubbed the back of his neck. "My guess is that Julia's credentials were as fake as these jewels and just as convincing.

She must have been part of a ring of thieves who took the time to make copies of the jewels and switch them for the real ones, which delayed discovery of the theft and gave them time to get away." He blew out his breath. "It's been five years since you've seen Julia? And since you'd never realized that your jewels were fake, you never filed a report with the police. So no one has been looking for them and, after five years, I'm not sure how good your chances are of recovering them. I'm sorry, Mrs. Sutton."

Cassandra put a hand to her throat and swallowed hard. "I can hardly believe it," she murmured. She looked at J.D. then at Rick. Her eyes met Corrie's and she shook her head. "Now what can be done?"

"First, we'll have to make sure Wilder's right, Mother," Rick said, patting her shoulder. "And then we'll file a report and do our best to find Julia and see if we can't recover your jewels." He cleared his throat. "We'll need to gather all the information we have about your jewelry, the insurance policies, anything we can turn over to investigators. Then we'll see...."

Cassandra straightened up and twisted her shoulders as if to shake off a chill. She raised her chin and looked Rick in the eye. "Patrick, I'm being selfish. This isn't important. Not compared to what you're going through right now. There will be plenty of time to deal with this after we clear your name. For now, I don't want to distract you or Detective Wilder from that task. I will get everything together and I'll file a report, but I don't want you—any of you," she added, looking around the room, "to give this anymore thought. I want your focus to remain on proving Patrick's innocence. Is that clear?"

"Yes, ma'am," they all answered, including Rick. Corrie allowed herself a small smile. Despite everything that was going on, the uncertainty of what the next day would bring, there was an obvious unity among them. She was relieved to know that Cassandra was never her enemy, and was not allowing a misunderstanding to stand between them now, although it pained her that it was probably too late.

We could have been friends. I might have liked having her as a mother-in-law, Corrie thought sadly and looked away, blinking, before anyone noticed the tears in her eyes. J.D. cleared his throat.

"It's late," he said. "Nothing is going to be settled or investigated tonight. I suggest we all try to get some rest so we can continue the investigation in the morning. I'm sorry we had to barge in on you like this, Mrs. Sutton."

She shook her head. "I couldn't sleep anyway. I might as well go ahead and start gathering all my paperwork for my jewelry, as well as look up the employee file for this Julia."

"Mother, don't tire yourself out," Rick said, his brow furrowing. "Waiting till morning isn't going to hurt anything."

"I'll be very surprised if any of us gets any sleep tonight," Cassandra remarked dryly. "I suspect the three of you will probably be brainstorming for a few hours. I'll be fine," she said firmly, ushering them to the door of her suite. "Maybe by tomorrow this will all just have been a nightmare and things will be back to normal. Good night," she added, before anyone could respond. They all murmured a response and Rick planted a kiss on his mother's cheek before they all stepped into the hall and the door shut behind them.

They made their way toward the stairs silently, each wrapped in his or her own thoughts. J.D. paused at the top of the stairs. "She's right," he said. "I won't be sleeping anytime soon, although you probably could use some rest, Sheriff."

"Not going to happen," Rick said bluntly. He looked at Corrie and she shook her head. He turned back to J.D. "I'm sure Luz has some piñon coffee in the pantry and she has a dual coffee maker. We're going to need plenty of caffeine, so let's get started."

Corrie fought back a yawn as she drained her third cup. Her eyelids were growing heavy and she marveled that both Rick and J.D. seemed alert as usual, if not more so. She couldn't even feel any irritation that they were both pretty much ignoring her as they hashed and re-hashed every minute detail of the last few days as well as events from five years earlier. She watched Rick closely as he told J.D. about the months leading up to Ava's birth. His face was impassive and his voice toneless; he had detached himself from the emotions surrounding his failed marriage and the death of his child in order to see what he might have missed during that terrible time in his life. Corrie marveled at the fact that he had once dived deeply into the bottle to escape thinking clearly and now realized that he had only trapped himself by doing so; his only hope of being cleared of Meghan's murder lay in looking closely at what he had once avoided.

"Did you think it was suspicious that Meghan wanted your mother to let Luz come work for the two of you, after she had been with your mother for so many years?" J.D. pressed.

"I did," Rick sighed, "but, at that point, nothing seemed to make Meghan happy so the fact that she was so adamant about wanting Luz to work for us, and the fact that having Luz around would make me feel like I wasn't so isolated, made me ignore any suspicions I had."

"How'd your mother feel about it?"

Rick shrugged. "On the one hand, she was relieved. She knew I was going through a lot, even though I didn't tell her much, and she obviously couldn't be there for me every minute. I think she felt the same way I did—having Luz in my household kept me from being too alone, made me feel that someone was on my side. She actually didn't want to hire a replacement for Luz, said that she could manage, but Meghan insisted on it, saying she would find someone from a reputable agency, even stating that we—well, I, actually—would pay for the temporary help." Rick gave a pained half-smile. "I had no problem with it, but it was odd, considering that Meghan hated it if I spent money on anything or anyone besides her."

"Your mother could certainly afford to pay for a new housekeeper without your help," J.D. remarked.

"More than I could at the time," Rick affirmed. "Not that I was hurting for money but, as I told Meghan, it was my family that was wealthy, not me. I went along with it because it seemed to make Meghan happier than she had been and having Luz there was a buffer between us."

"She wasn't happy about the baby, you told me," J.D. said, his voice gentler than it had been. Corrie shifted in her seat and both men looked her way. Maybe they'd forgotten she was there. She gestured for them to ignore her and continue their conversation. She got up to get the coffee pots to refill their cups and give her face time to return to its natural color. Avoiding Rick's eyes, she returned to her seat and tried to make herself invisible again.

Rick's face had also reddened slightly and he looked down into his cup. There were a lot of things that Corrie knew about his life and his struggles that he hadn't told her about—things she'd heard through the grapevine and things she herself had witnessed. She still recalled the night she'd heard that Meghan had served Rick with divorce papers. Though she'd kept her distance from him during the turmoil of the months of Meghan's pregnancy, she and Billy and most of the village had been aware that things weren't going well between Rick and Meghan. They had made sure to attend Ava's funeral and were stunned to discover that

Meghan wasn't there. Corrie had stifled the urge to ask him about Meghan when she hugged him after the graveside service—the first time she had been that close to him since their breakup in high school—but Delbert Otero, the mail carrier whose route had included the Black Horse Campground, Rick's apartment complex, and the hospital, had run into them at Dulcie's Bakery a few weeks after the funeral and whispered to them that he had witnessed Rick and Meghan's final fight as she checked herself out of the hospital the day after giving birth, while Ava fought her losing battle for life. "You ask me, it's over for them," Delbert had muttered, "but I dunno if Rick's gonna make it, losing 'em both pretty much on the same day." Dulcie Barreras, the bakery owner, was wiping down a nearby table and had overheard. She quickly made her way over to their table, shaking her head.

"It IS over," she murmured, as she made a show of filling their already-full coffee cups. "I heard that Rick got divorce papers delivered to him this morning... heard he called out from work and he NEVER does that...." Her voice trailed away as she moved back to the counter to serve more customers.

The words had sent a chill down Corrie's spine. She remembered seeing Rick's face as he stared at his daughter's grave and realized she was looking at a man who had lost the will to live. Without saying a word to Billy, she had slipped away from the campground that evening and gone to Rick's apartment. She had hoped he wouldn't have been there, that he had caved in to his mother's insistence that he come home to Tunstall for a while to regroup. Her heart had plummeted to her feet when she saw his truck in the parking lot of the apartment complex.

She had raced up the stairs, hoping against hope that Luz had remained at Rick's, although she knew that the housekeeper had returned to the Sutton house before Ava's funeral. Rick's apartment was dark. She rapped on the door. "Rick! It's Corrie!" Silence was the only response. Inexplicable panic flooded her heart and she knocked harder. "Please, Rick! Open the door! I just want to see if you're all right!" For a second, she wondered what his neighbors would think of her, but there were few cars in the parking lot and, at the moment, she didn't care what anyone would think. She decided she'd go to the apartment manager, though he'd probably think she was crazy to want him to open up Rick's apartment, but alarms were going off in her mind and her gut. She turned toward the window next to the door and saw that the blinds weren't closed all the way. It might be too dim to see inside but....

She went to the window and peered in. A muted light from the kitchen area cast a weak glow throughout the living room. When Corrie's eyes had adjusted to the shadowy interior, she gasped at what she saw. Rick was seated on the leather couch, hunched toward the glass coffee table, his elbows on his knees. A bottle of Crown Royal sat on the table, with a glass beside it. The pale light made the amber liquid gleam inside the cut crystal, but what horrified Corrie most was that Rick's service pistol also lay on the table and his eyes were fixed on it.

"Rick, no!" she had screamed, her fists pounding on the window pane, hoping she could break it, but it was too strong. Rick had to have heard her. His head slumped forward, but he didn't look her way. She was terrified of stepping away from the window, certain he wouldn't do anything if he knew she was watching, but she had to get to him somehow. Frantically, she glanced up and down the walkway outside the apartments, astonished that no one had heard her and come out. She spied a plant in a heavy, terracotta pot about three doors away. She jumped to her feet and ran to grab the plant. It was awkward and heavier than she had thought, but she hoped she could throw it hard enough to shatter the window. As she drew back to throw it, she heard a sound that made her heart stop... a loud, shattering bang....

She had dropped the pot, Rick's name frozen in her throat, and forced herself to look through the blinds again. Shaking uncontrollably, whimpering cries of "No, no, no...." escaping her lips, she blinked back tears and braced herself for what she would see.

The room was empty. Rick was gone. The top of the coffee table was shattered, along with the bottle of liquor and the tumbler. The pistol lay among the shards of glass. She blinked, relief making her knees weak. From somewhere inside the apartment, she heard a door shut. She crumpled to the floor, her heart hammering in her chest and she rested her throbbing forehead against the wall. "Thank you, thank you, thank you...." tumbled out of her lips and tears cascaded down her cheeks.

She had no idea how long she had huddled there, then she heard the sound of an engine starting. Her head jerked up and she looked over the railing in time to see Rick's truck backing out of its space. She had no idea how he had gotten to the parking lot without her seeing him, but her legs were shaking so badly she could barely wobble her way down the stairs. By the time she got to her own vehicle, his taillights were fading down the road. It took several minutes for her to calm down enough to be able to drive. Then, not knowing where Rick had gone, she went home.

Billy had been waiting for her, grim faced. She had stumbled into his arms, unable to say a word, but her sobs told her father all he needed to know. "It will be all right," Billy had soothed her. She wanted to snap at him how he could know such a thing, but she had also needed badly to hear those words.

Two months went by, while everyone in the village wondered about Rick's whereabouts. Cassandra Sutton had left town, to parts unknown as well, prompting even more speculation. Corrie had run into Luz at the general store and while she struggled to decide whether she should ask her about anything, Luz touched her arm and softly said, "Don't worry," then turned and bustled away.

Her head jerked up when J.D. spoke her name and she scrambled to bring herself back from the past. "I'm sorry, what did you say?" she stammered.

J.D.'s brow was furrowed, but he refrained from asking her what she had been thinking about. At least, not directly. "Do you recall hearing any scuttlebutt in the village around the time the sheriff's daughter passed? Anything regarding this Julia, or Ronald Brown, for that matter? We're running out of leads. We need something, and we need it soon."

She pursed her lips and spoke slowly as she thought hard, J.D.'s urgency spurring her sleepy brain to wake up. "Not that I recall. I mean, there was plenty of, uh, talk around that time, but I don't think it specifically had to do with those two people." She avoided Rick's eyes, knowing he was well aware that the talk had been all about him and Meghan. As far as she knew, what she had seen the night he left was unknown to everyone in the village except herself. She shrugged. "It was common knowledge that Rick's mother had hired a temporary replacement for Luz, so it was no shock when she left and, as far as I know, no one questioned her leaving. This is the first I've heard anything that suggested she was fired instead of just having been let go."

Rick let out a hollow laugh. "Trust Mother to do everything she could to keep it as quiet as possible." He shook his head then paused. He glanced at Corrie sharply. "Did you say Delbert Otero overheard Meghan and me at the hospital?"

"Yes," Corrie said and felt her cheeks heat up. "Listen, Rick, don't be mad at Delbert. I'm sure it was concern over you...." She

217

stopped when Rick stood up, his eyes brighter and more alive than they had been for days.

"I might be mistaken, but I think Delbert's mail route also included the funeral home. And didn't that witness at the insurance office today say he worked at the funeral home?"

J.D.'s face was grim as he nodded. "Possibly he was working there five years ago, around the time Ronald Brown was employed there?" He glanced at the clock and grimaced. "It's after midnight, Sheriff. I suggest we at least try to get some rest. We have a busy day tomorrow."

Chapter 25

Corrie was up early the next morning, but not before Rick and J.D. were already seated at the kitchen island, finishing up the breakfast that Rick had prepared for them. She shook her head and went to the coffee pot. "Did either of you actually take your own advice and get some rest?" she muttered as she filled her cup, thankful they had left some coffee in the pot.

Rick stood up, looking more clear-headed and bright-eyed than he had in the last few weeks. He went to the refrigerator and took a glass pie plate out. "Today is Luz and Manuel's day off," he said. "She always leaves ready-made meals for mother and she made a couple of quiches yesterday. She didn't want to take the day off, with everything that's going on, but I insisted on it. I made some home fries to go with the quiche and she left about a gallon of her salsa in the fridge, which might last us through the day."

Corrie smiled. Luz's salsa was legendary in the county. RaeLynn had spent the previous day as Luz's shadow in the kitchen and throughout the house, helping wherever she could, and she had borrowed several cookbooks from Luz's collection to take up to her room before bed. Corrie didn't doubt that RaeLynn had probably stayed up as late as they had, poring over them. Corrie helped herself to a slice of quiche and set it on a plate with a generous pile of potatoes and slid it into the microwave to warm up. She glanced at J.D. who was scrolling through his phone. "And what did you do, Detective? Play solitaire?"

"Very funny," J.D. said, getting up to refill his coffee cup. "I made sure we had some decent coffee along with the sheriff's preferred brew." He took a sip and raised an eyebrow at her. "Did you get any sleep?"

"Maybe. I know I closed my eyes a few times," she said. She set her cup down. "Did you come up with anything?"

J.D. shrugged. "We're trying to put this puzzle together but we're not sure if all the pieces came from the same box." He returned to his stool at the island and pushed a notepad over to her. The microwave dinged and Corrie retrieved her plate and sat down with her breakfast, hiding her surprise that Rick and J.D. were being so open with her about the investigation and wondering if Mrs. Sutton's words had made an impression on them. She looked at the notes with interest as J.D. went on, "It's just a list of known facts along with some things that need explanation or confirmation, like whether or not this witness, Warren Bradley, was working at the funeral home five years ago and if he knew Ronald Brown or heard anything about him possibly having met Meghan."

Corrie glanced up at Rick, but he seemed calm. He gave her his usual half-smile which reassured her that he was back in control of himself. She turned to J.D. "You would think that he had to have met her, if they were making the arrangements for...." Her voice trailed away as Rick shook his head.

"Meghan left Bonney before Ava had died. I was the one who made all the arrangements and I met with the owner of the funeral home, Martin Abeyta. I honestly don't recall having met with anyone else, especially Ronald Brown. Martin knew my mother's family and he took personal charge of the arrangements for Ava. One thing we're checking into today is just when Ronald Brown's employment ended with the funeral home."

Corrie looked up. "Is it just me, or does it seem weird to you that Ronald Brown and Julia both seem to have left their jobs right around the same time?"

"It's not just you," J.D. assured her. "You know how the sheriff feels about coincidences. Can't say I blame him, either," he added. "Neither Ronald Brown nor Julia were locals, both were hired about the same time, and both left their jobs—and town—at the same time."

"That's right, it's strange that they seemed to come to Bonney just to work those jobs and then leave. Did they have any ties to the community?" Corrie asked.

"You and the sheriff have lived here all your lives. If you two don't know...." J.D. shrugged. "We're going to make some inquiries, naturally, but it's been five years. We don't know how clear people's memories will be."

"Mine are perfectly clear." Cassandra Sutton appeared in the doorway, dressed in deceptively simple athletic wear which probably cost more than Corrie's monthly insurance premium. Not a strand of her hair was out of place and her face was perfectly made up. She had a manila folder under her arm. She set it on the kitchen island and accepted a cup of coffee from Rick. "Good morning, all. I see we've been busy." She tapped a finger on the folder. "This is the employment file on Julia Estrada-Howell. It includes the name of the agency that she was referred from, plus the dates of her employment. Naturally, all I have is information from the time she was working for me, but I'm sure I don't have to tell you how to do your jobs."

"Thank you, ma'am," J.D. said as she slid the folder toward him. He flipped it open and scanned the sheets within. "I'll start by looking up this agency...." Cassandra held up a hand.

"I'm sure my research skills aren't as good as yours, Detective Wilder," she said, "but I did make a quick internet search and couldn't find a listing for the agency."

Rick frowned. "Are you sure, Mother?" She gave him a small smile.

"No, as I said, my research skills are limited to being able to look up shopping websites and taking care of my bills and making payments. Of course, it's possible the agency went out of business some time ago...."

"Nothing ever completely disappears from the internet," J.D. interjected. "But I have an officer who is a whiz with computers and research. If there's anything about them at all, anywhere, I'm sure he'll find it." He glanced at the clock. "It's early, but I'm sure he's up, if not already on duty. Let me get hold of him." He left the room, punching in a number on his phone.

Corrie felt a slight air of constraint fall over the kitchen. Cassandra was watching her and Rick over the rim of her coffee cup. Corrie felt as if she should excuse herself, but she felt rooted to her stool, her breakfast forgotten. Rick had busied himself getting his mother a small dish of yogurt topped with fresh berries. She thanked him with a smile and then sighed and shook her head. "Are you all right?"

Corrie exchanged a glance with Rick. It wasn't clear who Cassandra was addressing. Rick spoke up. "I guess I'm doing fine, Mother, all things considered...."

"I meant the two of you," she interrupted. Her glacial eyes swung toward Corrie and she squirmed in her seat.

"Cassandra," she began, but Rick's mother waved a hand.

"I can tell that you two have had a falling out," she said dryly. "In spite of everything, I know your friendship has weathered a lot and I've always admired your loyalty to each other. All I want to say is this: Meghan couldn't destroy that while she was alive, so don't you let her destroy it now that she's gone."

Corrie felt heat creep up into her cheeks and she couldn't look at Rick. She managed a tiny nod and Rick mumbled gruffly, "Yes, Mother." She was grateful when J.D. came back into the kitchen, looking grimly satisfied.

"Officer Camacho is on it. I took pictures of the employment

221

papers and texted them to him. It might take a while, but I asked him to try to track down Julia Estrada-Howell and see what he can find out about her."

"I knew I should have had a background check done on her," Cassandra Sutton said with a sigh. "But Meghan was so insistent on hurrying to hire her before someone else snapped her up, I didn't... what is it, Detective?" she said, startled. J.D. was staring at her.

"Meghan hired her," he said quietly. He looked at Rick. "Did she run a background check on this Julia?"

Rick rubbed his chin. "I don't know," he said after a few seconds. "She was so insistent on taking charge of hiring a temporary replacement for Luz that I just let her do it all. She seemed glad to do it and eager to take care of the whole thing and... I didn't want to rock the boat," he added. His eyes narrowed. "What are you getting at, Wilder?"

J.D. held up both hands. "I don't know, really," he confessed. "I just find it odd that she suddenly took on the task of hiring someone new for someone else... unless it was going to benefit her in some way."

"She got Luz to look after her and Rick's home," Corrie pointed out. "Meghan wouldn't have had to lift a finger and Luz is an amazing cook. Why wouldn't she want to do what she could to get her?"

Rick was shaking his head. "But she didn't have to hire a housekeeper for Mother. All I had to do was say that I wanted Luz and both Mother and Luz would have agreed to it. You're right," he said, turning to J.D. "That was out of character for Meghan."

"One of several things that were out of character for her," J.D. said. Rick looked grim.

"Mother, do you think Martin Abeyta would be willing to meet with us before he opens the funeral home for the day?"

"I'm sure he will," Cassandra said as she rose from her seat. She glanced at the wall clock and saw it was just after six in the morning. "I'm supposed to meet some friends for breakfast in Ruidoso at eight. I'll call him now and see how soon he can meet you. Martin takes calls day and night," she added, turning to J.D. who was beginning to protest that it was too early to be bothering anyone. She waved away his concern. "He wants to be available if anyone needs his services," she explained as she left the kitchen. Rick followed Cassandra out into the great room, speaking to her in hushed tones. J.D. studied Corrie closely.

"Are you doing all right?" he asked quietly, touching her arm. She managed a smile and covered his hand with hers and gave it a squeeze.

"All things considered, I suppose I could be doing much worse," she said, keeping her voice low. "I'm still homeless and I still don't know who burned down my campground or why and I'm still not sure what the insurance company will do. My claim, assuming it does get approved, will probably be delayed due to Meghan's death." She drew a deep breath, trying to figure out how to best say what was on her mind, but she looked up into J.D.'s silver-gray eyes, so full of concern and repressed tenderness, and she tightened her grip on his hand and blurted, "I need to find another place to stay, J.D. I can't keep staying here much longer."

"Whoa," J.D. said, sinking onto the stool beside her. "Easy now. What's wrong? Did Mrs. Sutton say anything...?"

"No," Corrie said, shaking her head for emphasis. "Good Lord, no. Rick and his mother haven't said anything to make me feel that I, or the rest of my staff, have worn out our welcome. But we can't stay here forever...."

"Three days is hardly forever," J.D. said, giving her shoulder a little shake. "Come on, what's bothering you?"

She shrugged, and holding back tears seemed like a struggle. "Just that... it's hard to keep on acting like everything is okay between Rick and me. I mean," she shook her head again, "it seems like everyone thinks that now that Meghan is gone, all that needs to be done is clear Rick of her murder and everything will be just fine between us. Like the last fifteen years hadn't happened." She drew in a shaky breath. "I don't know how to explain it," she finished weakly. J.D. gave her a smile.

"Not everyone thinks everything is okay," he said. "And no one is expecting you to act like it is. Look, Corrie, don't think we've forgotten about you and the Black Horse just because of what happened to Meghan."

"It's all connected, I know," she said with a sigh. "But I thought that if we found out who burned my campground, it might tell us who murdered Meghan, and vice versa. It wasn't that guy she married in Mexico, and now it seems like the man who might have done it was here in Bonney when Rick's daughter died. It's all a big, jumbled mess in my brain," she said, dropping her head into her hands. J.D. squeezed her shoulder.

"We'll get to the bottom of this, Corrie. I promise." He stood up and glanced at the wall clock. "What have you got planned for today?"

"I don't even know what day it is," she groused with a shrug. "I know that the Pages and Myers were going to work on their own insurance claims and see about setting up a new address for their mail." She paused, realizing that, with the Black Horse gone, neither the Pages nor the Myers really had anything to tie them to Bonney. Would they think this would be a good time to step away, go on with their lives elsewhere? A chill touched her heart. She knew that Jerry and Jackie considered themselves family and would steadfastly refuse to leave unless she was settled in... somewhere. Was that fair to them? She wasn't a child; their duty to her and her parents that they took on when she lost her mother years ago was completed. She couldn't ask them to do any more than they already had. But the thought of losing them along with the Black Horse.... She shrugged again, shaking off the cold feeling. "I don't know, I'm sure I've got a lot to do. What are you and Rick doing?" she asked, hoping to divert his attention.

He was studying her closely, sensing how fragile she felt and deciding against pushing her too hard. "I've got Camacho checking up on Julia and the sheriff and I are going to go talk to the funeral director...." His voice trailed away when Rick came back into the kitchen, his cell phone to his ear, and a dark, thunderous look on his face.

"No, sir," he said forcefully, beckoning to J.D. "Ms. Stratham is no longer in charge of any arrangements. My daughter's remains will remain where they are, interred at the San Ignacio cemetery. I understand, but I'm on my way over there to discuss.... What? What about it?" Rick paused with his hand reaching for the doorknob. He shook his head, as if the person on the other end could see him. "There won't be any transfer of my daughter's remains. I'll be talking to you shortly." He sighed irritably.

"What's going on, Sheriff?" J.D. asked sharply. Corrie stared as Rick slapped a hand on the kitchen island, his face red with fury.

"Meghan had me sign that contract to have Ava's remains moved to Dallas. Martin Abeyta says that contract is still in effect."

"How, Rick? Meghan's dead," Corrie said bluntly. She stood up and planted her hands on her hips. "Surely that cancels the contract, doesn't it?"

"I would imagine it would," Rick said. J.D.'s head jerked up.

"Did she give you a copy of the contract?" he asked.

Rick blinked. He frowned and shook his head. "No," he said. "She didn't. She just gave me the copy of her marriage certificate, just like we agreed."

"You read the contract you signed, right?" J.D. said, his voice growing more urgent. Corrie stepped forward and grabbed J.D.'s arm.

"What are you getting at?" she asked. He looked grim.

"I'm willing to bet that the contract he signed wasn't just between him and Meghan. In fact, I can almost guarantee that Meghan wasn't a single party in that contract."

"What are you talking about, Wilder?" Rick snapped. "Why would Meghan want to have anyone else on the contract? It was strictly between us, it was about Ava! Why would anyone else have anything to do with it?"

"Meghan might not have planned it," J.D. said. "But if she had someone write it up for her, whoever did it might have wanted it between Meghan as part of an entity and you. As for why? That someone wanted to make sure that if something happened to Meghan, the contract wouldn't be nullified."

Corrie shook her head, as bewildered as Rick looked. "Why are you so sure that someone else was involved, J.D.? What evidence do you have?" He spun to look at her, his gray eyes as sharp as a steel blade.

"Because someone murdered Meghan and I'm positive it wasn't a crime of passion. Someone wanted her out of the way and someone got her—and Alex Durán—out of the way. The funeral home is taking care of Alex Durán as well as Meghan, isn't it?"

Rick shook his head in a daze. "Possibly Durán, since they're waiting for someone to claim him. As for Meghan, surely her family will want to make their arrangements."

"Let's go find out," J.D. said, slapping Rick's arm and urging him toward the door. "We need to see if Mr. Abeyta remembers Ronald Brown from five years back and we might stop by Meghan's office and see if that contract is anywhere to be found." And they were gone before Corrie could say another word.

Corrie paced the main room, causing Renfro and Oliver to glare at her for disturbing their rest, although her sneakers didn't make much sound on the hardwood floor. RaeLynn, perched on the edge of the leather sofa, implored her to sit still for just a few minutes. "You're only making yourself more nervous," she added.

Corrie couldn't argue with her. However, sitting still wasn't going to help either. "I'm sorry, RaeLynn, I know I'm probably driving you nuts. I'm trying to make sense of everything but I feel like *I'm* going crazy." She paused and took a deep breath. She massaged her temples. A half-formed idea shimmered at the edge of her brain, something she had heard, or thought she had heard, teased her memory. "We're missing something," she murmured.

"I'm sure Rick and Detective Wilder will figure it out," RaeLynn said, hopefulness being the prevalent tone of her voice. "We all know Rick could never hurt anyone. They'll find the proof that someone else killed Meghan and...."

"They have to," Corrie said glumly. She tried not to think of what would happen if they couldn't find another suspect in Meghan's murder. Surely there had to be evidence that someone besides Rick could have....

Me. Corrie shuddered and wrapped her arms around herself. *I could be a suspect. After what I said about wanting to kill her....* But she had an alibi, a solid one, for the time that Meghan was killed. They needed something else, someone else, any little thing that could....

She and RaeLynn jumped when the doorbell rang. They looked at each other as it rang again and again. Finally Corrie hurried to the foyer to open it, remembering that Luz and Manuel were off for the day. She paused, her hand on the knob and looked at the security pad next to the door where a screen showed who was standing on the porch. She frowned for a second as the woman, clad in a heavy winter coat and wearing a scarf around her head glanced around before pressing the doorbell again.

"Who is it?" RaeLynn asked, her face white and her eyes round with fear. The woman began to pound on the door and Corrie suddenly recognized her.

"It's Sheila Larsen, from the insurance company," she said as she pulled the door open.

"Corrie!" Sheila gasped as she practically fell across the threshold. She gripped Corrie's arm, but it seemed to be more from anxiety than from concern about losing her balance. "Oh, thank God someone's home! I was afraid I came all this way and no one would be here!"

"Calm down, Sheila," Corrie said, stepping back and allowing the agitated woman to enter. RaeLynn moved forward to shut and lock the door since Sheila kept a tight grip on Corrie. "Come in and sit down," Corrie said soothingly as she tried to lead her to the seating area near the fireplace.

"I'll go make some tea," RaeLynn offered. Sheila shook her head.

"I need to talk to the sheriff," she said urgently. "This can't wait! I heard that he's a suspect in Meghan's murder!"

"I guess the grapevine is as active as ever," Corrie said dryly. "If you need to see Rick, why did you come here? Why didn't you go to his office?"

"Because I heard the state has taken over the investigation and it sounds like they believe Sheriff Sutton did this! I know he and Meghan had lots of problems—she was always saying terrible things about him, although I'm sure she was making things up to be dramatic—and it makes him look guilty, but I'm sure he had nothing to do with her murder! He's too honest, too much of a good person, no matter how awful she was. He would never hurt anyone, not even her! I wanted to bring this to him," she added, pulling a large manila envelope out from under her coat and handing it to Corrie. It was addressed to Abeyta Funeral Home with Rick's return address at his apartment. She looked up at Sheila, frowning.

"What is this? Why did you bring it here?" she asked. Sheila grimaced.

"I was going to take it to his place in town," she explained. "But I saw that the investigators were there, probably searching his place, so I looked up the address for his family home. We have both addresses on file with the company. I wanted him to have this...."

"What is it?" Corrie interrupted. She stared at the envelope, marveling that it wasn't trembling along with her hands.

Sheila took a deep breath. "It was supposed to have been mailed a few days ago, before the fire at the Black Horse. I don't know what it is. It's got to be something personal. Meghan left it on my desk and I just put it all together with the mail I needed to take to the post office. But then she suddenly decided to shut down the office and I never got around to it. When I went in to the office

228

yesterday, as I passed by my desk I saw the pile of mail and felt guilty that I hadn't sent it all out... I mean, a lot of what needed to be mailed out pertained to people's claims and I hate to make people wait on answers. So I picked it up and put it in my tote bag, because I thought if Meghan was in a bad mood and told me to leave, I could at least send all this out." She bit her lip and tears formed in her eyes. "Then I found her... and I forgot all about the mail." She drew a deep breath. "I heard that nothing was missing from the office. I assume no one else knew about the outgoing mail... I'm not sure what to do now," Sheila whimpered, tears running down her cheek. "I mean, I thought I should report it to the police before I went to the post office but when I saw that there was something addressed to the funeral home, I... I was confused. I had no idea what it was, but I couldn't understand why something coming from our office would have the sheriff's return address. I was afraid to tell the police. I was afraid they might use it against Sheriff Sutton. I don't know what to do," she said miserably. "I don't want to get in trouble with the police for tampering with evidence or...."

"You did the right thing, Sheila," Corrie heard herself saying. She tried to avoid RaeLynn's incredulous look. "I'll be sure to let Rick know about this. And I promise you, he'll do the right thing with it. He didn't kill Meghan," Corrie added firmly, relieved to see Sheila nodding eagerly. "So there's nothing here that will make trouble for him. I'm sure of it," she went on with more confidence than she felt.

"I'm so glad I came here," Sheila said, releasing a huge sigh and giving Corrie a smile that indicated she'd had a huge weight lifted off her shoulders, even as Corrie felt herself being crushed by the information she'd been given. WAS she doing the right thing? Was SHE now the one who was suppressing evidence? She banished the concerns from her mind. The only thing that mattered was whatever was in the envelope... and she hoped it wasn't going to create more problems for Rick. She cleared her throat.

"Thanks again for bringing this out here," she repeated. "I'm sure you had more important things to do than driving way out here." She paused, then stared at Sheila in confusion. "Um, Sheila... how did you get through the gate?"

"The gate?" Sheila looked puzzled. "Well, it was open, of course."

Corrie blinked. The gate was open? Normally someone would have to press the buzzer at the gate to request permission to enter and have someone open the gate from the house. Luz and Manuel were both gone so how could Sheila have gotten through the gate, unless it had been left open...? That was unlike Rick or Cassandra; they were both meticulous about making sure everything was done properly. They had to be under a lot of stress to forget to shut the gate. She shook her head. "Okay," she said. "I'm sure if Rick has any questions, he'll get back to you."

Sheila Larsen's face registered apprehension, then resignation. "I'll talk to him," She said reluctantly. "But I hope those other cops won't ask me anything. I don't want to lie but I certainly don't want to help them put handcuffs on the sheriff!"

Corrie cringed at the image. She hoped she wasn't the one doing that instead of Sheila. She saw the older woman out and stood watching as she got in her car and drove away. She glanced at the security screen and frowned. The picture changed to the feed from a camera at the gate. It showed the gate standing wide open as Sheila's car came into range of the camera sensor. Corrie shook her head. There must be a way to close the gate from the house, but she had no idea how and she wasn't about to try to get hold of Rick or Cassandra to ask them. She shut and locked the front door and turned her attention to the envelope in her hands.

"What do you think it is?" RaeLynn asked, twisting her hands together. Corrie gave her a wry smile and shook her head.

"I have no idea, but I'm not about to open it and look. As much as I'd like to," she added. It wasn't a thick envelope, so whatever it contained was only a couple of pages at most.

"It could be a clue to who killed Meghan," RaeLynn went on. Corrie shot her a suspicious glance.

"RaeLynn...," she began but RaeLynn shook her head.

"I'm not saying you should open it without Rick's permission," she said. "But can't you call him and tell him that Sheila brought this over? He might want you to open it to see what's inside," she urged.

"That's true," Corrie said. She could already hear Rick chewing her out for wanting to snoop through his personal papers. She grimaced, thinking of how close she had come to looking through his mail from his father. She turned and headed for the office.

"What are you doing?" RaeLynn asked, inexplicably keeping her voice to a whisper as she hurried after Corrie.

"Trying to avoid temptation," Corrie muttered. She opened the office door and went to the desk. She pulled the drawer open and cast a guilty glance at the bundle of letters. She took the envelope that Sheila had given her and slipped it into the drawer, under an address book, planner, the pen tray, and the letters. She pushed it as far back as it would go then shut the drawer. Turning to RaeLynn, she drew a deep breath. "Now I'll call Rick and, in case he says to leave it alone, it'll be easier to do that if it's in this drawer rather than having it in my hand."

As they pulled into the parking lot of the Abeyta Funeral Home, J.D. fought back a shiver that had little to do with the icy wind that dropped the morning temperature to just below freezing. The place was deserted and dark at this early hour; no other staff but the funeral director were on duty before nine in the morning. Martin Abeyta was waiting for them at the back door when they pulled in.

"Sorry to have you come in so early in this weather," the sheriff said, as the director ushered them into the building.

"No need to apologize, Rick," the man said, shaking J.D.'s hand, "I know this can't be easy for you, with all that's going on right now and then having to deal with painful stuff from the past." He led them down a long hallway, past an elegantly appointed lobby, toward his office at the opposite end of the building. J.D. had braced himself before entering—anytime in the past that he'd had reason to be in a funeral home, there had always been an odor of antiseptic mixed with exotic floral fragrances and... something else that made his stomach churn. He was glad that the doors to the chapel and viewing room were firmly shut and the only thing he smelled was the welcome aroma of freshly-brewed coffee. Martin Abeyta invited them to sit and poured them each a cup of coffee before settling behind his desk. He took a sip from his own cup and came right to the point. "You want to know about the arrangements Meghan made, regarding transferring your daughter's remains to Dallas."

"Those arrangements are cancelled due to Meghan's death," the sheriff said. It wasn't a question, but Abeyta looked pained.

"Rick," he said then hesitated and looked at J.D. as if to ask him for help. J.D. had no idea what was going on and knew his face conveyed that. Abeyta sighed. "I got a call yesterday evening after... after the news broke about Ms. Stratham's death. It was a man who claimed to want to verify that the arrangements were going to proceed as planned. I was surprised and I asked him why, since Ms. Stratham was deceased. He said that he had a contract stating that Ms. Stratham's company had the right to enforce her wishes, despite the fact that she was no longer alive. I found that hard to believe, but I checked and saw that we DID have a note regarding a contract for the exhumation and transfer signed by our office and signed by a representative of Meghan's company...."

"Wait a minute," the sheriff said, raising a hand. "What representative? And what about my wishes? I'm... Ava's father," he managed to choke out, "and whatever agreement I had with Meghan was nullified by her death."

"Not according to the contract we have," Abeyta said. He opened a folder on his desk and pushed a paper across the desk toward Sutton. "It shows a line for your signature on an agreement between you and Stratham Enterprises, not just Ms. Stratham. By law, as long as any members of the parties making the agreement are alive, then the contract must stand."

"What?" Sutton snatched up the paper and stared at it in disbelief. J.D. disregarded common courtesy and stood up to read over the sheriff's shoulder. Sure enough, at the bottom, next to Sutton's blank signature line was Meghan's name, next to a signature line that read "legal representative, Stratham Enterprises". The sheriff shook his head. "This can't be right," he stammered and shook his head. "Why would Meghan's company want to have anything to do with our daughter's final resting place?"

Martin Abeyta shrugged. "Rick, I have no idea. However, our copy of the contract doesn't have your signature on it. The person who called said Meghan had the original contract that WAS signed. Her office was supposed to have had it mailed to us, but it hasn't arrived yet."

The sheriff's head jerked up and his eyes met J.D.'s. J.D. raised a brow. "Sheriff, do you remember signing anything regarding Ava's transfer?"

"Yes, I did," Sutton said, his voice low. "But it was supposed to be between Meghan and me, not anyone else, certainly not Meghan's company. Why would she want to have them involved in a purely personal matter?"

Abeyta cleared his throat. "Rick, I'm sorry, but if this contract does arrive here, I don't have a choice but to comply with the arrangements Meghan made. The person who called said they would take legal action, if necessary."

Sutton shook his head. "No way, Martin. Sorry. Not until I talk to whoever at Stratham Enterprises is supposed to be enforcing this contract. Do you know who it is?"

Martin Abeyta shook his head. "No. I never talked to anyone but Meghan, not until this call came in yesterday." He shifted uncomfortably. "And before you ask, no, I didn't get his name. He seemed agitated and just wanted to make sure things would go forward as planned."

"And are they?" J.D. asked.

"Well, no," Abeyta said. "Because we don't have that contract with Rick's signature on it." He had to have noted the confusion on J.D.'s and the sheriff's faces and he went on, "See, when we handled the plans for Rick's daughter, he was the only one who had any legal right to make decisions. If he signed a contract to allow Ms. Stratham—or anyone else—the right to make those decisions, we'd have to abide by that. But since we don't have that contract, we can't go forward with Ms. Stratham's wishes."

"Did you tell the caller that?" J.D. asked, suddenly feeling his gut twist. Abeyta nodded slowly. "Then what happened?"

"He said he'd make sure we'd get it and hung up," the funeral director said. He turned to Sutton. "So, for the time being, your daughter's final resting place won't be disturbed. I made it clear to the caller that nothing will be done until I have that contract in hand."

The sheriff looked relieved, but J.D. felt a cold dread settle on his shoulders. It seemed that Sutton didn't seem to be aware of the implications of what Abeyta was telling them—the fact that the contract he had signed had gone missing since Meghan's death was just another nail in the sheriff's coffin. It gave the sheriff another motive for getting rid of his ex. J.D. cleared his throat. "Mr. Abeyta, I'm sorry to change the subject but we also wanted to ask you some questions about a former employee. He happened to be here when the sheriff's daughter passed away. Does the name Ronald Brown ring a bell?"

Abeyta frowned. "No, but then that was five years ago. I'm sure we'll have information in our files." He got up and headed for the file cabinet in the corner. He searched through two drawers before bringing two folders to the desk. "Employee records for five years ago," he said, pushing one file toward Sutton, "and records of funerals from the month Rick's daughter passed. I'm afraid I don't have the complete file here, it would be in our storage room."

"Would this information include who handled the

arrangements?" J.D. asked. Sutton focused his attention on the employee file and didn't glance at the other one. J.D. couldn't blame him. He flipped open the folder as Abeyta answered.

"It should," the funeral director said, "but I've had a couple of different secretaries over the years who kept records differently. Since I rarely have to look this information up, I never worried about it."

Sutton finished flipping through the file in his hand and shook his head. "No Ronald Brown in the employee records. But that's no surprise. You said the information you received indicated he was working under a different name."

"Yeah, but they didn't know what it was," J.D. said. He quickly looked over the scant amount of paperwork on Ava Sutton's funeral. He shook his head. "No names." He glanced up at Martin Abeyta. "How much employee turnover do you have?"

"Quite a bit," Abeyta sighed. "I get a lot of interns, people getting some experience before moving on to other jobs, either in the funeral business or other areas where they have to come in contact with the deceased. Since I don't exactly have a waiting list of people wanting to work here, I take anyone who's willing to come to this tiny little town to help me out."

Sutton took out his phone and brought up the photo of Ronald Brown. He held it out to Abeyta. "I know it's been five years, but does this guy look familiar to you at all?"

Abeyta took the phone and stared at the screen. "Maybe. This guy might be a bit heavier, a little more bald. But as for a name," he shook his head and started to hand the sheriff's phone back. "I'm sorry, but I don't… wait," he said, taking the phone back and scrutinizing the photo more closely. He pursed his lips. "I do remember one of the guys I had employed around that time. He still works for me occasionally and is extremely reliable. George Williams is his name. He's kind of a jack-of-all-trades, including mortician. He comes around two or three times a year and helps out. I remember," he went on, "that he had a complaint about one employee around that time and I'm positive it was him!" he said, indicating the picture on the screen.

"What kind of complaint?" J.D. said.

"He didn't really elaborate," Abeyta said. "Just said that there was 'something not right' about him." Abeyta's eyes looked faraway as he sifted through his memories. "They butted heads a few times. This guy had already been here a few months when George came back to do his usual six week or so stint. That was right before," he paused, his gaze cutting toward the sheriff and then cleared his throat. "Well, anyway, George said this guy was pretty unfriendly, didn't want to let George work with him, was rude when he spoke to him, but mostly ignored him. I remember George saying that this fellow would get really irate if George ever stepped in to assist with any, er, preparations. I was concerned because I didn't want to lose either one of them—as I said, I don't have an excess of employees. This guy made it a point to tell me, flat out, that he would tend to Ava's funeral by himself and he didn't want George to butt in." He blew his breath out and shook his head. "I hated to tell George about it, but he took it in stride. Which was nice of him, seeing as how he knew the story," he added, nodding toward the sheriff. "He commented that, seeing it was going to be a, uh, closed casket service, he wouldn't make any waves and let this guy handle it."

"Can you get hold of this George Williams?" J.D. asked Abeyta. The funeral director shrugged and held out his hands.

"I can try," he said. "Usually he gets in touch with me. I have a number for him, but I've never called it. He's told me he only has it for emergencies. He's due to come around in another month or so, but I'll try." He pulled out his cell phone and punched in a number. He waited a few seconds, then looked at J.D. and mouthed "Voice mail" to him before he spoke up. "Hey, George, this is Martin Abeyta in Bonney. Give me a call when you get a chance, I have a few...." He stopped when they heard a knock on the front door of the building. Abeyta frowned and got up from his desk and made his way toward the entrance, with J.D. and the sheriff right behind him, J.D.'s hand on his weapon. A tall, gangly man with a bushy salt-and-pepper beard that was being whipped around his face by the wind stood framed in the glass doors, a cell phone to his ear. He pointed at Abeyta and they could hear his voice through the doors:

"You want to talk to me, Marty?"

Chapter 27

"Yeah, I remember him," George said, sipping a cup of coffee after having been introduced to both LEOs and shown the picture of the man who called himself Ronald Brown. He eyed the detective's badge clipped to Wilder's belt and raised a brow. "He in some kind of trouble?" He shook his head and went on before anyone could answer. "Sorry, dumb question. Of course he's in trouble, or the cops wouldn't be asking about him. What do you need to know?"

"His name would be a good start," Wilder said. "Do you remember it?"

"Called himself Rob Cowen." Martin began flipping through the employment records until he found it and he pushed it across the desk to Rick. "But I could tell that wasn't his real name. Couple of times, I spoke to him and he didn't respond right away. I kinda ribbed him about it, said, 'Man, you need a name tag or something? You forget your own name?' That's when he'd get irritated and snippy with me. Then one time I thought I heard him give his name on the phone as 'Ron'. He caught himself, pretended that he had to clear his throat, tried to make it seem like I heard him wrong." George set his cup down and shook his head. "But what bugged me most about him was his girlfriend."

"Girlfriend?" Rick glanced at Wilder, wondering if he'd heard wrong. Wilder looked perplexed. "He had a girlfriend? What about her?"

George stroked his beard and narrowed his eyes. "She was shady, even more shady than he was. She'd come around, two or three times a week, pull him out of work to talk to him for about a half hour, real secretive, then take off quick. Tried to be friendly once, asked him about her and all, and he just told me to mind my business. Real rude. Not jealous, though. Just made it clear he didn't want me asking any questions." As if he could read Rick's mind, he went on, "She was nice-looking, dark hair and eyes, kind of petite. I think she worked as a housekeeper or something. Once she showed up, kind of unexpected like—at least, he seemed surprised and not real happy to see her—and she was in a uniform—black with white trim, with an apron. That was the last time I saw her, come to think of it," he said, sitting up straighter. He shot a keen glance at both Rick and Wilder. "I'm not sure, but I think he called her 'Judy' or 'Julie'."

Julia. What had his mother's housekeeper been doing talking to Ronald Brown? Rick took a steadying breath and resisted the urge to glance at Wilder. "Is that all she did, just come talk to this guy?"

"First time that I saw her, I thought she was bringing him a sack lunch," George said. "He went out to meet her and she got out of her car with a brown paper bag in her hand. He kinda snatched it from her and they had a little spat. After that, whenever she came by, she'd wait for him in the car until he came out to see her."

"You never saw her give him a bag again?" Wilder asked sharply, while Rick's heart began to pound. George shook his head.

"No, but once or twice, I saw him give her a shopping bag. I don't know what was in it. By that time, I'd learned my lesson and I didn't ask him any questions." He shifted in his seat. "I never said anything to Marty. Didn't want to make any waves, didn't want this guy to get mad and leave Marty in a bind. I wasn't going to be around much longer, my time here was almost up. Besides, I never saw him do anything wrong. He was just a jerk. But now it looks like maybe I should've said something. What's this guy done?"

"Too much to get into," Wilder said. He glanced at Rick and jerked his head toward the door. "Let's go, Sheriff."

Rick thanked Martin and he and Wilder hurried out to the Tahoe.

"We have to find that contract," Sutton said as they drove toward the sheriff's office. J.D. reached over and grabbed the sheriff's arm.

"Not so fast, Sheriff," he said. "You need to be careful." Sutton shot him an incredulous glance and J.D. went on, "Don't you get it? That contract is another motive for getting rid of Meghan. Without your signature, she couldn't have Ava moved!"

"I'm more concerned about why she would want to have Ava moved even if she weren't around. Think about it, Wilder," he said, a renewed urgency in his voice and eyes, "Meghan wasn't a morbid person. She wouldn't do anything that didn't benefit her directly. Someone else wanted to make sure that Ava got moved even if Meghan wasn't around!"

J.D. stared at him, his mind spinning. Sutton had a point. Why would Stratham Enterprises have any interest in where the sheriff's daughter was buried? Only Meghan would care... unless there was someone in her organization to whom it mattered....

But why? For what reason?

The sheriff went on, "You said that your source told you that Ronald Brown had a lot of diverse interests in Mexico. And now George just told us that my mother's housekeeper was meeting him regularly. Did Brown have anything to do with jewelry?"

"Yeah, jewelry stores. He knew how to make and repair jewelry or he had someone who could and that's how he was able to replace real jewels with fake ones and avoid raising alarms before they got away. And he dealt in real estate and was connected to employment agencies. That must be how he got Julia hired on with your mother." His eyes met the sheriff's and they were as wide as J.D.'s. "And Meghan was the one who actually found Julia and hired her! Do you suppose...?"

"Meghan was after Mother's jewels? Somehow that doesn't seem as farfetched as I might have thought at one time." The sheriff's jaw rippled. "It all fits," he muttered. "Meghan met Alex Durán in Mexico. Durán and Brown were accomplices...."

"What odds that this Julia was Alex Durán's wife?"

Sutton nodded. "Brown got them jobs, they stole jewelry and other valuables, Brown would sell the jewelry or replace the stones and sell them, and the cycle would keep going. Meghan, for some reason, decided to get involved... probably because she already knew she wouldn't be the rich socialite wife she wanted to be. She found out who my family was and decided she could pull off the heist of a lifetime. She'd be set even after we divorced."

J.D. let out a low whistle. A lot of it made sense. But why didn't Meghan just leave with the jewels once she and Sutton divorced? Why did she keep coming around? Could it be sheer vindictiveness that kept her coming back and demanding that their child be moved to Dallas? That didn't jibe. "You think anyone is going to believe this?"

"We'll find out once we get that contract and see who actually signed it. I have to admit that I never saw Meghan's signature. I wasn't thinking straight. She insisted I sign it first. After that, all I cared about was getting the copy of her marriage certificate and having her approve Corrie's insurance claim." He drew a deep breath. "I don't know if it will be enough to prove I didn't kill Meghan, but I'm hoping it will convince those investigators to track down and take a closer look at Ronald Brown... and find out if he was the one behind the fire at the Black Horse."

239

"I never thought in this day and age that I'd have to deal with phone lines being down," Corrie muttered, slamming down the receiver in frustration.

Once upon a time, she had been given a cell phone—a combination gag gift from both Rick and J.D and serious attempt to keep her safe. She had not bothered to replace it after it was destroyed in an attempt on her life although both men, along with Jerry and Jackie, had bugged her to get a new one. And RaeLynn had never felt the necessity to own one. Both women spent most of their days at the campground where a phone was always nearby. Now they were both stuck with the need to get hold of Rick and J.D. and no way to contact them. RaeLynn had gone to see if the Pages or Myers would let them use their cell phones, only to discover that they had gone out to breakfast and tend to errands in town. They had left a note on the door of their RV, stating that they didn't want to disturb them so early in the morning and that they would be home sometime in the afternoon.

"What about email?" RaeLynn suggested. "Surely both Rick and Detective Wilder have email on their phones."

"Right," Corrie said glumly. "Would you happen to know their email addresses? I don't think I've ever sent either of them an email."

RaeLynn's face fell. "No, I don't. Maybe email their offices? Or is there a way to message them? Surely someone there can get hold of them," she said.

Corrie agreed, hoping that she wasn't going to stir up a hornet's nest by asking for Rick to get hold of her. She had no idea where the investigation was at this point and she wasn't likely to find out anything any time soon. She and RaeLynn went up to the room where J.D. was staying, stopping briefly to let Renfro and Oliver into her bedroom, and the two women hesitated outside the door, looking at each other. "I feel like I'm barging in," Corrie murmured. RaeLynn nodded, staying back. Corrie took a deep breath and opened the door. The room was as neat and sterile as a hotel room. Of course, J.D. didn't have many more possessions than Corrie and RaeLynn did; everything except the clothes on his back had been burned along with his cabin. Corrie's hopes had soared when she saw that he had left the desktop computer on, but were dashed when she saw that he had logged out of his email account. She hoped that there was an instant message option she could use. She found the website for the Bonney Police

Department, relieved that the internet connection was working, and quickly typed out a message asking for someone to let J.D. or Rick know that she needed to speak to them as soon as possible. She added that the phone lines were down when a pop-up message informed her that she should call 9-1-1 if there was an emergency, which stirred up feelings of uneasiness.

What would they do if there were an emergency?

She sat back and drummed her fingers on the desktop. RaeLynn hovered over her, wringing her hands. "How long do you think it'll be till they answer?" she asked.

Corrie bit back a grin; RaeLynn was far more anxious than she was. "I don't know. I guess it depends on how soon someone sees the message." She assumed that there was someone at the police department who was monitoring incoming emails and messages but, in light of what was going on, was it high on their priority list to have someone sitting at a desk all day? She decided to send an identical message to the sheriff's department as well. They waited five long minutes until it was apparent that they weren't going to get an immediate answer. Corrie sighed irritably. "I guess I'm going to have to sit here all day, waiting for someone to respond."

"You want me to get us some coffee?" RaeLynn offered. Corrie really didn't want any, but realized that RaeLynn needed something concrete to do.

"Sounds good," she said and RaeLynn nodded eagerly and scurried away. Corrie shook her head, wishing something would happen. She had a feeling she had a long wait ahead of her.

RaeLynn found herself growing impatient with the coffee maker. It was a state-of-the-art model that had taken her about twenty minutes to learn how to use and she had been grateful for Luz's patience, but now she wished that one of the features was some kind of fast brew option. She took a few minutes to rummage through the fridge and prepare a snack of grapes, apple and cheese slices, and fresh strawberries. Not that she expected that either she or Corrie were hungry, but it would give them something to do while they waited for an answer.

A soft "beep" alerted her that the coffee was done brewing. She set the fruit platter on the counter and turned to grab a couple of mugs. She gasped.

A heavy-set man with a scruffy face and dark, glittering eyes stood in the doorway. He had a gun pointed directly at RaeLynn.

"Keep your voice down, missy. You're coming with me and you better hope your friend gets down here quick."

Corrie was getting irritated. Surely it shouldn't take so long for law enforcement agencies to respond to a question on their websites? She had sent a polite "nudge" message to both the police and the sheriff's department after five minutes, followed by a slightly less polite message ten minutes later. "Urgent. This is Corrie Black. I need to see Detective Wilder and Sheriff Sutton immediately." Still no answer from either place. And how long did it take for RaeLynn to brew a pot of coffee anyway?

You need to calm down, she told herself. Her impatience propelled her out of the chair to pace out her restlessness. It occurred to her that maybe RaeLynn decided to bring up some snacks along with the coffee. Maybe she needed a hand. As much as Corrie hated to leave the room, she reminded herself that a watched pot never boils and sitting and staring at the screen wasn't helping her peace of mind. She forced herself to tear her gaze away from the computer and leave the room.

As soon as she crossed the main room and entered the dining room, she felt a sudden jolt of uneasiness. It was eerily silent in the house. "RaeLynn?" she called out. There was no answer and she couldn't hear any sounds from the kitchen. She pushed open the kitchen door and looked around. A full pot of coffee sat on the burner and a plate of fruit and cheese was on the counter. The refrigerator door was slightly ajar. A chill ran down her back and her mouth felt dry. "RaeLynn?" She hesitated then slowly backed toward the door, her mind running over possible scenarios: Had RaeLynn let Renfro out? No, he and Oliver were up in her room. Had Jerry and Jackie returned and RaeLynn had gone out to help them with something? But she had seen RaeLynn's jacket hanging near the door and it was too cold to go out without it. The bathroom? Unless she was sick, why would it be taking her so long and why wasn't she answering Corrie?

She turned to head back to the main room and suddenly the man she knew as Ronald Brown stood in front of her. "About time you came downstairs," he growled. Corrie stepped back and then saw the gleam of the gun in his hand. "Don't move."

"Where's RaeLynn? What did you do to her?" she stammered. He moved forward and grabbed her arm, yanking her roughly toward him. He pressed the gun into Corrie's side.

"She's safe, for now. And so are you. I need that envelope."

"Envelope?" She hated to sound so clueless, but her mind was scrambling to find a way out of her predicament. "What envelope?" She bit back a gasp as the gun barrel dug into her ribs.

"You know what envelope," he snapped. "I followed that woman out here. I saw her taking the office mail to the post office and she didn't have it in her hand when she went in. I figured it was a long shot, but I thought she still had it. When I saw her go by the sheriff's office and then his apartment, I knew she wanted to give it to him. So I had to see where she was taking it." He chuckled. "Once I saw her head out of the village, I knew where she was going. I took a shortcut and got here first. I was going to take it from her and split. But then I got a better idea."

While Corrie was glad that Sheila Larsen hadn't been hurt, she was sure that Ronald Brown's idea of "better" didn't apply to her and RaeLynn. "What good is that envelope going to be to you if anything happens to us?" she asked.

"You and your friend are my guarantee that the sheriff does what I say," he said. "Now where is it?"

Corrie drew in a silent breath. At least it didn't sound like he was planning to kill them once he got the envelope. But what was in it that he wanted so badly? "Must be pretty important," she said. Brown's grip on her arm tightened and she winced.

"It is," he said simply, "and you're stalling. Where is it?" he demanded, shaking her roughly.

"Okay, okay," she said through gritted teeth. His hold on her loosened slightly and she drew a shaky breath. She was out of ideas; all she could do was give him the envelope and hope that she and RaeLynn got an opportunity to get away from him. "It's in the office."

"What office? That one?" he asked, gesturing in the direction of the closed door. Corrie nodded, noting that the door was closed all the way. He pushed her toward the office, stopping beside a small table and picking up a key that lay on it. Corrie frowned.

"You locked RaeLynn in the office?" She glared at him. "How did you know where to find the key?" she asked.

"A little bird told me," he muttered. "Same little bird that told me the code to the front gate. She said that in spite of the fact that the sheriff's mom lived here, the security measures were pretty lax. They haven't changed codes or keys in years. Small-town mentality. I'm surprised they don't leave everything unlocked at night." He stuck the key into the lock and waved the gun at Corrie. "Don't get any ideas or I'll shoot her first and then come after you," he warned. He unlocked the door and tossed the key back on the table. "Step away from the door and don't try anything funny! You got that?" he shouted.

"Yes." Corrie was surprised to hear RaeLynn's voice was firm and steady. Ronald Brown shoved the door open and propelled Corrie in ahead of him. He glowered at RaeLynn who stood near the desk, her arms wrapped around herself. She had pulled the rolling office chair out from behind the desk and had been sitting in it. Now she moved behind it, using it like a shield between herself and the man with the gun.

"All right," Brown said, releasing Corrie with a push but keeping the gun trained on her. "Where's the envelope?"

"What envelope?" RaeLynn asked, moving toward Corrie and catching hold of her arm. Corrie flinched as she felt RaeLynn's nails dig in and tug her closer. She tried to pat RaeLynn's hand reassuringly, but RaeLynn caught her fingers in a death grip even as she held on to the back of the office chair.

"She knows what I'm talking about. No need to keep pretending," he sneered. He waved the gun again threateningly. "The envelope?" he repeated.

"It's in the desk drawer," Corrie said, trying to tug her fingers loose, but RaeLynn's hand tightened even more. Ronald Brown gave her a warning look and he stepped behind the desk. He pulled the drawer open and took his eyes off them long enough to look down.

RaeLynn shoved the chair toward Ronald Brown and lunged for the door, pulling Corrie along with her. Ronald Brown let out a yell. Corrie caught a glimpse of the man falling over the office chair in his way as she and RaeLynn dove out into the main room. A bullet ripped through the door panels as RaeLynn ducked and slammed the door shut. "The key!" she gasped as the sound of Brown's swearing reached them through the heavy wood. Corrie snatched the key up from the table and jammed it into the lock. RaeLynn dragged the small table in front of the door for good measure. "Let's go!" she cried.

Corrie hesitated for a second. Running out the door made them sitting ducks; Ronald Brown had a car, but they were in the middle of nowhere, without a vehicle, and there was no place for them to hide. She grabbed RaeLynn's hand and tugged her down the hallway. Deep in her memory, she recalled the layout of the house and knew there was a door that led outdoors from the basement. She hoped that Ronald Brown was more concerned with getting the envelope and getting away, so their best bet was to hide until he left. A cold hand clamped on her heart. If Rick and J.D. got her message, it could mean that they would be walking into an ambush, but what else could they do? "Come on," she urged RaeLynn as they ducked down the hallway and headed for the stairs to the basement.

Chapter 28

J.D. and the sheriff pulled up in front of the insurance office, where they saw the fire investigators' car parked along with Eldon LaRue's patrol car. Apparently, a compromise had been reached: Eldon had convinced them that he could handle the investigation in a fair and impartial manner but the state insisted on looking over his shoulder. J.D.'s stomach tightened; he wondered what would happen when they explained why they were there.

Officer Camacho stood in front of the door and his eyes widened when he saw the sheriff. He looked at J.D. "Detective Wilder, um, I was told not to let anyone come in," he began.

"Then let the chief know we need to talk to him right away. We'll talk out here," he added. Camacho nodded and poked his head in the door, calling to Eldon.

LaRue came to the door with Agent Jackson right behind him. He stared at the sheriff. "What are you all doing here? You know we can't allow you in here while the investigation is going on!" He looked at J.D. and raised a brow. "Something happen?"

"Yeah," J.D. said. He nodded toward the office. "We just heard that there could be evidence in the office that proves that someone else had a motive to kill Ms. Stratham."

"What evidence?" Agent Jackson said, pushing forward. "Who did you hear this from?"

"Abeyta Funeral Home says they have a contract to move my daughter's remains to Dallas that was signed by a representative of Meghan's company, Stratham Enterprises," the sheriff said. His voice held a slight tremor and Jackson's eyes narrowed.

"Yeah, so?"

"So we need to see if Meghan actually signed that contract or if someone else did," Sutton said. He turned to LaRue. "There's no reason why someone else would have signed that contract. It was supposed to be between Meghan and me and the funeral home."

"You're saying someone might have killed your ex-wife and signed that contract? But why? What reason?" Eldon said.

"That's what we're trying to find out," J.D. said. He turned to Agent Jackson. "We won't touch anything. You'll be right there. All we're doing is looking for a contract with Abeyta Funeral Home signed by Sheriff Sutton and Meghan Stratham or a representative of her company."

Jackson sighed. He jerked his head toward the door. "Doesn't look like anything is missing," he said dourly. "If someone was looking for anything, they might have gotten scared off by someone before they found it." He eyed the sheriff suspiciously. To his credit, Sutton didn't respond and kept his expression stony. J.D. reined in his temper as Jackson led the way into the building.

They stopped in the outer office. J.D. turned to the sheriff. "Well?"

Sutton looked around the office and shook his head. "I met with Meghan in her private office," he said, indicating the closed door. Agent Jackson smirked.

"You mean, where she was killed?" he clarified. Sutton spun on him, his eyes flashing with anger.

"Yes, that's where she and I spoke, Agent Jackson, and that is where I signed the contract. And that's where that contract should be, since the funeral home never received it."

Jackson grunted and opened the door to Meghan's office. Nothing seemed out of place; only Meghan's body was missing from the way J.D. had seen it the day before. He glanced at the sheriff who was staring at the spot where Meghan had been. "You okay?" J.D. asked him in a low voice.

"Yeah," Sutton said, shaking himself. He nodded toward her desk. "That's where I signed the contract. She said she was going to send it to the funeral home right away."

Jackson pulled on a fresh pair of gloves and went to the drawer. As he was pulling it open, Eldon said, "Wait a minute."

They all turned to him. He was frowning, looking from the desk back to the front office.

"What?" Jackson snapped.

The chief shook his head. "If she was having it sent out right away, it wouldn't have been in her desk. It should have been in the outgoing mail tray on her secretary's desk." He pointed at the empty tray. "When did that get emptied?"

Sutton's eyes widened. "That tray was full when I left here yesterday."

"You're sure?" J.D. said sharply. The sheriff nodded. J.D. turned to LaRue and Jackson.

"Get hold of Sheila Larsen, the secretary. Ask her if there was any mail on her desk when she found Meghan." LaRue stepped to the door and barked orders at Officer Camacho. LaRue was frowning as he rejoined them and pushed his ball cap back on his head. "The office hadn't been open all week. If anyone sent out mail, it would have been Meghan." He glanced at the sheriff and Sutton shook his head. Eldon sighed. "No, I guess not. She would have had her employee do it, wouldn't she?" Camacho poked his head in the door and beckoned to LaRue. "That was fast," LaRue muttered.

"Chief, Ms. Larsen just pulled up," Camacho said. He glanced at J.D. and the sheriff. "She said she needs to talk to the sheriff as soon as possible."

"What about?" Jackson said, pushing past J.D. and the sheriff to stand in the doorway. The middle-aged woman stopped in her tracks and looked past Agent Jackson. Her eyes widened and she pointed to the sheriff.

"I need to speak to Sheriff Sutton. No one else. It's important," she said.

"What about?" Jackson repeated. Sutton stepped forward, ignoring the agent.

"Ms. Larsen, whatever you need to tell me, just say it. It's all right with me for everyone else to be present." Jackson started to speak but LaRue cleared his throat sharply and the agent relented with a sour expression on his face.

She looked around with uncertainty. "Well...." She hesitated, then nodded. "All right, I think I'd better." She straightened her shoulders. "Would it be all right if we stepped inside out of the cold?"

They moved into the front office and J.D. studied her closely. She was far more in command of herself than she had been the day before. She glanced toward Meghan's office and gave a little shiver. J.D. stepped over and pulled the door shut and she gave him a grateful smile.

"All right, Ms. Larsen, what's this all about?" Eldon asked. His tone made it clear that he, not Jackson, was in charge. She seemed to relax slightly.

"Well, I just want to tell Sheriff Sutton about an envelope that was supposed to have been mailed out from our office. It was addressed to Abeyta Funeral Home and... and the return address was your apartment here in Bonney."

The sheriff's face registered shock. "What was in the envelope?"

"I don't know," Sheila said uncomfortably. "Meghan put it in my outgoing mail tray a few days ago, before she decided to close down the office...."

"Wait," Sutton said, his face growing paler. "It was in your outgoing basket a few days ago? Not yesterday?"

"Oh, it was there yesterday," Sheila said quickly. "When I

came in, I saw that the mail hadn't gone out, so before I went into Meghan's office, I… I took the mail and put it in my tote bag. I had planned on going by the post office when I left and then I saw the envelope…."

"And you mailed it out?" J.D. asked at the same time the sheriff asked, "You're sure that it was there a few days ago?"

"No. Yes." Ms. Larsen shook her head. "I mean, yes, it was there a few days ago. I saw Meghan slip it into the pile and then about an hour later she decided to close the office down and told me I had to leave right away." She took a breath. "And no, I didn't mail it out after I picked it up yesterday." She hesitated and glanced at the investigator and the chief. "I heard that Sheriff Sutton was a suspect in Meghan's death. And I knew he and Meghan had been having, er, problems lately…." J.D. closed his eyes and groaned to himself. That was the last thing that Jackson needed to hear. Ms. Larsen went on, "and I thought it was odd that something that had the sheriff's personal return address on it was being mailed from our office, so when I saw that, I thought it might be best if I gave it to him and let him decide what to do about it."

J.D. and Sutton exchanged a glance. "You have that envelope here?" J.D. asked, standing up straighter.

Ms. Larsen's eyes were wide as she shook her head. "No," she said. "I mean, hasn't Corrie called you?"

"Corrie?" Now the sheriff's eyes and voice were as sharp as razors. "What does Corrie have to do with this?"

"Well, I went out to your family home this morning, Sheriff," Sheila Larsen said. Her face reddened slightly. "I was going to take it to your apartment here in town, but I saw that the investigators were there…."

"WHAT?" Sutton spun around and glared at Jackson, whose jaw had dropped. "You searched my apartment?"

Jackson's face went white. "Well, what did you expect, Sheriff? You're a suspect and we had a warrant…," he sputtered.

"Good thing you did and we're going to want to see it," J.D. growled. Eldon LaRue looked to be on the verge of a stroke.

"You went over my head?" he roared. He grabbed Jackson by the front of his jacket. "Are you out of your mind?"

"Forget it!" Sutton shouted. He grabbed J.D.'s arm and started tugging him toward the Tahoe. "Corrie has the envelope! It's at the house. We need to go get it!"

"Detective!" Camacho barged into the office, his cell phone

to his ear. "A message came through to the office on our website! Corrie's trying to get hold of you and the sheriff! She's been trying to call you but the phone lines are down...."

"What phone lines?" Sutton asked sharply. He glanced at J.D. but Camacho went on.

"Dispatch called the phone company after they got the message to report the outage," he said, his eyes wide with concern. "They said there aren't any outages in the area, Sheriff, so they checked your home's lines and found there was a line break...."

It was all J.D. could do to keep up with Sutton as he ran for his vehicle.

Corrie and RaeLynn hurried down the stairs, trying to make as little noise as possible while straining to hear if Ronald Brown was after them. They reached the basement where, to Corrie's dismay, three hallways branched off from the bottom of the stairs. Which way led to the door that opened outside? Corrie racked her memory. "Which way do we go?" RaeLynn breathed, still clutching Corrie's arm.

"One of these hallways leads to a storm cellar," Corrie whispered. Memories of the hide-and-seek game they played at Rick's twelfth birthday party tumbled into her mind but, like a puzzle dumped out of a box, she couldn't figure out which piece went where. She shook her head. "We'll have to check them all. I can't remember...."

"We don't have much time!" RaeLynn hissed. Corrie looked at her, perplexed.

"Don't worry," she said, trying to soothe RaeLynn who was trembling uncontrollably. "He won't waste time looking for us. He'll grab that envelope and then get out of here...."

RaeLynn shook her head. "He won't find it," she cried softly. She tugged her shirt out of her waistband and pulled out the envelope. "I figured he was after it... so I took it out of the drawer when he locked me in the office and hid it. When he doesn't find it...."

Corrie felt her heart drop. Then, from up above them, came the sound of a door flying open. She grabbed RaeLynn's hand and pulled her down the nearest hallway and into the first door they came to. Corrie yanked the door open and they stumbled into the dark room. She managed to stop herself from slamming the door shut behind them and then fumbled with the doorknob. "No!" she gasped under her breath.

"What? Lock the door!" RaeLynn sobbed in a whisper.

"There's no lock!" Corrie breathed. She felt around in the darkness until she found a switch by the door and turned on the light. She looked around and realized the chill she felt wasn't just from fear.

They were in the wine cellar.

Her eyes met RaeLynn's and tried to fight back the panic that welled up inside her. For a brief moment, a memory of her and Rick hiding in the wine cellar flashed through her mind and she felt a stab of terror as it occurred to her that it wouldn't take Ronald Brown long to find them. They were going to have to fight back.

She grabbed two bottles off the nearest rack and handed one to RaeLynn. "Do you still bat left-handed?" she whispered. RaeLynn looked confused, then comprehension dawned on her face and she nodded eagerly. Corrie motioned her into place on one side of the door while she ducked back on the other side. "You swing low, I swing high," Corrie instructed. "And don't hold back! Knock it out of the park!" RaeLynn's jaw tightened and she nodded again. Corrie breathed a silent prayer as she flicked the light switch off. It had been months since she'd swung a baseball bat and a wine bottle was very different. The best they could hope for was to stop Ronald Brown long enough to give them a chance to get away.

She held her breath and drew back when she heard running footsteps heading their way. In the darkness, she sensed RaeLynn tensing in preparation. If they were lucky, Ronald Brown would be so intent on catching them that he would just barge through the door. After all, he had a gun—he shouldn't have any reason to be cautious in facing them. But if he suspected a trap....

Corrie choked up on the neck of the wine bottle as the footsteps stopped outside the wine cellar and the door was yanked open. Ronald Brown stepped through the door, his gun held ahead of him, and he paused to let his eyes adjust to the darkness.

RaeLynn's bottle connected just below his waist, eliciting a painful yelp from Brown as he started to double over, his face thrusting forward just as Corrie swung her bottle with all her might. She shuddered as the crunch of the bottle connecting with Brown's face traveled up her arms and she turned away to avoid flying glass and wine. With a strangled roar, Brown dropped to his knees, the gun skittering across the floor as his hands flew to his face. RaeLynn snatched another bottle off a shelf and brought it down squarely on top of his head. He slumped to the floor with a moan and Corrie and RaeLynn leaped over him and sprinted for the stairs.

"Hurry!" Corrie cried, pushing RaeLynn ahead of her as they ran up the stairs. Muffled cursing came from down below, spurring them to move faster than they ever had in their lives. A few steps from the top, the door at the top of the stairs swung open and they froze.

A woman they had never seen before stood in the doorway, pointing a gun directly at them. "Where do you think you're going?" she snarled.

"Who are you?" Corrie stammered as the woman gestured for them to come all the way to the top of the stairs. She was attractive, olive-skinned with dark hair and eyes, and only a few years older than they were. She backed up as they climbed the rest of the stairs, keeping the gun trained on them.

"Trust me, it doesn't matter to you!" she snarled. "Ronald said you had the envelope but he's taken too long to get back to me. I don't know what you did to him, but I want that envelope. Now!"

Corrie sucked in a deep breath and turned to RaeLynn who was staring with wide, terrified eyes. "Go ahead, RaeLynn," she said softly. They had no choice now; she nodded at RaeLynn who reached under her sweater slowly and drew out the envelope.

Suddenly Cassandra Sutton appeared silently behind the woman, her eyes cold and hard. In one swift move, she swung an umbrella overhead and caught the woman's gun arm with the hooked handle and yanked it downward. Corrie and RaeLynn dodged as the woman stumbled, startled off balance, and fired the gun into the wall, then they tackled her to the floor. The woman screamed as Corrie wrestled with her for the gun and screamed even louder as Cassandra brought the umbrella down again and cracked her in the wrist with the hardwood handle, causing her to release the weapon.

They heard the front door burst open. "Corrie!" Rick's voice echoed in the main room and Corrie felt herself weaken with relief.

"Over here!" she shouted. "Ronald Brown is in the wine cellar!" she went on as Rick and J.D. appeared at the end of the hallway with their weapons drawn. "He's got a gun!" she added as Eldon LaRue and Officer Camacho also appeared and took charge of the furious woman as Rick and J.D. dashed past them and down the stairs.

Cassandra coolly walked over and looked at the woman who was now securely cuffed and being restrained by the chief and Officer Camacho. "Why, hello, Julia," she said, then turned to Eldon. "Chief, I'd like to report a robbery and also thank you for apprehending the perpetrator... and yes, I will be pressing charges."

Chapter 29

"I suppose this was probably the best occasion I could have been saving those bottles of Château Lafite Rothschild for," Cassandra said without a trace of regret as she sipped a small glass of sherry. "Although I would have preferred to have had Manuel pouring a glass for everyone instead of mopping it up off the floor."

Three hours after the commotion had died down, they were all seated in the main room, all looking both drained and relieved. Manuel and Luz had cut their trip to Las Cruces short because Luz had "gotten a bad feeling" and had insisted on returning home immediately. They, along with the Pages and the Myers, had arrived to a scene of several law enforcement vehicles from the village, the county, and the state in front of the house and, once the shock had worn off and they had determined that everyone was safe, they immediately began "damage control", as Rick put it. Luz had insisted on making everyone something to eat while Manuel went with the LEOs to examine the damage in the wine cellar. Rick and J.D. had herded everyone into the dining room while they assisted with taking the two intruders into custody. Julia had been hauled in for breaking and entering and assault with a deadly weapon, along with suspicion of theft. Ronald Brown was treated for a broken nose, fractured jaw, concussion, and various cuts and bruises at the scene before being arrested as well.

A very subdued Agent Jackson had stood by while Chief LaRue and Officer Camacho took statements from everyone, then mumbled something about charges being dropped.

"I'm sorry, what did you say?" Cassandra's imperious voice rose, and she fixed her glacial eyes on the agent.

"Don't worry, Mother, I heard him and so did Eldon," Rick said, patting her shoulder. Jackson gave Rick a grateful nod before hurrying after the patrol cars carrying the prisoners to the county jail. "I'll let them sort out who has jurisdiction," Rick added, making no move to accompany them. Eldon LaRue gave Rick a surprised glance and shrugged.

"No matter who it is, they won't get away." He motioned to Officer Camacho. "Let's go talk to George Williams and Martin Abeyta and get their statements as well."

"Wait," Corrie said as they started to leave. She gestured to RaeLynn. "Here's that envelope that everyone was so intent on getting their hands on." RaeLynn handed it to Corrie. "Maybe you can find out what it contains that was so important."

Rick's face was grim as he studied the envelope. "It's Meghan's handwriting," he confirmed. He carefully opened it and drew out a single sheet of paper. He read it over and frowned. "It's what Martin said it would be," he said. "It's a contract stating that I give all rights to Meghan and her company, Stratham Enterprises, regarding," he swallowed hard, "Ava's final resting place." He blinked and then his jaw tightened. "But this isn't my signature. This was signed a few days ago, not yesterday."

"What did Meghan have you sign then?" J.D. asked.

Rick shook his head. "I have no idea. Nothing was found in the office except shredded documents in the waste can. Nothing else with my signature or Meghan's."

J.D. raised a brow. "We'll have someone reconstruct those shredded documents," he said, "but I'm willing to bet that she had you sign some random document just to prove that you signed something. It was strictly between the two of you, and she knew that you would honor your agreement, no matter how much you hated to."

Rick nodded and scanned the document once again. "It's like Martin said. The agreement is between me and Stratham Enterprises, not just me and Meghan. And it makes no sense. If Meghan's gone, why should anyone else care where Ava is buried?"

"It matters enough that someone was willing to kill for it," Corrie said with a shudder. RaeLynn's face paled and she shivered, wrapping her hands around the mug of hot tea that Luz had given her. "What's the connection between this Julia, and Ronald Brown, and Meghan?"

J.D. gave her a grim smile. "Ronald Brown started blabbing out accusations about his accomplice the minute he saw us." He ran a hand over his head and gave his ponytail a tug. "Turns out this Julia was Alex Durán's wife... and she was the one who shot him."

Stunned, Corrie stared at him. "And how is Ronald Brown connected to them?" She looked at Rick in confusion. He seemed resigned and unwilling to say much. Pieces were falling together, but the only way that they made sense was almost too incredible to believe. "And what's Meghan got to do with all this?"

J.D. glanced at Rick who gave him a brief nod. J.D. cleared his throat. "Alex Durán and his wife had been working for Ronald Brown for a while. They'd move from resort to resort or from job

256

to job, perfecting the art of robbing wealthy people without anyone catching on to what they were doing. One of the many businesses that Ronald Brown ran was an employment agency, so he was able to find them places to work and provide authentic references. He also owned several jewelry stores where he was able to fence the jewelry that was stolen and also replace the stones in jewelry that was switched out from wealthy victims who hired housekeepers from Brown's employment agency. When Meghan pulled her little stunt in Cabo, Durán saw that she might be a very lucrative connection for their 'business' but she didn't want to play. Durán decided to keep the marriage certificate, in case he ever needed it in the future. In the meantime, Ronald Brown did some research, found out about the sheriff's family wealth, and got himself hired on with Stratham Enterprises where he managed to gain Meghan's trust—of course, never letting her know that he was acquainted with Alex Durán. Incidentally, he was the one who convinced Meghan to buy out the insurance company, just to expand his own operations and have a way to get inside information about the locals and their finances.

"Brown admitted that Meghan hadn't wanted to get pregnant, especially since she had already decided she was going to divorce Sutton, but when it happened, Brown encouraged her to insist on having Luz move in with her and the sheriff in order to get Julia hired on here. She agreed, but she didn't know the true reason: that Brown wanted an opportunity to get hold of Mrs. Sutton's jewelry. It worked except for Mrs. Sutton having decided to look in her armoire and found the pieces missing. Julia was supposed to have returned the jewelry before it was discovered missing and she was too late." He looked at Cassandra who had turned to look at her son. "That was what she was doing when she was meeting up with Brown at the funeral home. She would hand off the real jewels to him and he would return them to her once he switched the stones. It worked for six months, then just before Ava was born, she was found out and fired. Since it looked like the jewelry had been returned intact, nothing was ever done. The theft wasn't even reported." He took a deep breath and Corrie realized that he hadn't told them the most disturbing part of the story yet. "And then something went wrong and Ava was born prematurely and not expected to survive. Meghan had decided she had had enough. She didn't feel she could keep up appearances any longer and she bailed out, not even bothering to notify Ronald Brown.

"Brown, in the meantime, was having a hard time keeping

suspicion at bay. George Williams actually recognized Brown as a petty thief from back in the day. One of George's many jobs in the past had been security at a high-end jeweler where Brown had been employed as a repairman. He'd noticed that jewelry had gone missing then suddenly reappeared whenever Brown was tasked with working on it. Again, because it always turned up, no one reported any losses, but Brown was doing the same thing he did with Mrs. Sutton's jewelry—taking the pieces and replacing the real jewels with fake ones. He had amassed millions of dollars in stolen jewelry, but he left that job when he noticed Williams getting suspicious. He had hoped that Meghan would be able to get him access to the jewels, but Mrs. Sutton wasn't the type to loan out pieces to anyone, even her daughter-in-law."

"I never trusted her," Cassandra said sharply. "I know she managed to convince Patrick she was honest and trustworthy and loyal, but something just never sat right with me. I wish I'd said something at the time, but I didn't want to ruin Patrick's happiness."

Corrie felt the words like a stab in the heart. *Rick's happiness.* Something he apparently hadn't found with Corrie. She bit her lip and stared down at her hands, clenched into fists as if holding herself together. She felt J.D.'s eyes on her, but she didn't dare look up. He took a minute to clear his throat and take a sip of water before he went on.

"Anyway, we know Meghan got Julia hired on and she succeeded in switching out the jewels but not before she was caught. Brown knew that George would get suspicious if Brown skipped town right when Meghan did, so he got the idea to stash the jewels in...." J.D. paused and looked at Rick whose face was ashen. "He stashed the jewels in Ava's casket. He figured that he'd have time to retrieve them before she was buried, but George had said something to Martin Abeyta about his concern that there was something off about Ronald Brown. Mr. Abeyta dismissed Brown without warning, right before the funeral, claiming that he no longer needed his services. Brown tried to protest, but he didn't want to tip his hand so he left without a big fight."

Corrie's head jerked up, and horror filled her. She looked at Rick, her vision blurry with tears as the realization struck: "That's why Meghan was so adamant about moving Ava to Dallas!" Rick nodded mutely. She looked at J.D. but she couldn't formulate any words.

J.D. drew a deep breath. "That was Ronald Brown's idea. He

figured that enough time had passed and nothing had come up about stolen jewels, so when he found out that the sheriff was petitioning for an annulment, he thought it would be the perfect way to get Ava moved to Dallas without raising any suspicions. So he had Meghan start pressuring Sutton about that. She didn't know where he had hidden the jewels and she had no idea why he wanted her to have Ava buried in Dallas, but she went along with it, mainly because she was enjoying torturing the sheriff. Brown was losing his patience and Meghan wasn't getting anywhere with getting the sheriff to allow her to move their daughter. So Brown got hold of Alex Durán and had him come to Bonney, hoping to spur Meghan to action. Durán and his wife, Julia, had had troubles when Meghan came into the picture ten years ago. Julia was jealous; she didn't trust her husband. She followed Alex here and to the Black Horse where they quarreled as he was going to set it on fire. Her jealousy got the better of her and she ended up shooting him and she started the fire. She was the one who emptied Alex's wallet and left his car abandoned. Adding a murder to arson just made things worse for Brown, until he saw that there was a way to implicate the sheriff, but it would mean getting rid of Meghan." He paused and then Rick spoke up.

"He said he got Meghan to write up the contract and forge my signature," he said, his voice strangled. "He convinced her to make the contract between me and Stratham Enterprises, where he was a partner, instead of just between the two of us. She signed her death warrant by doing so—she was so used to following Brown's orders without question and she was so focused on getting her hands on the Black Horse that she never wondered why Brown wanted Ava moved to Dallas. All she was interested in was that, not only was she going to get a chance to rub things in Corrie's face, she was going to get a chance to get her hands on the Black Horse as well. Brown and Meghan would be able to buy it for cheap and then he told her that he had a buyer lined up to purchase the property."

Corrie shot to her feet. Her anger rose up in her chest, choking her. "All this time... it was the campground she was after? She didn't even know about the jewels?" Her chest heaved; she felt as if she were going to be violently sick and she impatiently blinked tears away. She looked at Rick and J.D., shaking her head. "Why? Why did she want the Black Horse so badly?"

"Because Ronald Brown wanted it...," Rick began and Corrie

spun on him.

"You're defending her?"

"No," J.D. stepped forward, holding his hands up. "No, Corrie, he's not. Ronald Brown put the idea in Meghan's head about taking the campground, but when she found out what it was worth and what her cut of the sale would be, along with the knowledge that she was going to hit you where it hurt the most by not paying your insurance claim and taking advantage of you by buying it for so much less than it was worth, she did everything she could to make it happen." J.D. took a deep breath. "She knew how much the Black Horse meant to you... almost as much as—" He broke off abruptly and shrugged. He turned to Rick.

Rick sighed and swiped a hand over his face. "Anyway, once Ava was moved to Dallas, Ronald Brown would get the jewels from her casket and be able to sell them without anyone suspecting they were stolen. And then, after they bought the campground from Corrie...."

"Why?" Corrie broke in. "The campground is destroyed. I've already come to accept that it would take so long to rebuild that even trying would be pointless. Even if they convinced me to sell it, which I don't know that I would, especially to Meghan or her company, what good would it be to them?" She swiped tears off her cheeks, dimly surprised that she was crying. With a start, she realized that she had finally admitted that the Black Horse was beyond saving. It reminded her of the time, weeks after she had buried her father, when she found herself automatically going about Billy's regular duties at the Black Horse with tears coursing down her face as she realized that she had come to accept that he was gone.

There was silence in the room for several minutes; no one seemed to have an answer. Cassandra stood up at last and went to Rick and laid a hand on his shoulder. "You don't have to... disturb Ava," she said hoarsely, her lips trembling. "I don't care about the jewels. Just leave them where they are."

A spasm of pain crossed Rick's face. He patted his mother's hand and glanced at J.D. who grimaced. "Mrs. Sutton, ma'am," he said quietly, "we, uh, have to confirm the allegations and we need the jewels as evidence." He paused and glanced at Corrie. She felt sick to her stomach again.

"Very well," Cassandra said quietly. She shook her head. "I'm going to call Mr. DiMarco. I'm sure he needs to know about all this and I'll have him answer the questions I know everyone will be asking. I'll be in my suite," she finished abruptly and she hurried up the stairs.

Silence settled over the room again. Corrie realized they were all waiting for her to say something but she didn't know what she could say. She looked from Rick to J.D., hoping they were going to give her some more answers, but it was plain to see that there were only more questions. She swallowed hard. "So... now what?"

J.D. seemed reluctant to answer. He said slowly, "We need to go talk to Eldon and the investigators. This case is far from closed, but at least the sheriff has been proven innocent." Somehow, Rick didn't seem as relieved as he should have been. He merely shook his head as if tired of the whole business. She couldn't blame him. She felt like she had been awake and her mind spinning for weeks. Had it really only been two days since the Black Horse had burnt down? Only yesterday since Meghan was murdered? She looked at RaeLynn and saw the same haunted expression of exhaustion that was on everyone's face. She turned to J.D. and Rick who were both getting up and heading toward the door.

"Do I need to come, too?" She was hardly surprised when they glanced at each other and shook their heads.

"We have their confession," J.D. said. "Brown and Julia were both Mirandized before they started throwing the blame at each other and Chief LaRue and Agent Jackson both heard it. You and RaeLynn have been through enough for one day. If we need to talk to you, it can wait till tomorrow." Rick had said nothing, but his eyes were fastened on Corrie. She caught his gaze and held it. Was he trying to tell her something? There were still so many questions.... She turned away and cleared her throat.

"Okay," was all she managed. They went out the door but she felt frozen in place. RaeLynn approached her hesitantly.

"Are you okay?" she whispered. Corrie turned and looked into her wide, tear-glazed tawny eyes. She looked around the room, seeing everyone's concerned faces, their eyes full of concern and sympathy. And she felt numb.

"I don't know," she answered.

Chapter 30

The rest of the day passed in a blur. Corrie felt like she was sleepwalking. The police—she couldn't remember which department—took her and RaeLynn's statements over the phone, but it was a mere formality. Meghan had apparently not completely trusted Ronald Brown and had kept records of all of their conversations and dealings and, when he discovered that there was proof of all the thefts and his illegal operations, he tried to make a deal in exchange for his confession. The police still had enough evidence to convict, but Brown's confession meant a trial would be avoided. Julia hadn't fared much better. In her rush to implicate Brown, she ended up admitting to her husband's murder.

It was no surprise that Rick and J.D. hadn't returned by the time Corrie and the rest of the household went to bed. She was surprised, however, when she ventured into the kitchen at her usual waking time and found only J.D. sitting at the island with a cup of coffee. He looked up from scrolling through the daily news articles on his phone and gave her a smile. "Morning," he said. He got up and went to the coffee pot and filled a cup for her. "Can't break the habit of getting up early?"

She gave him a wan smile and thanked him for the coffee. "I don't know what else to do. I think I'm just on auto-pilot." She took a sip of her coffee as he resumed his seat and she glanced around. "Rick's not up?" she asked.

J.D. let out a snort and shrugged. "He probably is, but he's not here." He set his phone down and looked at her seriously. "He stayed in town last night. Said he needed to be alone for a while." Corrie spun to look at him and she half-rose from her seat, nearly spilling her coffee. J.D. caught her wrist. "Easy," he said, his silver eyes boring into hers. "He's all right. I told him I'd be checking in and he'd better answer every time I did or I'd be glued to his side twenty-four/seven. He told me about that night," he said, his voice growing softer. "He told me you were there. He said it would never happen again. He couldn't hurt you like that again."

Corrie swallowed hard and glanced away. *Not like that, but in other ways....* "Okay," she breathed, willing her heart to slow back down to its normal rate. She shook her head and straightened up. "So now what happens?" she asked, turning back to face J.D. She wasn't sure if she needed to explain what she meant—she didn't care about what would happen to Ronald Brown and Julia, but she was still homeless and in the most awkward way possible.

Of course, J.D. understood. "You should be receiving a check from your insurance company any day now," he said. "Meghan did authorize payment on your claim immediately before she…. Anyway, the investigation has been wrapped up into the fire at the campground, so you're free to do whatever you want with the property."

"That's just it," Corrie said. "What am I going to do with it? The campground is destroyed. How much is it going to cost to clean up the land and rebuild? How long will it take? The main building—my home—is completely gone," she went on, surprised that she wasn't tearing up. "I have to find a place to live and I have to decide what to do with the… property."

J.D. nodded. "I know. But there's no rush, Corrie. You know you have a place to stay until you make these decisions."

"I can't stay here forever," she said. She expected J.D. to say something but he didn't. "I can't," she reiterated as if he had argued with her. "I won't stay stuck, I have to move forward, I have to… to do something." She had clenched her hands into fists, feeling helpless. She drew a deep breath. "What am I going to do?"

"Listen to me," J.D. said, catching her hands in his. He waited until she raised her eyes to look into his. "You don't have to decide right this minute. Or even this week. You do have time, Corrie." He squeezed her hands and took a deep breath. "Look, I'm going to say something and I hope you don't take it wrong or hate me for saying it. I know you're hurting right now and you've lost so much and gone through a lot, but you need to hear this. You have a blank slate now; everything is completely fresh. To put it bluntly, you no longer have the campground so you no longer have that responsibility. And, believe it or not, you don't have any obligation to rebuild it, if you don't want to."

Corrie's mouth dropped open in shock. "What about Jerry and Jackie? And the Myers? What are they going to do?"

"Whatever they want to do," J.D. said earnestly. "Haven't you always worried that they would never move on to enjoy their retirements as long as they felt obligated to stay and help you with the campground when you were struggling? They have plans, Corrie. Plans they've put aside out of loyalty to you and your father. They'll be fine… as long as you're fine. And that goes for RaeLynn, too," he added. "She's stronger than you think. She's got the freedom to do whatever she wants to do, thanks to you, as well as the confidence to make her own way. You have to stop worrying about everyone else. Just take care of yourself for a change."

Corrie's breath caught in her throat. What J.D. was saying was true, but also frightening. Her entire life had been built around the Black Horse. Her family roots were there; her childhood memories, as well as most of her grown-up ones, revolved around the campground. It had been her home from the day she was born, her parents had built it from the ground up and left it to her, their legacy. Could she walk away from it? Could she build her life on a different foundation? But she had loved the campground—she had loved the work, the people she met, the guests who enjoyed her hospitality. How could she let that go? "I don't know, J.D.," she whispered.

"Like I said earlier, you don't have to make that decision right now," he repeated. He squeezed her hands once more and got up to refill their coffee cups. "One thing at a time," he said. "Once you get your insurance claim paid, you'll have enough to live on while you figure out the rest. And if you decide to sell the property...."

"Do you think I should?" she asked, setting down her cup before she dropped it. This was the question she struggled with the most and she couldn't stop her hands from shaking. J.D.'s face was solemn.

"You're afraid you're betraying your dad and his legacy if you sold it," he said perceptively. She bit her lip and gave a slight nod. He shook his head. "Look at it this way, Corrie. The campground is gone and not because of anything you did. You wouldn't be selling the Black Horse; you'd only be selling the land. The Black Horse isn't there anymore."

She shivered and half-laughed. "You're right," she said, tears clogging her throat. She took a deep breath. "I don't even know what I would do with the land now. I'm afraid to go look at it. I have no idea what condition it's in."

J.D. grimaced. "I'll be honest... it's pretty awful. I wish you didn't have to see it again. Just remember it the way it was."

Corrie swiped away sudden tears. "Billy said, at the end of his life, that he wanted me to remember him in his prime, not the way he looked when he was wasting away." She shook her head. "At first, it was easier to go on without him by remembering him when he was so sick and suffering. It made it easier for me to let him go because I didn't want him to be in pain anymore. But now… I only see him the way he was before, when he was at his healthiest and happiest."

"You'll do the same with the Black Horse," J.D. assured her. A muted buzz echoed in the kitchen and he reached for his phone. "It's the sheriff," he told her before he answered. "Did you get any sleep at all? What? Yeah, of course, she's up. She's right here." He raised a brow. "You're sure?" Corrie sat up straighter, noting the look of surprise on J.D.'s face. "Okay, I'll tell her. Are you coming by? Okay, talk to you later." He set the phone down and gave Corrie a grim smile. "I didn't expect this to happen so fast, but do you think you'll be ready to talk about selling the property in the next few hours?" he asked.

"What?" She blinked. "What are you talking about?"

"While going through the files in Meghan's office, Officer Camacho found a file labeled 'Offer on the Black Horse'. In it was a draft of a contract for Stratham Enterprises to buy the land on which the Black Horse stands from you and then another one between Stratham Enterprises and a potential buyer, once ownership is transferred."

"Meghan was already planning to sell the Black Horse to someone else, even before she knew I would sell it to her?" Outrage flooded Corrie, making her feel as if she were running a fever. J.D. nodded.

"I don't blame you for being angry, Corrie, but before you write off this information as irrelevant and decide to keep the property out of spite, let me fill you in on some information which should be arriving right about…." A soft tone sounded from his phone and he swiped open his email. Corrie forced herself to wait quietly while he scanned the information and he let out a low whistle.

"Well? What is it?" she demanded. He got up and took her hand, tugging her to her feet. He jerked his head toward the stairs.

"Let's go up so I can print it out for you to read. It might help you make your decision."

It was well after nine o'clock and Corrie was pacing impatiently in the main room, waiting for the potential buyer to show up. After reading the email that Rick had sent J.D. with the attached documents found in Meghan's office, sitting still was a near impossibility. J.D. had convinced her to eat breakfast, then she showered and, thanks to Cassandra Sutton's offer of anything in her voluminous closet, found something besides a t-shirt and jeans to wear. RaeLynn had helped Corrie twist her long hair into a loose chignon, framing her face with soft tendrils that effectively juxtaposed the ruby-red jacket and skirt of the "power suit" Cassandra had suggested. The Pages and Myers, along with RaeLynn, had reluctantly agreed to wait in the dining room to hear what happened when Corrie met with the potential buyer. J.D. had agreed to be present, along with the Sutton family lawyer, Anthony DiMarco. Corrie sat down then stood up again, shooting J.D. a hostile look when he chuckled.

"He's late," Corrie said, offering an explanation for her impatience. J.D. smiled.

"I'm sure he was surprised when he heard where this meeting was to take place," he said. "If Mr. DiMarco had a local office, we'd have arranged to meet in Bonney. Relax, Corrie. We've had time to do more research and make sure that, if he agrees to purchase the property, he's paying what it's actually worth."

Mr. DiMarco looked up from his papers. "Having the comparisons of other properties has given you quite an edge, Miss Black. I'll say quite honestly that Ms. Stratham was offering you an embarrassingly low amount for the property. It's my opinion that she was hoping you would be too emotional to do your homework and she would be able to take advantage of you. If this potential buyer had offered her even two-thirds of the value, she would have made a tidy profit over what she planned on paying you. I advise you to let me do the talking if he decides to argue about the worth of the land."

"Other than that, you're doing the talking," J.D. told her. "Just don't back down."

"Is there something you know that I don't?" she asked, pausing in her pacing to give J.D. a narrow-eyed glare. He shook his head, but that maddening grin wouldn't leave his face. The doorbell rang and Corrie turned toward the door and sucked in a deep breath. She glanced at J.D. once more.

"Don't back down," he said softly.

She forced herself to wait as Manuel went into the foyer to open the door. She heard the murmur of voices and she straightened her jacket and tried to compose her face into an expression of confidence that she didn't quite feel. Manuel ushered the man into the main room. "Miss Black, Mr. Englewood to see you, ma'am."

"What?!" Corrie sputtered, shock making her poise vanish in an instant. It was nothing, however, compared to the expression of astonishment on Conrad Englewood's face as he strode into the room with a leather briefcase.

It took him a full ten seconds to recover his voice. "Is this a joke?" he stammered. He looked around the room, flinching slightly at the sight of J.D., but clearly expecting to be dealing with someone other than Corrie. "Where's Meghan?" he demanded.

Corrie drew her breath in sharply. "Meghan?" she asked. She looked at J.D. and he shrugged. "You mean you don't know?"

"Know what? All I know is, I was supposed to meet her at her office in Bonney and get this deal wrapped up...."

"Wait, what deal?" Corrie snapped. "You mean the deal you've sworn for months that you weren't making with her?"

He had the decency to blush. "That was before the fire at the Black Horse," he said. "She told me she would have a deal hashed out with you afterward.... I don't have to explain this all to you!" he snarled, recovering his composure. "Now where is Meghan?"

"You've missed all the news, Mr. Englewood," J.D. said, folding his arms across his chest. "Ms. Stratham passed away yesterday afternoon."

Conrad Englewood stared at him, his eyes round and his mouth hanging open. Corrie said nothing; she sensed that it would be best to let J.D. deal with this part of the meeting. "What are you talking about? Meghan's dead? When did this happen? What happened to her? She was just fine a couple days ago...."

J.D. straightened up and moved toward Englewood, his jaw set and his gaze unwavering. "She was murdered, Mr. Englewood. She was involved with some rather unsavory characters and she trusted the wrong people. Count your blessings that the person who killed her didn't get to you first."

"What do you mean?" Englewood said, a tremor of fear in his voice. His gaze darted around the room. "Who killed her?"

"A man by the name of Ronald Brown," J.D. began and this time, Englewood let out a startled squawk, his face went dead white, and he dropped his briefcase. J.D. raised a brow as the man made no move to pick it up. He seemed frozen in place. "Something wrong, Englewood?"

"That's—that's impossible," he stammered. "Ronald Brown is... he's...."

"In custody and has confessed to the murder along with various other crimes including fraud and theft. Is there something you need to tell us?" J.D. asked.

Conrad Englewood groped for the arm of a leather wingchair and he dropped into it, lowering his head into his hands. His shoulders began to heave and he let out several wheezing breaths. Corrie looked at J.D. in alarm. She hadn't expected this reaction. She took a step toward him and J.D. held up a hand, warning her to stay in place. "Englewood?" J.D. said.

"I'm all right." The words came out in a muffled gasp. "I'm all right. It's just...." The man went into another spasm of hiccupping sounds. J.D. turned to Mr. DiMarco but the lawyer had stepped up beside Corrie and already had his cell phone out.

"Englewood, we're calling an ambulance," J.D. began but Conrad Englewood sat up straight and shook his head, mouthing "no".

He was laughing hysterically.

Corrie took a step back, stunned into silence. J.D. was also speechless. Mr. DiMarco recovered first. "Mr. Englewood, please pull yourself together and explain yourself, before I notify the police of your suspicious reaction to news of a murder...."

"No, no, no... no, I'm all right." Englewood swiped his hands over this face, fumbled for a handkerchief, and drew a deep breath. "I'm sorry," he said, his voice more composed. "I just... I'm shocked. You took me by surprise. I just think this is hilarious...."

"Care to explain why you find Ms. Stratham's murder funny?" J.D. snapped. Conrad immediately sobered and stood up.

"I don't," he said somberly. The snail tracks of his tears contrasted sharply with his frown. "I can't believe she's dead. But the fact that Brown killed her... you're sure about that?"

"He confessed," J.D. said, watching the man closely.

Englewood sighed. "I should have known this was too good to be true. What was this, a stunt to get me to implicate myself? Because I promise you, Detective, I had nothing to do with all this. I've always been just a messenger. A very well-paid one, to be sure, but I keep my nose clean, I don't ask questions, and I'm discreet." He stopped and stared at each one of them in turn, noting their perplexed expressions. Corrie had a lot of questions, but she was so confused that she couldn't articulate any of them and it seemed like J.D. and Mr. DiMarco were just as mystified as she was. Conrad shook his head. "Wait... what am I missing? Did you know about my connection to Ronald Brown?"

"Keep talking," J.D. said, keeping his expression and tone neutral. Englewood dropped back into the chair, shaking his head dazedly.

"This is why Meghan always told me to let her do the talking," he sighed. He straightened up. "Okay, here's the deal and I'm telling you everything because one thing I am not is a murderer... or a thief, for that matter. Did I know Ronald Brown was a thief? Yes, I did. I was paid very well to not see anything I wasn't supposed to see and to keep my mouth shut. I never thought he'd be capable of murder, though."

"You worked for Ronald Brown? But I thought you worked for Meghan." Corrie finally found her voice. Englewood glanced at her in surprise. Perhaps he'd forgotten she was there. He smiled weakly.

"That's me, the middleman," he said dryly. "I've been double-dipping for years and it's been quite entertaining, not to mention a challenge, to keep both Meghan and Ronald from knowing they were both paying me to do the exact same thing, often against each other. No matter which of them won or lost, I always came out ahead. But this... this was the best yet. Or so I thought."

"What's 'this'?" J.D. asked. Corrie was sure he already knew the answer, just like she did, and she felt her anger begin to swell inside her. She bit her tongue hard when Englewood looked her way. He almost looked apologetic.

"Well, it's been no secret that I've been trying to arrange the purchase of Miss Black's campground for some time...."

"And you kept insisting it wasn't Meghan who was interested! I knew you were lying!" she cried. Englewood shook his head and stood up.

"No, I wasn't," he said calmly. "I mean, I wasn't lying when I said I wasn't representing Meghan. She did want the Black Horse, but she wanted to handle it herself. Personal reasons," he added, looking uncomfortable. "I was representing Ronald Brown."

There was another silence in the room. "But Ronald Brown worked for Stratham Enterprises," J.D. said.

"Ol' Ron was just as loyal to one employer as I was," Englewood said dryly. "He wanted the campground, not for Stratham Enterprises, but for his own self. Meghan was going to present a low-ball offer and then resell it at a tidy profit. I don't know how she thought she'd ever get Miss Black to agree to it, but since I wasn't asked to get involved I didn't really care. Not Ronald. He was willing to outbid Meghan, but Miss Black wouldn't even talk to me."

"And why did Ronald Brown want the campground?" Corrie asked. Her head was spinning and her chest hurt. Nothing was making sense.

Conrad Englewood shifted uneasily. "Well, he didn't want the campground so much as he wanted the land. He had another buyer in mind... they wanted to build a kind of truck stop, 'travel center' he called it, with a convenience store, restaurant, souvenir shop, maybe work out a deal where he could have slot machines in it. He'd done the research and discovered that the location was perfect. Of course, once he bought the campground, he'd have to raze the main building and cabins and...." He gasped as Corrie strode toward him.

"Easy, Corrie," J.D. stepped in immediately, but she ignored him.

"That's what they were going to do with my beautiful, peaceful campground? They were going to cut down trees and tear down my home and...." She couldn't speak anymore; tears were choking her words off and she turned away, not surprised that Jerry and Jackie and RaeLynn had come out of the dining room, and it was all she could do not to collapse into Jackie's arms. She turned to glare at the man, who looked like he was facing a firing squad. He was holding his hands up as if that would protect him from the angry gazes of the people in the room. "That's why my campground was burned down?"

"I had nothing to do with that!" Englewood protested. He looked panicky and he shook his head vehemently. "Miss Black, on my honor...."

"You don't know what the word means!" she cried. "Why should I believe you? Give me one good reason why you shouldn't be charged with arson as well!"

"I didn't know Ronald would go to those extremes! I swear I didn't! You have to believe me! I was only supposed to arrange the purchase! Ronald promised me a fifty percent cut when he sold it and that would be enough for me to leave both him and Meghan behind and get on with my life!" His words were tumbling out of his mouth so quickly they barely made sense. Corrie almost didn't hear the doorbell ring again and she saw Manuel, out of the corner of her eye, hurry to the foyer.

J.D. stepped forward. "I don't know what the sheriff had planned here," he muttered, "but you'll have to come down to the station to answer a few questions, Mr. Englewood...."

"What's going on here?"

They turned toward the door. Rick, dressed in a sport jacket and tie, stood beside a distinguished looking man in a three-piece suit and expensive coat. Rick stared at Conrad Englewood. "What's he doing here?"

"You tell me," J.D. retorted. "Isn't he the buyer you were sending over here to talk to Corrie? You could have warned me!"

Rick's mouth dropped open. "What? No, he's not the buyer! This gentleman," he said, indicating the man beside him, "is the potential buyer. Arthur Reynolds. He owns a string of travel centers and truck stops throughout the southwest."

"What?" Now it was Conrad Englewood's turn to look stunned and his face had gone white. "Reynolds? What are you doing here?"

"I told you, Englewood, I wasn't interested in doing business with you," Mr. Reynolds said, looking down his long nose at Englewood. "Didn't you get my message this morning?"

"I got your message! It said you were going forward with the purchase...."

"On my own," Reynolds clarified. He glowered at Englewood. "Maybe you should listen to your messages all the way through. I imagine you just heard those words and ran out the door." Englewood had the decency to blush.

"I did. I thought... I had Meghan on one hand wanting to meet with me and I had heard that Miss Black was staying here so I just... I thought I was still representing you," he finished weakly. Arthur Reynolds shook his head in disgust.

"I heard about the fire at the campground. I wasn't comfortable with how quickly Ronald Brown reached out to me about the deal we were working on for me to purchase it, so I contacted the sheriff's department to see what was going on with the investigation." He turned to Corrie. "Miss Black, I'm sorry, this must be so distressing for you. Ronald Brown had been telling me for months that you had been planning to retire and sell the campground. The sheriff has set me straight on that and filled me in on what was going on. I can't tell you how horrified I was to hear that your home was destroyed in order to sell the property to me. I did inform the sheriff that I am still interested in the property but I have no intention of dealing with anyone but you, directly." He shot a dirty look at Englewood.

Conrad Englewood's face went as white as snow. He started to sputter a protest, but Mr. DiMarco stepped forward. "Mr. Reynolds, if you'll give me a moment to speak to Miss Black, we'll meet you in the office shortly to discuss the situation. The sheriff will show you the way and we'll have some coffee brought in." Reynolds glanced around the room, not sure what was going on but willing to stick around and see. He nodded and Rick gestured for the businessman to follow him. Manuel hurried away to get the coffee. Mr. DiMarco gave a discreet cough and gave J.D. a pointed look.

"Well, Englewood, I guess you've overstayed your welcome... not that you ever were," J.D. said. He jerked his head in the direction of the door. Englewood seemed rooted to the spot.

"But... we had a deal," he began plaintively.

"You had a deal with Ronald Brown. Not with me and, apparently, not with Mr. Reynolds anymore." Corrie straightened up. "And now, I'm going to talk to Mr. Reynolds about what I'm going to do with MY property. Good-bye," she said and strode into the office.

Corrie stared at the number on the offer in front of her. Surely she was seeing things. Or dreaming. That's it... the whole morning had been a dream. She actually hadn't woken up yet, hadn't talked to J.D. in the kitchen, hadn't met with Conrad Englewood; she was still asleep and her mind was spinning wild, improbable, impossible dreams. She was going to need a lot of coffee when she woke up.

A discreet cough made her blink and she looked up into the face of Arthur Reynolds, who seemed mildly perplexed at her reaction. Rick was standing behind the man and the expression on his face was that of a man trying not to laugh. His blue eyes were twinkling—something she hadn't seen in a long, long time. She wondered if he'd had anything to do with the amount that the Reynolds Corporation was offering her for the land on which Billy and her mother had built their dreams, the land that had been her home for so many years, the land that was now hers to sell. If she wanted to.

"Mr. Reynolds... I'm not sure what to tell you," she stammered.

Arthur Reynolds nodded. "I understand you might still be in shock, Miss Black," he said. "After all, you only lost your home a few days ago. However, I have been interested in it for a long time, after I was told you were interested in selling it and retiring. I'm sorry that I was misinformed and I don't mean to be heartless, but if you're not going to rebuild and you have no other plans...."

He let his words trail off and Corrie drew a deep breath.

Rick had emailed J.D. information that Meghan had in her files, surveys and studies done of the inherent value of the Black Horse property. Corrie had had no idea that it was considered a prime piece of property for a truck stop or travel center between Ruidoso and Roswell. The value of the property far exceeded what Billy had had it insured for ... but Mr. Reynolds was offering far more than what Corrie had decided to ask. While she had no idea what she'd do with that much money, she could feel Billy urging her to accept the offer and figure it out later. She glanced at Mr. DiMarco and the attorney's face told her that he would forever brand her as the dumbest client he'd ever represented if she let the opportunity pass. She took a deep breath.

"Mr. Reynolds, I'm going to leave all the details for Mr. DiMarco to iron out, but I accept your offer," she managed to say without her voice breaking. Mr. Reynolds looked pleased and relieved, which puzzled Corrie, but he stood up and offered her his hand.

"I can't tell you how happy I am... and if it will ease the transition a little, I would be glad to name it 'The Black Horse Travel Center'...."

"No!" Corrie said sharply, nearly drawing her hand back. Mr. Reynolds looked surprised but she shook her head emphatically. "I'm sorry, Mr. Reynolds, but no, I don't want you to name your truck stop after my campground. It's my family name and the campground is gone. If the Black Horse were to ever come back... well, please don't take offense, but it will not be as a truck stop. I don't want my father haunting me," she added. Mr. Reynolds laughed heartily.

"Well, that's fine, Miss Black. I'll speak to your attorney and we'll get this wrapped up as soon as possible. We'd like to break ground and hopefully have it ready to open by the summer season, if all goes well...." He droned on but Corrie barely heard him. The freedom to do what she wanted that J.D. had told her about was now a reality and it made her feel both terrified and exhilarated, excited and also lost.

The Black Horse Campground was gone.

But she was still here.

Chapter 31

"Congratulations."

Corrie looked up with a start. Both Rick and J.D. were raising a glass to her. J.D.'s held three fingers of Crown Royal Reserve, Rick's held iced tea, as did RaeLynn's. Somewhere, perhaps in the dim recesses of the wine cellar, Rick had managed to find a bottle of Jo Mamma's White from Noisy Water Winery and had presented Corrie a glass of the sweet wine. The Pages and Myers all held their beverage of choice and Cassandra had insisted on Manuel and Luz joining them in toasting the sale of the Black Horse. Corrie wondered if any of them had any idea of how she was really feeling.

She wasn't even sure how she was feeling.

She smiled, but it felt forced. Everyone could tell that she was hurting. Even though it seemed that she had had an amazing stroke of good luck, the fact was that she had lost everything—her home, her business, her connection to her parents. She now had more money than she ever dreamed of having and with it came the opportunity to do anything she wanted with her life.

And all she wanted was the Black Horse back.

The one thing her money couldn't buy.

She straightened up. "This is a lot to process," she began. She struggled to smile. "I don't want you all to worry. It's time I took the next step, but I have to figure out what that step is going to be. However, I also don't want you all to feel like you have to take it with me. We've been family for a long time and I hope that will never change... but we don't have to all be under one roof." She turned to the Pages and the Myers. Jackie, Dana, and even Red had tears in their eyes; Jerry, true to his nature, was looking away but his walrus mustache was quivering. She swallowed hard. "It's time to retire, you guys," she said, trying to make her voice light. "No more setting the alarm, no more worrying about guests, no more planning your time off around everyone else's vacation times."

"About time," Jerry said gruffly, although everyone heard the hitch in his voice.

"Oh, honey," Jackie sobbed, jumping up and embracing Corrie. "We both loved the Black Horse as much as you did! Don't listen to him!"

"She never has. Why should she start now?" Jerry choked out, fumbling with his handkerchief and burying his face in his hands.

Corrie couldn't help but laugh, even with tears streaming down her face. "I know you did, and I couldn't have kept it going without your help. But I want you to enjoy your life, free of any responsibilities. Billy would want it, too," she added.

"Well, you're not getting rid of us that easily," Jackie said stoutly, as Jerry got up and wrapped his arms around Corrie in a bear hug. "After all, we still need a home base to park the RV. So wherever you end up, we probably won't be too far away."

Red and Dana also hugged her. "Oh, sweetie, don't think we won't miss you," Dana said, her voice trembling. "Our daughter and her family have been after us to move to Phoenix to be closer to the grandkids... but we hate summers in Arizona so we'll be coming back to visit as often as we can!"

Corrie laughed shakily. She looked up and her eyes met J.D.'s. He was watching her intently, as if trying to see if she really was okay. Her heart twisted. What would J.D. do now? He was now an important part of the Bonney police department, but his home—his little cabin at the Black Horse—was gone. Would he use that fact as an excuse to leave Bonney? Of course he could find another place to live, but....

Out of the corner of her eye, she saw RaeLynn sitting perched on the very edge of one of the leather couches. She was staring down into her glass of iced tea, a million miles away. Corrie's heart lurched. She had often wondered what RaeLynn would do if she had sold the Black Horse. How often had she assured her that it would never happen? What was RaeLynn thinking now? Did she feel betrayed? Corrie felt a stab of guilt, even though she knew that she'd had no choice. She felt J.D.'s gaze boring into her and she looked at him again. She could almost hear his words out loud: *You wouldn't be selling the Black Horse; you'd only be selling the land. The Black Horse isn't there anymore.*

She wasn't sure she believed it yet, so how could she convince RaeLynn?

The house was quiet. Rick listened to the muted crackling coming from the fireplace in the main room. Everyone else had gone to bed a few hours earlier. He stood in the shadows of the hallway and watched Corrie, curled up in a leather recliner, staring into the dancing flames. He hadn't seen her looking so lost in years, not even when Billy died. She'd still had the campground then, a part of Billy she thought she would always have.

She looked up, having sensed his presence, and sat up straight. He moved toward her. "Hey," he said, "how are you doing?" He sank into the chair across from her.

She shrugged. "Still a little overwhelmed. I couldn't sleep. I hope you don't mind that I came in here to sit."

"Of course not," Rick said. He noted that she was wearing sweat pants and her Black Horse Campground t-shirt... probably the only thing she had left from the campground. He was wearing faded jeans and a University of New Mexico t-shirt. He saw her glance at him and then look down, a faint blush touching her cheeks. He wondered if she was thinking about the UNM football jersey she used to wear to sleep in. He cleared his throat. "Can we talk? There are some things I need to tell you."

Her head jerked up and she frowned. "What things?"

He took a deep breath. "Things I should have told you years ago." He stood up. "Let's go in the office. I don't want anyone to interrupt us."

She nodded and followed him into the office. He gestured for her to have a seat and then shut the door. He sat down behind the desk and noted that she was sitting with her arms crossed tightly across her chest. "Are you cold?" he asked. She shook her head and uncrossed her arms. She folded her hands and leaned toward him.

"What is it, Rick?"

He blew out his breath. He wasn't sure how to start, but he knew that Corrie didn't have the patience to wait for him to ease into the conversation. "I want to talk to you about... us."

She stiffened and sat up. "What 'us', Rick?" she asked. Her voice and eyes had hardened. She gripped the arms of the chair and he wasn't sure if it was to make sure she remained seated or if she was trying to keep from hauling off and slugging him. He couldn't blame her. "Are you saying that because Meghan is gone, we can go back to the way things were fifteen years ago?"

"No," he said forcefully. "I'm not that insensitive. She was my wife. No matter what happened to us towards the end, I did love her at one time and did my best to respect her."

Corrie looked away, her shoulders heaving. Rick bit back a sigh. This wasn't going the way he had wanted it to. "I should go back to bed," she said quietly. "I have a busy day tomorrow. I need to find a place to stay." She stood up. Rick did, too.

"Don't run away, Corrie. We have to talk."

"There's nothing to talk about."

"I have a lot of explaining to do. I owe you a lot of explanations."

"That's right, you do," she said, surprising him. She turned toward him, her hands on her hips. "You can start by telling me what I did wrong, Rick."

He stared at her. "What are you talking about? You didn't...."

"I must have, Rick," she said. She went on before he could respond, "Years ago, we were closer than I could ever imagine being with anyone else. Years ago, I thought... I thought that you and I...." She looked away and swallowed hard. "For years, I blamed Meghan," she said softly. "It was so easy to put the blame on her because I... I still loved you. So I let myself believe that she... stole you from me. That she took someone that belonged to me. But that wasn't true, was it?" she asked, her eyes hard on his. "Because you had already decided that, no matter who you were going to spend your life with, it wasn't going to be me."

"That doesn't mean I didn't love you... or that I still don't." He came from around the desk and, without meaning to, stood between her and the door. She raised an eyebrow at him and he moved back toward the desk, leaving a clear path. She stayed put. That gave him a glimmer of hope. He raised his hands. "Please, let me explain. Then, if you want to leave... well, I guess I can't stop you."

She eyed him narrowly, but she made no move toward the door. She also didn't sit down so Rick leaned a hip against the desk. He rubbed the back of his neck while she waited silently. "I don't know exactly where to start," he said. She still said nothing. "All right," he said. "Let's start with when Billy got sick, back when we were in high school."

Corrie's eyes widened. "What's that got to do with anything?"

"Remember when you called me from the hospital in Albuquerque? You'd just heard your dad's diagnosis. Some form of cancer and the only treatment option was some experimental one that wasn't covered by his insurance." He paused. "You sounded so devastated. You were crying so hard I could barely understand what you were saying. I just knew that you were over a hundred miles away, your dad was dying, and I'd never felt so helpless in my life." He cleared his throat. "Do you remember what happened next?"

Tears were streaming down her face. "Billy wanted to come

home. He said that there was no way he could afford the treatment if his insurance didn't cover it... and he wasn't about to try to sell the campground in order to pay for treatment. He wanted me to have the campground, to have a future, even if he was gone."

Rick nodded. He steeled himself and looked her straight in the eyes. "I called my father," he said hoarsely. "I told him... I needed him to... take care of Billy's treatment. I wanted it all paid for. I told him it was the least he could do after tearing our family apart, that I didn't care about him leaving me any of his inheritance. He agreed, but on one condition. I had to break up with you." He looked down and he was surprised to see his hands were shaking. He went on numbly, "I argued with him, said never mind, that I'd go to my mother for help but then I realized that I... couldn't. My father was trying to get her to file for divorce so he could legally marry Natalie... Billy's niece. They had a pre-nup— whoever filed for divorce would have to pay alimony—half of their personal wealth—and mother had more money than he did. He'd never file, not if he wanted to stay with Natalie. He'd never have given up the money. Natalie was Billy's niece and my father convinced me that it would be devastating to my mother to ask her to help the uncle of her husband's mistress. I felt trapped, but all I cared about...." He sucked in a shaky breath, raking his fingers through his hair. He could still hear Corrie's sobs over the phone line, still feel the nearly overwhelming urge to go to her and hold her and tell her it would all be okay, still relive the feeling of being powerless... a feeling he hated more than anything else. He had hated it when he was seventeen, he still hated it now, fifteen years later.

And he was feeling it again.

Corrie stared at him in shock. "You? You paid for Billy's treatment?"

"My father did, he made the arrangements," Rick said. "But it was my idea. And I never wanted you to know. I didn't want you to feel that... you owed me in any way."

"Billy didn't know, either?" Her voice was a haunted whisper. Rick let out a sharp laugh.

"Do you think he would have agreed to it, under those conditions? You know he'd have never allowed it. He would have never traded his life for our—your happiness."

"But *you* did? And you never told me? How could you keep this a secret?" she breathed.

"Because I made a promise," he said heavily. "I promised to

never tell... I agreed to give up my inheritance from my father in order to pay for Billy's medical treatment. Even my mother didn't know. When I turned eighteen, I signed away my rights to any inheritance from my father. Mother no longer could access my bank records so she didn't know I wasn't getting any interest payments from him. It didn't matter; I didn't care about the money and what I was getting from her was more than I needed. The only thing I wanted was the only thing I couldn't have," he finished, his eyes fastened on hers.

"Rick, how could you? Why didn't you talk to me about this?" Her hands clenched into fists. "You had no right to make that choice without talking to me, to Billy!"

"Listen to me, Corrie," he said, catching her by the upper arms. She didn't fight, didn't resist. She just stared at him, her eyes glazed with tears. "If Billy had known, do you think he would have lived? He would have refused the treatment. You know he would have! And if you had known, then what? What would you have told me? Would you have made that choice—me or your father?" He shook his head. "I couldn't ask you to make that choice, Corrie. And I couldn't ask Billy. He wouldn't have done anything to hurt you or me! He was the father I wished I'd had all my life! He would have sacrificed himself for us... but I gave you almost another fifteen years with him. I know I hurt you to do it," he said, releasing her and stepping back. "But, God help me, I'd do it again. The look on your face when you told me the treatment worked, that he was in remission...." He stopped, tears choking him. He swallowed hard. "I did it because I love you. I never stopped loving you and I never wanted to break up with you. I dreaded having to do that. I held off as long as I could, but my father was pressuring me, reminding me of the promise I made."

"You and your damned sense of honor!" Corrie snapped weakly. She shook her head and looked away, swiping tears off her face. "I guess I should say 'thank you'," she muttered.

Rick's heart twisted. "You don't have to thank me," he said hoarsely. "Believe me, you don't owe me anything. I loved Billy, too. I did it for him as much as I did for you."

She drew in a shaky breath and wrapped her arms around herself. "There's just one thing I don't understand, Rick," she said. She paced back and forth a few times. Rick said nothing; he knew she wanted to get her thoughts in order, be able to speak to him calmly. She stopped and turned to face him and took a deep breath. "Meghan," she said. "Why did you go find someone else, if you still loved me? Why did you have to go marry someone…?" Her voice trailed away.

Rick sighed and shrugged. "Every time I saw you, I saw hope in your eyes. A hope that we would get back together. And I believed that the best thing I could do to help you get over me was to make sure I wasn't available." He gave her a half-smile. "I underestimated how tenacious and loyal you can be," he said softly. "I wanted you to move on, find someone else, make a life for yourself. I thought the best way to do it was for me to make a life with someone else."

"You married Meghan," she said hesitantly, "just to get me to forget about you?"

"No," Rick said, shaking his head. "I wouldn't have married her just for that. I had made up my mind to stay away from you, to keep my promise, but I still wanted to get married and have a family." He cleared his throat. "Meghan was different back then, Corrie. She wasn't you, but she was someone I could love. And I *did* love her," he said, folding his arms across his chest, as if that would calm his pounding heart. "Turns out I loved who I thought she was. I wouldn't have married her otherwise. I take marriage seriously. I hoped you would find someone…."

There was a soft tap on the door and they both jumped. Rick frowned; it was after eleven p.m. Who would be up? He went to the door and opened it.

J.D. Wilder stood in the doorway. "Wilder? Is something wrong?" Rick asked.

"Sorry to interrupt, Sheriff," the detective said, glancing from Rick to Corrie, one brow raised. "But I could hear your cell phone going off from down the hall." He handed the phone to Rick. "It was your attorney, DiMarco. I don't know why he was calling at this hour…."

Rick's heart nearly stopped. He took the phone from Wilder. "Thanks. I need to call him right away," he stammered. He avoided Wilder's and Corrie's eyes as he strode down the hall, his heart pounding, knowing this was the call he had been half-expecting and half-dreading….

"What's going on?" J.D. asked Corrie. She looked dazed, as if she had just woken up from a deep sleep or a dream. "Are you all right?" He jerked his head in the direction that the sheriff had gone. "The sheriff okay?"

"Yeah, we're fine, J.D. Thanks," she said. She rubbed her

upper arms and forced a crooked smile. "We've been, uh, clearing up a lot of things. It's been pretty intense."

J.D. felt his stomach drop. He'd been concerned ever since Sutton had managed to expedite the settlement of Corrie's insurance claim and then the sale of the Black Horse. He had seen Corrie looking lost and confused. Was she going to be swayed by the sheriff's actions? Could she forgive and forget that easily? He cleared his throat and again nodded toward the door. "So what was that all about? Do you know why the Suttons' attorney is calling the sheriff so close to midnight?"

Corrie shook her head. "I have no idea." She looked at J.D. "Sorry his phone woke you. You've had a hard day."

J.D. shrugged. "Trust me, I wasn't asleep. Looks like you weren't either," he said.

"Things are so different than they were last night. And the night before. And the night before that," she said. She sat down and motioned for J.D. to sit also. He lowered himself into the rolling desk chair. He tried to study her discreetly but she noticed and shrugged her shoulders. She gave him a faint smile. "Rick explained a lot of things—things that happened years ago… it's a lot to process," she added, shifting in her seat.

J.D. nodded. "Is it going to make a difference?" he suddenly found himself asking. He could have kicked himself. What was he thinking? What kind of question was that? And couldn't he have picked a worse time to ask?

Corrie didn't seem surprised by his question, but her face looked somber. "I'm not sure, J.D. There's… there's a lot to think about."

J.D. refrained from asking anything else. He sensed that there was a lot that either Corrie or the sheriff were going to tell him eventually, but he was going to have to be patient. He sat up as he heard footsteps approaching the office door.

He and Corrie both turned as the door opened and Sutton stood framed in the doorway. One look at his face and they both jumped to their feet.

"Rick, what's wrong?" Corrie asked. Sutton shook his head and J.D. went to his side.

"Sheriff, you need to sit down. You look like you've seen a ghost." The sheriff waved away his assistance.

"I'm all right," he said hoarsely. "It's okay. Everything is…." He let his voice trail away and closed his eyes.

"Rick, talk to us!" Corrie said, taking his arm and shaking it.

"Something happened or Mr. DiMarco wouldn't be calling you in the middle of the night, now tell us what's wrong!"

The sheriff took a deep breath. "My father passed away an hour ago."

Chapter 32

Rick left early the next morning for Montana, with no clear idea of when he would return. He and Cassandra had had a long conversation into the early morning hours after receiving word of his father's death. Corrie guessed he had filled her in on a lot of things of which she was unaware... or maybe she had been aware all along but said nothing. J.D. offered to drive Rick to the airport in Ruidoso where he had chartered a private plane to fly him to Albuquerque. Rick spoke to Corrie briefly before he left. "We'll talk more when I get back, if you want to. I know you have a lot to think about. I'll be in touch." He had brushed the back of his forefinger against her cheek, his blue eyes intense, but he refrained from kissing her... even though there was really no reason for him to hold back. Corrie wasn't sure if she felt disappointed or relieved.

She received a text message from J.D. after he had dropped Rick off at the airport. Rick had given him the keys to his apartment, so he was going to stay there instead of driving all the way back to the Sutton house. He told her not to worry, that he was going to get some much-needed sleep and she should do the same.

She didn't wake up until eight in the morning, surprised that Renfro and Oliver hadn't roused her. She went downstairs and found that RaeLynn had let them out while Corrie was sound asleep and they were now curled up in front of the fireplace in the main room. RaeLynn's eyes had dark circles under them, their usual amber color muted to a pale brown. "You look like you should have slept in," Corrie told her as she helped herself to a cup of coffee and a piece of Luz's cinnamon coffee cake.

RaeLynn gave her a tentative smile. "I doubt either of us slept much. I heard you go to bed sometime after two a.m. Is everything all right?" Corrie realized that she very much wanted to talk to someone and found herself telling RaeLynn everything that she had learned last night, including the reason why Rick had broken off their relationship back in high school. RaeLynn listened without saying a word, only getting up a couple of times to refill their coffee cups. When Corrie finished, RaeLynn let out a long sigh and shook her head. "Wow," was all she said.

"It's a lot to take in," Corrie said. "But what do you think?"

"I always knew that Rick never stopped loving you," RaeLynn said. "When he broke up with you back then, just about every girl fantasized that she'd have a chance to be with him."

"Including you?" Corrie asked, faintly amused but not surprised.

RaeLynn scoffed. "I've never had any illusions about my chances with Rick... or any guy like him," she said, not seeming to be bothered. "But I saw what those other girls didn't want to see: That he was still in love with you. I saw the way he looked at you when he thought no one was looking. No one ever noticed me, so it was easy for me to catch him with his guard down. I couldn't understand why he did it... and I guess if I'm going to be honest, I still don't understand." Corrie sighed.

"Rick made a promise to his father...."

"His father was an awful man," RaeLynn said, her brow furrowing. "He hurt Rick's mom and Rick as well. Rick was just a kid and for his dad to just suddenly vanish from his life over a girl half his age... and he was terrible to your cousin, too." RaeLynn nodded, fiddling with a napkin on the table. "He made her be 'the other woman'. If he really loved her, he wouldn't have done that to her. How could she trust a man who would cheat on someone to be with her? No," she said, shaking her head, "I can't feel sorry that he died. I'm not even sorry that I feel that way, either," she added.

Corrie managed a smile. "It's okay, RaeLynn. I understand. I feel bad for Natalie, though. She was dazzled by the attention from a rich man. Billy tried to warn her, but she wouldn't listen." She stopped and shook her head. "She's going to be the one most hurt by Rick's dad's death. They were never married. I don't know if he was honest enough to make sure she would be all right if anything happened to him." RaeLynn made a small sound in her throat, not completely willing to be sympathetic but too kind-hearted not to be moved by the plight of a young, naïve girl who might have thrown away her life by breaking up a rich man's marriage.

Luz bustled into the kitchen with a stack of folded kitchen towels. "Oh, good morning, Corrie," she said. "Would you like some breakfast?"

"I think two pieces of your coffee cake will do me, Luz," Corrie answered as she helped herself to a second helping.

Luz smiled, pleased, then her face grew serious. "Mrs. Sutton asked me to let you know that she has gone to stay with some friends near Tucson for a few days. She says she has some thinking to do, as I'm sure you're aware. She said that you and

286

your friends are welcome to stay as long as you wish and to feel at home. Manuel and I are at your service."

"That's very kind of her, Luz, but...," Corrie began but Luz shook her head.

"Mrs. Sutton said you would probably argue, but she insisted," Luz said. She smiled at RaeLynn. "I think it would be nice to have people in the house and I know that RaeLynn would like to pick my brain for cooking lessons and recipes, wouldn't you, RaeLynn?"

"If it's not too much trouble," RaeLynn said, blushing. Corrie could see that RaeLynn was excited at the thought and she realized that, really, there was no place for them to go. She got up and excused herself to go up to her room. She had a lot of thinking to do, herself.

J.D. arrived at the Sutton house late in the afternoon. The weather had cleared enough for him to be able to ride his Harley. He had tied up a lot of loose ends at the police department and answered a lot of questions that Eldon LaRue had. He had swung by the sheriff's department as well, just to make sure that Dudley Evans didn't need any help and to let him know that he was available if they needed him. Dudley assured him that he would call if necessary and then asked J.D. to let him know if he heard from the sheriff.

He entered the house and found Corrie sitting in one of the wing chairs in front of the fireplace. She had several papers scattered over the coffee table and she was making notes on a pad. She looked up when he walked in and she smiled. "Long time no see, stranger," she teased.

He grinned. "Has it only been about fifteen hours?" He glanced around. "Are you the only one here?"

She set the notepad down and stood up. "RaeLynn and Luz kicked me out of the kitchen. I can't wait to see what they've got planned for dinner. Red and Dana are leaving for Arizona tomorrow, so they're making something special. Jerry and Jackie are scouting out a place to move their RV, even though Cassandra told them they were welcome to stay as long as they want to. The same goes for all of us." She tilted her head and looked at J.D. "Is everything all right? You seem a little distracted."

"Depends on what you mean by everything," he said. "The village and county are in good hands. Eldon tried to give me leave of absence for as long as I want, but I feel like staying busy. I'll be staying at the sheriff's apartment. It's a little more convenient to work and I can keep an eye on things for him while he's gone." He paused. "Have you heard from him?" he asked.

"I was going to ask you the same thing," she said. She sat back down and he dropped into the chair beside her. "Did he tell you anything on the way to the airport last night?"

"Yeah," he said. The sheriff had told him everything, actually, but he guessed he didn't need to tell Corrie that. He swiped a hand over his head and sighed. "He said he hadn't planned on having to take care of two funerals at once...."

"Two funerals?" Corrie looked startled, then comprehension showed in her eyes. "Oh. Meghan's. He's taking care of it?"

"He said the plans that she'd made for their daughter's interment in Dallas would be used for Meghan's final arrangements. Her parents are struggling financially; apparently, part of Meghan's shady business dealings were to help them out, so Sutton—of course—offered to take care of her funeral for them."

"Sounds like Rick," Corrie said with a wry smile. "Did he say he was planning to take care of his dad's final arrangements, as well?"

J.D. recalled the conversation he'd had with the sheriff on the way to Ruidoso. "Not in so many words," he admitted. "He said he'd be surprised if his father had even had a life insurance policy. He said his father was all about keeping up appearances and lived way beyond his means." He gave Corrie a pointed look. "He said he wasn't sure, but he thinks you might have seen the letters."

It wasn't a question and Corrie had the grace to blush. "I didn't read them," she said. "I was surprised, though. I had assumed that he hadn't heard from his father in years."

"He hadn't," J.D. said. "His dad started reaching out to him a couple years ago. He was pressuring Sutton to try to talk his mother into filing for divorce... he needed the alimony settlement. He'd gone down a bad path a few years ago—drinking, gambling, womanizing...."

Corrie blinked. "What about Natalie?" she asked, sitting up straighter.

"He was still with her. Or rather, she was still with him at the end. He wrecked his liver and was dying slowly. All his girlfriends left him but she stuck with him. I guess she was still hoping she would get something when he died. The sheriff's going to be taking care of a lot of loose ends for his dad, including making sure that Natalie has something to live on, though not as lavishly as his father had her accustomed to. That's why he won't be back right away. Mr. DiMarco has his work cut out for him." He waited a few seconds, studying Corrie's face. "You know about the deal he made with his dad," he said slowly. "If he'd had any concerns about it, they're now gone. His father's death has pretty much canceled any obligation the sheriff had to that agreement."

Corrie's face reddened slightly. "I know," she said. She looked directly into J.D.'s eyes. "That doesn't mean that I can just forget the last fifteen years, J.D. He knows that."

J.D.'s chest tightened. Was he crazy for having a scant hope? He shook his head and changed the subject. "What are you working on? Planning on a European getaway?"

"I have no idea what I'd do in Europe," Corrie said. "I'm antsy to find something to do. The insurance settlement and the sale of the land won't keep me forever and I'm too young to retire. I'm making plans for my next move."

"Which is?" J.D. leaned forward and glanced at the paperwork she had spread out on the table. He picked up a sheet and raised his brows. "You're planning to reopen the Black Horse?"

"I'd like to," she said, leaning back in her chair. "I just don't know where yet… or what I'm planning to make of it. Maybe another campground, maybe a bed-and-breakfast. I'm looking at properties." She paused and shifted in her chair. "It might not be here in Bonney, though."

J.D. blinked. Had he heard wrong? "You're thinking of leaving Bonney?"

"Are you surprised?"

"That's putting it mildly," J.D. said. "I never thought you would even think of leaving Bonney. I mean, it's your home."

"I'm not talking about moving to the moon," she said. She gave him a crooked smile. "Charlie and Joanie are going to be married soon. He wants me to mend fences with Billy's family. He said there's land to be had… maybe it's something I'd consider. It would be a lot of work, but I'm used to it."

"I see," J.D. said. It made his heart hurt to think of Corrie leaving Bonney. What would it mean for him to see her leave? Would he want to stay in Bonney if she were gone? What would the sheriff do? Would he be willing to leave Bonney?

She seemed to sense his inner turmoil. "You're the one who convinced me that I should take the opportunity to make a fresh start, no obligations," she said.

"You're right," he said, hoping he could mask his feelings. He knew he was doing a lousy job of it. "Just didn't realize it could involve you leaving Bonney."

"I didn't, either," she said, with a slight tremor in her voice. "I honestly don't know what I'm going to do. I'm still trying to figure things out." She stood up and gathered all the papers. "But I've had enough for one day. I'm going to see if Luz and RaeLynn need any help. You're staying for dinner, right? With Red and Dana leaving in the morning...."

"I'm not brave enough to say 'no' to Luz's cooking," he said, forcing a smile. The truth was, he didn't want to spend one more minute away from Corrie than was necessary. No one knew what the next day would bring. "I just need to gather up whatever stuff I have in my room upstairs...."

"Aren't you coming back when Rick returns?" she asked, her face registering dismay.

For some reason, it made J.D. feel a little better. He chuckled. "I guess that remains to be seen," he said. "But as long as I'm staying at the sheriff's place for a couple of weeks, I do need more than one change of clothes." Her face relaxed and J.D. felt his heart lighten.

A lot could happen in a couple weeks.

Chapter 33

San Ignacio Catholic Church, Bonney County, New Mexico, early March

Corrie stepped out of the church after Sunday morning Mass and breathed in the spring air. She had zipped her jacket to her chin before leaving her pew, as it had been quite chilly when she arrived an hour earlier, but now she was half tempted to remove her jacket completely. The morning had warmed up considerably once the sun had peeked over the mountaintops.

After the harrowing events of the previous month, snow had fallen regularly which had saved the tourist industry by enabling Ski Apache to open to one of their busiest months in history. Corrie tried not to think about what a great spring break season the Black Horse was missing out on... normally, she and her staff would be scrambling to accommodate the number of guests who would be using the campground as their base for a winter vacation. Bonney had received a decent amount of snow, but the temperatures hadn't been brutally cold; only the tent sites would have been empty.

Now only the ski resort had a healthy amount of snow and spring had decided to arrive early in the valleys. Over the sounds of the parishioners greeting and chatting with each other and cars starting up in the parking lot, she could hear the faint sounds of heavy machinery coming from the direction of the former site of the Black Horse and it was as if a cloud covered the sun and made her pull her jacket tighter around herself. The snowfall had delayed Mr. Reynolds' plans to begin work on his travel center. Now they were working round the clock, it seemed, to try to be ready to open by Memorial Day weekend. She hadn't been able to bring herself to go by to see the work; she had gone once to see the ruins of the campground before the Reynolds Corporation began razing what was left of the store. J.D. had taken her. Snow had covered up the worst of the burn scar but, for Corrie, it was enough to confirm that she had made the right choice in selling the property.

She made her way to the Bronco; Jerry and Jackie had gone to visit their children while their grandkids were on spring break and they left their vehicle for Corrie to use. She unlocked the ancient SUV and glanced toward the adjoining cemetery and froze in surprise.

Rick was kneeling at the foot of a small grave. His daughter Ava's grave.

Corrie made her way over to him, not sure if she should intrude on his privacy, but it had been nearly a month since he had left to tend to his father's final arrangements. She'd only received a few text messages—cell phone service was spotty where his father had lived—and he explained that there were a lot of things he needed to focus on before he came home.

Rick was brushing leaves and twigs away from the small, white granite stone. He picked up a tapered glass vase that contained a bouquet of pink and white carnations. It looked like a strawberry ice cream soda, with a gold number 6 perched on top. He set a small brown-and-white stuffed horse beside the bouquet, with a white ribbon tied around its neck with pink letters spelling out "Happy Birthday" on it. Corrie felt her heart twist as she paused a few feet away. The tributes stood out in stark relief against the freshly turned earth; Cassandra's jewels had been recovered, though Corrie doubted she'd ever wear them again. Rick had removed his Stetson and bowed his head for a few minutes. He crossed himself and then glanced over his shoulder and she drew closer.

"She probably would have been asking for a pony for her birthday this year." He sounded amused, a hint of sadness in his tone. Corrie smiled through her sudden tears.

"And you would have probably gotten her one."

He chuckled softly. "Yeah," he agreed. He stood up and brushed dirt from the knees of his dress slacks and replaced the Stetson on his head. He smiled at Corrie and then glanced around the cemetery. "I never told you how much comfort it gave me to know that she was buried just below where your mother was buried. And now with Billy there as well," he said, indicating the matching stones just up the slope from Ava's grave. "I feel better knowing they're watching over her."

Corrie swallowed hard. She hoped she wouldn't start bawling. "When did you get back?" she asked when she could speak.

"I flew into Albuquerque yesterday afternoon. I went to see a friend at the Carmelite Monastery in Santa Fe and went to Mass at the Cathedral. I left to come home early this morning because I've never been away for Ava's birthday." He took a deep breath. "It's been a crazy last few weeks," he said dryly.

Corrie gave him a twisted grin. "You're telling me," she said.

She took a deep breath. "How is my cousin, Natalie?" she asked

Rick shook his head and shrugged. "It's been hard on her," he said. "My father was almost penniless when he died. She got stuck with a huge amount of medical bills. The worst shock was that, even though he had a sizeable life insurance policy, she wasn't one of the beneficiaries." He hesitated a moment before going on, "He'd named me and two children he'd had with two other women as beneficiaries."

Corrie's mouth dropped open. "You have siblings?"

"Yeah," Rick said. "Two half brothers. I met them at the memorial service... they were cordial but they don't seem to be too interested in maintaining any kind of relationship. I can't blame them; they didn't have any fond memories of my father and he never bothered to acknowledge them while he was alive. I'm nobody to them. They're satisfied just to take the money and get on with their lives." He cleared his throat. "I took care of my father's final arrangements and his medical bills and I gave my share of his life insurance to Natalie. He refused to have children with her and he left her pretty much destitute. She had nothing."

"She could come back to New Mexico...."

Rick shook his head sadly. "I mentioned that to her. She says she's too ashamed to come back. She said there's no way she can face you." He took a deep breath. "She had pretty harsh words with Billy before she left, words she now regrets. She couldn't even bring herself to come to his funeral. And she said she had loved him so much when she was a child."

"Who didn't love Billy?" Corrie said with a hitch in her voice. She hadn't been surprised to hear what Rick had done for his father and for Corrie's cousin as well. She cleared her throat. "RaeLynn's preparing brunch. She went to Mass last night because Manuel and Luz took the weekend off to go visit family in Las Cruces. She was anxious to try her hand at making a big Sunday brunch on her own. I was beginning to wonder if it was only going to be three of us eating it."

"Wilder on duty this morning?" he asked, understanding her need to change the subject.. Corrie nodded.

"He'll be heading back to the house shortly. We'd better go before RaeLynn starts worrying that her brunch will be ruined." She started to turn away, but Rick caught her hand.

"Have you been thinking?" he asked softly.

"Too much," she answered quickly. She glanced in the direction of the church parking lot. Most of the cars were gone. No one was near; they were alone. The warm sunny morning had suddenly become simultaneously stifling hot and freezing cold.

"And?" he persisted. "It's been a month. What have you been thinking?"

"What should I be thinking?" she snapped, feeling irritated. "We've hardly talked since you left! I have a lot of questions and no answers."

"What questions?" he asked, as they started to make their way toward the Bronco. He had released her and shoved his hands into his pockets. Corrie recognized his customary defensive pose and it irritated her further.

"Where do you want me to start?" she said. "How about 'why didn't you tell me about what your dad asked you to do?' Okay, maybe you had to go along with his demand, but you could have told me about it! I wouldn't have liked it, but at least I wouldn't have spent the last fifteen years thinking I did something to make you hate me!"

"I never hated you," he said, his brow furrowing. "Did you really think that?"

"I thought your MOTHER hated me!" she said. "I thought she was the reason you broke up with me! And she thought that I broke up with you! You never bothered to explain anything to anyone! And why? Because you're so stubborn you won't talk to anyone! You want to fix everything yourself!"

He held up a hand. "Corrie, I didn't want to worry you...."

"Thanks, but you failed miserably, Rick! That's all I've done is worry and wonder!"

"I made a choice that I didn't want to force you to make!" he said, catching her by the upper arms. "Can't you understand that I couldn't put that choice on you?"

"I can understand why you didn't want to, Rick. I do understand. But you didn't have the right to make that choice without telling me!" she cried, not sure if what she was saying was making sense. He sighed and let her go. He took a step back.

"Okay," he said quietly. "You're right. I'm sorry."

She blinked and almost fell over. "What?"

"I said, 'You're right. I'm sorry'. Yes, I said it. You don't have to rub it in," he said dryly. "I realized that all these years I've been saying I'm sorry for hurting you, but I haven't said that I'm sorry for what I did to hurt you." He pushed his Stetson back and scratched his head. "That probably made about as much sense as what you said," he muttered. He shrugged and shook his head.

"Okay, so... does that answer that question? Can we go on to the next? We need to wrap this up before we go to brunch. I don't want you stabbing me with a butter knife in front of RaeLynn and Wilder."

Her mouth dropped open. He gave her his usual half-smile, that maddening half-smile, and leaned against the Bronco. Her heart trembled, her knees grew weak, and she stamped her foot in frustration. "You are absolutely infuriating, Rick! I don't know what to make of you! One minute I want to strangle you and the next I want to hug you! First, you make me want to cry and then you make me want to laugh! I've spent the last month wanting so bad to see you again and right now, I swear, I never want to see you again!"

"That's fair. So are you saying you will?"

She stared at him. "What are you talking about? Will I what?"

"Marry me?"

She felt the world spin. She caught the door handle of the Bronco to keep herself upright. Her brain was completely blank and, at that same time, she was flooded with more emotions than she could process. "Marry you? *MARRY YOU?* This? This is your idea of a proposal?" she sputtered. He continued to grin at her and she continued to rage. "What is wrong with you, Rick? We're in the middle of a huge fight and you just throw out a marriage proposal?"

"Well, I was hoping that you'd forgive me for all the stupid things I've done over the last fifteen years first, before we move on to talking about marriage...."

"Oh, that's romantic!" Corrie scoffed. Her face was burning and she became aware that Father Eloy could probably hear them from inside the church. She was glad the entire village wasn't around to hear them. "This is how you planned to propose to me?"

"No," he said. He took her hand and dropped to one knee. "I didn't buy a ring because I wanted to make sure I get you one that you really like and won't want to take off, but I did plan to propose in a more conventional manner. So, Corrie Black, *mi Corazón*, my heart, will you marry me? Will you put up with me and my bull-headedness, forgive me for being thoughtless and hurting you and be willing to do it again because I admit I'm not perfect but I promise to do my best not to let it happen again? Will you...?"

"Stop!" Corrie cried. She was half-laughing, half-sobbing,

partly furious, partly touched, and overwhelmingly confused. He stood up, still holding her hand, and offered her his handkerchief. She took a few minutes to wipe her eyes, blow her nose, and pull herself together. "Rick, are you serious?"

"I'll try not to take offense to that, but yes, I am, Corrie. We—I mean, I—took a fifteen year detour to get to this point, but this is what I've always wanted and I'm hoping that it's what you wanted, too… and still do."

She had calmed down and looked up into his eyes. They were dark and serious, with an ocean of feelings just below the surface. He was keeping his emotions in check, proving that he had given it a lot of thought and wasn't just reacting emotionally.

He was doing far better than she was.

She took a deep breath. She should have been expecting this, she should have given it more thought. Rick had always been there; even when he was married, he'd still been a part of her life, albeit peripherally, but there was nothing that had prepared her for this actual moment. She had dreamed of it, but it had always been the impossible, unattainable dream. She honestly had no idea how to respond.

"Rick," she began. The look in his eyes intensified and she was startled to see that he was actually holding his breath. He wasn't so confident; despite the fact that he knew she was forgiving and generous and loving, he also knew that she had every right to turn and walk away and never give him another chance to hurt her again.

"I… I want to take this slow," she said. "Everything is a mess right now. I've lost my home and business and I'm still trying to figure out what I want to do. I need time; I don't want to make my problems your problems."

"You're missing the point of marriage," he said, catching her chin with his fingers and looking deep into her eyes, into her soul. "I want to help you with your problems. I want to help you find solutions and I want to stand beside you as you find your way. Corrie, I'm not going anywhere, no matter what you decide. I'll always be here for you. I've made mistakes and maybe I can't make them all right, but I'm always in your corner. I'll always be your friend." He released her and stepped back. "I know this took you by surprise. I understand it's a shock. I won't rush you. We'll take it one step at a time. One thing I never realized about you is that you don't settle. You could have found someone, years ago, and he would have been the luckiest and smartest man in the world to have you in his life. But evidently you didn't and you wouldn't settle for just anyone, even though I wasn't available anymore. I don't want you to settle for me, either. The truth is, you don't need me. You don't need anyone, Corrie. You'll be fine on your own; you always have been. But I'm hoping that maybe you might *want* to have me around. Either because you're a glutton for punishment or maybe you just like my company," he added. He flashed her a smile and she found herself smiling back and she let out a laugh.

"All right," she said. "But for now, we'd better get back to the house before RaeLynn has our heads for making her brunch wait."

J.D. let himself into the Sutton house, reminding himself that only Corrie and RaeLynn would be there this weekend. The wonderful aroma of bacon and coffee wafted from the kitchen area and his stomach growled. He followed his nose into the dining room and saw that the table wasn't set. "Hello?" he called.

"Hello!" RaeLynn called back. "Detective Wilder? We'll be eating in the breakfast nook. Is Corrie home yet?"

Home? J.D. shook his head. Obviously a slip of the tongue but he grinned. "Not yet," he answered. Of course, RaeLynn had made herself right at home in the kitchen as Luz's shadow. He went into the kitchen.

The island had been transformed into a buffet. A platter of bacon and sausage sat next to a basket of homemade biscuits. A huge bowl of fresh fruit took center stage beside a cast-iron skillet of home fries. Small crystal bowls holding a variety of jams and fruit butters were clustered around a butter dish next to a pitcher of fresh orange juice. RaeLynn straightened up from the oven with a deep-dish spinach and mushroom quiche in her hands and made her way to the island. J.D. took the dish from her hands and set it on the trivet that was obviously placed for the quiche. RaeLynn smiled at J.D. nervously. "Well? How does everything look?" she asked.

"Absolutely amazing!" J.D. said. "I'm glad I didn't stop to grab a donut on the way here to hold me over. I haven't eaten since before midnight."

RaeLynn looked pleased and bounced on her toes a little. The sound of the front door opening reached them. "Oh, good, Corrie's here!" she said. She turned toward the counter and grabbed the coffee pot from the warming plate.

"Something smells wonderful!" Corrie said as she came in

the kitchen door. J.D.'s smile froze as he saw the sheriff walk in behind her.

"Oh, Rick, you're back!" RaeLynn said. "Oh, I'm so glad I made plenty!"

"Plenty? Were you expecting the whole village to show up?" Sutton joked.

"Welcome back, Sheriff," J.D. managed to say. His appetite had vanished; he saw the way the man was looking at Corrie and the way she looked at him. It was apparent that Corrie had made up her mind.

And somehow he wasn't surprised.

"I think we made a dent in your brunch, RaeLynn." Corrie smiled as RaeLynn bustled around the table refilling the coffee cups.

"I'm glad everyone liked everything. I was so worried," RaeLynn said as she took her seat again. She looked like she was about to burst with pride.

"Luz has some competition in the kitchen," Rick said. "She's taught you well. I didn't think anyone could ever make biscuits to rival Luz's."

"She's going to teach me how to make tortillas, too," RaeLynn said happily.

"Oof," J.D. said, patting his stomach. "Homemade tortillas are my weakness. I hope they're not going to be a regular thing. I've been neglecting my trips to the gym."

Corrie smiled as she listened to them chatting around the table. She had avoided J.D.'s eyes when she came in with Rick; somehow, she knew he was aware of what had transpired between her and Rick. She would have to talk to him, soon. There was a pang in her heart at the thought of J.D. deciding that there was no reason for him to stay in Bonney if she were to marry Rick. She looked toward him and wasn't surprised that his eyes were fastened on her. He glanced at Rick, then back at her, and gave her a resigned shrug. She felt a hitch in her stomach. What did that mean?

She stood up. "I think I'd better help RaeLynn with the dishes before I go into a coma," she said, but Rick and J.D. jumped up.

"No way," J.D. said before Sutton said a word. "The sheriff and I got the dishes. It's the least we can do."

"Oh, no, you don't have to...," RaeLynn said, but Rick waved away her protests.

"No, he's right, RaeLynn. But before we do, I need to talk to Corrie."

Corrie froze, holding a stack of plates. He wasn't about to bring up his proposal right now, was he? "Uh... talk about what?" she said, setting the dishes down before she dropped them. He motioned them all to sit down and she exchanged a puzzled glance with both RaeLynn and J.D. It was evident that neither of them knew what Rick was talking about.

He cleared his throat. "It's been a month since a lot of stuff happened," he began. "A month since the Black Horse burned down. I know that Corrie's been giving it a lot of thought, but, as far as I know, hasn't made a decision. Correct?"

"Not yet," Corrie managed to say. She felt her cheeks burn. She had told Rick that she had to figure out what she was going to do with her life and she honestly didn't know. She knew what she WANTED to do, but so far, she had no prospects. There were no properties available for what she wanted; the property on the reservation had fallen through since Charlie and Joanie decided they wanted to raise horses and would need the land. Corrie had been glad for them, even though Charlie felt guilty that he had raised her hopes. Beside, things were still tense between her and the rest of her father's family and she didn't feel comfortable being under their constant scrutiny. They needed more time and Corrie felt better being in Bonney, anyway.

But she hadn't found what she wanted in Bonney, either.

Rick was watching her as if he could read her thoughts. He cleared his throat. "I might have some information that will make things a little easier to figure." He straightened up. "I called Mother after I got back to New Mexico yesterday. She's been talking about moving to Arizona and making Tucson her primary residence. She's got a wonderful condo there and it's not as isolated as this place." He leaned forward. "As I told Corrie, I won't be inheriting anything from my father, so I worked out a deal with my mother. Instead of receiving my inheritance when I turn forty, I get the ranch now. Mother says she's not planning to go anywhere in the next seven or eight years, so she wanted to make sure I was willing to make that trade. I don't need the money," he said. "And I don't really need the house, either. But I was wondering what you would think of this," he looked around, "becoming the Black Horse Inn."

Corrie's jaw hit the table... or at least, it felt like it. She sat back, stunned, and glanced at RaeLynn. Her hands were up over her mouth, her eyes as wide as saucers. Corrie shook her head. "Wait," she stammered. "Are you saying your mother wants to sell the ranch... to me?"

"No," Rick said. "The ranch is mine. I'm offering a partnership. Use the money from your insurance claim and the sale of the campground to make improvements, remodel, whatever you need to do, but you run the place. Just like you did the campground. You have carte blanche, Corrie. You have a total of eight bedrooms with adjoining baths upstairs and two suites, plus four suites downstairs. There are also several RV hookups out back that we've used for ranch hands in the past. I'll let you plan the rest, but this is a way for the Black Horse to go on. We'll work out a deal where you basically pay me to use the property. I'm a very easy landlord," he said with a half-smile. "I won't get in your way and you can run your business however you want. No strings attached," he added, his face growing serious. "Absolutely none."

Did her face turn red? Did J.D. and RaeLynn realize what he meant? Did she believe him? She stared at him and his face was impassive, although she could read his thoughts as if they were written over his head. He had meant what he had said at the church. He wasn't going anywhere. And he was offering her another chance at Billy's dream. Her dream. Excitement rose in her chest. She knew what Rick was thinking; maybe the house wouldn't be hers on paper, but it would be hers, completely and absolutely. Rick's honor... yes, that was all she needed to depend on.

"I accept," she managed to croak out. RaeLynn let out a squeal of delight and Corrie laughed. Rick gave her one of the biggest smiles she'd ever seen and she looked at J.D. who gave her a resigned smile.

As if he'd been expecting this.

Rick was putting the last of the dishes away as Wilder wiped down the kitchen counters. "You're awful quiet," he said. The detective straightened up and shook his head.

"Not much to say." He shrugged. "Except maybe 'congratulations'."

Rick paused and turned around. Wilder was leaning against the kitchen island, his arms folded across his chest. Rick raised a brow. "She hasn't said 'yes'," he said.

"Yet," Wilder countered. He tossed the cloth he'd been using into the laundry bin. "How can she say no when you've given her what no one else could? You've given her the Black Horse back. No one can compete with that, Sutton."

"That's not part of the deal," Rick said harshly. "She can still say she just wants to be friends and she'd still have the Black Horse." Wilder raised a brow.

"You think she believes that?"

"Just because you don't?" Rick shook his head. "Whether either of you believe it doesn't matter. It's the truth. The Black Horse is hers." He didn't know what else to say and it was apparent that neither did Wilder. They stared at each other for a long time.

Finally Wilder laughed. "I guess I knew all along the two of you would be together. No matter how much I wanted to believe I had a chance...."

"You still might. She hasn't said 'yes' yet."

"Mere formality," Wilder said, waving his hand. "I'm not a jealous man, Sutton, but I wouldn't want to share her with you. She loved you first and always will. It's time I accepted it."

"You're not leaving Bonney, are you?" Rick asked, alarmed at the finality in the detective's tone. Wilder gave him a crooked grin.

"Nah. Probably not. Eldon's given me heads up that he's thinking of retiring. He's got too many bad memories tied to Bonney. And life here is pretty good. Good people. And Corrie's my friend," he added. He straightened up and looked Rick in the eye. "She believed in me and trusted me when I came to town, when no one else would. You don't find someone like that every day. And I'm willing to have her just as a friend, if nothing else, because I'm not stupid enough to throw away a friendship like that. You don't have a problem with that, do you?"

"Not at all," Rick said without a trace of a smile. He held out his hand.

Wilder gripped it tightly.

The next few weeks went by in a frenzy of activity. Corrie hired architects and carpenters to help her redesign and remodel the new Black Horse Inn. An elevator would be installed for the convenience of older guests and those who didn't want to haul their luggage up the stairs. Bathrooms were updated and, with apologies to Rick's mother, the dark opulent décor that Cassandra had favored was replaced with a lighter, cozier farmhouse feel. Together with RaeLynn, she designed a business plan to incorporate a combination of a luxurious bed-and-breakfast with the friendliness of the campground. Myra, having found out she was having twins, was glad to know she would have a full-time job that enabled her to bring her babies with her. Spa services, such as facials and manicures and pedicures, would give Dee Dee another income source. Buster was happy to relinquish his job in the village to be a full-time maintenance man, assisting Manuel with the chores and groundskeeping. And RaeLynn, under Luz's guidance, would be a stellar cook for breakfasts, family dinners, and tea-time treats that would be offered to the guests in the afternoons.

J.D., much to Corrie's amusement, had become Rick's roommate in town. It was far more convenient than driving in from the Black Horse, although he still managed to show up almost every evening for dinner, unless duty called him away. Rick was also staying in town, only coming out to check on the progress of the Black Horse about every other day and often staying for dinner, especially when RaeLynn wanted to show off a new recipe.

One evening, Corrie heard Rick's Silverado come up the road and she glanced at RaeLynn in surprise. "Were we having the guys over for dinner tonight?" she asked.

RaeLynn frowned. "I don't think so. Detective Wilder said he had to work late and Rick doesn't usually come on a Wednesday."

Corrie waited for Rick to come in and was surprised when she heard a knock at the door. "Now what is he up to?" she muttered as she went to the door and opened it.

Rick stood on the porch with a bouquet of flowers. He wasn't in his uniform. He was in faded jeans and a dark blue t-shirt. He swept off his Stetson. "Good evening, Corrie. I hope you aren't too busy tonight?"

She stared at him, perplexed. "Uh, no, not at all."

"Good," he said. He handed her the bouquet. "I know it's bad manners to ask a lady on a date at the last minute, but if you don't have plans, would you care to have dinner with me?"

"Dinner?" she stammered. She glanced down at herself, still wearing the jeans she'd been painting in and the faded Black Horse Campground t-shirt. "I'm not really dressed for it…."

"Sure you are," he said, taking her hand. He tugged her toward the front steps and led her down to the truck. He lowered the tailgate and grabbed a footstool. "This should make it easier to climb up. Now have a seat and give me a minute." He went to the passenger side door and returned shortly with a pizza box and a bucket filled with ice and a few bottles of Coke. "Is the 'Regulator' combo still your favorite? Pepperoni, sausage, mushrooms, onions, and green chile?" Corrie laughed.

"I thought it came with olives, too?"

"You hate olives. I asked Tony to put 'em just on half."

"Rick, what are you doing? What is all this?"

He jumped up on the tailgate and grabbed a bottle out of the bucket. He popped the cap and gave it to her. "You said you wanted to take it slow." He smiled. "Remember our first 'official' date? I'd just gotten my driver's license, but Billy didn't want me to take you out after it got dark...."

Tears filled Corrie's eyes. "So you picked up a pizza and sodas from Tony's and we had our first date in the parking lot of the Black Horse." He tapped his bottle against hers.

"Kind of fitting, don't you think?"

Dedication and Acknowledgements

This book is dedicated to the many small-business owners who have struggled through the last two years, adapting and adjusting to meet the challenges that have come their way, especially independent bookstore owners who do their best every day to keep their doors open and allow authors to keep their books available to everyone. John Hoffsis at Treasure House Books and Gifts in Albuquerque and Becky Ewing at Books Etc. in Ruidoso, this one's for you.

Heartfelt thanks to:

Paul, for always and everything,

Cynthia, for her invaluable insights and spot-on editorial comments,

Carla Morrow for her killer book cover designs. Be sure to visit her page (www.dragonladyart.com) to see more of her work, and credit to Egor Vikhrev (on Unsplash.com) for the cover photograph.

Noisy Water Winery crew for being a great cheering section,

For the family and friends who are always in my corner,

And my publisher, Mike Orenduff, for always asking when the next book will be ready!

Other books in the Black Horse Campground Series

End of the Road
Book 1

Corrie Black, owner of the Black Horse Campground, hopes for a successful summer season, but the discovery that long-time guest Marvin Landry has been shot dead in his own RV and $50,000 in cash is missing does not herald a good beginning, especially since the victim's handicapped wife and angry stepson show little interest in discovering who murdered him. Is the appearance of a mysterious biker with a shadowy past and a recently deceased wife merely a coincidence? Despite opposition from former flame, Sheriff Rick Sutton, Corrie is determined to find the murderer. But will she find out who is friend or foe before the murderer decides it's the end of the road for Corrie?

No Lifeguard on Duty
Book 2

At the Black Horse Campground in Bonney County, New Mexico summer means warm sunny days, a cool refreshing pool... and murder? Corrie Black welcomes the summer with a party to celebrate opening the pool. The shock of discovering Krista Otero's body in the pool the morning after the party is bad. What's worse is that the death wasn't an accident. And Krista's closest friends all have something to hide. Corrie is determined to find out who used her swimming pool as a murder weapon and her home as a base for illegal activities. But someone wants to keep Corrie out of their business... even if it means killing again!

No Vacancy
Book 3

"Close the campground Saturday. This is your only warning. Your life is in danger." So reads the note shoved under the door of the Black Horse Campground store as Corrie Black and her staff celebrate the first "no vacancy" day of the season. When a man suspected of writing the note is found dead in a cabin, it seems the threat is gone. Until the man's identity is revealed. Someone who knew a lot about the Black Horse family, a lot more than even Corrie knew. With the help of Bonney County Sheriff Rick Sutton and former Houston PD Lieutenant J.D. Wilder, Corrie digs into secrets her parents kept from her. But the deeper she digs, the more she finds out things that could change her life forever... if not end it!

At the Crossroad
Book 4

Trouble often comes in threes. It's no different at the Black Horse Campground. On his first day as detective with the Bonney Police Department, J.D. Wilder finds three cold case files on his desk – three women who disappeared over a fifteen year period. It seems no one has ever properly investigated them. Then a woman from his past arrives to ask for his help. Again. The timing couldn't be worse, since he's finally about to ask Corrie on a date. But Corrie also has a visitor from her past show up. And Sheriff Rick Sutton has his hands full dodging his ex-wife, Meghan, who insists on digging up a painful memory. When three bodies are discovered that prove the missing women were murdered, J.D.'s investigation reveals that all of their visitors have some connection to the victims. But which one of them killed three women? And will there be a fourth victim?

A Summer to Remember
Book 5

Police detective J.D. Wilder's attempt to focus on his budding romance with Corrie Black, owner of the Black Horse Campground, is thwarted when the cold cases he thought he had solves are reopened, and the killer is poised to strike again. But who held a grudge against the three cold-case victims? And who is the next target? With the help of Bonney County Sheriff Rick Sutton, J.D. probes the memories of Bonney residents who knew the victims and begins to make connections.
Then another death occurs, and Corrie is attacked. The attacker and the cold-case murderer could be the same person, but Corrie's condition is critical and she's lost memories of recent events, including the identity of her attacker and even having met J.D. Will she survive long enough to remember what happened? Or will she end up as a memory?

Fiesta of Fear
Book 6

Fun. Games. Food. Murder.... Corrie Black, owner of the Black Horse Campground in Bonney County, New Mexico, has her hands full. She has offered to host the annual San Ignacio church fiesta at the campground, she's helping her best friend Shelli deal with a missing ex-husband and troubled teenager, and she's trying to keep the peace between the parish's two most vocal members. When the high school principal is found dead in the church cemetery, Corrie needs answers: Who are the 'ghost girls'? What is causing Shelli's son to get into so much trouble? What is causing the tension between the church secretary and the church treasurer? Are these connected to the murder? And most importantly to Corrie, what is the secret her coworker and friend, RaeLynn Shaffer, is hiding? With the help of Bonney County sheriff, Rick Sutton, and Bonney Detective J.D. Wilder, Corrie tries to unravel the threads that connect all the mysteries to the fiesta and the Black Horse Campground. But the threads turn into a net that could snare Corrie and her friends in a deadly trap!

On a Dark and Deadly Highway
Book 7

When RaeLynn Shaffer is found on the highway near the Black Horse Campground—drugged, beaten, and unconscious—the mystery behind her disappearance weeks earlier only grows deeper. Soon it's apparent that she wasn't meant to be found alive, and what she knows could be fatal to the people she cares about, especially campground owner, Corrie Black. Despite the fact that RaeLynn can't identify her kidnappers, Bonney Police Detective J.D. Wilder and Bonney County Sheriff Rick Sutton take their hunt to find RaeLynn's assailants across the state of New Mexico to find out who wanted her dead and why.

As they investigate deeper, deadly connections come to light and a dangerous storm puts the entire village in peril as desperate men take violent measures to silence RaeLynn and everyone who tries to help her. Corrie, Rick, and J.D. put their lives on the line to save RaeLynn, but can they find out who was behind her kidnapping and what it is they're willing to kill for?